# WATCH OVER ME

## MILA GRAY

SIMON & SCHUSTER BFYR

New York   London   Toronto   Sydney   New Delhi

For Karthi

SIMON & SCHUSTER BFYR

An imprint of Simon & Schuster Children's Publishing Division
1230 Avenue of the Americas, New York, New York 10020
For information about special discounts for bulk purchases, please contact
Simon & Schuster Special Sales at 1-866-506-1949 or business@simonandschuster.com.
The Simon & Schuster Speakers Bureau can bring authors to your live event. For more
information or to book an event contact the Simon & Schuster Speakers Bureau
at 1-866-248-3049 or visit our website at www.simonspeakers.com.
Also available in a hardcover edition
Interior designed by Tom Daly
The text of this book was set in Chaparral Pro.
Manufactured in the United States of America
First Simon & Schuster Books for Young Readers paperback edition December 2020
10 9 8 7 6 5 4 3 2 1
The Library of Congress has cataloged the hardcover edition as follows:
Names: Gray, Mila, author. | Title: Watch over me / Mila Gray.
Description: First Simon Pulse hardcover edition. | New York : Simon Pulse, 2019. |
Audience: Ages 16 up. | Audience: Grades 10–12. | Summary: Told in two voices,
eighteen-year-old Zoey Ward struggles to protect her mother and siblings from her
violent father, and her brother's best friend, Tristan, a member of the Coast Guard,
tries to make her feel safe.
Identifiers: LCCN 2019032636 |
ISBN 9781534442818 (hardcover) | ISBN 9781534442832 (eBook)
Subjects: CYAC: Family violence—Fiction. | Brothers and sisters—Fiction. | Family
problems—Fiction. | Dating (Social customs)—Fiction. | Love—Fiction. | United
States. Coast Guard—Fiction.
Classification: LCC PZ7.G7798 Wat 2019 | DDC [Fic]—dc23
LC record available at https://lccn.loc.gov/2019032636
ISBN 9781534442825 (paperback)

Please be aware that *Watch Over Me*
includes the following content:

**Gun Violence**
**Domestic Violence**

National Domestic Violence Hotline
Thehotline.org

1-800-799-SAFE (7233)
1-800-787-3224 (TTY)

# The End

# ZOEY

I see the decision get made—the resolution crosses his face, and in the same instant I move in front of Tristan to shield him.

There's a deafening bang, followed closely by a second bang, and I fly sideways and hit the ground. Tristan falls too.

Pain shoots through me like comets streaking across a black sky. My vision turns starry.

I look up and see the monstrous shape of my dad looming over us. He blinks, seemingly astonished. Maybe it's shock at what he's done. Maybe it isn't. Light bursts around him in a dazzling halo. I can't breathe—the pain is almost as bright as the light.

I've been shot, I realize. But what about Tristan? Is he okay?

Thoughts dart like eels through my mind so fast and so slippery I can't grasp on to them. The only thing I can hold on to, like a beacon in the darkness, is the thought of Tristan. Please let him be okay. I don't care if I die. Just let him be okay.

My dad drops to his knees in front of me like a dark avenging angel. For a moment, I think he's about to beg forgiveness for what he's done. I stare up at him, but his expression shows no remorse, not an ounce of sorrow. He's baring his teeth like an animal about to shred his prey.

My ears are ringing so loudly that all other sounds are dulled. Time has slowed to a near stop. My heart seems to be following suit.

Tristan is all I can think of as the light starts to fade. I led him here. This is all my fault. Where is he? I desperately want to see him. I can feel something behind me. Something heavy and unmoving. A body? His body? I want to roll over and reach for him, but I'm paralyzed.

I desperately need to know that he's okay.

But what if he isn't?

What if he's dead?

What if I'm dying too?

# The Beginning

## ZOEY

There's no dark in Las Vegas. It's the brightest city on earth, and I haven't seen the stars in three years because of it. So bright, in fact, the city can be seen from outer space.

There's no quiet in Las Vegas either. Even out where we live, miles from the strip and its herds of tourists, there's constant noise: the roar of traffic sliced with sirens, thumping music; arguments interspersed with cackles of laughter and the incessant drone of TV chatter drifting through open windows.

I miss quiet, but I don't miss the dark.

I finish the washing up and tidy Cole's homework away into his backpack. His notebooks are covered in colorful cartoon doodles, but as I shove one into his bag, I pause, realizing they aren't cartoon doodles at all. Underneath his name—COLE

WARD—written in big block letters of uneven sizes, he's drawn a man holding a gun. Bullets are flying from it, and half a dozen stick figures lie sprawled across the page, tongues lolling, limbs severed, and red marker used for blood.

My hand shakes a little as I study the picture. Why is a nine-year-old boy drawing pictures like this? Is it normal? Perhaps all nine-year-old boys who spend time playing video games draw pictures like this. But even as I try to excuse it, I know deep down that it isn't normal.

I sink down at the scarred kitchen table and debate what to do. I can't tell my mom, that's for sure. It'll be too much for her to deal with. She's finally managed to get on a good track, and I'm anxious not to do anything that might send her plummeting back into the dark place.

The best thing to do, I decide, is to speak to Cole. The violence could be Will's influence. It makes sense, given that our older brother is a marine and Cole hero-worships him. Or it could be he's just copying something he saw on TV or online. I try to police his screen time, but I'm not always home, and my mom isn't great with discipline. She doesn't like conflict. Maybe I should speak to his teacher, even though last time she made it very clear that it's my mom who should be taking responsibility for Cole—not his teenage sister.

I shove the book in Cole's bag and make a mental note to talk to him tomorrow before school—if I have time, that is. I have an early shift at work. Which reminds me that I need to get moving so I don't end up too late to bed. There's still laundry to do and lunches to prepare for tomorrow.

I stick my head around the bedroom door and see Kate isn't yet asleep. She's sitting cross-legged on the top bunk wearing the unicorn onesie I gave her for Christmas. She's texting on her phone, her fingers flying at five hundred emojis a minute. I swear that phone is glued to her hands, and not even a crowbar could remove it.

"Hey, it's late," I say to Kate, but she's wearing her headphones and can't hear me. "Kate!" I say louder, and she glances up, her hair blazing around her head like a fiery sunset. "Bedtime."

She rolls her eyes as though I'm just one big annoyance, put on earth to end her Snapchat streak, but miracle of miracles, she stops texting and yanks out her headphones.

"Good night," she says, and reaches for the little unicorn reading light by her bed, twisting its horn to dim the brightness. When we first moved here, I tried making the room nice for her. She was unhappy about the move and even more so about having to share a room with Cole. The books on the shelf are gathering dust, though, because the only thing she reads these days are texts and Instagram stories.

She shoves her phone under the covers, and I know as soon as I'm gone she'll be back to texting. I make Cole's bed on the bottom bunk. He sleeps there normally, but he and Kate had a screaming argument earlier, so he went to sleep in Mom's bed.

As I close the bedroom door, my phone rings. It's another call from an unidentified number, the third one today. The first one I answered, hoping it was about a job I'd applied for at a restaurant closer to home, but it wasn't—only silence greeted me on the other end. I hung up fast, before it rang again a few seconds later. And when I finally answered, all I could hear was someone on the other end, breathing loudly.

There was no answer when I said hello, just more breathing. Whoever it was proceeded to call a few hours after that.

And now, at ten o'clock at night, they're calling again.

My breathing hitches, and my heart beats abnormally fast. It's not him, I tell myself angrily. If it were him, I'd hear the pip-pip-pip of the federal inmate phone system and then an automated voice asking me if I wanted to accept a call from a prisoner at the Penitentiary of New Mexico. I know this because a few years ago he tried to call me. This was when I still had my old phone number. I rejected the call, then changed my number.

It can't be him, I repeat to myself. There's nothing to be afraid of. I switch off my phone and put it down on the table, trying to shake off the bad feelings slinking over me. Without warning, memories lunge out at me from the darkness, where I've tried to bury them: Cole's screams, Kate's sobs, my mother's face bursting under a flurry of punches, the fridge door hanging on one hinge. Then the blue and white and red flashing lights outside; my dad's angry roars. *You bitch! I'll fucking kill you.*

The phone rings again. I startle. How long have I been standing here staring into space, remembering things I'd rather forget? It's the landline this time. I walk toward it, debating whether I should answer. Something tells me not to, but another voice in my head, a belligerent one, demands that I do. I grab the phone. "Yes?" I say.

Silence greets me.

"Who is this?" I whisper, heart hammering furiously.

There's another second's silence, and then I hear the click as whoever is on the other end hangs up. As I stare at the phone, there's an enormous BOOM. The window shatters, and glass flies across the room. A wall of heat rushes toward me as a crackle and a deafening roar fill my ears.

Shielding my face, I squint through the broken window. Oh

my God. It's my car, parked just outside on the driveway in front of the house. It's on fire.

I stumble back from the window, chased by smoke and heat, and run to the bedroom, throwing open the door and screaming at Kate to get up.

"Fire! Move!" I yell before rushing out and into my mom's room to wake Cole. I come to a halt in the doorway. The room is empty.

"Cole?" I shout, ducking down and looking under the bed. He's not there. And he's not in the closet, either. I ransack the room looking for him.

Smoke is now billowing in through the broken window, and I start coughing. I push past Kate, who has staggered from bed and into the living room.

"Call 911!" I shout at her.

The front door is the only exit, and we can't get out, thanks to the fact the car is parked right in front of the door. Behind me, I can hear Kate on the phone to the dispatcher. "F-fire," she stammers. "Th-there's a fire."

"Cole!" I scream, turning every which way, trying to figure out where he might be. I check the bathroom, the kitchen, the closets—everywhere I can think of—but he's nowhere to be found. Coughing, I yell his name again, but he doesn't answer. The smoke is so thick and choking we can barely breathe. I grab Kate by the arm and drag her back into Mom's bedroom.

"Come on," I say to Kate, pulling her over to the window. "We need to get out of here."

The neglected courtyard outside is shared by the two dozen or so houses that back onto it. It's meant to be a communal meeting area with grills, concrete picnic tables, and a play area for little kids, but the play area is taped off because the rusting climbing frame and broken swings are a liability, and the only people who use the picnic tables are drug dealers.

Someone in the courtyard runs over and helps Kate out of the window, catching her as she stumbles. The person then helps me. I recognize him as a neighbor, a guy in his fifties, who I think works as a bus driver. His name is Winston.

"Have you seen my brother?" I ask him as he helps me down.

He shakes his head as panic ripples through me. I scour the crowd of a dozen or so neighbors—some in pajamas—rushing out of their houses to see what's happening. There's no sign of Cole. In the distance, I can hear the sirens of the fire truck.

I take Kate's hand and pull her around the side of the house, to the street. The car is still burning furiously, and the flames have started to stroke the roof of the house and melt the guttering. As I watch, sparks dance through the broken window and land on the curtains in the living room. They burn so fast and so brightly that they incinerate in seconds, and now the flames, hungry for more, leap toward the sofa.

Two fire trucks screech to a halt in front of the house, and we watch as firefighters go running past, carrying a hose. One team douses the car, and in less than a minute the blaze is under control, sputtering and finally vanishing with a hiss and a billow of black smoke.

The other firefighters have turned their hose on the house—sending the spray through the window and on the flames consuming the living room, while two others have taken an axe to the front door. They smash it down, then rush inside. I sink to my knees on the sidewalk, Kate collapsing beside me, sobbing. What if Cole's inside? What if he was hiding?

The fire in the living room is quickly put out, but it feels like we wait hours until the firefighters exit. One of them approaches Winston, who I see point me out to him. He walks over with a solemn expression on his face, and my heart starts to hammer. Kate grips my hand tight. The firefighter kneels down beside me. He's about fifty years old with a bushy moustache and blue eyes. "My name's Lieutenant Franklin," he says. "This your house?"

I nod. "D-did you find . . . ?" I stammer. "My brother. I don't know where he is."

He frowns and shakes his head. "There's no one in the house."

I let out a sob of relief. Kate does too.

"How old is he? Can you give us a description of him?"

I turn back to Lieutenant Franklin and try to focus. "His name is Cole. He's nine. He has brown hair, brown eyes, freckles. He was wearing Spider-Man pajamas."

Franklin repeats all of this into his radio, and the dispatcher confirms it.

"Is that all?" Franklin asks me. "Any other identifiers?"

I open my mouth, but nothing comes out. How else to describe my little brother? I haven't done him justice. He's smart as a whip, I want to say, even though he hates school. He loves to make up jokes, really bad ones. He's currently obsessed with Genghis Khan and LeBron James and Lionel Messi and he wants to be a race car driver when he grows up, unless of course he can be a famous soccer player. None of this information is going to help them find him, though. But how many nine-year-old boys in Spider-Man pajamas must there be walking around Vegas at this time of night?

"When did you last see him?" Franklin asks me.

"I put him to bed around seven thirty. I went to look for him after the explosion, but I couldn't find him. I don't know where he is."

I'm fighting back tears. I want to go and look for him—I *should* be looking for him—but Kate is gripping my arm, holding me firmly in place. She hasn't said a word this whole time. She seems to be in shock. Someone has placed blankets—those foil ones—over our shoulders. "Please," I whisper to Franklin, "you need to find him."

"Don't worry," he tells me. "All the patrol cars in the area are looking for him. We'll find him." He nods at me reassuringly.

"Where's your mother?" Franklin asks.

"She's at work," I tell him. "She should be home soon."

He frowns at that, and I sense he's making a judgment. He's probably thinking, What kind of a mother leaves her children at home to work a night shift? It irks me. I'm almost nineteen, and I'm not a kid. There are no laws being broken. Besides, he doesn't know anything about us. He doesn't know that my mom's job is the best thing that's happened to her in a long time, that it's given her back a sense of purpose and self-confidence. She might not be earning very much money, but she's earning something—enough to put a roof over our heads and get us off food stamps. This is what I want to say to him, but I don't.

"And your father? Is he around?" Franklin asks.

I shake my head. "No."

"You should call your mother," he says to me.

"My phone's inside," I say, nodding at the house.

"Okay, I can have someone contact her. Where does she work?"

"The Luxor," I tell him. "She has a job doing hair and makeup for the show there."

"That the aerial one? With the acrobats and the trapeze people?"

I nod. My mom got us tickets for Kate's birthday a few months ago. Special-rate ones. It was one of the best nights we'd ever had. Afterward, Cole spent two months swinging off every pole and rail he could find, until he fell leaping from a wall and took a chip out of his elbow.

"What's your mom's name?" Franklin asks me.

"Gina Ward," I tell him, mumbling it, my mind back on Cole. Where did he go? And more important, *why?*

"Does she have a car?" he asks.

"No. She takes the bus."

Franklin nods. "I'll have someone pick her up." He steps away, and I watch him talk into his radio, and then I just sit there on the curb, trying to comfort Kate and not to think about what might have happened to Cole.

Ten minutes later, as we watch the firefighters roll up their hoses and wait for my mom, Franklin returns. He crouches down beside us. "They found your brother," he tells me.

The relief bursts out of me. Beside me Kate clutches my hand. "Oh, thank God—where was he?"

"A few blocks away. A patrol car spotted him. He ran. They had to chase him down."

"What?" I ask, stunned. Why would he run?

"They're bringing him here," Franklin tells me. "Do you mind . . . ?" Franklin says, gesturing with a nod of the head for me to follow him a few feet away, out of earshot of Kate.

I prize my arm out of her grip and follow him. He gestures toward the car. "It looks like arson. It burned with the kind of intensity we normally see when an accelerant is used."

*Arson.* I say the word in my head as I stare at the smoking, mangled ruin that was once a Toyota Camry with 175,000 miles on the odometer.

"You're lucky," the fireman goes on to say. "If you'd had more fuel in the tank, it would have been an inferno. It could have taken out the entire block."

"Oh my God," I whisper, my heart clanging in my chest.

"Know anyone who might have a grudge against you?"

I open my mouth to say no, but then stop. Yes. I do know someone with a grudge against me. Someone who threatened once to kill me. But he's in prison. And he doesn't know where we live. It can't be him. But that's the second time I've thought that tonight, and I'm not a believer in coincidence.

Franklin shrugs. "Might just be bored kids. It happens." His eyes drill into mine as he says it. "Young boys in particular often go through a phase where they get interested in fire, playing with matches and things."

I don't understand what he's implying at first, and then it hits me with a jolt. "You think it was my brother who started the fire?" I ask, a note of anger in my voice.

He's quick to walk it back, shaking his head. "That's not what I'm saying."

But it's what he's thinking. I scowl at him, angry but also wrong-footed, because I'm wondering if Franklin might be right. Is that why Cole ran away? Because he didn't want to get into trouble? I can't believe that Cole would ever do something like this. I mean . . . I don't *think* he would do something like this.

"You got renters' insurance?" he asks. "The house has got a fair amount of fire and smoke damage."

"No," I say, my heart sinking.

He squeezes my shoulder. "The place isn't going to be inhabitable for a while," he says. "Do you have somewhere you can stay?"

I stare at the broken front door and the soot-covered walls of the living room. "No," I tell him. We don't have anywhere.

# TRISTAN

W hat the hell were they thinking?" Gunnie asks me as we hurry to the water's edge.

"They were thinking it was a great day to try kayaking for the first time."

Gunnie mutters under his breath. He has a low tolerance for "idiots and morons," which in his mind refers to ninety-nine percent of the population.

I'm grinning because, while two kayakers are now clinging to their capsized kayak half a mile from shore in freezing water and choppy conditions, I get to ride the Jet Ski. I can't lie; bouncing over the waves on route to rescue people does make the *Fast and the Furious* soundtrack play loudly in my head. Officially, it's not called a Jet Ski. It's a personal rescue watercraft. But really, it's a Jet Ski.

"I'll get to rescue people while riding a Jet Ski and flying helicopters," I told my family when I joined the Coast Guard and they wanted to know what the hell I was thinking.

"He couldn't be Tom Cruise in *Mission: Impossible*, so this is his plan B." My sister, Dahlia, smirked.

I laughed along with them all, but to myself I had to admit that Dahlia had pretty much hit the nail on the head. I was thinking more Tom Cruise in *Top Gun*, though. It's an old movie from the '80s, and old movies from the '80s are one of my many obsessions. No one does heroics, throws a bottle of liquor, or woos women like Tom Cruise in '80s movies, except maybe Tom Cruise in movies today.

Gunnie and I rev the Jet Skis and take off, following the coordinates from the helicopter team. I can see the orange bird in the sky anyway, hovering over the kayakers' location. One day I'm going to be up there in the helicopter—that's my dream, to make pilot one day—but for now, while I wait for a place to open up at flight school, I'm happy out on the water.

This stretch of coast, just north of San Diego, is beautiful but also deadly, with strong undertows. Even experienced boaters and kayakers get into trouble, not to mention swimmers. We rescue dozens of people each month. But it's not all rescue missions, as I tell people when they ask if a coast guard is the same thing as a lifeguard. Coast guards are a branch of the military; lifeguards are not. We seize drugs and weapons that are being smuggled by sea into the US. We deploy to war zones to assist in military operations. Lifeguards do not.

Gunnie and I reach the kayakers in a couple of minutes. The water closer to shore is a brilliant topaz blue, but out here it's the color of brushed steel, and the waves are being whipped by a wind that makes it hard to steady the Jet Ski alongside the people who need rescuing. They're both exhausted from the cold and from treading water. The kayak must have sunk, and I wonder at how lucky they are that they were able to call for help. A few more minutes out here, and I bet the woman would have drowned.

The guy is wearing a life jacket, but the woman he's with isn't. What a gentleman. I reach my hand to the woman, and she takes it gratefully.

She climbs on behind me and slumps against my back, shivering so hard all I can hear are her teeth chattering. I hand her a life jacket to put on.

"I'll have you back on land in no time," I tell her.

"Thank you," she says as Gunnie pulls the man onto his Jet Ski. He's professional enough not to call the guy an idiot to his face, but I know that's what he's thinking. I turn around and tell the woman to hold on. She's glowering at the guy, who I assume must be her boyfriend, and I wonder if this little misadventure is going to lead to their breakup and hope it does. Guy's a jerk.

After the couple is back safely on land and the incident report is all typed up, my shift is finally over. I grab a shower and change, pulling my motorcycle helmet from my locker and checking my phone.

"Hot date?" Gunnie asks.

I shake my head and keep my lips sealed. My love life is a constant source of entertainment for Gunnie and the rest of the crew. They think I'm some kind of player, and, as most of them are married, they like to live vicariously through me. They have the wrong idea. I mean, occasionally dates lead places, but mostly where they lead is nowhere. I've had a million first dates and no second ones.

My sister, Dahlia, thinks I'm scared of commitment, which isn't true. I've committed to a lot in my life: my job, for one, my friends, my baseball team, hunting down the best burger on the West Coast, and collecting baseball cards. The latter with a fervor and dedication that Dahlia used to mock me for when we were kids. She doesn't anymore since the collection in my shoe box is worth close to eighty thousand dollars. She'd argue her own collection of shoe boxes is worth about the same, but I would argue mine brings greater joy, despite the fact I can't wear mine.

I'm not scared of commitment. I just haven't found a person that I want to commit to, I tell her.

I hurry outside toward my bike, where the girl I rescued just an hour ago is standing. I slow down a beat. She's all dry now and wearing shorts and a white tank top. And, I can't help but notice, no bra.

"Hi," she says to me.

"Hi," I answer.

She smiles a little coyly. "I just wanted to say thank you. I'm not sure I told you how grateful I am for you saving my life."

"You're welcome," I answer, a little bemused. She's waited for me all this time just to tell me that?

She looks up at me through her lashes and bites her bottom lip. I smile. She's flirting with me, and she's pretty. Very pretty, in that blond Southern California way; maybe a few years older than me, around twenty-five. She twirls a strand of hair around a finger. "It was so scary. I thought I was going to drown for sure," she says.

I nod. "Yeah, rough seas today. You should have been wearing a life jacket."

She nods. "My boyfriend said we didn't need them, but then when we capsized he took the emergency one for himself."

"And he's still your boyfriend?" I ask her, resting my bag on my bike.

She shakes her head and looks me straight in the eye. "No."

I notice she's found the time to reapply her makeup—she's wearing mascara that makes her eyelashes look like arthritic spiders' legs, and her lips are a red gloss that matches my bike. She rests her hand on the handlebars. The gesture annoys me. It's presumptuous, like she's touched a part of my anatomy without my permission.

"I was wondering if I could buy you a drink to say thanks," she says to me.

I pause, recognizing that part of my wants to say yes, but there's a blurry professional line.

"I'm busy tonight," I tell her.

Her face falls. She swallows her dented pride, and I feel bad. "But I really appreciate you taking the time to say thanks."

She brightens at that. "Well, maybe another time?" she asks hopefully.

"We're not meant to date people we rescue," I tell her.

"Who said anything about dating?" she answers, giving me a mischievous look that makes it abundantly clear she's after one thing and one thing only—and it's definitely not my brains or charm.

"Here's my number," she says, handing me a piece of paper. She steps closer to give it to me, her breasts inadvertently on purpose brushing my arm. For a beat, I do think about it. I mean, it's been a while.

"Call me if you change your mind," she says, and presses the piece of paper into my hand, her fingers lingering for a moment on my wrist. I glance down. She's written her name, Brittany, and her number, alongside a cartoon girl drowning.

From the corner of my eyes, I see Gunnie exit the building, and so I go for the quick escape. Swinging my leg over my bike, I say a hurried good-bye before revving the engine and tearing out of the lot.

# ZOEY

You can't stay here," Aunt Chrissy says, wringing her hands, twisting the half-dozen rings she's wearing around and around as though trying to unscrew them from her fingers. "You know I would let you if I could, if we had space, but you know how Javi is." She looks at me pleadingly as she says it, and I nod.

"He gets home from work at five a.m., and he needs to sleep," she goes on. "There just isn't room for all of you here."

"We understand," I say, forcing a smile. "We just didn't know where else to go."

Chrissy walks over to my mom and puts her arm around her. My mom is looking shell-shocked, as though she's just received news of a death in the family. "We lost almost everything," she murmurs, bewildered. "Who would do this?"

I haven't told her what I suspect. That it's the same person who's been making the phone calls.

Chrissy pats her on the shoulder. "Let me make you all something to drink. You want some hot chocolate?" She looks at Kate, who is sitting on the sofa, recovered from her shock and now texting like she has to make up for all the lost time, and at Cole, who is sitting beside her kicking his heels against the floor.

"No," he spits. "I want my things."

"We can't get them," I tell him. "It's not safe there. Not until we find out who started the car fire."

"When's that going to be?" he shouts.

I take a deep breath. "A few days."

"Where are we going to stay until then?" my mom asks, and I realize she doesn't have an answer. She's waiting for me to supply one. Aunt Chrissy, much as I love her, can't help us. She's barely scraping by working housekeeping at a hotel on the Strip, and her boyfriend, Javi, is a creep.

"I want to go home," Cole yells, jumping up and running over to my mom. I intercept him, but he darts around me. "I want my Xbox," he shouts in her face. She flinches backward, and I have to get between them again and pull him away.

"Cole," I say gently, "come on. We'll get your Xbox, okay? Don't worry."

He looks at me then, and I see the scared little boy hiding behind the angry little monster. I knead his shoulder muscles—taut as tightrope wires—and he starts to relax slightly. Sometimes touch, just a hand on his back or a gentle stroke of his hair, can be enough to defuse him. It doesn't work this time—just as I think I've got him calm, he pulls away from me. "Get off me! I hate you!"

I stare at him, taken aback. What did I do?

I still haven't confronted him about the fire. When the cops brought him back, he was sullen and untalkative, refusing to look me in the eye and claiming that he'd heard the smoke alarm, jumped out the window, then run away because he was scared. He wasn't in his pajamas, though; he was wearing jeans and his sneakers and a hoodie. I didn't question it, but I know that Franklin noticed.

Was it him? I wonder about it, but honestly, I can't even go there. Not right now. We need a roof over our heads. That's the priority. I do a quick calculation. We have maybe enough money to pay for a motel for tonight and possibly tomorrow, but then what? I work in a coffee shop and make ten dollars an hour. My mom makes just a little bit more than I do, and between us every cent goes to rent, bills, and getting by. We don't have enough money to put a deposit on a new place.

"I guess we could try the shelter," my mom says, looking at me as though she wants me to make the call.

I grit my teeth. I'm not going back to a shelter, not with Cole and Kate. I'm not putting them through that again: the sense of uncertainty, the living with a revolving door of strangers, most of whom aren't exactly the kinds of people you want to be neighbors with. My mom, dark-haired, petite as a sparrow, and delicately featured, looks like a teenager. People often mistake us for sisters, and right now I feel like I'm the oldest sister, and I wish to hell I didn't.

"What about Romeo?" Kate suddenly announces.

"Oh no," my mom murmurs.

"Oh God," I say at the same time.

"Where's Romeo?" Cole asks, almost as alarmed as Kate.

"I'm sure he's fine," I say. "He's a cat. Cats are smart. He probably jumped out the window."

"We have to go back for him!" Kate shouts, jumping to her feet. "He'll be scared. What if he runs off?"

Romeo is a house cat. He doesn't ever go outside, given the

traffic and other dangers lurking on the block in the form of two rottweilers and a Doberman.

"We'll go back for him," I reassure Kate, who is now verging on hysteria, tears spilling down her cheeks. "We'll go back, okay? I promise." I put my arm around her, but she wrenches away from me in anger.

Cole scowls at me too, and I see hate flash in his eyes— something I've never seen before. It shocks me to my core. It must be the fire that's unsettled him. He's looking for someone to blame. Or am I mistaking it? Is it guilt? He looks like he's about to start yelling, but Chrissy intervenes and gives him the TV remote, which thankfully distracts him.

Just then, Aunt Chrissy's phone rings. She grabs for it and steps into the bedroom to take the call. I edge toward the door and crane to listen. After we got here an hour ago and I whispered my suspicions to Chrissy, she called a few friends back in Scottsdale to ask if they'd heard anything about my dad getting released from prison.

"Did you . . . ? What? . . . Okay . . ." I can hear Chrissy talking, her voice breaking. And that's when I know for sure. I peek through the gap in the door. She's standing with the phone to her ear, her other hand pressed against her mouth. "Oh my God," she whispers.

My legs buckle.

Chrissy exits the bedroom, her expression almost as fearful and afraid as my mother's. She looks at me. "Your dad got early release," she says under her breath so my mom and the others can't hear. "My friend says he saw him in town at Jim and Rob's—you know that bar?"

I nod.

He's out. That's all I can process. Why did no one tell us?

"And then he vanished," Chrissy continues. "Word is he left town a few days ago."

It feels as if a knife is being shoved between my ribs and right into my heart. He's out. All I can see is his face—the snarl on his lips as he told me that one day he'd find me and kill me. The fire was no accident. It was arson. And it was him. A warning, a threat, or an actual attempt to kill me. I don't know.

Chrissy grips my elbow. "It's okay," she whispers.

I look over at my mom sitting at the table, her mascara smudged around her eyes from the tears she shed earlier. I have to tell her that the man who almost beat her to death, the man I testified against and got sent to jail for eight years, is out after serving only three.

"How does he know where we are?" I ask Chrissy, my voice trembling.

She shakes her head. "I don't know."

We changed our last name; we moved to where no one knew us, except for my mom's sister, Chrissy. None of us are on social media, apart from Kate, but she uses an anonymous name and all her settings are private. She knows the drill. My eyes dart to the door of Chrissy's apartment.

I'm so stupid. We are not safe here.

"We need to leave," I say in a whisper. We need to get out of here right now.

Cole is fixated on the TV, and my sister is on her phone. How can I tell them we have to go? How can I tell them that they need to abandon their friends and school and the life we've built and start over yet again?

I have to fight the instinct to sprint for the door. But I can't run. It's not possible because a) I don't have a car anymore, and b) even if I did, I have nowhere to run to.

And I can't leave the others.

"I'm going to call the police," Chrissy says. "You could get protection."

I shake my head at her. "The police? Really? You think they'll do anything?"

Chrissy looks away, down at the ground. She knows how I feel about the police. My dad was a cop. The police did nothing to help us before. They rallied around one of their own. It took him almost killing my mom and me and a neighbor providing witness statements for them to actually charge him with anything. So no, I have no faith in the police actually doing their job and helping us. And even if they could do something, it would only be a restraining order, and that's not going to stop him. It didn't stop him before.

I hear a noise and turn around. My mom has pushed back her chair and risen to her feet. "He's out, isn't he?" she asks.

Chrissy looks at me. I nod my head. "Yes."

Somehow, my mom manages to stay standing. After a moment, she clears her throat. "I'm going to call Will," she says.

I glare at her, angry and upset, but I can't argue. What other choice do we have?

# TRISTAN

You want another beer?" Will asks.

It's past midnight, and I have to be up at six to hit the gym before work (another thing I'm committed to—take that, Dahlia), but I say yes because this is the last time I'm going to see Will for eighteen months. He's redeploying to Afghanistan in two days' time.

"Let me get this," I tell him, pulling out my wallet.

Will's an old friend of mine from elementary school. When my parents divorced and I moved from Scottsdale to California with my mom eight years ago, Will and I stayed in touch. Will joined the marines straight out of high school. I joined the Coast Guard after I graduated college. Whenever Will's back from a deployment, we get together to shoot pool and drink beer, sometimes with his friend Kit.

I order two more burgers, a nonalcoholic beer, much to Will's ribbing, and another Bud for him. He's way over the limit, so I'll drive him home after this. "How you feeling about going back?" I ask.

He shrugs. "I'll feel great about it if I make it home alive and with all my limbs attached."

He's nursing his beer and looking glum, and I want to throw my arm around his shoulder and tell him not to worry, that he's going to be fine. But I don't because I know the words will ring hollow. He's seen so many friends die in combat, so many return wounded. I glance at him out of the corner of my eye, wishing there was something I could say. A part of me always feels like a coward because I joined the Coast Guard, not the marines or the army, and the chances of me seeing active combat are low. I also joined as an officer, making my way straight from college to officer candidate school. Will started at the bottom as a private, and though he's made corporal, that's as far as he's likely to go. He could go further—he'd make a great officer—but Will sees his time in the military not as a career but as a prison sentence. This deployment is his last before he can get out, and he's counting down the days until freedom.

He clinks his beer against mine. "To staying alive," he says.

"To staying alive," I repeat, saying a silent prayer that this isn't going to be the last time I see him, then cursing myself for even thinking the thought. It's bad luck.

Will's phone rings as he downs his beer, and he pulls it out of his back pocket, immediately frowning at the name on the display. "Who is it?" I ask him.

"My mom," he answers. I can see the concern on his face. It's late for her to be calling. "Hello?" he says, picking up.

I watch him go stock-still, and I feel a growing sense of unease. His expression has turned stony as his fist slams down on the bar and stays there, tightly clenched. "Okay, I'm on my way," he says into the phone before hanging up.

"What's going on?" I ask.

"He's out."

There's only one thing that means. His dad is out of prison. "I thought he got eight years?" I say, absorbing the news with the same amount of shock as Will.

He shakes his head. "Yeah, turns out that means three, with good behavior."

I swear under my breath. "Is your mom okay?"

Will shakes his head. He's reaching for his keys, on the bar. "I've got to go."

I stand up. "Why? What's happened?"

"He's found them. My dad's found them."

"What did he do?" I ask.

"He set fire to Zoey's car. At least that's what they think. Their apartment caught fire too. There's smoke damage. They're okay, but they've got nowhere to stay." He looks at me then, and for a fraction of a second, I see the little boy I used to know: the kid I became best friends with after we both ran to stop an eighth grader from beating up little Randy Meisterburg. "I don't know what to do," he says.

I put my arm around his shoulder. "It's okay. We'll figure it out."

He nods at me.

"Come on," I tell him, steering him toward the door. "Let's go."

# ZOEY

Will keeps looking at me in the rearview mirror, and I keep looking away, staring out the window, tracking the sun as it rises over the desert and makes the sky bleed red. Cole is lying on my lap, fast asleep. I stroke his hair, wishing he were always this still and at peace. Kate is asleep too, in the row of seats behind me, curled up in a ball, her phone clutched tightly in her hand.

My mom is sitting up front. Will's driving, but it's Tristan's car. When he and Will arrived at Chrissy's, I was busy trying to wrangle Cole and Kate into leaving and didn't say much to either of them. I have little to say to Will anyway.

Tristan is beside me in the car, and Cole has stretched his feet out across his lap. I reach out and try to pull them off, but Tristan smiles and shakes his head. *No worries*, he mouths.

I look away, too embarrassed to hold eye contact. Back when we all lived in Scottsdale, back when things were bad, he was a constant visitor to the house. He knows everything about my family. Will's told him. And I think he even saw some of it with his own eyes.

I remember one time opening my bedroom door, thinking that it was Will knocking—that he had heard me crying—and finding Tristan standing there instead. He didn't say a word, just stepped into the room, wrapped his arms around me, and held me while I sobbed against his chest. I think he was about fourteen. I must have been eleven. I don't even remember why I was upset, only that I was crying so hard I could barely breathe—great hacking sobs erupting out of me. Does he remember that day? How he distracted me by telling me the plot of the movie *Alien*?

When I cast a surreptitious look sideways at Tristan again, it's hard to believe he's the same person who held me in his arms back then. He's so different now, so grown-up in a way that makes me feel weirdly uncomfortable and also makes me want to keep staring. The last time I saw him he was fifteen and gangly limbed, all jutting elbows and knees with skinny shoulders and a concave chest. Now he's the opposite. Over six feet, with shoulders broader than Will's. His biceps aren't even flexed and they're filling out the arms of his T-shirt. He's got dark brown hair like Will's and the most unusual color eyes: a caramel brown speckled with amber flecks.

He looks like a marine too—with his physique and the way he carries himself—but I'd be surprised if he was. Tristan was an honor student with a clear path to college. His parents were rich and successful. I think his mom worked in marketing for a big outdoor clothing company and his dad was a professor of something. I mean, if anyone was bound for an Ivy League college and then a successful career, it was Tristan. And then there's the car he picked us up in—an expensive Lexus SUV. I remember he was always obsessed with cars. And with baseball. And that he could eat more food than I'd thought was humanly possible.

I want to keep looking at him, marking all the changes, but he senses me and looks over. I turn quickly away and study the desert beyond the car. But now it's my turn to feel him looking at me. It makes my stomach screw up into a tightly knotted ball and my face flame hot. I'm torn between happiness at seeing him again and mortification at him seeing us like this. I hate that we need his help.

"Are you hungry?"

Tristan's holding a protein bar out to me. I shake my head, then instantly regret it. I'm starving. But for some reason I've said no and I can't walk it back. I think it's because I don't want to take anything more from him. It's enough that he's driven all this way to Vegas, and now we're driving all the way back to wherever he lives near San Diego to stay somewhere he's found for us.

"Are you sure?" he asks. "Twelve peanuts, three eggs, and two dates died to make this. And it's delicious."

I look at him. He's giving me a one-sided smile, and it reveals the deep dimple in his left cheek. It triggers a memory of him. How he was always trying to make people laugh, cracking jokes and playing the fool, anything to raise a smile. I know that's what he's trying to do now, but I'm not in the mood to laugh.

"I'm fine, thanks," I tell him, and chastened, he places the protein bar on the armrest between the two front seats.

"Well, it's there if you want it later," he says.

As I stare out the car window at the mountains rising in the distance, I have to fight back tears. How is it possible we are on the road again, with nothing save the clothes we're wearing? I don't know exactly where we're going, or how we're going to survive when we get there. I start to fret about all the details—how I need to call the coffee shop where I work and Cole and Kate's schools to let them know we're not coming back, and how I need to cancel all our utilities and . . .

"You'll like it," Tristan says.

I swipe at the tear rolling down my cheek and turn toward him. Is he talking about the protein bar?

"I mean Oceanside," he explains, "where I live. You'll like it."

I know he's trying to make me feel better, but he could tell me we were moving to a mansion in Hawaii or a penthouse on Fifth Avenue and it wouldn't raise a smile, because what he doesn't know is that it could be the farthest place on earth, the most protected place on earth—hell, it could even be Mars . . . He'll still find us. And when he does, then what? It might just have been better to stay in Vegas, in our smoke-damaged house with no windows or door. At least we would have known the confrontation was imminent. Now I'll just be looking over my shoulder the whole time, not knowing when it's coming.

"My landlord has a spare unit," Tristan says. "It's across from mine; this couple who were renting it just moved out. It's small, but it's nice."

Across from his? He'll be there, a voice in my head tells me. He'll be close by. I'd be lying if I said the knowledge didn't make me feel relieved.

After a little while, I sneak another look in Tristan's direction.

"Is the apartment near the beach?" I ask him.

Tristan grins at me. "Yeah, it's right by the beach. You can hear the waves crashing if the windows are open."

Wow. It feels wrong to smile given the circumstances, but then, looking at Tristan and finally daring to meet his eyes, I can't help myself.

# TRISTAN

Zoey's leaning against the door, frowning slightly in her sleep. She holds Cole in a tight embrace, as if she's scared he'll escape somehow while she sleeps. I'm a little hesitant to wake her, but I reach out to tap her on the shoulder. She startles awake in fright, shrinking back against the car door. For a split second, I see the terror in her eyes before she remembers where she is and the fear fades.

"We're here," I tell her.

She looks out the window, rubbing her eyes, and then shakes Cole awake. "We're here," she says to him quietly.

Cole stirs, and I brace myself for the oncoming typhoon. The kid's a handful, though Zoey seems the most able to cope with him, or perhaps she's the only one of the family who tries. Their mom seems to have checked out, though that's hardly surprising.

Zoey looks like her mother—the same hazel-colored, almond-shaped eyes and curly brown hair. The same flawless skin, though hers is splashed with freckles. Zoey's taller than her mom, and slender, though it's hard to tell what her figure is like because she's wearing such baggy clothes and because I'm trying really hard not to perv. Like, *really* hard.

It didn't just take me by surprise when I saw her again. It almost knocked me off my feet. I don't know why, but I was expecting her to look the same as she did the last time I saw her, six years ago—a short, skinny kid with freckles—but instead I walked into that apartment and found myself face-to-face with a girl so stunning she literally took my breath away.

I can't stop staring at her lips and the cute gap between her two front teeth, which I get a glimpse of when she very occasionally smiles.

Kate, who has barely glanced out the window to look at their new place, looks like their dad, with paler skin and reddish-brown hair that's taken on an electrified look after a night spent tossing and turning in the back of the car.

"Did they find him?" Kate asks me, a twinge of hope in her voice that pains me to have to quash. She's talking about the cat they had to leave behind. She had been hysterically crying about it when Will and I arrived last night at their aunt Chrissy's. Her face is still tearstained.

"I haven't heard," I tell her. I put a call into the fire station last night to ask them to check and am still waiting to hear back. "I'll let you know as soon as I do," I reassure her.

We climb out of the car—everyone stretching and yawning. Kate looks around with a scowl on her face, and Cole rubs his eyes. "Where are we?" he demands, glowering at the apartment complex in front of us.

"You're going to stay here for a while," I tell him, glancing at my watch. The landlord, Robert, told me he'd be by around two to meet his new tenants. I've already explained the situation to him—waking him up at one in the morning to beg him to let them have the place, which he had marked for renovation. He was reluctant at first, but Robert's a good guy, and as soon as I mentioned that they were fleeing a domestic violence situation, he agreed. I threw in a couple of sweeteners, too—telling him I'd help with the renovations if he gave them a six-month lease, enough time to get them back on their feet.

I look over at Zoey's mom, Gina, wondering if I did the right thing. She looks like a lost child, and Will has to put his arm around her and steer her toward the door. The apartment is part of a complex of eight. Their block of four faces two other duplexes, making a little square with the front side facing the street. They'll be in one of the upstairs apartments. I live directly opposite but on the ground floor.

"The key's in the lockbox," I tell Will as we all pile up the stairs. I give him the code, and he opens the door.

Cole pushes inside first. "Where's the TV?" is the first thing he asks.

Zoey winces apologetically and gently admonishes him.

"I don't know if there's a TV, but we can sort that out."

Zoey frowns at me, her mouth tightening—the only indication she's annoyed. "You don't have to do that."

"It's no problem," I tell her.

Will sat his mother down at the little Formica table in the kitchen area. I go over to the window and pull back the curtains. "Look, you can see the ocean."

Cole comes running, skidding to a stop beside me, eyes wide with wonder at the glistening strip of blue in the distance. It's the first time I've seen him lost for words. Kate, too, has come over to look, her phone hanging limply in her hand. I think I see a slight softening of her perpetual scowl, but I might be mistaken. I look at Zoey, who stands beside me, so close our arms are almost brushing. Her eyes seem to blink back tears. "Are you okay?" I ask quietly.

She darts a glance my way and then gestures at the apartment. "I don't . . . I mean . . . I don't think we can afford . . ." A blush rises in her cheeks.

She's talking about the rent and the deposit. "It's fine," I reassure her. "It's handled. We can talk about it later."

A little furrow appears between her eyes. I know she wants to ask how, but before she can, Cole tugs on her hand. "Can we go to the beach? Can we?"

She smiles a little at his excitement, and I can see how hard she finds it to say no to him.

"Okay," she says, looking at me as though for permission. I realize in that moment she could probably ask me anything and I'd agree to do it, just on the off chance she might smile.

"Is there a pier?" Cole asks.

I nod. "Yeah, there's a pier."

"Does it have an arcade? And a Ferris wheel?" he asks, his eyes widening with excitement.

I shake my head. "No, but you can fish off it."

"Fish?!" he exclaims. "Cool. Can we do that now?"

I shake my head. "I don't have any equipment. But we can do it another day." I gesture to Will. "I'm going to take these guys out to the beach and for some lunch."

Will nods. "I need to stay here with Mom and make some calls." He means to the police. He needs to find out what the deal is with their father and his parole rules. He needs to alert them to their suspicion that his dad set the fire and also try to get some local services to help out with resettling his mom and siblings.

Zoey turns to Kate. "Do you want to come?" she asks her sister.

Kate shrugs, nonchalant, her expression still stony, but there's a glimmer of excitement in her eyes and she hurries after Cole.

"Don't you have to go to work?" Zoey asks me as we head out the door together.

I shake my head. "I called in and took a personal day."

She frowns again, and I wonder what I said or did to cause it.

I stand aside to let her go ahead of me down the stairs, my eyes tracking her movements. I don't know if she feels my gaze because she turns and looks at me over her shoulder. I flush and clear my throat. "How do you feel about trying the best burger in Oceanside?"

# ZOEY

It's so loud, like a living creature—wild and untamed. There's something both terrifying and electrifying about the scope and scale of it. I try to pinpoint the exact place where the sea meets the sky, but they blur into one brilliant blue expanse.

Cole has raced to the water's edge and is already throwing off his sneakers in a wild dash to dip his toes into the water. Kate, trying to seem cool and nonchalant, is not far behind him. I smile as I watch them, tucking wind-whipped strands of hair behind my ears. Tristan keeps looking at me out of the corner of his eye, and I worry it's because I look like a mess, but I don't have a hairbrush or a toothbrush or even deodorant, so there's not much I can do to fix that. I wrap my arms around myself and try not to shiver as the wind picks up, spraying salt water against my bare arms and face.

"Are you cold?" Tristan asks.

I shake my head.

"You're shivering," he says, and he pulls off his sweater and gives it to me.

I shake my head. "No, I'm fine," I tell him, but he keeps holding it out to me, and now he's smiling, revealing that deep dimple in his cheek.

"Come on," he says again. "You're freezing. Either that or you're really excited."

I lift my eyebrows at him, puzzled.

"My mom's dog shakes like that every time he sees a ball." He sees that his joke has fallen flat and hurries on, clearing his throat. "Not that I'm saying you're like a dog." Another pause. "You should really take my sweater," he says.

Reluctantly, I do. "Thanks," I murmur. For a moment I just hold it, feeling too awkward to put it on. It's warm from his body. It feels too intimate to actually wear it.

"I don't have cooties," he says.

I give him a look that says *ha ha* and finally pull it on. It's too big on me, of course, but it's so warm that I feel cocooned and, for a split second, even safe. It also smells of him, of citrus and something muskier, too, that makes me want to bury my nose in the fabric and breathe in deeply.

I don't; instead I glance at Tristan, who is watching Cole and Kate at the water's edge.

"Their first time seeing the ocean, huh?" he asks, nodding in Kate and Cole's direction.

I rip my eyes from Tristan and look. The two of them are dancing in the shallows, Cole shrieking with laughter as each wave laps his feet. "Yes. Can you tell?" I ask.

He grins and sits down in the sand, and after a beat I join him. I make sure to leave a good distance between us and pull my knees up to my chest. There are a few people out and about, and I scan each and every one of them. I can't shake the fear that my dad's followed us here. After three years of peace, I can't believe I'm back to living with this creeping sense of paranoia and terror. Is this what it will be like from now on? Forever? I think I might cry.

"Are you okay?" Tristan asks.

I open my mouth to tell him yes, but what comes out, much to my surprise, is "No."

"It's going to be okay," he tells me.

I've heard that before, from the police, from lawyers, and from social workers, and even then I knew it was all lies. It might be okay for a little while, but it never ends up staying that way for long. It's like having a fatal illness. It will only end one way. But I can't tell him this. It's not what he wants to hear. He wants his reassurance to make me feel better, so I just force a smile and let him think it has.

"I figured we can go have lunch," he says, "then head back to meet Robert, the landlord."

Why is he helping us? I'm grateful, of course, more than he knows, but I also hate the feeling that comes with it: that I owe him more than I can ever repay. I stare at the water, not knowing what to say.

"You know Will's leaving tomorrow?" he adds.

I nod.

"He misses you."

I pull a dubious face. Will misses me? Right, sure he does.

"I know you're pissed at him," Tristan goes on. "He's told me."

I dig my hands into the sand.

"He feels really bad, you know," Tristan goes on, "that he wasn't there."

Tears prick my eyes, sharp as needles. I blink rapidly to clear them. Will was around for a lot of the bad times, but he wasn't around for the worst of it. He joined the military as soon as he could. I was fourteen when he signed up. He left me to deal with everything by myself, and look what happened. I couldn't protect Mom on my own.

"I'm sorry," Tristan says, and it riles me because the last thing I want or need is his pity. "You shouldn't have had to deal with that all by yourself. It must have been hard."

That's an understatement. But something catches in my chest. I think he might be the first person who's ever recognized how hard it was.

"What you did, testifying against your dad, that was really brave."

I shrug, unable to look at him, conflicted by wanting to reject his pity while also recognizing his sympathy means something to me. "Yeah, well, I didn't have any other choice," I tell him.

"Yes, you did," Tristan argues. "And what you did took courage. Huge courage."

"And what was the point?" I ask quietly, the tears threatening to fall again. "He did three years, and now he's out and he wants revenge."

Tristan draws a breath, and when he speaks there's a growl to his voice. "He's not going to hurt you or your mom or anyone else."

I look sideways at him. From the way he's staring at me, with such fierce intensity, it's clear he wants me to believe him. I give him a faint smile—it's all that I can manage right now. But I look away quickly, to hide the truth that I don't believe him at all.

Suddenly, I feel a hand on mine. I look down. Tristan's fingers lightly touch my wrist. "I'm not going to let him hurt you," he tells me.

For several seconds, neither of us says a word. I can feel the heat of his fingers on my wrist, and his gaze holds me, refusing to let go. It's impossible to look away. I can feel an opening in my armor, a chink that lets in light, or maybe it's hope. And when I look into his eyes, I can feel myself being drawn into them.

I flash back to how he held me at fourteen, in his long, skinny arms, his chest lean but solid. For a heartbeat, I wonder what it would feel like to be held by him now—and my body responds in a way that shocks me. My heart speeds up; my skin burns where his fingers still rest on my wrist. Why is he staring at me still? Why are we both staring at each other without looking away?

I drag my eyes from his, my pulse skittering. He pulls his hand away. I can't be lured in like that by the feeling of hope that he offers. It's a trick. A con. Even if he thinks it's real. Hope's cruel like that.

Cole is suddenly diving down into the sand in front of me, his jeans soaked to the knees and his face flushed, and I'm grateful for the interruption.

"You have to try it." He grins. "The water's freezing!"

I shake my head, looking for Kate, who is still standing down at the water's edge, talking on her phone. "Maybe later," I mumble. "We need to go." I don't know why I say it. We don't have to go, but suddenly sitting here on the sand beside Tristan feels uncomfortable. I feel anxious, too anxious to sit.

I start to stand up, but Tristan leaps to his feet and holds his hand out to me. I pretend I haven't seen it, but when I glance his way and see the tiny look of hurt on his face I regret it.

"I'll take you out fishing sometime on my boat," Tristan tells Cole as we walk up the beach.

"You have a boat?!" Cole asks.

"Well, my dad does," Tristan answers.

"You can sail it?"

Tristan nods. "I'm in the Coast Guard."

"What's that?" Cole asks, screwing up his nose.

"It's a branch of the military—the smallest one. We run search and rescue and—"

"Do you kill people?" Cole asks.

Tristan's eyebrows shoot up in surprise, but he covers it with a laugh. "Well, most of the time I don't need a gun, not if I'm saving people from drowning. But sometimes we're taking down bad guys."

"Bad guys like who?" Cole asks, his face lighting up.

Tristan nods. "People doing bad things like smuggling and drug trafficking." He looks over at me as though to check that it's okay for him to tell Cole the truth, but in doing so catches my shocked expression. I had no idea he was in the Coast Guard. I wonder why Will never told me, but then I remember we haven't spoken properly in years.

"Do you get to shoot the bad guys?" Cole asks, and I poke him with my elbow.

"I have never shot anyone," Tristan says, turning to Cole, an expression of seriousness on his face. "And I hope I never do."

"But you have a gun and you know how to shoot it?" Cole asks.

I try to tamp down the niggling concern I have about his obsession with guns. It reminds me of the pictures he drew in his school notebook—something else I still need to deal with.

"I have a military-issue weapon, yes," says Tristan, "but I don't carry a gun." He leans down closer. "I'll tell you a secret. I don't really like guns. That's why I joined the Coast Guard: I wanted to help save lives, not take them. And also, I loved the sea, and I wanted to be on the water, but I also wanted to be a pilot, and this way I didn't have to choose. I could do both."

"You're a pilot?" Cole asks in wonder.

"Hoping to be," Tristan answers, grinning wide.

He's slowed his pace to match mine so we're walking alongside each other, and I sense him looking in my direction.

"My dad's a policeman," Cole says, a note of pride in his voice.

I almost stumble. Tristan's right there, his hand cupping my elbow, shooting me a look of concern. I nod at him to tell him I'm fine.

"Look!" Tristan says, making a rapid conversation change. "That's where we're going for lunch." He points at a little café on the beachfront. "First person there gets to order three scoops of ice cream for dessert."

That's all the encouragement Cole needs. He's gone like lightning, streaking toward the café.

Tristan glances my way again. "He doesn't know?" he asks me.

I shrug. "Cole was five when they arrested him. We kept it from him as much as we could. I had to tell him Dad was going to prison, but I told him it was because he did something wrong and hurt our mom and so he had to pay for it."

"How'd he take that?" Tristan asks.

I sigh. "I don't know. He doesn't ever talk about him usually. Occasionally he asks when Dad's getting out of prison. I guess at some point I should tell him he's been released."

We walk for a few moments in silence, watching Cole as he sprints toward his ice cream reward.

"He seems . . ." Tristan breaks off.

"Difficult?" I answer for him.

He shakes his head. "No. I was going to say that he seems like he has a lot of energy."

I laugh under my breath. "Yeah, he does. He's good at sports, but in Vegas there was no park or anywhere for him to go. I think he'll like being near the beach."

We reach the café, and Tristan holds the door open for me. "I can take him to the park and play soccer with him if he likes. And baseball."

I smile as I pass him, getting a hit of the same scent that's on his sweater. "He'd love that," I say, but he must spot something in my expression, because he stops smiling and narrows his eyes at me.

"What's the matter?" he asks, and I realize it's almost impossible to hide anything from him. I'm not used to that. My poker face has always been flawless, honed from years of having to hide in plain sight so as not to trigger my dad.

"Nothing," I say, because how can I put into words everything I'm feeling: overwhelmed and embarrassed and grateful and afraid and exhausted?

He studies me for a beat before answering. "For whatever it's worth, I think this could be a good place to call home."

Home. I think about that, about what it means. I guess it means a place you long to come back to. A place where you feel safe and happy, a place where you want to make memories. I've never had that. In fact, in my entire life I've never felt safe, and I've never lived anywhere that I look back on fondly. I don't have many memories because most things I want to forget.

Tristan pulls out a chair for me at a table near the window, and I fluster at the gesture. I'm not sure anyone has ever pulled out a chair or opened a door for me in my entire life. I've had a door slammed in my face and on my fingers, but never held open for me.

I sit down and Tristan sits opposite me, and for a few seconds it's just the two of us looking out at the ocean and the endless blue sky, and it feels like this moment, this very small, insignificant moment might be something I could store in my memory.

Soon, Cole and Kate join us, and Tristan looks at me and smiles. And for the first time since we saw each other again, I don't look away first.

# TRISTAN

As Cole and Kate rush over to the ice cream counter to pick out flavors, I glance at Zoey. I'm trying not to stare too much, but it's hard because it's like she has magnets in her skin and I'm filled with iron ball bearings. I can't stop studying her face, and it reminds me of being out on the water, watching the horizon, scanning for signs to predict the weather. Her eyes fall and her lips turn down when she seems the most impassive, struggling the hardest to hide the turmoil underneath. She doesn't like people seeing her worries, I don't think. Maybe that's because she doesn't like to worry her brother and sister.

All I can think about now is a memory of Zoey at age nine, her head normally buried in a book, joining Will and me watching a movie in their house. The movie was funny, though I can't recall why, because all I remember is Zoey laughing so hard she fell off the couch.

I'd give anything to see her laugh like that again. I know that's my thing—trying to solve and fix problems. Whether it's an engine or someone drowning, it doesn't matter. My sister has a habit of telling me that some things aren't my problem to solve—but this one feels like it is. I've been wanting to solve this one for a long time, ever since Will came over to my house when we were thirteen with a black eye. His dad had punched him in the face after Will had stepped between him and their mom.

He made me promise not to tell anyone what had really happened, and I had to listen to him lie, even to my own parents, that he'd taken a ball to the face in a game of baseball. I hated myself for lying, but I was scared that if I told the truth I'd lose his friendship, and Will's friendship meant more to me than almost anything else. It still does. So I covered for him and lived to regret it.

I used to wonder what might have happened if I'd told my parents the truth that day. Might they have been able to do something? Could they have called the cops, or social services? Could they have helped Will and his family? But Will's dad was a cop himself—that's what made it so hard. And Will had told me that if I said anything the police would take his dad's side, and if his dad found out he'd told anyone, he'd only beat him worse. I didn't want that to happen, so I stayed quiet. I thought I was protecting him. Now I know that I wasn't. But worse than that, I wasn't protecting Zoey, either. If I had spoken up then, maybe none of this would have happened and they wouldn't be where they are now, living in terror. I know that their dad hit Will, but I don't know if he hit Zoey, and the thought that he might have makes me ill with guilt and rage. The thought of anyone hurting her . . .

Zoey tries to make polite conversation throughout lunch, distracting a moody Kate from worrying about the cat and Cole from worrying about his Xbox, but I can tell her mind is on other things, so I take over, running through my repertoire of jokes to keep Cole occupied.

"Two goldfish are in a tank. One says to the other, 'Do you know how to drive this thing?'"

Cole laughs. Kate looks at me like I'm an alien. Zoey doesn't even hear. She keeps glancing nervously at the door every time it opens. Her foot is tapping a slow but steady rhythm under the table, so much so that it makes me want to reach out and put a hand on her knee to help keep it still.

She's barely eaten anything either, having ordered only a glass of water and some fries. She ate half, giving the rest to Cole, who followed my advice and ordered a bacon double cheeseburger, but I've barely seen Zoey eat since she snuck the protein bar I left her in the car while she thought I was asleep.

I ask her if she wants ice cream too, but she shakes her head. A flash of worry crosses her face as she watches Cole and Kate ordering at the counter, and immediately I figure it out and wonder how I could have been so stupid. She's worried about paying. Shit. "This is on me, okay?" I tell her, just as the waitress brings the check.

"No," she says, reaching to take the check from the waitress's hand. "Please, you've done enough."

I grab the check, and it becomes a tug-of-war. "You can get it next time," I tell her. Reluctantly, her cheeks flaming, she lets go.

I've no intention of letting her pay next time, but it's the only thing I can think of saying. I worry I've damaged her pride, but I know they don't have the money, especially with everything they now need to buy in order to get back on their feet.

She lowers her head. "I'll pay you back. I just need to get to the bank."

I nod. "Were you working in Vegas?" I ask, trying to change the subject.

"Yes, but only part-time, in a coffee shop." She casts a look at me, as though expecting me to be judging her negatively. "I was about to start community college."

I remember how smart she was. She was in all the enrichment programs they offered at our school. I wonder if the reason she didn't go to college was financial or because she couldn't leave her mom to manage alone. It seems so unfair.

"There's a great community college in San Diego," I tell her. "You could sign up for classes there."

She nods vaguely. "I need to get these two into school first," she says with a sigh, looking over at Cole and Kate. "There's so much to figure out. I need to find a job, too."

"I think I might know of one," I say. "My friend Kit just opened a restaurant in town."

Zoey looks at me with undisguised hope, and I realize that what I want more than anything is to protect her like I wasn't able to do before. It feels like nothing less than she deserves and nothing less than I owe.

# ZOEY

I hate being beholden to anyone, and for some reason being beholden to Tristan is worse. I don't want him to see me as a victim or needy or a burden. I'm worried about how we'll cover the rent on the apartment, though I haven't brought it up. It's such a nice place—way better than we could ever afford.

I know it's partly furnished, but we still have so much to buy. We don't have bedsheets or kitchenware, and the priority is new clothes and shoes for Cole and Kate and a phone for me. Every time I try to make a mental list of all there is to do, panic and anxiety threaten to overwhelm me, making my heart race so hard I can feel it trying to hammer a pathway out of my chest.

"One thing at a time," I hear Tristan say, and for a second I wonder if I spoke my anxiety out loud, but he's talking to Cole, who is asking him about the Xbox Tristan has offered to lend him, and when they can go and play soccer and when they can go out on the boat.

"Who's she texting all the time?" Tristan asks me, nodding at Kate, who, as usual, is managing to walk and text at the same time.

"Her friend Lis," I tell Tristan. "I think she's trying to get her to find the cat."

"I'll call the fire station when we get back, see if they've got any news." He pauses before asking, "Have you heard from the police?"

He means about my dad. "They were checking in with my dad's parole officer to see if he was in Scottsdale last night." I keep praying that the answer is yes, though if my dad has an alibi, then that leaves the possibility that maybe it was Cole who started the fire after all, and I'm not sure I want to deal with that possibility either.

"What?" Tristan asks, narrowing his eyes at me.

"Nothing," I say, annoyed at how transparent I am to him.

"He's not going to find you here," Tristan reassures me again, thinking I'm worrying about that and not about the fact my little brother might be a pyromaniac. "I spoke to a friend of mine who's a local cop," he says. "He told me that because of your situation you don't have to register your address with the DMV, so your dad won't be able to trace you."

I glance at Cole, who is running ahead. I don't want him to hear, and I think that's why Tristan has waited until he's out of earshot to talk to me about it. "I know," I tell him. "But he's a cop. He knows how to find people."

"*Was* a cop. I can't imagine he has too many friends left in the department."

I shrug. "You don't know my dad."

He frowns.

"He's charming," I tell Tristan, pulling my arms around my body, grateful again for the warmth of his sweater. "He fools people all the time. He fooled you, didn't he? And your family. Everyone always loved him. That's why it was so hard to summon the courage to admit what he was doing. We didn't think anyone would believe us. And when we did speak up, we found out we were right—a lot of people didn't believe us."

"I did," Tristan says quietly but firmly. "I knew. I believed you," he adds.

I look up at him—he's a head taller than me—and I smile briefly. He doesn't know it, but those words are everything. He looks away quickly.

We arrive at the apartment complex, and I notice a white Mazda parked outside. Immediately, I'm on edge before Tristan spots the car and says, "Robert's here. He's the landlord. He's great," he reassures me.

I follow him up the stairs to the condo's front door. Will's inside sitting at the kitchen table. My mom is flitting around the kitchen making tea, and though there's a slight manic-ness to her movements, she's smiling. The reason for her smile walks through the door. He's a man of about fifty, with gray tufty hair and crystal-clear blue eyes. "And you must be Zoey," he says, beaming at me, hand extended.

He shakes my hand and fixes me with a look that radiates, for want of another word, pure goodness. "It's lovely to meet you," he tells me.

"You too," I say, and then add, "Thank you. We really appreciate you letting us have the apartment."

"It's my pleasure." He gestures at the kitchen. "I'd been planning on putting in a new kitchen and bathroom, so I apologize for the state of them."

I look at the kitchen, which seems perfectly fine to me, way better than the kitchen we had in Vegas. "Everything's great," I tell him. "Please don't apologize."

Tristan looks at a box of cakes on the table. "These from Kit's new place?" he asks Robert as he takes a bite out of one. Cream oozes out of it, and he licks it off his lips. For some reason, I can't stop staring.

"Yes. There was a line out the door this morning."

Tristan offers the box of cakes to me. "Try one."

I do, and it's just about the best cake I've ever eaten. But I'm also starving, so that could be why.

"Um," I say, clearing my throat and turning to Robert, "should we talk about the rent?" I glance at my mother, not wanting her to hear. Usually, I like to keep all the financial stuff to myself. My dad was the one who handled all the money, and when we left him, my mom found it hard to manage. It was just easier for me to take over the housekeeping and the money management.

"It's all sorted," says Robert, smiling at me broadly.

"What?" I ask, confused.

"Your mother and Will and I have everything settled," he explains.

My mom and Will both nod at me. "It's all good," Will says.

I want to ask them what that means, but I can't, not with Robert and Tristan both standing here, listening.

"I also brought a few things over—things that have been left behind from my other rentals—kitchenware and such." I look toward the boxes he's pointing at and notice one is overflowing with saucepans and utensils.

"Thank you," I say, suddenly remembering the few things we left behind in Vegas. I get a flash of the mug that Cole made for me once on a school trip to a pottery place. And the painting that Kate did of birds in a tree that hangs on the wall in our now-burned living room. All my books, ones I've salvaged over the years from thrift stores. They're silly things, with no value other than sentimental, but it hits me then what we've lost. We'll get everything back, I tell myself. We might even be able to move back home once the repairs are done, if we find out it wasn't my dad who set fire to the car.

But when I look around this little apartment, at Cole and Kate digging through the box of cakes, at my mom pouring tea for Robert, and . . . at Tristan, who's teasing Cole, painting his face with cream from one of the pastries, I wonder if that's still what I want.

# TRISTAN

leave Will and his family to get settled and head straight to Kit's new restaurant, Riley's, packed with customers even in the lull between lunch and dinner.

I find the owner in the kitchen, elbow-deep in flour, surrounded by hectic chefs and waitstaff.

"It's busy out there," I say.

Kit raises a flour-dusted hand to high-five me. "Yeah, we haven't stopped since we opened. It's crazy."

"Your mad baking skills are the talk of the town."

"I don't like to brag"—Kit grins—"but my buns are pretty damn good."

"I don't need to know what Jessa says about your buns." I laugh.

Kit grins even harder, as he always does at the mention of Jessa. I can't help but smile. I've always wondered what it would be like to feel the way Kit so obviously does about Jessa—like he's the luckiest man alive and can't quite believe it. Even just mentioning her name, it's like someone turned a light switch on inside of him. And Jessa's the same whenever she's around him.

"What's up?" Kit asks, kneading the dough, his eyes darting around the busy kitchen, checking that everything is running smoothly.

"You look like you could use an extra pair of hands."

He stares at me skeptically. "Dude, I know there's a 'Help Wanted' sign on the window out front, but don't you have a job? You know, saving people and all that?"

"Not for me. Will's sister. She needs a job. And you need staff, so . . ."

Kit stops kneading. "I didn't know she lived in town."

"They just moved here. It's a long story, and . . ." I break off. It's really not my story to tell. I'll let Will give him the details. "Anyway, Zoey needs a job. She's really amazing. You'll love her."

Kit cocks an eyebrow at that, his gaze narrowing. "Really amazing, huh?"

"Yeah, and she's got experience, too."

"Sounds like *you* want to give her a job." Kit smirks.

I roll my eyes, but Kit's smile widens.

"Will know you got the hots for his sister?"

I snort. "I don't have the hots for her." I'm not about to let Kit's imagination go off the rails. "Look, I'm just trying to do her a favor. The situation's not great. Their dad's out of prison. She could use the money."

Kit's expression shifts, the smile vanishing. "Shit, seriously? How'd he get out of prison? I thought he was in for years."

I shake my head. "Parole."

"How's Will?" Kit asks.

"He's leaving tomorrow," I say. "You should call him."

"Yeah, I'll do that." Kit was in the marines, so he knows exactly what it's like to leave home for long stretches at a time. "Have Zoey come by, or give her my number."

"Thanks, Kit," I say, watching him divert his attention back to the task at hand.

I take a second to think about all Kit's done—from being a marine to running his own restaurant—and wonder if he ever saw life beyond being a soldier. If he ever allowed himself to think that far ahead. If Will does. I've never thought of any job beyond being a pilot. Even when I'm done with the military, I know I'll still want to fly. I enjoy the solitude of the sky, the silence—so different from the sea. I like the freedom of being able to go anywhere around the world, having wings. The thought of being stuck in one place, surrounded by the din of a busy kitchen, giving orders to staff, dealing with customers, would drive me crazy.

"I'll get out of your way," I say to Kit as I back out of the kitchen.

Kit raises a hand in good-bye. "And I promise I won't tell Will you have the hots for his sister."

I open my mouth to protest, but he's already turned away, dealing with some kitchen crisis.

By the time I get back to Zoey's, it's evening. I knock on their door and hear Zoey inside, asking, "Who is it?"

"It's me," I reply, wishing that I didn't hear the edge of fear in her voice. "Tristan."

I hear the sound of the locks turning and the chain being removed, and then Zoey opens the door. She looks tired, with dark circles under her eyes. I guess I am too—it's been a long twenty-four hours.

"Will's not here," Zoey says to me. "He took Cole and Kate shopping."

"I wanted to see you, actually," I say. Zoey looks surprised to hear this, so I hold up the bags I'm carrying. "I brought a few things from my sister."

She frowns. "She's an assistant," I explain quickly. "To an actress. You might know her. Emma Rotherham."

There's zero response from Zoey as I pass her the bags. "She gave me some things. Clothes and shoes. I told her about you and what had happened, with the fire, and she went through Emma's closet."

Zoey is staring at me like I'm talking gibberish, but I carry on. "Dahlia said she gets sent samples all the time that she never even wears. I think you're the same size." I try not to let my gaze travel south when I say that and instead maintain strict eye contact, but it's awkward because I've just implied that I've appraised her body well enough to make the assumption about her size. Which would not be a lie. She works hard to hide her body, so maybe I have it wrong, but I don't think so.

"Will you stay for dinner?" Gina asks, coming up behind Zoey and wiping her hands on a tea cloth. "I'm cooking pasta. Robert was kind enough to lend us enough kitchenware to open our own restaurant, and Will took us grocery shopping earlier."

"I, er . . ." I look at Zoey to see if the invite to dinner extends from her, too, but her mouth is pursed and she's frowning yet again. It's clear I'm the cause of the frown, but I don't know why, and it's also clear she isn't happy about the invite. What did I do?

"I'm busy," I say quickly to Gina, making an excuse, even though the smell of garlic and onions frying is making my mouth water and I've got nothing more exciting to do at home but watch Netflix and chill, without the "chill" part. "I'll just leave these here," I say to Zoey, setting the bags down at her feet.

Still, Zoey says nothing.

"Thank you," Gina says, speaking up. "It's so kind of you." She touches my hand. "Really. We appreciate it. Don't we, Zoey?"

Zoey's glowering at the bags like they've just insulted her. And it suddenly dawns on me that maybe she's looking at it like charity. Damn it. I should have thought about that. I wanted to help, and it looks like I've done the exact opposite. I don't understand why, though. Part of me wishes she'd stop being so damn stubborn and accept the help. It's like a drowning person not taking the hand being offered to pull them into the life raft because they're too proud and want to prove they can make it back to shore alone. Even if potentially they might drown.

"I'll see you around," I murmur, and head out the door. "If you need anything," I say to Gina, "just give me a call."

Zoey's mom smiles at me and waves me off, but Zoey doesn't move.

# ZOEY

'm taking a shower," I tell my mom, but as soon as I've locked the door behind me I collapse down onto the toilet seat and bury my face in my hands. I don't know what I'm so bothered about. They're clothes. And I need clothes. I should be grateful, but that's the thing. I'm sick of having to feel grateful because it makes me feel pathetic.

I haven't had more than a minute to myself all day. I'm so tired I can barely see straight, and emotions are tumbling around inside me like loose change in a dryer. I don't know which emotions hit me hardest, but I know that I'm afraid. Actually, "terrified" would be more accurate. And I don't want the others to see my fear, so I've been hiding it, which is exhausting.

I haul myself to my feet, strip, and step into the shower, closing my eyes and letting the water wash away the day. I turn the tap to the hottest it will go, hoping it will somehow sear away the sadness and the fear. When that doesn't work, I start to cry. I only ever cry in the shower, where no one will hear me. Living in close confines forces you to find clever ways to hide your secrets. But straightaway someone knocks on the bathroom door.

"Just a minute," I shout, and take a few deep breaths, my palms flat against the tiles, my head bowed, trying to pull myself together. Finally, I turn off the taps and get out, wrapping myself in a clean towel from the pile Robert left us. It reminds me of cocooning myself in Tristan's sweater earlier at the beach.

There's another knock on the door. "Okay, okay," I say, pulling it open. But it's not Kate. It's my mom.

"Here," she says. "The clothes Tristan bought." She hands them to me. "I had a look through; there's some really lovely things."

I take the bag reluctantly.

She studies me, then puts the bags down and pulls me in for a hug. It surprises me so much that a sob rises up my throat and I have to swallow it down before it can burst out of me.

When I was a little girl, my mom and I were always close, but for the last few years we've been more like housemates than mother and daughter. Our conversations are never about boys or dating or friends; they're about paying bills and dividing up chores.

As she hugs me, I realize how long it's been—so long that I'm now taller than her. And because of that, it feels odd, like I'm the parent and she's the child and I'm the one who should be comforting her. She pulls back after a while, giving me a smile that doesn't do much to mask the sadness in her eyes, a sadness I had thought was gone for good and hate to see has returned.

She strokes my wet hair behind my ear. "Come on, let me comb your hair."

I let her pull me toward the sofa. I close my eyes and enjoy how soothing it feels. We used to do this all the time when I was a little girl. She would braid my hair every morning before school, every day a more elaborate style. Tears start to well up again, and I fight them. If I thought that my mom could handle it, that she could hold me and soothe me without breaking down herself, then I would turn to her and cry into her shoulder like I imagine other daughters do with their moms.

My mom finishes and puts the comb down. Her hand rests on my shoulder, and I turn to her, tears welling despite my attempts to stop them. But then I find that she's fighting back tears herself. She grips my hand, and the tears start to flow down her cheeks. I blink away my own.

"It'll be okay," I tell her numbly, and pat her hand.

I can't afford to be a little kid right now. We can't both break down. I need to be strong. And I can't be mad at her. She's probably more afraid than I am. My dad almost killed her. He would have done it if I hadn't called the police. She must be reliving that scene every time she closes her eyes. I know I do.

My mom nods at me, her lip trembling. "It's going to be okay," she repeats, then adds very quietly, "I'm sorry."

Sorry for what? I wonder. It's not her fault that we're in this position. He fooled her as well as he fooled everyone else. He was good-looking and charming and fun at first, and he was her ticket out of a miserable childhood and an even more miserable town. We all make bad choices in life, but most of us don't spend the rest of our lives paying for them. I could never blame her. My father is the one with the anger, the temper. He was the one who raised his fist and hit her. Hit Will.

She wipes at her tears, gets up, and rushes over to the stove, where the pan of water is threatening to boil over. Just then, Cole comes charging inside the apartment, with Will and Kate following behind him.

"I'm starving!" Cole shouts. "Is dinner ready?"

"In a minute," my mom answers him.

Kate comes over to me. "Here," she says, thrusting a plastic bag my way. "I got you what you wanted: underwear and socks."

"Thanks," I say, but she's already walking away.

I take the plastic bag and then, reluctantly, the two bags of clothes that Tristan brought and disappear back into the bathroom. I need to get over my pride. It's not like I'm in any position to turn down free clothes.

Much to my surprise, half of the clothes still have their price tags attached, and they are all, without exception, designer labels. Most of it I would never wear in a million years, not because the clothes aren't nice, but because I could never afford them. I usually just wear whatever baggy, oversize clothes I can find at the thrift store.

There are a few dresses and a pale blue silk shirt with a five-hundred-dollar price tag still attached. It makes me sigh, both with wonder at how beautiful it is and with anger at how a shirt can cost the same as an entire month's grocery budget. I noticed a few things that might fit Kate and think that the new clothes might cheer her up and distract her from the missing cat.

I tear the tag off the denim shorts and find the new underwear Kate bought me and get dressed, deciding that the silk shirt is too nice to wear. In the end, I ignore the sweaters, too—they seem too luxurious to wear and too tight—and pull on Tristan's sweater instead.

When I come out of the bathroom, I find Cole complaining again about being hungry and Will helping my mom with the dinner. I hand the bags of clothes to Kate, who, as predicted, gives the first real smile since we got here and runs into the bedroom to try things on. Then I help Cole lay the table.

"Is that Tristan's sweater?" Will asks as I reach past him for cutlery.

"Yes," I mumble.

He doesn't say anything, so I glance up and catch the tail end of a scowl. My face heats up. Oh God, what's he thinking? That I have a crush on his friend?

My mom puts the food on the table, and I shout for Kate, who emerges wearing one of the new sweaters—an emerald-green one—which clings to every curve. "This is the only thing that fits," she tells me grumpily. "Everything else is made for a miniature supermodel."

"Actually, they're made for Emma Rotherham," I tell her.

Her eyes go wide. "What?"

"Tristan's sister works as her PA. They're her things."

"Oh my God!" Kate squeals. "I'm wearing one of Emma's sweaters?"

I nod. "It suits you," I tell her.

She purses her lips. She knows it looks good, and though she's trying to act like she doesn't care about my opinion, I know she's happy for the compliment.

"I thought you said you didn't have any clothes," Will says pointedly.

I pretend not to hear as Mom serves dinner. Cole reaches across the table for his plate and knocks a glass of water into my lap, soaking me. "Damn," I hiss, jumping up as water cascades over the table edge.

My new shorts are soaked.

Mom admonishes Cole, who starts yelling back at her that it wasn't his fault, and then Kate is sighing loudly and pulling out her phone and texting, her normal response when she doesn't want to deal with any family drama.

"Cole," Will shouts, handing me a tea towel to dry myself. "Sit down, be quiet, eat your dinner."

Cole shuts up and, glowering, sits down and starts angrily digging into his pasta.

"It's my last night; I just want to have a nice family meal," Will says, sitting down. "Kate, who are you texting all the time?"

"No one," she huffs, putting the phone away.

Cole looks angrily among us all, and Kate just stares at her phone, as though wishing she could operate it telepathically. Will raises his eyebrows at me, then pulls a face. It's what he used to do when we were little. We'd communicate in a series of expressions and under-the-table kicks. A Morse code between siblings who early on learned not to aggravate their father. This look, the raised eyebrows and the twitch of a smile at the edge of his mouth, means *Is everyone else in this family crazy but us?*

Once upon a time, I'd have nodded and then kicked him under the table, but this time I just ignore him and excuse myself, escaping into the bedroom to change out of my wet shorts, but I've got nothing to change into, since Kate has the bag of clothes in her room. I don't want to go back to the table and pretend to be a happy family. Instead, I wander to the window and look out. It's dark. Anyone could be out there watching from beyond the amber halo thrown by the streetlight. My eyes land on the apartment opposite.

I wish I hadn't been so rude to Tristan when he brought the clothes over. He didn't deserve it. Mind you, I'm glad he didn't stay for dinner, given how it's turned out. The light is on in what I guess is his kitchen or living room. I wonder if he lives alone.

Does he have a girlfriend? I hadn't considered it until now, but it seems obvious that he must. He's good-looking, there's no denying it—sweet, funny, and smart too. He's the whole package, as my aunt would say. I wonder what his girlfriend is like.

Just then there's a tap on the door, and Will walks in. He sees me standing by the window and comes over to stand by me. "Your dinner's getting cold."

"I'm not hungry," I say.

"Are you okay?" he asks.

I nod. "I'm fine."

"Don't lie," he says, turning to face me. "You're not fine. How could you be with all this going on?"

I sigh. "What do you care?"

"What's that supposed to mean?" he asks, frowning at me.

I could bite it all back like I normally do. I could pretend everything's fine between us, but I don't. All the anger and resentment that I've stored up for the last few years comes rushing out of me. "You show up once every year or so," I hiss. "You're never around; you don't care whether I'm fine or not!"

"Of course I do," he answers, looking shocked at my outburst.

"Bullshit," I shout, startling him as much as myself.

"Seriously?" he asks. "You're going to call bullshit? After everything I've done?"

It's my turn to look taken aback. I laugh bitterly, sarcasm dripping from my voice. "Okay, you came and picked us up and brought us here. Thank you. I appreciate it. What do you want? A medal?"

He stares at me for a few seconds, seeming more hurt than angry. "That's not what I meant," he says finally, through gritted teeth.

"Then what did you mean?" I ask.

"Nothing," he mutters.

"No, tell me," I demand, hands on hips. "I'm all ears. I want to know what else you've done while I've been at home for the last five years taking care of everyone, making sure there was food on the table and the bills got paid and that Cole and Kate were looked after, and that Mom didn't fall into depression?"

Will doesn't answer me.

"Please tell me, what have you done?" I push, and when he still doesn't answer I take a step toward him, keeping my voice low so the others can't hear. "You chose to leave. You chose to look out for yourself. Not for us."

He stares at me silently, then shakes his head. "You're right," he says. He stares at me for another few seconds before he turns on his heel and walks toward the door. He stops and looks back at me. "I'm sorry," he says so quietly I barely hear him.

It knocks the wind out of me to hear him say it, but one measly apology isn't enough, and I have so much anger toward him I can't act like that suddenly makes it okay. He left us. He left me to deal with Dad by myself. I can't forgive him for that.

Will's looking at me as if waiting for me to say something, but when he realizes I'm not going to, he turns away and walks out the door.

# TRISTAN

glance up at the window and sense rather than see Zoey, watching us. I wonder what she and Will argued about. He won't tell me.

"Just keep an eye on them for me, okay?" Will says to me.

I turn back to him. "Of course, bro." He doesn't need to ask. That's a given.

"I'll try to keep watch on my dad," he mumbles, "speak to his parole officer, but it'll be difficult from over there." He frowns, frustrated, and I put my hand on his shoulder.

"It's going to be okay," I tell him, realizing I said the exact same thing to his sister a few hours ago. Will gives a vague nod in response. He doesn't believe me either. It's like he and Zoey are prisoners on death row who've given up any hope of reprieve.

Will nods his thanks. "I'm sorry," Will says. "To put this all on you."

I shake my head. "Hey, don't be stupid. You'd do the same for me."

He nods. "Luckily, you don't have a psycho for a dad, so I don't need to."

I smile. "Fair point," I answer dryly.

"I gotta go."

I nod. This part is always the hardest. "Take care over there. Don't be a hero."

He gives me a wry smile at that. It's our catchphrase, what we've been saying to each other since we were kids and I climbed into a tree to rescue a cat, followed by Will having to eventually call the fire department to come rescue me and the cat.

"No chance of that," Will answers.

I raise one skeptical eyebrow. He likes to act modest, but the truth is he's been cited for bravery. When it comes down to it, Will might not be a natural soldier, but he's not a coward, either. He'd put his family—and in this case, his fellow soldiers—first in every situation.

He kicks up the stand on his bike and revs the engine.

"Hey," I say to him just as he's about to pull away. "Why did Mickey Mouse get shot?"

He shakes his head, already groaning and rolling his eyes.

"Because Donald ducked."

"Can you work on your jokes while I'm gone?" he asks.

"What's wrong with my jokes?" I call after him as he drives away.

# ZOEY

I hear an engine roar to life outside the apartment, and suddenly it hits me: Will's leaving tomorrow. And I just let him go without even saying good-bye. What if he doesn't make it back?

I shove the thought aside. Of course he'll make it back; he always does. But I can't let him go like this. I sprint to the window just in time to see Will revving his bike. I bang and bang on the window with my fist, but neither he nor Tristan hears me, and then he's gone and it's too late.

Tristan watches him drive away too, then turns and looks up at my window, frowning, before walking back to his apartment and shutting the door. Will must have told him what a bitch I was.

Kate and Cole are both exhausted, the events of the last twenty-four hours starting to catch up with them, and for once it's easy to get Cole into bed. He and Kate are going to share the small room with twin beds, much to Kate's annoyance, and my mom and I will share the double, though I'll probably end up sleeping on the sofa as I usually do. I prefer to sleep near the door so I can be sure to hear if someone ever tries to break in. Even after my dad was sent to jail, that didn't change—the fear has never gone away. It's ingrained in me too deep, and now, following the fire, I think it'll be even worse.

My mom has just taken her nighttime pill and is getting ready for bed. Another layer of sadness has descended on her because of Will's leaving. She's wringing her hands as she sits on the edge of the bed. "Will said he'll send us some money," she tells me.

"I'll get a job tomorrow," I tell her, not wanting Will's money.

"What about school?" she asks me.

"I'll call tomorrow and get Cole and Kate registered."

"No," she says, still chewing on her lip. "I meant your school. What about college?"

"We need money," I say gruffly.

She sighs but says nothing because she knows I'm right, and yet it still hurts that she doesn't try to argue with me. I haven't said anything about her getting a job because I'm not sure she'll be ready to look for one. She isn't good with new situations. She suffers from anxiety. I wish I could shake her by the shoulders and tell her to get it together because I'm tired of being the grown-up, but I can't. She's too fragile. It would be like shaking a child. It's not her fault, I remind myself for the millionth time. My dad did this to her.

"Did you hear anything?" I ask. "From the parole officer?"

My mom swallows and nods. "Yes, just now. Will texted to say he'd heard back. He said . . . your father . . . he's in Scottsdale. As far as the parole officer is aware, he hasn't left town. He just checked in on him, and he's there right now."

A boulder lifts off my shoulders. But then I realize that

though it means we're safe for tonight, it doesn't mean he wasn't in Vegas last night. He could have driven there and back in time. He isn't wearing an electronic tag. They don't know his whereabouts 24/7.

"Do you think it was him?" my mom asks me, her voice barely a whisper.

I don't answer straightaway. I'm weighing what I believe against what I think she needs to hear. I remember the strange phone calls last night, and I think about Cole, too. In the end, I shake my head and say, "No." It's what she wants to hear, and the truth is I really don't know.

After she's fallen asleep, I take our dirty clothes and head outside to the laundry room behind the condo. Knowing my dad is in Scottsdale, that there's an actual confirmed sighting of him there, makes me feel brave enough to venture out into the dark, but I make sure to take a kitchen knife anyway.

After sticking my still-damp shorts in the dryer, I think about heading back to the apartment, but then, without warning, I find myself bent over the washer, sobbing. I let it all out: my fear and my exhaustion and my upset at fighting with Will. I'm pouring out hot tears, and my lungs feel like they're going to burst inside my chest. As I struggle to catch my breath, I hear a sound just outside the door—a footstep. I grab for the knife on top of the washing machine and spin around.

Through my tears, all I register is someone blocking the door, silhouetted against the light.

"Whoa, it's just me. It's just me," Tristan says, holding up his hands and staring at me like he thinks I'm crazy. "Do you want to put that down?" he asks, nodding nervously at the knife. "I'm kind of attached to my limbs."

I realize I'm thrusting the knife in his direction and quickly drop it to my side, wiping my nose with the back of my sleeve, which I realize too late is his sleeve because it's his sweater. Then I remember I'm not wearing any shorts either and his sweater is only just covering my underwear.

"Sorry," I mumble. Is it possible to die of embarrassment? Because if so, then I think I'm pretty close to flatlining.

"It's okay," he says.

I stare down at the ground, and Tristan takes a step forward and slowly reaches for the knife, prizing it out of my hand and setting it down on top of the dryer. He must think I'm a total psychopath. My shoulders start to shake again. I don't want to cry in front of him. I forbid myself from crying in front of him, and I swallow hard to stop myself, which feels like I'm swallowing the actual knife. But then Tristan takes another step forward, and just like when I was eleven and he was fourteen, he wraps his arms around me and pulls me against his chest.

I think about protesting, about pulling away, but even if I made up my mind to, my body wouldn't let me, not just because it feels so good to be held but because it feels so good to be held by *him*.

I'm pressed against his chest, my head resting just below his chin. I can't even remember the last time someone held me like this. And then it dawns on me. It was him. Back when I was eleven. My hands are flat against his stomach, and I can feel the topography of muscle beneath his T-shirt. With my ear pressed to his chest, I can hear his heart beating, strong and steady beneath my ear. I can feel the warmth and strength of his arms, and his hands, one on the center of my back and the other on my shoulder, holding me tight, pulling me closer.

Over my sobs I can hear him saying, "Shhhh," and his lips brushing the top of my head, sending a shiver down my spine that I don't fully understand. It's not a shiver that ends when it reaches the soles of my feet, but rather it turns and travels all the way back up my spine.

Eventually, my breathing starts to calm down, to fall into sync with his, and I become acutely aware of other things, like how good he smells. I breathe in deeper, a great heaving breath that manages to calm me even further. I know I should probably pull away because I'm no longer crying, but I don't want to. I feel safe in his arms.

He mumbles something I can't hear, so I have to lean back a little. When I do, his arms drop away, and I feel like I might sink to the floor. I wipe my hot mess of a face with my sleeve.

"I hope you're going to wash my sweater," he says.

Mortified, I glance at him. He's grinning at me, revealing the dimple in his cheek. "I'm joking," he says quickly, seeing my expression.

"I'm sorry," I mumble.

"No," he says, shaking his head. "Don't be. Are you feeling better?"

I nod. Though the truth is I'm not as good as I was twenty seconds ago. I feel bereft, if that's the right word to describe what I'm feeling. No, it's not bereft. That would suggest a much greater loss. He held me for a few minutes. Why am I making such a big deal out of it?

He's looking at me, though, really studying me, and I grow even more self-conscious under his scrutiny. I wipe my face again, trying not to imagine how red and puffy I must look.

There's a moment where we both stand there looking at each

other and I feel as if he's inviting me to step into his arms again, as if he's actively fighting from pulling me toward him, but I know I can't get used to that feeling. It's false. There is no safety anywhere, and it's dangerous to kid myself otherwise.

The washer beeps, letting me know the load is done, and relieved, I rush to open the door and take out the wet clothes.

"Here, let me help," Tristan says.

"No, it's fine," I say, getting in his way.

He backs off. "Oh, right," he says quietly. "You don't like help."

My head whips around. "What?"

"You don't like help," he says, daring me to contradict him.

"That's not true. I . . ." I trail off. It's true, so why am I bothering to argue with him? I'm just annoyed because what does he expect? I've had to do everything on my own for the last five years. I pull my shorts from the dryer and stuff the wet clothes in. Tristan moves to turn it on, but I push in front of him and do it myself. He laughs under his breath.

"Okay, maybe it's a little bit true," I say grudgingly.

# TRISTAN

Um, do you mind . . ." She does a twirling motion with her finger, and I wonder what the hell she means, but then she holds up a pair of shorts.

I still don't get it, but then I glance down at her legs and wonder why I hadn't noticed until now that she's not wearing anything except my sweater. It's riding up at the tops of her thighs, giving me a peek of her underwear. Wow. Okay. Look away, Tristan, look away. I give myself the order, but it takes a few seconds for my brain to obey, and the image stays with me, burned onto my brain like a cattle brand on flesh.

I can't unsee what I've seen, and that tiniest glimpse of white and the image of her bare legs has stirred something inside me that is going to be a very visible problem in a few seconds. I turn around quickly, to protect both our modesties, and start thinking of unsexy things like Gunnie doing push-ups on the weight bench and . . .

. . . I hear her pulling on a pair of shorts and doing up the zipper, and immediately thoughts of Gunnie evaporate, and all I can think about is the sound of that zipper, and now I'm imagining what it would be like to slowly, very slowly, pull it down and ease the shorts over her hips and . . . Wrong. So wrong. What is with me? My problem is getting bigger. I focus on the square root of pi.

"Okay," Zoey says.

I give myself a mental shake and a stern admonishment before turning back around. "You want to go for a walk?" I ask, running a hand over my head and hoping she hasn't noticed how flustered I am.

"What?"

"The dryer will take a while. We can walk around town. I can show you some of the sights."

"In the dark?" she asks me, one eyebrow raised.

It's a good point. Hadn't thought of that. What am I going to show her in the dark? I don't know. I just wanted to get out of the close confines of the laundry room and into the cool night air, but I didn't want to leave her out here alone waiting for the dryer to finish, and, okay, I also just didn't want to leave her, period. I think back to what Kit said earlier about me having the hots for her. He was just teasing me, but as soon as he said it, I realized it was true. I was attracted to her. *Am* attracted to her. Shit.

"Okay," she says quickly before I can even come up with a response to what nighttime spectacles Oceanside has to offer. I can think of only one thing I do for excitement around here at night. Okay, two. The first involves my bike and a long straight road through the desert, and the second involves . . . Why do I keep going there? Back the hell up, soldier, I tell myself. You just started thinking about kissing her, and now you've jumped all the intervening stages and gone straight to sex? Shit. Like it wasn't bad enough thinking about kissing her, I have to go and open that Pandora's box too? It's too late, though, to unthink the thought, and my mind starts shooting off in all sorts of directions, picturing Zoey's upturned face, her lips parted ever so slightly in a smile, her naked legs tangled with mine, her naked body laid out beneath me, before I force myself to quit thinking altogether. What is with me? It's Zoey. I've known her since she was tiny. I'm best friends with her brother. She's terrified, and her whole life is a mess; this is the last thing I should be thinking about.

"Are you coming?" she asks.

I startle. But she's just waiting for me, wondering what I'm doing. I follow her outside, noting that she pauses and looks hesitatingly back at the knife she's left on top of the dryer.

"You can bring it if it makes you feel better," I tell her.

She shakes her head. "No, it's fine," but she sounds unsure. We start walking toward the street. "I didn't mean to go all *Psycho* on you back there. You scared me is all."

"No," I say. "I'm sorry I snuck up on you. I should have thought of that." I remember the look on her face when she turned toward me holding the knife in her hands—the terror in her eyes but also the shard-like glint of anger. She wasn't going to go down without a fight.

I hate Zoey's father for doing this to her—making her so afraid. I wonder where he is right now. Is Zoey right to worry that he could find them here?

"He's in Scottsdale," Zoey says as though she's heard my silent thoughts.

I nod. "Do you still think it was him who started the fire?"

I hear her sigh. "I don't know."

We're walking side by side. I really want to put my arm around her, and it's not because I'm drawn to her or because I'm attracted to her, which I'm not even bothering to deny anymore. I want to put my arm around her because more than anything I want to make her feel better, to reassure her that I'm going to look out for her, watch over her, as Will asked me to.

She's chewing her lip, and then suddenly she looks at me. "If it wasn't him who started the fire, then the only other person it could have been is Cole."

"What?" I come to a sudden stop.

She shakes her head, upset. "I know it sounds crazy, but . . . you've met him."

"But arson?" I ask her. "He's just a kid."

"I know," she says, her voice wrung out with stress. I figure this is the first time she's spoken of her suspicions with anyone. "But he ran away straight after the fire. The firefighters thought it could have been him who set it."

"Has he ever done anything like this before?" I ask.

Her top lip pulls up in a sardonic smile. "What? Blow up a car? No."

I can't help but laugh. She glares at me for a moment, but then she bursts out laughing too. I wish I could keep making her laugh, keep hearing it, because it's the best thing I've heard all day. But soon she falls silent, pulls herself together, and we keep walking.

"I'm not sure which option I prefer," she says. "Either my dad's trying to kill me, or my brother is an arsonist."

"Those aren't great options," I admit.

"I found these drawings yesterday that Cole had done. They're of people shooting one another. It's like a massacre of stick figures."

"Okay," I say slowly.

"That's not normal, is it?" she asks, looking at me.

"I wouldn't know," I finally answer, aware she's looking for reassurance that I can't give. "My friend Didi is a psychologist, though. If you'd like, I can ask her to recommend someone he could talk to."

"We can't afford it," she says. "And I know there are free counseling services, but I'm worried that if anyone finds out, social services will get involved. Or the cops." She kicks the curb and walks on. "I'm so bad at this."

I catch up to her and take her by the elbow to pull her around to me. "Hey, you're doing an amazing job."

She looks up at me, chin defiantly jutting but eyes watering. "No, I'm not."

I take her by the shoulders. "Yes, you are. You're amazing." I don't mean it in just the way she thinks but in every single way possible. I've seen her today, putting herself second to everyone, holding it together in front of them all. I've seen the kindness she reserves for Cole, who'd frankly test the patience of a saint. I've seen the patience she shows her mother, even though she'd be within her rights to feel mad at her for letting her bear the weight. I've seen her pride and her dignity and her strength, even when she's feeling humiliated and broken and weak. I've been with her for close to twenty-four hours, but it's more than enough time to realize that she's amazing. And she doesn't deserve any of this.

I stare into her eyes, willing her to know that I'm telling the truth and shocked, too, by just how much this girl has gotten under my skin in such a short time. She shakes her head sadly, takes a deep breath, then pulls away, and I wonder if she saw something else in my look, beyond my reassurance, because color rises in her cheeks.

"So, what sights are you going to show me?" she asks.

I try rapidly to think of what's open in Oceanside past midnight, but the options are few and far between. Then I remember the pier. "This way," I say, taking a right and heading to the beach.

It could be my imagination, but I think she's edged closer, so our arms are almost touching as we walk. Don't read anything into it, I tell myself. She's dealing with a lot, and for all I know she might even have a boyfriend. Or a girlfriend. It wouldn't surprise me if she told me she hated all men after seeing what her dad did to her mom.

"So, are you still a nerd?" I ask her as we walk.

"What?" she asks, turning to me surprised. "Who are you calling a nerd? *You* were the nerd!"

"True." I smile. "But what I remember most about you is that you always had your head buried in a book, and you were obsessed with Greek myths."

She cringes. "You remember that?"

"Oh yeah. I remember the costume you used to wear all the time. What was it? A gladiator?"

"No," she answers, a little outraged. "I was Athena! A Greek goddess."

"Right." I laugh, remembering the white tunic, plastic armor, and headdress she wore for months when she was about seven. "Isn't she the goddess of wisdom or something?" I ask.

"Yes, and war," she tells me, her mouth curling into a smile that does something to my gut. Is she flirting with me?

"It was cute," I tell her. Am I flirting back?

She snorts, flashing a quick glance in my direction. "Cute? You definitely did not think I was cute."

"Yes, I did." Still do, I add silently. And definitely not in a seven-year-old-cute way.

She snorts again, this time in disbelief. "You thought I was annoying—don't deny it."

"I didn't!" I argue. "I swear to God. I mean, you were a little competitive—"

"When you let me play!" she answers, laughing. "You and Will were always leaving me out."

"Sorry," I say, shrugging, because it's true. Will and I would often leave her out. In our excuse, we were ten and she was seven. And a girl. And all she wanted to do was play make-believe games that involved dressing up.

"You had that penguin phase too," I remind her.

"Oh God." She laughs, showing the gap in her teeth. "I forgot about Boris."

"Boris?"

"We went on a visit to the zoo with school. There was a penguin called Boris. He looked really unhappy, like he was desperate to get out of there." She pauses. "I wanted to break into the enclosure and free him. I hate zoos. You know, I read that penguins in captivity often have to be given Prozac for depression."

I smile as I listen to her, because it's great to hear her chatter away and see the darkness lift off her like a storm front passing over, revealing sparkling blue skies.

"Why are you smiling?" she asks. "It's sad." But she's smiling too. "Poor Boris. I wrote to the zoo's board of directors, demanding they free him."

"Did they?"

She shakes her head. "No. Of course not."

"Why did the penguin cross the road?"

She stares at me, only half-amused.

"To prove he wasn't a chicken."

She shakes her head, but there's a twitch of a smile at the corner of her mouth. "You're still collecting bad jokes, then?" she says.

"What do you mean?" I say, though I know exactly what she means.

I remember once going around to their house because Will hadn't been at school for a few days. Zoey answered the door and took me upstairs to his room, where I found him drawing at his desk. And when he turned, I saw he had a black eye. Will told me he'd gotten the black eye from being hit in the face by a ball. I didn't say anything, though I had questions. He got mad at Zoey for letting me in and yelled at her to get out of his room. She burst into tears, and I felt bad that somehow I was the reason.

I gave him his homework and told him I'd see him at school. But before I left, I knocked on Zoey's door and found her crying on her bed. I sat down next to her, feeling awkward and uncertain.

"Knock, knock," I said eventually.

"Who's there?" She sniffed.

"Europe."

"Europe who?" Zoey asked.

"No, I'm not."

Zoey stared at me for a full five seconds, then burst out laughing.

I told her a few more bad jokes until the tears had fully stopped. I liked Zoey. I thought of her sort of like a sister, not like Dahlia, exactly, but Zoey was someone I wanted to look out for and take care of, the way Will did.

"Can I tell you a secret?" she whispered, glancing nervously at the door.

I nodded.

She leaned in closer. "It wasn't a ball."

She rocked away from me, her eyes never leaving my face, a vulnerability and fear in her eyes that I still recognize today. I didn't know what to say to her then. I was only a kid myself. I didn't ask if it was her dad, but I knew it was.

In the end, feeling like a coward, I took her hand and squeezed it. "It'll be okay," I said, and told her another joke.

"I remember you used to always tell bad jokes," Zoey says to me, pulling me back into the moment.

"*Bad* jokes?" I say. "I seem to remember you laughing at them."

I don't tell her how that day I went home and memorized jokes especially for her, how making her laugh became one of my obsessions.

I look at her and see she's smiling, and I get the same little sense of satisfaction I used to get when I made her smile as a kid.

"Are you still collecting baseball cards?" she asks with a slight smirk.

"No," I answer, thinking of the collection sitting in a shoe box in my closet. "Not really. Are you still the Napoleon of board games?"

"What do you mean?"

"You always had to win. Like I said, you were very competitive."

"You always let me win. That's what made me mad."

"I didn't let you win," I argue, a little annoyed she saw through my ten-year-old self's ruses.

She cocks an eyebrow at me.

"Okay, not all the time," I admit. "Just the Game of Life. I know how much you wanted to win it."

She sighs. "I loved that game." Her smile fades. "Don't think I'm ever gonna win it in real life, though." She says this last part with a bitter laugh.

"I'll play you again sometime," I tell her. "Fair and square. Okay, give me your foot."

She stares at me, bewildered. "What?"

I point at her foot. "Give me your foot. I need to give you a boost."

"Why?"

"We're going over." I point at the gate we've stopped in front of.

She looks at the sign stuck to the gate. "It says 'Pier Closed.'"

"To other people," I tell her. "But I'm Coast Guard." I'm totally bullshitting, and she knows it.

"Couldn't we get in trouble?" she whispers, glancing around for anyone watching, but it's late and no one is around.

"I'll tell anyone who finds us that we thought we saw someone about to jump off the end of the pier and raced out here to save them. We'll be heroes."

She takes a deep breath, then sticks her foot out toward me. I grin, cup my hands beneath it, and boost her up and over the gate. She's athletic, gripping the top, swinging her legs over, and jumping down lightly to the other side. I follow her, noticing as I'm halfway over that a cop car has appeared with something like perfect timing, and is pulling to a halt on the street fifty meters away from us. Shit. I land in a crouch, grab Zoey's hand, and start running down the pier.

"What?" she hisses. "Why are we running?"

I pull her into the shadows alongside the wooden building that houses the ticket office and arcade. "Shhh," I say, glancing over her shoulder, noticing the cop is now out and lumbering over toward the pier entrance. Shit. Did he see us? He must have.

"Oh my God," Zoey whispers, her hand clenching mine tight. "What are we going to do?"

Being arrested was not part of my planned entertainment for this evening. I really should have thought this through. "Shhhhh," I say under my breath, watching the cop pull out a flashlight and start probing the shadows.

I pull Zoey closer, and she shrinks away from the light, pushing up against me. I cradle her as close as I can, deciding that if we're spotted I'll just take the rap and pray I can talk us out of it. Zoey's holding her breath, and when the cop rattles the gate to check it's locked, she tenses even further and we're pressed so tightly together that for a second I forget entirely about the cop and about the fact we're going to be arrested. All I can focus on is the smell of her hair and the feel of her body, which is just as perfect as I'd imagined—softer, too, in all the right places. And I really shouldn't be going there, but then she tilts her head up so she's looking at me.

This is exactly what I imagined just twenty minutes ago, and for a beat, as I stare at her lips, which are parted ever so slightly, I think about what it would be like to lean down and kiss her. It feels like the universe has set it up. It's just like a John Hughes movie.

I wonder if she's thinking the same thing, because her breathing has become rapid all of a sudden and I can feel her chest rising and falling against mine, her hands gripping my arms, but even though we're looking at each other, our faces are in shadow, so it's hard to tell what her expression is. Maybe she's not thinking the same thing at all. Maybe she's glaring at me, furious about the situation I've gotten us into and the trouble we'll be in if the cop spots her. Maybe the electric buzz I feel building like a static charge between us is in fact fueled by her fury, not by lust.

I seek out her eyes, trying to find the message in them. They're gleaming, watchful but also wary, and it gives me another pause. The cop moves away a few feet and starts shining the flashlight on the other side of the pier. I wait for Zoey to step back out of my arms or at least put a few inches between us, but she doesn't. We're both just frozen, the only sound the waves and my heartbeat, which to me sounds even louder than the waves.

Slowly, cautiously, I let my hand trace its way down her back to her waist. I hear a sharp intake of breath from her, which could be either startled surprise or something more. I freeze, uncertain which it is, but she doesn't move away, and then, to my own surprise and relief, I feel the very slight incline of her body toward mine, as she presses even further up against me. There's no mistaking it, is there? She does feel it too. There is an attraction, and it does go both ways.

It would be so easy to slide my other hand up her back. My fingers itch to stroke up her neck, to cup her cheek and then raise her lips to mine. There's nothing stopping me. I don't need to worry about Will—I know he wouldn't be mad. He's not that kind of brother. But is this the right thing to do, given everything Zoey's going through? Would it be taking advantage of her? And that's what stops me in my tracks, because the truth is I don't know what it would be.

*Complicated* is the answer that my brain fires back. Imagine kissing her and then things don't work out. It's not what she needs right now. Besides, you also told her brother you'd watch over her, not try to get into her pants. Act like a friend, not like a jerk.

# ZOEY

His hands drop from my waist, and he practically pushes me away. "He's gone," he says.

I glance over my shoulder and see the cop is getting into his car and starting the engine, but I'm too humiliated to care about the cop. Tristan's shoving his hands into his pockets and won't look at me. Oh God . . . What an idiot . . . I thought he was going to kiss me. And I think I *wanted* him to. But of course he doesn't look at me like that. I'm Will's sister, and besides . . . why would he ever like me? My face burns with embarrassment.

But then I remember the way his hand stroked down my back and lingered on my waist. I can still feel the imprint of it. Or am I misremembering what happened, like witnesses do after a crime?

I back away from him, tugging down the bottom of the sweater and wrapping my arms around my chest. "So . . . this is what you wanted to show me?" I ask, trying to act indifferent.

"This way," Tristan says, heading for the end of the pier.

I follow him and notice my stomach is fluttering. What is with that? We keep walking, reaching the end of the pier, and I stop and take a deep breath. It's like we're on the prow of a boat far out at sea, floating under the stars, and I haven't seen them in so long that I think I might cry.

"It's beautiful," I whisper.

"Yeah, it is," Tristan answers.

I turn to him and find him looking at me. "You know, I haven't seen the stars in so long," I tell him.

He frowns at me, not understanding.

"Vegas. The light pollution." I shrug. "You don't see the stars."

"It's the best thing about flying at night," Tristan says. "The stars feel so close, like you could reach out and touch them."

I stare up at the sky. I can't imagine. I've never been on a plane. "It must be amazing," I say, sneaking a look at him as he stares up at the sky. In profile, I notice the strong line of his jaw. "What's it like?"

"Flying?" he says, looking at me, his whole face lighting up. "It's the best feeling on earth." He stops. "Well . . . almost."

I flush, blood pounding to my cheeks.

He gazes up at the sky, shaking his head. "It feels like total freedom. It's so quiet and so still, and the world seems so small. It gives you a whole new perspective on everything."

I wish I could live on a plane, in that case. I wouldn't mind that freedom and peace or the knowledge I could escape any-time, anywhere.

"One day I'm going to travel the world," he says.

I gaze out at the horizon. I'd be lying if I said I wasn't jeal-ous. I've always wanted to travel, but I know I'll never have the chance or the money to go anywhere.

"See those three stars right there? That's Orion's Belt. If you follow it up, that triangle of stars above it, that's Orion." He points, and I tilt my head and try to put it together. I can't quite see it.

He steps closer so our shoulders brush. "That really bright star is the top of the triangle," he says.

I nod, finally seeing it. "Orion was a hunter. He hunted with Artemis," I explain. "She killed him with an arrow."

Tristan glances at me. "Geek," he mutters, nudging me in the side with his elbow.

I laugh and nudge him back, and for a moment I feel completely happy.

I lean over the end of the pier and stare down into the dark, swelling waves below and then back up at the stars. A plane is inching its way between them as though playing dot to dot. It reminds me of Will, about to board a military plane and head to the other side of the world.

"I got in a fight with Will," I admit to Tristan. I'm not sure why I tell him, but there's something about him that makes me want to open up and share. He's a good listener. And maybe it's also because Tristan knows me, knows my story. I can't hide the truth from him.

"He told me," he answers, coming to stand beside me, though leaving a good arm's distance between us. He obviously doesn't want me getting the wrong idea.

"What did he say?" I ask, bristling a little. Did Will say something horrible about me? Does Tristan believe it? Tristan shrugs, chewing on his lip.

"It's easy for him," I mutter. "He just gets to walk away every time things get hard."

Tristan turns to look at me, and I catch the flare of surprise in his expression. My cheeks burn. I didn't mean to say that. It's too personal and revealing. The silent part of what I said hangs there. I don't get to walk away. I'm always the one left behind.

"Can I tell you something?"

I nod warily.

"You're wrong about Will," Tristan says.

I cross my arms and turn to face him, bristling.

"He didn't abandon you. He did it for the signing bonus."

It's like I've been punched in the gut, all the air leaving my lungs. "What?"

"He wanted the signing bonus to pay for your mom and you guys to get away from your dad. He figured the money would help you start over."

My legs feel unsteady. "What?" I say again, staggering backward, covering my face with my hands. I think I might faint. Suddenly, I feel Tristan's hand on my lower back. I whip around, shaking it off. "Why didn't he tell me?"

"He gave the money to your mom. Your dad found it. He took it and . . ." He pauses, as if struggling to find the right words. "Remember that time she ended up in the hospital with the broken wrist?" I nod. Oh my God. *That* was the cause of it? I remember the rage my father flew into. It was like a tornado hitting the house dead-on. "Will blamed himself," Tristan goes on. "Thought it was his fault. He didn't want you to find out."

I feel sick and clutch my stomach as it starts to churn like the ocean below us. "How is that his fault?" I ask. "I can't believe he didn't tell me."

"I know," Tristan says quietly, shoving his hands in his pockets. "I told him to, but he didn't want to. And he'll be pissed at me when he finds out that I've told you."

"Why did you?" I ask.

He pauses. "Because he asked me once before to keep a secret, and it was the stupidest thing I ever agreed to. You needed to know. It's not worth you guys falling out over this."

Oh my God. The shock of what he's just told me makes me dizzy. How wrong I've been. How unfair. "I need to call him!" I blurt. "He's leaving tomorrow. I need to talk to him." I stick my hand in my back pocket for my phone before remembering I don't have one. I left it in Vegas.

"Here," Tristan says, "use mine." He hands it to me, and I see the lock screen image. It's a photograph of Tristan with his arms around a gorgeous, dark-haired girl. She's laughing as though he's tickling her. There's a stabbing feeling in my chest, like someone just shunted a knife between my ribs. So he does have a girlfriend after all.

Tristan takes the phone and scrolls to Will's number. He presses dial and hands the phone to me. The call goes straight to voice mail.

"Hey, Will," I say. "It's me. Call me back. I don't have my phone, so maybe try Kate in the morning before you leave." I hang up and give Tristan back the phone. I hope Will calls. I need to speak to him before he goes away. I need to make things right between us.

"You want to go home?" Tristan asks me.

I nod, and we start to head back up the pier. Neither of us says a word. I'm still processing what he told me about Will, feeling guilt mixed with anger, but I'm also processing the lock screen image on his phone. I don't know why it bothers me so much. I should know better than to let myself crush on anyone. I've seen how that ended up for my mom. Love just causes heartbreak and suffering. I've experienced heartbreak once myself, and I vowed to never let it happen again, to never again be so weak or so stupid to fall for a guy or his lies, or let anyone hurt me. It's a good thing that Tristan has a girlfriend, I tell myself. That way I won't make the mistake of falling for him.

Tristan cups his hands again to boost me over the gate, but I ignore him and struggle up and over by myself.

We walk until we reach the condo, and I head to the laundry room and grab my dry clothes. He comes with me.

"Don't forget the knife," he says, laying it on top of the laundry.

"I'll wash your sweater and give it back to you," I mumble.

"No," he says. "Keep it. It's fine."

I hurry out of the laundry room, Tristan following behind.

"Good night," he says as he veers off toward his place.

"Good night," I answer, the words catching in my throat. I head for the stairs to our apartment.

"Hey, Zoey?" Tristan calls out softy.

I turn.

"What's black-and-white and black-and-white and black-and-white?"

I shake my head, already laughing despite not knowing the answer.

"A penguin rolling down a hill." He grins.

I run up the stairs to our apartment, laughing but also feeling an ache in my chest that I don't think will be going away soon.

# TRISTAN

The first thing I do is put on a record, something to take my mind off everything. Then I drop to the floor like I'm at training camp and do fifty push-ups. I need to work out all the energy that's coursing through my body like a lava flow. There's frustration—of several kinds—and I feel like I'm at the start line of an Ironman race, not at the tail end of thirty-six hours with no sleep.

No matter how hard I push myself through the fifty sit-ups and then fifty pull-ups, though, I can't seem to banish the image of Zoey looking up at me: the way her eyes seemed to glimmer in the darkness, and the way she held her breath, as though anticipating something. I think about her lips again, how full and perfectly heart-shaped they are, and wonder what it would it be like to kiss her.

I do crunches next, grunting as I push myself into a sweat, wondering if Will is going to be mad that I told her the truth but wondering more what Will would say if he knew the thoughts I'm having about his sister. They're so out of left field I feel like I've been slugged by a right hook to the face that I didn't see coming. I've known Zoey almost my whole life. I've thought about her on and off over the years, keeping up on her news from Will, but I never in a million years expected to ever feel this way about her. I don't fall for people like this. I never fall for anyone. What the hell's going on?

I think back to when we were kids. I know I used to feel protective of her and that I always tried to watch out for her and find ways to make her smile, but it was a brotherly thing. But now it's definitely not the same. Yes, I want to still protect her, and the same instinct to make her laugh is also there, but I'm not doing it so selflessly. I want to make her smile, but more than that, I want her to smile at *me*.

Shit.

I'll keep my distance and just keep an eye on them from afar as I promised Will. That's best all round. The only problem is I'm working tomorrow for three days straight. There's some kind of smuggling operation we've been called in to deal with. I won't be around to keep an eye on them, but I'll have time to get my head straight, and maybe when I get back all these feelings will be gone.

I'm dripping with sweat by the time I stagger into the shower, and even then I can't banish the images of Zoey wearing just my sweater, the flash of her underwear. Goddamn it. I turn the taps as cold as they'll go, but it doesn't help. I get out of the shower, turn off the record, and switch on the Weather Channel. Focusing on hurricanes in the Atlantic might help.

While I'm trying to wind down, I sort through my clothes for tomorrow. We'll be undercover, so that means civvies. I empty out my jean pockets and find the piece of paper the girl I pulled from the water the other day scribbled her name and number on. Brittany. I'd forgotten all about her. I'm about to toss it when I stop. Maybe Brittany's just what I need. She did only want sex, after all. Maybe it would help expend some of my energy and stop me thinking about Zoey so much.

Before I can change my mind, I grab my phone and send a text to Brittany. It's late for a booty call, but who knows. Maybe she's also up late. I could kick myself the minute I've sent it, and a part of me is relieved when she doesn't respond. It was a dumb idea. I get my things together for the morning and flop into bed, staring at the ceiling.

I fall asleep eventually, but when my alarm wakes me what feels like five minutes later, I sit up, feeling like a bunch of rhinos stampeded through my head. I take another cold shower, this time to try to zap the energy back into me, but it takes three cups of coffee, a protein shake, and two bowls of cereal before I feel even vaguely human.

It's still dark out when I throw my bag over my shoulder and roll out the door. I glance up at the window to Zoey's room, wondering if she's asleep, wondering too if I should knock on her door and say good-bye. But instead I jog over to my bike and start the engine.

Three days. When I get back, everything will be different.

# ZOEY

A re you waiting for one more?" I ask, pointing at the empty setting at the end of the table.

"Yes," one of the girls sitting at the table tells me.

I nod and keep pouring water into the glasses, trying not to let my hand shake and the water spill. I can't believe the manager, Tessa, put me in charge of this table, and on what's only my second night on the job. As I move along, filling water glasses, I take a sneaky glance at my boss, Kit, who is only twenty-six but already owns a chain of award-winning restaurants, and at the girl beside him, his fiancée, Jessa, who I instantly recognize as the actress from that movie about spies in the Second World War! Holy . . .

"Oh God, I'm so sorry!" I look down at the now-soaking-wet tablecloth and Jessa's now-soaking-wet lap. Oh God, Kit's going to fire me. I just drenched his fiancée with water.

"It's fine," Jessa says in a whisper, smiling. "Don't worry."

I look around. The others haven't even noticed; they're all too busy listening to Kit telling a story about how he took some kid called Riley surfing for the first time and what a natural he's going to be. Jessa discreetly mops up the water in her lap with a napkin and gives me another reassuring smile, which almost makes me forget how to breathe. She's so completely mesmerizing to be close to, as though she's been doused in some kind of magic fairy dust that makes her glow.

Kit reaches a hand under the table and places it on her lower belly. Jessa gazes at him with a look of total adoration on her face, her cheeks flushing. I draw a sudden breath of understanding, and Jessa looks up at me, her eyes widening. She knows I've seen—not Kit's hand, but the small bump that's now visible thanks to the fact her soaking dress is clinging to it.

She's pregnant—maybe four months. It's obviously not public knowledge, and she must want it to stay that way. I smile and nod at her. She smiles back. I return to filling the water glasses, but I can't get the image of Kit reaching for her out of my head. And then there was the way she smiled at him as though there were no one else in the room. I've never seen a couple like that before. A couple who look at each other the way lovers in movies look at each other. My mind automatically conjures up Tristan. It keeps doing that. I don't know why, because I keep ordering it not to. I miss him. It's strange, but I do. I can't stop thinking about him, about his smile and the way it felt to be held by him, about how easy and how fun it was to talk to him.

When I think about the way he stared down at me in the shadows of the pier, butterflies start to flutter in my stomach. And each time I try to angrily swat them away. He has a girlfriend, and even if he didn't, I don't want to feel this way. Men are only trouble—I don't have to look any further than my mom to know that. Love, as far as I can tell, never works out. It just ends in heartbreak, or worse. Even so, I can't stop thinking about him.

Kit clinks a knife against his water glass and stands up, holding his glass in one hand. He turns to Jessa, and a look passes between them, one of such intensity and desire that it makes me blush. "I just wanted to wish a very happy birthday to my beautiful soon-to-be wife, Jessa," Kit says, his eyes glued to hers.

It seems like beneath the words there's a whole private, other-level conversation happening, and like everyone else in the room, I can't stop staring at them. Whatever chemistry they have is so strong it's almost visible.

"Okay, you two, get a room!" A girl with dark, curly hair opposite Jessa laughs, breaking the spell.

"You can talk, Didi!" Jessa retorts, laughing at her friend.

The man beside Didi, a broad-shouldered guy with an easy smile and a week's worth of scruffy beard, lifts his glass. "Happy birthday, Jessa!"

The other people at the table all join in with the toast, and I feel an enormous twang of envy as I look around at them all, laughing and chatting. Never mind love, I've never had that, either. I don't even know what it would be like to eat a dinner with friends because I've never done it.

"Would you bring some bread?" the girl—Didi—asks me, grounding me back to earth. "I've got a carb craving that absolutely must be sated."

I nod and rush off to fulfill the order, anxious not to mess anything up. On my way to the kitchen, a middle-aged man who is eating with his orange-tanned wife grabs my wrist as I pass his table.

"Sweetheart, can you bring me the wine menu?" he asks, directing the words at my chest, not my face.

I tug my arm from his grip, nodding and forcing a smile. As I turn around, I slam straight into someone.

"Sorry," we both say at the same time.

With a start, I look up. It's Tristan. "Sorry," he repeats.

I shake my head, mute. In only three days, I'd forgotten just how gorgeous he is. My memory didn't do him justice. At all. And now all those resolutions to forget him are ironically forgotten.

"How's it going?" he asks.

I shrug, unable to formulate words. It's only now, seeing him again, that I realize I've been ignoring the hollow ache I've been carrying around in my chest for the last few days. But seeing him makes the ache vanish, and I'm finally able to draw a full breath.

He's waiting for me to answer, but I can't, and now he's staring at me quizzically.

"Tristan!" someone yells, and his eyes dart over my shoulder and I see him break into a smile. He waves at one of the girls at Kit's table: a girl in a fuchsia-pink dress that sets off her perfect, glowing skin. She's beckoning him over to the empty chair beside her. It's the girl from his lock screen. His girlfriend.

"Guess I'll see you around," he mumbles without even looking at me, in too much of a hurry to take his seat beside her.

I hurry off, dazed, feeling like I'm fighting off blows from invisible fists as I stumble past tables, making for the kitchen. As I reach it, a waiter walks out, carrying three plates of food in his hands. I dance out of the way, stupidly turning my head back toward Kit's table. Tristan is sitting down next to the girl in the pink dress. He's turned toward her, his arm resting on the back of her chair like Kit's was on Jessa's. Her face is animated, and she reaches forward and picks some lint off the collar of his shirt, then kisses him on the cheek.

Tristan whispers something in her ear that makes her throw her head back and laugh, and as he does, his gaze meets mine across the room.

In that infinitesimal moment between heartbeats, it feels as if time has stood still—like he's looking right into my soul, trying to tell me something—but then the kitchen door swings back the other way, and I hear the chef yelling at me. When I glance back, Tristan is no longer looking in my direction but is focused completely on the girl he's with, and I laugh bitterly at my imagination.

# TRISTAN

Dahlia narrows her eyes at me. "What's wrong?" she asks. I laugh under my breath. The downside to having a twin sister. She swears we're psychic, and sometimes I think she might be right. "Lot going on," I tell her, hoping it's true enough but vague enough to shut her up.

"At work?" she presses. "Or is this about Will?"

Dahlia knows about Will and his dad. I had to tell her because we needed her car to go and pick up his family from Vegas and because she gave me clothes for Zoey. But I would have told her anyway. We don't have secrets. At least, not until now, we haven't. For some reason, I don't want to tell her about Zoey. It feels too personal, too pointless as well, especially as I've already decided nothing can happen.

Seeing her again didn't just take me by surprise. It was like those old cartoons where the Road Runner drops an anvil on Wile E. Coyote's head. Here I was thinking and hoping and praying the feelings would vanish, that I'd realize all I felt toward her were brotherly feelings, but instead it's like a virus has silently spread and is now infecting every cell in my body. My only hope is that this is the fever spiking and the virus will soon be gone. Because what I'm thinking about when I look at her definitely doesn't fall into the brotherly feelings category.

I'm having to work on not looking in Zoey's direction, but it's almost impossible. Even though I keep my gaze fixed on Dahlia, I'm finely tuned to Zoey's presence in the room.

"Are they okay?"

"Huh?" I turn my wandering attention back to Dahlia, ordering myself to focus.

"How did the clothes fit?" Dahlia asks. "Did she like them?"

"You can see for yourself," I say, nodding toward Zoey, who's busy serving a table on the other side of the restaurant. She's wearing a silk shirt tucked into a short black skirt. My gaze slips down to her legs before I reprimand myself and look away. But not for long. It's like my eyes are on a string that's tied to her wrist, and she keeps tugging on it.

"What?" Dahlia asks, turning in her seat to follow my gaze. "Our waitress? That's Zoey? Will's little sister?"

I nod.

"My God, she's gorgeous."

Dahlia only saw Zoey once or twice, back when we lived in Scottsdale, so I didn't expect her to recognize her, but I can tell she's astonished. "How old is she now?" she asks me.

"Eighteen," I say, trying to sound casual.

"Oh my God," says Dahlia, a little too loudly.

Shit. I know what's coming next and try to hush her down.

"You have a crush on her!" Dahlia whispers, leaning in toward me. Unfortunately, Dahlia's whispering is a normal person's shouting.

"Shhh," I hiss, glaring at her. "Keep it down."

Her mouth splits into a satisfied smile. "I'm right! You have a monster crush on her."

"On who?!" asks Didi, sitting on her other side. Her ears are specially tuned for gossip.

"No one!" I say through gritted teeth, aware that Zoey is walking toward us.

"The waitress," Dahlia tells her, pointing her out.

"Which waitress?" asks Didi, scanning the restaurant like a sniper.

"*Our* waitress."

"Does Tristan have a crush on the waitress?" Jessa asks, throwing a spotlight on me so the entire table turns toward me.

"Do you?" asks Walker, Didi's boyfriend.

Seriously, I could kill Dahlia right now. Everyone is staring at me, grinning like fools, waiting for me to admit or deny it. "No," I mumble, feeling my face start to burn.

"Liar." Dahlia laughs.

"I'm going to get you back for this," I whisper to Dahlia through gritted teeth.

She brushes me off. "Yeah, yeah, whatever. Have you kissed her?"

"Have you asked her out yet?" Didi asks at the same time.

"Bro, she's way out of your league." Kit laughs.

"Hey, give the guy a chance," Walker argues.

"She's so sweet." Jessa sighs. "What's her name?"

Oh, dear God. I'm in hell.

"Zoey," Dahlia tells her. "She's Will's sister."

Jessa's eyes widen. "Oh, Kit told me about her. It's so awful what happened to her and her family. Is she okay?" she asks me.

I nod, grateful that the conversation has moved on. "Yeah,

they're doing okay. They just moved into the apartment opposite mine. It's only until they get on their feet."

Dahlia interrupts. "Does she know you like her?"

I notice a customer at the next table, sitting with his wife, check Zoey out as she sets a glass of wine down in front of him. He leans back in his chair to stare at her ass. Anger boils through my veins.

"Have you told her?" asks Didi in a stage whisper as Zoey continues moving toward our table.

I roll my eyes, exasperated. "No. I haven't told her."

She pounces. "So you do like her!"

I fluster. Damn. I gave myself away. "Oh my God, what is this? The Spanish Inquisition?"

Kit smirks. "If you want my advice, talking as someone who has dated their best friend's sister, make sure you don't leave her underwear lying around your bedroom or any naked photos on your phone for Will to find."

"What the . . . !" I spit as Jessa shoves her hand over Kit's mouth to shut him up. "What are you even talking about?" I say over everyone's laughter. "It isn't like that. We're just friends. I've known her forever. I'm just looking out for her."

"Uh-huh," says Kit, his voice muffled by Jessa's hand.

Zoey is now within spitting distance. I turn to Dahlia and try desperately to one-eighty the conversation. "How's Lou?" I ask.

The others, still laughing, go back to their own conversations.

Dahlia plucks at the pink straps of her dress and smooths the creases in her lap. "We're taking a break."

I give her a look. Dahlia's girlfriend, Lou, is a musician, and she's on tour with her band right now on the East Coast. I'm guessing the decision was Lou's and not Dahlia's, because I can read my sister almost as well as she can read me. I can tell by the way she squares her shoulders that she's hurt. Dahlia dates both men and women, but Lou was the first person I know she really liked. "I'm sorry," I tell her.

"It's all right. Long-distance never works," she says with a shrug.

I put my arm around her and squeeze her shoulder. "Plenty more fish in the sea," I tell her, glancing at Zoey, who has approached the table and is taking Jessa's order.

"I know," she says. "You keep throwing them back."

We watch Zoey, clearly flustered, scribble down the order. As she writes, she glances up and her eyes catch mine, just for a second, before she looks back at Jessa, smiles, and moves on to Jo, Jessa's sister-in-law.

"She's totally into you," Dahlia whispers, glancing at Zoey while poking me in the ribs with her razor elbow.

She is? It's an endorphin hit just hearing Dahlia say it, and like that I can feel the virus in my bloodstream multiply in response. "No, she's not," I argue under my breath.

"Why haven't you asked her out?"

"I can't," I say. "It would be weird. And it's not what she needs right now."

"Kit dated Jessa. They were friends for years before."

I glance their way and frown at the sight of Jessa resting her head on Kit's shoulder.

Zoey's taking Walker's order now, and she's so close I could reach out and touch her. It feels like the restaurant just ramped up its thermostat a thousand degrees hotter, and I tug at my collar. It could be caused by Kit, Jessa, and Didi all staring at me, their eyes like laser beams, watching for how I will react when

Zoey stops by me. Or it could be the electricity that seems to be crackling in the air between us. Or maybe the virus is real and I'm getting sick.

"Have you decided?" Zoey asks, finally reaching me. She's looking down at her pad.

I feel the weight of everyone's eyes, hear the suppressed giggle from Didi, and manage to lose all capacity for speech. All I can think about is how fucking beautiful she is, how I want to lie next to her and study her face up close until I have every freckle memorized. She looks up from the writing pad with a question in her eyes. Shit.

"Um, the fish," I say, not having a single clue if there is even fish on the menu.

"The pine-nut salsa salmon?"

"Yeah . . . ," I say.

Another giggle from Didi.

My sister clears her throat. "You're allergic to salmon," she whispers.

Everyone is watching me with total delight, having to stifle their hysterics, and I can see it's making Zoey uncomfortable. She thinks they're laughing at her. She glances down at the table, and that little frown appears, tugging unhappily at her mouth. That mouth . . . Shit, again. I glance down at the menu. The words and the letters are all jumbled. I'm dyslexic, and when I'm stressed it's even harder to make all the shapes and symbols make sense.

"Why don't you have the steak?" Dahlia says, catching on to my struggle.

I nod. "Yeah, sounds good. I'll have the steak," I say to Zoey, closing my menu with a snap. And handing it to her.

"How would you like it?"

I manage to catch Kit grinning at me. I could kill each and every one of these people right now.

"Medium rare, right?" Dahlia says, putting her hand on my wrist to bring me back to the order. She smiles at Zoey. "That's how he likes it. I'll have the same."

I nod dumbly. Zoey nods and turns swiftly on her heel. She walks away as fast as she can without actually sprinting. The table erupts into laughter. I wince, hoping Zoey can't hear and that if she can, she doesn't think it's her they're laughing at. Jessa gets up and excuses herself to go to the bathroom, and I think about doing the same. And then maybe never coming back. Embarrassment feels like being buried in hot coals. I've never acted like that before in my life, except as a kid, when called on to read in class. What is with me?

"Wow," says Dahlia, leaning into me. She's not laughing. She looks in shock. "You really do have a crush."

I blush and frown at the same time. I wasn't even prepared to admit it to myself, and now it's out in the open, as obvious to everyone as a case of the measles. "Yeah, I do. But I don't know why—I mean, I barely know her."

"You've known her most your life."

"Yeah, but not really. I mean, it's only been three days since we saw each other again."

"I fell for Lou the second I saw her," she says. "She was standing in line ahead of me at a coffee shop. She was reading a book and I tapped her on the shoulder because the barista was waiting to take her order, and she turned to say thanks, and that was it. I was in love."

"You think it can really be that fast?" I ask. "It wasn't just lust?"

"Both. It was lust *and* love at first sight."

I shake my head. "She needs a friend. I don't want to make a move and screw things up."

"You never know: maybe she only wants a one-night stand."

I pull back, frowning in consternation. "Who said anything about a one-night stand? That's not what *I'm* looking for."

"Really?" she says, looking at me skeptically.

"I go on dates," I argue.

"For one night," she claps back.

I shake my head at her. "Because I can't ever find anyone I want to date twice."

"Who's to say Zoey would be any different?" she asks.

I press my lips together. Dahlia's pinpointed exactly what I've been worried about, and she knows it. But, I think to myself, we already kind of did go on a date—when we walked to the pier—and I really want to see her again, and I can't stop thinking about her. I've never felt this . . . I don't even know how to describe it. Why can't I get her out of my head?

"And you don't want to have a one-night stand with your best friend's sister," Dahlia continues, tearing a hunk of bread and stuffing it in her mouth. Dahlia is an anti-gluten-free campaigner, like Didi. "Imagine if it went wrong and she got hurt. Or if you did start dating and then broke up."

It's exactly why I didn't kiss her on the pier. It would be so awkward, living opposite her, knowing I'd promised her brother I'd take care of her. I've known her since we were kids. We're friends. At least I think we're friends. I don't want to hurt her— she's been through enough—and my track record is not great when it comes to women. I've never done a real relationship. And, God, why am I even thinking about it? I don't even know if she's interested in me like that. I could be jumping the gun and making massive assumptions. Maybe we should stick with being friends.

Dahlia sighs and pats me on the shoulder. "Much as it pains me to say it, my brother, I think you're right. You shouldn't go there."

"You're not telling me that because you're crushing on her too, are you?"

Dahlia smiles slyly and shakes her head. "No. I'm serious. She's been through enough. She doesn't need any more hurt." She pats me on the arm. "And you do have a reputation for breaking hearts."

# ZOEY

As I walk away from their table, I hear them all burst out laughing. My feet cannot carry me fast enough to the kitchen. A customer tries to get my attention as I hurry by, but I ignore him. I can't stop thinking about that girl Tristan had his arm around, the girl who told me how he liked his steak cooked, the girl who seemed to be mocking me with her smile. Clearly his girlfriend. It was as if she knew I had a crush on her boyfriend and was trying to humiliate me. But how could she know? Unless, of course, Tristan told them all about the other night on the pier.

I think about running out the back door of the restaurant and going home, maybe even farther than that. Sometimes I have these thoughts of jumping behind the wheel of a car and speeding off into the distance. Or about getting off a train in New York City, or handing over a boarding pass and buckling into an airline seat. I imagine what it would feel like to have a place to call my own, not shared with anyone else: a studio in Brooklyn, a clapboard Victorian with a veranda wrapped around it and a porch swing, a cabin in a forest next to a rushing stream.

I dream of all these places, and how it would feel to unlock the front door and step inside, to pull the door shut and not have to lock it behind me. But then reality crashes me back down to earth. My life is a rigidly determined path with insurmountable walls on either side. A prison, basically.

Someone catches me by the shoulder. I whirl around, my heart skittering in my chest, adrenaline flooding my system. It's Jessa.

"Are you okay?" she asks, looking at me, worried.

"I'm fine," I say, plastering on a smile, trying to shake off the lingering shadow of fright. It makes me realize that even though I've been telling myself my dad doesn't know where we are, I'm still afraid that he's going to find us.

"Did you need something?" I ask Jessa, panicking that maybe I forgot something. Did I take all the orders?

"No, no," Jessa says, shaking her head. "I just . . . I wanted to say that I know you just moved to town and things aren't that easy at the moment."

Her face is a little flushed, and I can sense she feels awkward. My first impulse is to react with embarrassment and even anger. Has Tristan told all of them about my dad and what happened? But then I remember that Will is friends with Kit, so perhaps she heard about my messed-up family situation from him.

"If you ever need a new friend, or just someone to talk to, I'm here."

"Thanks," I manage to stammer, taken completely off guard by the offer.

"I better get back," she says to me with a shy mile. "Take care, okay?"

I watch her weave through the tables toward Kit, every head in the restaurant swiveling to watch her pass.

The man who tried to get my attention earlier gestures to me impatiently. God, I'm so distracted I'm forgetting to do my job. I rush over to him and his wife, a woman in her forties who sighs loudly. "At last. Can we order? I'm starving. I'll have the mixed salad and the salmon. Dressing on the side." She gets up as soon as she's ordered and stalks off toward the bathroom.

I turn to her husband. "And for you?"

He doesn't answer straightaway, so I look up from my notepad. He's staring at me. Or to be more precise, he's staring at my body. "I know what I want," he says.

My back teeth crunch together. Asshole, I think to myself. He's at least forty-five, bald, and paunchy, with thick, wet lips, which he smacks together now as if tasting something good.

"The special today is sea bass," I say, reeling off the specials while feeling an awful helplessness and rage welling up inside me.

"Are *you* on the specials menu?" He grins, leaning back smugly in his chair. "I wouldn't mind having a taste of you. Maybe for dessert."

He laughs. And I stare at him, my fingers itching to pick up his wineglass and pour the contents over his head. But I'm also frozen, my feet rooted to the ground.

His smile becomes a smirk. "When do you get off work?" he asks, his eyes once again traveling down my body.

Pervert. I scream the word silently and, ignoring him, keep running through the specials.

"What are you doing?"

It's the wife. She's returned from the bathroom. "Have you still not ordered?" she asks, annoyed, flouncing down into her seat.

"I'll get the lamb," he says, looking at me. "Done pink," he adds, licking his lips.

I glare at him, imagining breaking a plate over his head too, and then manage to finally unstick my feet and walk away.

Shaking and raging, I put in the order and then bring out the main courses for Kit's table. I pull myself together, balancing four plates in my hands, and thankfully manage to make it to the table without dropping anything. I place Tristan's steak down in front of him, trying not to look his way or his girlfriend's, but my hand shakes.

"Is that guy bothering you?" he asks me under his breath.

"What guy?"

He nods at the pervert guy. "Did he say something to you?"

I shake my head. "It's fine."

"If he's bothering you, I'll—"

"I can handle it," I tell him tersely before racing back to the kitchen to collect the rest of the food.

When I finally sneak a quick two-minute bathroom break over an hour later, the restaurant is starting to empty out, and those remaining are finishing coffee and scraping their dessert plates clean. I have to force myself not to look at Tristan, though I'm painfully aware of his presence, so much so that I keep forgetting orders. If I'm not careful, I'm going to get fired.

I have one last thing to take out to Kit's table, and that's Jessa's birthday cake. It takes both hands to carry it because it's so big, and the candles are those sparkler things and they are sizzling in front of my face, so I can barely see where I'm going.

Someone has dimmed the lights, and as I exit through the kitchen door, walking backward so as to protect the candles from the draft, I feel something slide between my legs, up my skirt. I scream and spin around.

The cake flies off the plate and splats the guy who just stuck his hands between my thighs. It's the pervert guy. Chocolate icing and raspberries decorate his crotch, and he's glowering at me, his face turning a puce color.

I can't process the silence that's fallen over the room or the countless eyes drilling into me, because all I can feel is his fat, disgusting hand between my legs. Even though it's not there anymore, it's like it's left a chemical burn on my skin.

"You stupid bitch!" the man yells at me as he looks down at his ruined clothes.

I shrink backward against the door. I want to shout back at him, call him a pervert, and tell people what he did, but the words jam in my throat.

Murmurs start to fill the restaurant. Everyone is staring at me, covering their mouths in shock. They're all wondering who the stupid girl is who dropped the birthday cake and if they're going to get to witness her being fired. Kit is striding over to us. He gestures to a waiter to bring napkins. He doesn't look at me, and shame makes me feel like I've been doused with gas and set alight. I just ruined the cake. *And* Jessa's birthday. And I'm about to get fired. And Tristan and his girlfriend witnessed it, just to make things even worse.

The man starts yelling about me being incompetent and demanding that Kit comp his meal and pay for his dry cleaning, but Kit isn't looking at the man. He's looking at me now. Here it comes. . . .

"Are you okay?" he asks.

I startle. What? There's concern etched on his face. And then

Tristan is there, beside him, looking at me with the same expression of concern.

Tristan touches me gently on the shoulder. "Did he touch you?" he asks quietly.

Somehow I find my voice. "Yes."

Tristan turns to Kit. "I told you," he says, his voice a growl. "I saw him. He put his hand . . ." He doesn't want to say the actual words, but I can see him struggling to contain his fury.

"What are you talking about?" the man's wife shrieks, looking among us all.

Tristan glances at me, and I can see he's torn. He doesn't want to humiliate me in public by saying it out loud.

I step forward. "Your husband put his hand between my legs," I say, loud enough for everyone around to hear. I'm not going to feel ashamed or humiliated by something that this man did to me. I am not the one who did something wrong.

There's an intake of breath, and I feel dizzy, like all the air just got sucked out of the room, leaving me to breathe pure carbon dioxide. I realize that Jessa and Didi are standing beside me, flanking me, and it makes me feel so grateful.

The man starts to fluster as he looks around at everyone. "That's a lie. She's lying," he says.

I'm hurtled with force back to that day in court, hearing my dad say the exact same words when I took the stand and testified about how he beat my mother. *That's a lie. She's lying.* I remember looking around at the judge and the jury and wondering if anyone believed me. It was clear some of the jury didn't.

"I'm not a liar," I say, in a louder voice. "You harassed me earlier when I served you, and you just assaulted me."

It feels great to say the words and see the man try to bluster his way out of the accusation as he's facing Kit, Walker, and Tristan. All three of them look like they could rip this guy's head off his neck as easily as popping a champagne cork. He takes them in and visibly shrinks.

"You'll be getting a one-star review!" he shouts at Kit, grabbing his wife's hand and marching for the door.

Tristan strides in front of him, blocking his way. "You're not going anywhere."

"We're calling the police," Kit says, joining him.

I look around at the customers in the restaurant who are all staring, jaws to the floor, their food clean forgotten about as they're treated to this live reality-TV show.

"It's okay," I say. "I don't want to press charges."

"Are you sure?" Didi asks me, surprised.

I nod. "I don't want the police involved," I say, looking at Tristan as I do because I think he might be the only person here who understands why I don't want the cops called, and he does. He touches Kit on the arm and murmurs something into his ear. Kit frowns but nods.

The wife is glaring at her husband, and there's some satisfaction in her knowing the truth about him and believing me. She runs out the door, her heels clattering, and the man tries to follow her, but Tristan is still blocking the way. The man swallows as he stares up at him. He's squarely built, but he knows he's outclassed. Tristan's easy smile is nowhere to be seen. Instead, there's a simmering rage behind his eyes. The man seems to quake before him. "Apologize," Tristan says, his voice steel.

The man glances at Kit. "Sorry," he mumbles.

"To her," Tristan hisses.

The man turns to me, and I'm back there again in court,

sitting in the witness box, staring down my father. Only my father wasn't ashamed or contrite or apologetic. He was just angry.

*I'll kill you, you bitch!* His words as he was dragged out of court ring in my ears even as the pathetic man in front of me mumbles, "Sorry."

The man turns toward the door, which Tristan holds open for him. As he scurries out, Tristan once again blocks the way. "If I ever see you again," he whispers, "if you ever touch any woman again without their permission and I find out about it, I will hunt you down. . . ."

The man blanches. I know Tristan doesn't mean it, that he isn't that kind of person, but the man doesn't know it, and the look Tristan's giving him is enough to turn his legs to Jell-O. He scampers out, chasing after his wife, who has already stalked off.

After he's gone, everyone's attention swings back to me. "Are you okay?" Jessa asks, putting her hand on my shoulder.

"Your cake," I say, my lips wobbling as I take in the remains of it on the floor, the crushed raspberries making it look like a crime scene.

"It's just a cake," Jessa says, hugging me.

I can still feel the heat of the man's pudgy hand. I think I'm going to be sick. I look up. Kit's walking toward me, and Tristan, too, but I can't face them. I need air. I turn around and push through what feels like a crowd of people, making for the kitchen. I run through it, past the chef, and burst through the back door and into the alleyway behind the restaurant.

# TRISTAN

I run after her, finding her outside in the alley, beside a dumpster. She's doubled over, dry heaving. When I approach and put my hand on her lower back, she lets out a yelp and spins around in fright. I back away, hands in the air, astonished by the fear I see in her eyes.

"It's just me," I tell her.

She swallows, wiping the back of her mouth. Her whole body is shaking like she's in shock. I've seen it hundreds of times with people pulled from the water. I step slowly toward her. "It's okay," I murmur.

Slowly, she comes back into herself, her shoulders dropping, her breathing settling. "I thought . . ." She trails off. I don't know if she thought I was her father or even the man who just assaulted her. Either way, I'm mad at both of them for making her feel this afraid.

"Can I get you anything?" I ask.

She shakes her head. I want to cover the distance between us and pull her into my arms, tell her it's going to be okay, that I've got her, that I won't let anyone hurt her, but I don't.

"Is Kit going to fire me?" she asks.

I smile. "Of course not."

She takes a deep breath, relieved. "Thank you," she says.

I shake my head. I didn't do anything. In fact, I'm furious at myself for just letting that guy walk. I know she didn't want to call the police on him, but I hate that he didn't get punished. I wanted to chase him out of the restaurant and put my fist through his smug face. The thought of him touching her, putting his hands on her, makes me so angry I finally get the expression "seeing red."

Zoey shakes her head. "I hate it that people like him think they can do things like that and just get away with it."

"He didn't get away with it," I say, though really, he did. But I won't make her feel like it's her fault. It's not.

"But if you hadn't seen, if you hadn't said something," she says, "I don't think I would have. I just froze." Her face contorts with anger and frustration and then disgust. "I can't stop feeling his hand . . . ," she says, shaking herself like a dog trying to rid itself of fleas.

She begins pacing and then bends over again and starts taking deep breaths, almost hyperventilating. I can't just stand there and watch. I put my hand on her back, and this time she doesn't throw me off. I let my hand rest there for a while until her breathing starts to come under control. "I'm sorry," she mumbles again.

"Stop saying that," I whisper.

She straightens up slowly, and my hand regretfully falls away. She turns to face me, and there's just a few inches of space between us. She's looking at me with those huge eyes of hers wet with tears, her bottom lip still trembling. Without thinking about it, acting purely on instinct, I pull her against me, obliterating those unnecessary inches.

She draws in a sharp, startled breath, and I worry I've just made a huge fucking mistake. Some guy just touched her without her permission, and I've just done the exact same thing. I let go immediately, my arms dropping to my sides, and take a step back. "I'm sorry," I say, shaking my head in embarrassment. "I'm sorry."

She doesn't move for a few seconds, and I worry she's about to yell at me or slap me, but then she does something that totally surprises me. She takes a step forward, and this time it's her obliterating that dead space between us. I feel her hands lightly, tentatively circle my waist and my own wrap around her, holding her tight.

She looks up at me, her face doused by the light of the emergency exit sign, and this time there's no confusion like there was on the pier, when I couldn't read her expression. This time I see the wanting in her eyes crystal clear, albeit shadowed by a slight wariness or trepidation.

I can hear Dahlia telling me not to go there, but my hand is moving of its own accord, and before I know it, I'm touching her cheek, feeling the softness of her skin, like velvet, beneath my fingertips.

Her lips part softly, and I hear the intake of air as an invitation. My attention is drawn to the gap between her two front teeth and then to her mouth. And next thing I know, I'm tracing the heart shape of it with my thumb. Zoey tilts her head back a fraction of an inch, staring up at me, her breathing hiking. It's the only point of contact between us, my thumb to her bottom lip, but honest to God, it's probably the sexiest moment of my entire life. It's like a spell. And I don't want to break it. She's staring at me, her eyes half-closed, her breathing fast, waiting for me to kiss her, and my body's reacting like I've been shot through with an electric current and I need to close the loop or else my circuits are going to fry.

There's still a chance to break away, walk it all back, but I can't. I move my hand to cradle her face, and she surprises me by pressing her cheek into my palm, arching her neck sideways. She's waiting on me, and I have no idea why I'm holding back. Because, fuck . . . if I don't kiss her right now, I know I'm going to regret it for the rest of my life.

I draw her face toward mine, my other hand reaching for her waist, pulling her, with more urgency than I mean to, against my body. She closes her eyes, and my lips are just about to graze hers when—

"Tristan? You out here?"

We both pull apart, the spell instantly shattering. It's Dahlia. She's standing in the doorway, frowning at us. Did she see? I wish her twin psychic-ness would kick in right now and she'd hear my silent yells at her to go away. But maybe it's her twin psychic-ness that told her what I was doing out here with Zoey, and she deliberately came out here to put a stop to it.

Zoey, blushing, rushes past me toward the door as though her feet are on fire. "I gotta go," she mumbles.

"Hey," says Dahlia, who's standing in her way. "Are you okay?"

Zoey nods and rushes past her.

Dahlia watches her go and then looks at me, her lips pressed together in a prim line and her eyebrows arched. "Did I interrupt something?" she asks, faux-innocently.

I could say a few choice things right now, but my senses are returning, the blood flowing upward to my brain, and I'm starting to wonder if her arrival wasn't perhaps fortuitous. I give her a look, and she knows to drop it.

"We're doing take two on the birthday cake," she says. "You coming?"

I nod. "In a minute," I tell her. I need that and more to get ahold of myself and cool the hell down.

# ZOEY

K it has rustled up another cake for Jessa, or rather a plate of *pasteis de nata*, the little Portuguese pastries he's famous for. As I walk into the restaurant, I hear their table breaking into a second rendition of "Happy Birthday."

Everyone in the restaurant joins in, but I stand on the outskirts, looking in, painfully aware of feeling like a stranger in their midst. I watch Tristan and his girlfriend standing by Jessa. Did his girlfriend see us almost kiss? Out there, in the alley, I forgot about her completely. There was just Tristan. Nothing else. My whole body is vibrating like a tuning fork that's just been struck. He looks up and over at me, as if he can hear the note sounding, as if it's a note only he can hear. Our eyes meet before I quickly look away, reaching a hand to my cheek before I can stop myself. It burns where his fingers grazed it, and my lip thrums as though it's been stung. If his girlfriend hadn't appeared, he would have kissed me. But what kind of a guy sneaks around on his girlfriend like that? And how could I have gone along with it? I made myself a promise I wouldn't fall for anyone and wouldn't let myself get close to anyone. Why am I being so stupid?

Jessa blows out the candles, grinning, and I watch as her friends swarm her and have to turn away.

"How are you feeling?"

I find Kit at my shoulder. I shrug because I'm not sure what I'm feeling right now. "I'm sorry about the cake."

"Don't be," he says. "I'm sorry that happened to you. Next time a customer acts out of line like that, you come tell me or Tessa right away. We'll deal with it."

I nod, but really I'm wishing that I didn't always have to rely on others to fix my problems. I wish I could have dealt with that man myself. But most of all, I wish that these things didn't happen to me. It's as if I have the word "victim" tattooed on my forehead. I can't help but wonder if the majority of men are awful or if I'm a magnet for the all the bad ones. I'd like to think Tristan and people like Kit are different. But maybe they're not; maybe they just hide it better. My dad certainly did.

"We're closing up," says Kit. "I'm going to put on some music. We'll have ourselves a little dance party. Join us?"

"I should get home," I say.

Kit and Jessa look disappointed and exchange a glance. "Are you sure we can't tempt you?" asks Jessa. "Why don't you stay and have a little fun?"

"Thanks," I say, not wanting to be rude, "but I'm tired. I'm going to go home. I'll see you tomorrow."

Kit nods. "Thanks for tonight. You did great."

The praise means a lot. Jessa smiles at me and then gives me a hug. "Remember what I said. If you ever want to hang out, go for coffee or a walk on the beach, let me know."

I nod, a little speechless, then hurry toward the door, anxious to get away.

"How are you getting home?" Kit calls after me.

I hesitate a beat. "Um, I'll walk," I say.

"No," Kit says, pulling out his phone. "I'm calling you a taxi. I'll pay," he says when he sees me open my mouth to protest.

It's only ten minutes later when the taxi pulls up outside the condo. I hand the driver the ten dollars Kit gave me and get out. A motorbike pulls in front of me. It's Tristan. He's alone. No sign of his girlfriend.

I stop awkwardly and wait for him to park.

He pulls off his helmet. "Hey," he says, swinging his leg over the bike. My stomach flips at the sight of him.

"I would have given you a ride if I'd known you needed one," he mumbles. He doesn't seem to want to look at me. Is he embarrassed at the almost-kiss? Are we going to acknowledge it or pretend it never happened?

Neither of us says anything. I can't help but wonder where his girlfriend is. Did they fight?

"Good night," he says, and turns away.

# TRISTAN

I can't do it. I can't leave things hanging like this. I turn back to her. "I'm sorry," I say.

She frowns, cocks her head slightly to one side. "About what?" she asks.

I swallow. "I shouldn't have . . ." I pause, the words fizzling on my tongue. I can't say I'm sorry for almost kissing her, because I'm more sorry that I didn't. But I need to explain why we can't be more than friends. Though, as I stand here staring at her under the amber glow of the streetlight, I've already forgotten why that is. Something about it being complicated, though if someone asked me to spell "complicated" right now, I'd struggle.

"I'm sorry if I got you in trouble," she says quietly, looking down at her feet before darting a glance up at me.

I frown. "What do you mean?" I ask.

She looks embarrassed and touches a hand to her chest, as though covering her heart. "I thought . . . your girlfriend . . . did she—"

"What do you mean, my girlfriend?" I ask, shaking my head, confused.

"The girl in the pink dress," she says.

I burst out laughing. "Dahlia?"

Confusion dances across Zoey's face.

"She's not my girlfriend," I say, smiling. "That's my sister!"

Zoey's eyes widen. Her hand flies to her mouth. "Really?" she asks. "That's Dahlia?! I didn't recognize her and I had no idea she lived in Oceanside."

I nod, still laughing.

Zoey shuts her eyes. "Oh my God . . . I thought . . ." She breaks off. When she opens her eyes, she's smiling, and my heart does a massive somersault in my chest. I want nothing more than to cross the few steps that separate us and pull her into my arms. I want to kiss her, and it's pure torture just thinking about it. But I can't act on it. It wouldn't be the right thing to do.

Neither of us moves. And neither of us says anything. I'm frozen. I don't move toward her, but I can't walk away, either.

"Well," she finally says, "I should probably go to bed."

Bed. I shake my head, preventing my mind from picturing what it would be like to have her in my bed. All I manage by way of response is a nod and a kind of grunt. Zoey doesn't make a move to leave, though, and I wonder . . . Is she waiting for me to say something or do something? Fuck.

Before I can do anything, she walks away. Bigger fuck. Shit. I watch her, telling myself it's for the best. It's an infatuation, and it will go away. Best not to screw up my friendship with her or with Will by kissing her, or even worse, sleeping with her.

"Hey, Zoey?" I call out before I can stop myself. What am I doing?

She's on the steps, and she turns to look at me, unable to disguise the hope in her face. Shit. It's a killer, that expression. The same way she looked at me when we almost kissed in the alley. "What?" she asks.

I can't let her walk away. I need to kiss her. And caution and all the rest of it can go to hell.

"Can you come here?" I say.

Zoey frowns, and for a beat I wonder if I've read it wrong, but then she slowly walks back down the stairs and I start walking toward her. She pauses at the bottom of the stairs, and I keep walking, stopping when we're almost touching, barely a centimeter between us. The voice of reason in my head is just a dull background noise that I'm ignoring, my focus on Zoey's lips. Her breathing hikes.

My hand cups her cheek. I stare into her eyes. She looks at me, her face so open, like she's standing, holding her heart in her hands and offering it to me. The vulnerability gives me pause. But then she does something unexpected: she pushes up on tiptoe and presses her lips to mine.

I'm too shocked to respond. At least for the first three seconds, the time it takes a lit fuse to run up the rope and meet the dynamite. At which point, it's BOOM. World's on fire. No more thought in existence, let alone any internal debate.

I wrap my arms around her and kiss her back, finally getting to feel the lips I've been fantasizing about, and they're even softer than I imagined, and sweeter, too. She's tentative, but when I drop my hands to her waist and crush her body against mine, her lips part in a loud exhalation and the kiss changes from being sweet and tentative to the opposite. She opens up and lets me really taste her, her hands twining in my hair, pulling me closer, and my God, I want her.

My brain is shouting things at me that I ignore because all

there is is Zoey, bombarding every sense. The smell of her filling my lungs and making me never want to come up for air, the taste of her making my head spin, and the feel of her skin—smooth as silk—as my hands find their way underneath her shirt to circle her waist.

She's breathing as hard as me, as though we're both running a sprint. It's zero to one hundred in less than a second. Her hands tighten on my back, pulling me even closer. I'm so wrapped up in Zoey that I don't hear the car pull up behind me or the door slam. I don't hear anything until Zoey pulls away, and then I turn and startle, feeling a dreadful sinking sensation.

Fuck. Fuck. Shit.

"Tristan?"

Brittany—blond, fully made-up, wearing a black silk slip of a dress that might even be a negligee—is staring at me and Zoey.

All the blood is draining away from every extremity in my body and seeming to pool at my feet. This is bad. Very bad. I've made a very big mistake.

"What. The. Fuck," Brittany announces.

I swallow. I knew it was a bad idea to send that text when I left the restaurant today. It was a heat-of-the-moment, need-to-purge-Zoey-out-of-my-system text. I got carried away with Zoey and the unexpected kissing and forgot about it. That's not going to fly with either of them as an excuse, though.

Zoey looks at Brittany, then turns to stare at me with a fury that's biblical. She steps back and out of my arms. Her eyes are flint but also gleaming with tears. And her nostrils are quivering as though she's fighting back either a torrent of anger or grief, or probably both. I hate it. I hate having caused it. In fact, I hate myself more in this moment than I ever have in my life.

"I'm sorry," I start to say.

"If you wanted a threesome, you should have told me," Brittany says. "I would have been down for it, but some notice would have been nice."

Zoey looks at her, her mouth falling open. Then she looks at me as though wondering if that was actually my intention.

"No," I say in alarm, "that's not what I . . ."

Zoey shoves past me, not letting me finish, which is fair enough. I reach for her automatically, but she pulls her hand away like she's been bitten by a snake and races past me, not up the steps to her apartment but down the street. Brittany steps aside to let her pass, and Zoey doesn't even acknowledge her. I should follow her—I want to follow her—but my feet remain frozen. I'm weighted down by the knowledge of how big this fuckup is.

Brittany crosses her arms over her chest and shakes her head at me. "Is that your girlfriend?" she asks.

"No," I say.

"So what happened? Did you booty-call a few people at the same time in the hopes one of us would show up?"

"No," I say weakly.

"You're an asshole," she spits. "You know that, right?"

I nod. Yes, I am.

# ZOEY

run, and I don't stop running until I reach the ocean's edge. Great heaving sobs burst out of me as I take a few steps back and sink down onto wet sand, burying my head in my arms. How could I have misjudged him so badly? I told myself not to get close, and this is why.

I'm such a damn idiot. I punch my fist into the sand.

Something alerts me to another person's presence on the beach. I whip my head around, but it's impossible to see much beyond twenty feet. The chances are if I can't see them then they can't see me either. Still, my senses are ringing alarms. My brain automatically conjures thoughts of my dad, but what would he be doing here, on a beach, in the middle of the night? It can't be him. He doesn't know where we are.

I wonder if it could be Tristan, but he's probably back at his apartment getting it on with that girl. I scrunch my fists into the sand. I wish to hell we'd never moved here.

My senses prickle again. Someone is definitely out there in the darkness, close by. They must have heard me crying. I pick myself up, wiping my face, and start walking fast toward the street, but before I make it, someone bursts out of the dark and leaps in front of me. "Zoey!"

I suppress a scream. Jesus. It's Tristan. I'm so mad I don't stop. I shove past him at a run. "Leave me alone," I tell him.

"Please," he calls out, and jogs to catch up with me. "I've been looking for you. I need to talk to you."

"I don't want to hear it," I tell him.

Tristan curses under his breath, but he doesn't give up. He chases after me. "I know. I get it. I've been a jerk, and I understand if you never want to see me again or speak to me again, but just let me say this one thing first."

I keep walking, mad that he probably thinks I'm crying over him when I'm not. I'm crying over myself and how stupid I am. He races after me, catching me as I reach the boardwalk. He jumps in front of me, blocking my path, holding up his hands, trying to get me to stop.

"I'm sorry. I fucked up. I've never done this before. I mean . . . I've never felt this way about anyone. And I was scared that I would do this . . . that I would make a mistake and fuck up . . . And I have." He runs a hand through his hair, grimacing.

Lies. All lies. Does he really think I'm falling for it?

"I'm sorry. Please forgive me."

I decide the only way out of this is to feign indifference. "Okay," I tell him coolly, looking in his direction but almost through him. "I forgive you."

He double-takes. "You do?"

I nod and try to get past him.

"Nothing happened with Brittany," he tells me. "I swear."

"I don't care," I say, hating hearing her name fall so easily from his lips. Lips that just kissed mine.

"You don't forgive me. You're just saying it."

"I do forgive you. I just don't care. You're right. It was a mistake. I made one too. Let's just forget it."

He shakes his head. "No. You weren't a mistake, Zoey." He sighs, glancing around as though trying to figure out which excuse to try on me.

"I don't want to be a jerk," he says. "Dahlia convinced me it would be the wrong thing to ask you out—that it would only complicate things. What with everything going on in your life. And Brittany had texted me earlier in the evening wanting to hook up, and on the spur of the moment, after I left the restaurant, I texted her back because . . ." He breaks off, squeezing his eyes shut.

I stare at him. *That's* his excuse? "Because you wanted sex. And you were using her," I say.

He shakes his head. "She was the one who suggested it in the first place. Sex, no strings. I wasn't using her. We were using each other."

"Is that all you wanted?" I ask before I can stop myself. "Sex, no strings?"

"No," he says angrily. "Believe me. I would never want that with you. That's my point." His voice gets quieter. He stares me right in the eye. "You don't have to believe me, but I want more than that with you. Maybe it sounds stupid, but there's something there between us—I think you feel it too."

I make my face poker flat.

"Look," he says. "You can walk away, you can never talk to me again, and I won't blame you, but know that kissing you was not a mistake."

I take a step back to maintain the distance because when he

gets too close it makes it hard to remember why I'm so angry.

"I fucked up," he says. "I would never, ever hurt you, not intentionally," he says, his brown eyes boring into mine as though trying to will me to believe him.

"My father used to say that to my mother," I say quietly.

Tristan opens his mouth, then shuts it. He's taken aback, and I regret it the moment the words leave my lips. But then I shake off the regret because it's true. He stares down at the sidewalk for a few seconds, then looks up at me and nods. "I'm not your father," he says. "But I understand why you don't trust me."

I grit my teeth. As mad as I am, as hurt as I am, I still have to fight the urge to move toward him and let him wrap me in his arms.

"I'm sorry," he says, looking me in the eye. "Hurting you was the very last thing I wanted to do."

"You didn't hurt me," I tell him, lying through my teeth. My tone turns icy. "You taught me a lesson."

It's as if my voice has cut through his skin. He even flinches.

I'll never trust anyone ever again, I think to myself, and with that I keep walking, head high, the crack in my heart growing with every step I take. I hate it—hate my betrayed, betraying heart. It has no right to crack or break without my permission.

Tristan walks behind me. I can sense him there, twenty or so feet back. I'm guessing he wants to make sure I get home safely because that would be just the kind of Tristan thing to do, which again makes me mad for some reason. I don't want his chivalry. I never asked for it. I was fine before he came along. I don't need him watching out for me.

When I reach our street, though, I find my pace slowing. My brain allows myself to think about what would happen if I turned around and waited for him, if I believed his words and accepted his apology. If I told him I liked him too.

Uninvited, the memory of him kissing me enters my brain, and all I can think about is the way he stroked my cheek, the way he touched my lip, and more than anything, the way he looked at me. There was so much intensity but also clarity, like he saw me, all of me, the broken part and the unsure part and the frightened part—and he still wanted me.

A heat rushes through my body as I remember how safe I felt when I was in his arms. Honestly, I wanted him to never let me go. I felt like I had been drowning my entire life—and finally, he was there, pulling me out of the water, helping me to safety.

But I was a fool. I have to learn to swim by myself. That's the only way to survive in this world.

Maybe if I were another kind of girl, the kind of girl who doesn't learn from her mistakes, I'd stop right here, turn around, and wait for him to catch up to me. Then when he did, I'd tilt my head back and let him kiss me. If the world were a different kind of world, the kind you see on-screen, where love is made to look real, then maybe there'd even be a happily-ever-after.

But I'm not that girl. And it's not that world.

# TRISTAN

Self-loathing is a new experience for me. When I stare in the mirror, instead of being okay with what I see, I hate myself. The voice in my head is stuck on a loop, admonishing me like a furious drill sergeant, telling me what a useless, stupid asshole I am and how I'll never make this right, not in a million years.

A week has gone by, and I've thrown myself into both work and working out, trying to avoid Zoey in real life and the Zoey in my head. The first is easy enough because I'm never really home, and she's busy with her own life, but the latter one, the Zoey in my imagination, is harder to avoid because I keep getting flashes of her smile, her lips, keep remembering what it was like to kiss her.

The worst thing is knowing I hurt her. Even though she told me she wasn't hurt, I know it's bull. I lie awake in bed every night replaying that kiss, hearing her sighs as though she's right there with me, feeling the weight of her in my arms like some kind of missing limb. I've accepted this isn't some stupid infatuation. It isn't a passing thing. It's not going away, and living next to her is torture.

When I leave my apartment and head up the stairs to hers, I get a weird feeling in my stomach that I recognize as nerves. I've felt it before, like when I first arrived at grunt camp and when I first copiloted a plane—but I've never felt it before about someone else.

I'm hoping and silently praying Zoey answers the door. These snatched glimpses of her are what I live for, lame as that sounds. I'm like an addict needing a hit, and she's the drug I can't wean myself off of. I know it's bad for me, and it's only worsening my addiction seeing her, but I can't help myself.

My face falls when Kate answers.

"Hey," she says glumly, looking no less disappointed that it's me than I am about it being her. "Cole!" she yells over her shoulder. "Tristan is here!"

"Everything okay?" I ask. "How's school?"

She shrugs. No smile.

"That good, huh?" I ask.

My gaze slips over her shoulder. There's no sign of Zoey. Is she in the bedroom?

"She's out with my mom."

I look back at Kate. "What?" I ask.

She gives me a pointed look as though she sees through my facade, and I wonder if Zoey has told her and their mom about what I did. They aren't throwing things at my head, and I saw her mom the other day, and she was friendly, so I guess not.

"Zoey. She's out with my mom," Kate says.

I shake my head and try to look nonchalant, as though I don't know what she's implying. "You want to come play soccer?" I ask her, figuring it might do her good to get outside.

She shakes her head and gives me a withering look. Do

they pull all fifteen-year-old girls aside in school and teach them that?

"Any news on the cat?" I ask her.

She shakes her head, and despite the fierce expression on her face, her chin wobbles. She reminds me of Zoey in that respect: always hiding her softer side beneath an impenetrable armor and a solid scowl. "He's probably dead. He wouldn't know how to survive outside. He was a house cat."

"Don't say that," I tell her. "Cats have nine lives."

"No, they don't," she shoots back at me like I'm an idiot.

"Well, don't give up hope," I say.

This earns me another eviscerating look. Wow. The army should employ her in place of using bayonets. Thankfully, before I have to make any other attempts at conversation, Cole comes tearing out of the bedroom, showing off the brand-new soccer shoes Robert bought for him. He's happy to see me, grinning enthusiastically and snatching the soccer ball right out of my hands.

"Let's go," he says, already running down the stairs.

"See you later," I say to Kate.

She grunts and shuts the door on us. I jog after Cole.

"How are things?" I ask once I catch up with him and we're halfway to the rec center playing field.

"Good," he says.

"You liking school?"

He shrugs. "It's okay. I made a friend. Tan. His dad is a firefighter. You know firefighters came and put out the fire on our house?"

"Yeah," I say. "That must have been pretty scary, huh?"

He shrugs, indifferent, and I remember how he was several

streets away when the firefighters found him. He probably didn't even see it—unless, of course, he's the one who set it. "I think I want to be a firefighter when I grow up."

"Awesome," I tell him. "That's a cool job."

"Do firefighters have guns?" Cole asks, looking up at me with such an innocent expression it's hard to reconcile it with his pyromania and general obsession with deadly objects.

"No," I tell him. "Firefighters don't need guns. They're putting out fires. They need hoses."

He laughs, but I don't. The whole gun obsession is disturbing. I can see why Zoey was worried, and I keep coming back to the question of whether Cole was the one behind the torched car. Firebombing a car seems like a big job for a nine-year-old to pull off.

"I might become a policeman, though," Cole says, rattling on. "They have guns. My dad has a gun."

"I don't know if that's true," I say tentatively, knowing that his dad would have had to hand over his police-issue weapon when he was arrested. Not to mention that a person who's just out of jail, with a history of domestic violence, can't get a license for one.

"It is," Cole answers back stubbornly, his mouth pursing.

I don't press because I don't want to rile him up.

"Can I tell you a secret?" He grins at me like he's about to burst if he doesn't get it out.

"Sure," I say.

"My dad. He's out of prison," he whispers, his eyes gleaming with excitement.

I try to keep my voice level. "How do you know he's out of prison, Cole?"

Cole shrugs and won't look at me. "I just heard," he says. "My mom and Zoey don't think I know, but I do. They're keeping it a secret from me."

How did he find out? Did he overhear them? "I think they just wanted to protect you," I tell him.

His face scrunches up again. "They're liars," he says, spitting the word.

"No, they're not," I say. Then I kneel down so I'm level with him. "Cole, your mom and your sister aren't liars."

He scowls at me. "Yes, they are."

"Why do you say that?" I ask, keeping my voice light.

He looks away. "Because they are."

"Look at me," I say. Reluctantly, he does. "They haven't lied to you."

Cole spots something over my shoulder. "Look!" he yells, pointing.

I turn around. It's a seagull pecking at something in a trash can, its wings flapping loudly. Before I can turn back to Cole, he's off—racing toward the rec center playing field.

I let Cole expend the surplus of energy he seems to stockpile, running him up and down the field until his face is bright red and he's out of breath. I know it will only be for an hour or two and then he'll be back to full strength. The kid is powered by some kind of nuclear reactor or something.

"I think you might be ready to try out for the junior soccer team," I tell him.

"Really?" he asks, beaming.

I nod. "Yeah."

His face falls suddenly, and, glowering, he kicks the ball so it flies across the field.

"What's the matter?" I ask, puzzled.

"Nothing," he grunts.

"Don't you want to try out?" I put my hand on his shoulder, but he shrugs it off.

"There's no point," he says.

"Of course there is," I argue.

He kicks the dirt with the toe of his boot. "But I won't be here to play in the games."

I kneel down in front of him. "Hey, you're going to be here awhile," I tell him. "Long enough to play a season, maybe longer." Truth is, I don't know how long they're going to be here. However long it takes them to fix up their old apartment? Or will they decide to stay?

"No, I won't," he snaps. "I'm not staying here." He races off to retrieve the ball, and I stare after him, wondering what the hell he means by that.

# ZOEY

"This is nice," my mom says, sighing deeply as she stretches her legs out on the sand beside me.

She looks over at me and smiles. It's a wan smile, but there's a trace of real happiness beneath it—or maybe not happiness; maybe it's hope. Because we haven't heard anything more about my father, we're both slowly letting out the breath we've been holding these last two weeks. Of course, I still haven't told her my suspicions about Cole. When I asked him straight up if he knew anything about the fire, he yelled at me, telling me he didn't do anything.

My mom reaches and brushes away a strand of hair that's stuck to my face. "Is everything okay?" she asks.

"Yeah, everything's fine," I tell her, though my smile is forced. While the beach and the breeze have lifted some of my melancholy, they can't do much to shift the ache in my heart.

"It's so hot," my mom says. "Why don't you take off your T-shirt and shorts?"

I flush. I'm wearing the yellow bikini that was in the bag of clothes from Emma Rotherham, still with its tags attached, though it's hidden under my shorts and a T-shirt. I don't know why I put it on. It's pretty much dental floss on the bottom half, and as I sit here now, I can hear my dad's voice in my head, calling me a whore as I was getting ready to leave for my end-of-year school trip to a water park when I was fifteen.

"Cover yourself up. No one wants to look at you," he said.

I was wearing a pair of shorts and a T-shirt, only they were clothes from before my growth spurt, which meant the shorts rode up and the T-shirt was tight.

My mother intervened, and he hit her in the face, breaking her nose. I never did go to the water park. And the next day, feeling bad, my dad gave me a hundred dollars and told me to go and buy some new clothes. I bought extra large. But my dad wouldn't let it go. He'd still make comments and call me names. *Slut. Whore. Tease. Just like your mother.*

Fuck that.

Before I can stop to think about it, I tear off my T-shirt, then wriggle out of my shorts. For one shocking moment, I feel naked—and I hesitate, almost cowering, waiting for a reaction—but when I glance around, no one is looking at me, and I feel liberated, as though for all these years my father, without me even being aware of it, was controlling my choices from afar. His voice in my head was louder than my own. Wearing this bikini is like giving him the middle finger, and it feels amazing.

"That's better," my mom says, smiling at me. "I wish I'd made more of myself when I was your age."

"You're beautiful, Mom," I tell her, because it's true.

"I've got a job interview on Monday," she whispers, as if it's a secret.

Surprised, I ask, "Where?"

"A salon in town. A friend of Robert's wife owns it. She's looking for a senior stylist."

"That's fantastic," I say.

She shrugs. "It's quite high-end. They do a lot of weddings, and, well, I don't know if I'm good enough—"

"Of course you are!" I burst out, wishing she weren't so down on herself all the time. I hate it that my dad made her doubt herself so much and crushed her confidence. "You're more than good enough. You should have your own salon."

She laughs at that, as if I'm being ridiculous. "It's so sad about Robert's wife," she says with a sigh. "The way he speaks about her, he obviously loved her so much."

"When did she die?" I ask.

"A couple of years ago. She had breast cancer. He's still devastated." Her smile fades. Just one more reason not to fall in love, I think to myself. It always ends with a broken heart.

My mom clears her throat. "How are you and Tristan?" she asks. She's looking at me knowingly.

"What do you mean?" I ask.

"I'm not blind, Zoey."

Now I'm stumped for words. I don't talk boys with my mom.

"Do you like him?" she asks.

"Sure," I say, picking up a magazine and starting to flick through it. I'll act like I don't understand her subtext. "He's been really nice to us."

I can feel her narrowing her eyes at me. "I didn't mean it like that."

"Huh?" I ask, acting innocent.

"Did something happen between you?" she asks.

"Happen?" I pretend to study my horoscope in the magazine.

"I saw you last week, after work. You went around to Tristan's place."

"You were spying on me?" I ask her, astonished.

She shakes her head, looking hurt and bewildered. "No, of course not. I worry about you is all, especially with"—she takes a deep breath—"your father being out of prison. I like to know where you are and that you get home safe. I always wait up for you. I heard someone outside, and I looked out the window. . . ."

If she saw me looking out the window, then she must have also seen me kissing him. Did she see Brittany arrive and all that drama too? Why didn't she say something about it until now?

"And you've been ignoring him ever since and seem sad. Did something happen?"

I swallow hard, feeling like I'm swallowing the handfuls of sand I'm squeezing between my palms. She mustn't have seen it all. "He . . . I . . ." I break off. My mom touches my wrist.

"You can talk to me. I know I haven't always made it easy. I've been so wrapped up in my own . . . what was going on . . ." She stops and I smile at her. I know she finds it hard to admit her depression. "But I want to make this a new start," she says. "A fresh start. I like it here. I think it's good for you kids. And I want to be a better mother." Her nostrils quiver, and her eyes fill with tears.

I squeeze her hand. "You are a good mother."

She shakes her head. "No. I've left you to do the parenting and to take responsibility. It's not fair. What kind of a mother expects her teenage daughter to go to work?"

"I don't mind," I start to say, but she cuts me off. "Zoey, I want you to go to college, do the things that I never got to do, and instead I'm making you pay for all my mistakes."

"They're not your mistakes," I say.

She smiles at me skeptically. "They *were* mistakes. I should have left your father when you were a baby, as soon as he first raised his fists to me. I should have walked out that door and never looked back. Though I'm not sure, even back then, that he would have let me leave."

My mom reaches out and strokes my cheek, the way Tristan did, as though wiping away an invisible tear. "What did happen with Tristan?" my mom asks again.

Another painful swallow, and then it pours out of me. "I did something stupid."

"Did you sleep with him?"

I shake my head, embarrassed that she'd ask.

"I wouldn't judge you, sweetheart."

I chew my lip, my eyes tracking to the pier, thinking of how Tristan took my hand and pulled me to the end and how it felt like we were alone in the middle of the ocean somewhere. "I didn't sleep with him," I tell my mom. "We kissed."

"And?" she probes.

"And then a girl showed up. He'd booty-called her."

My mom tries to hide her shock. "Oh," she says. "I see."

"He says that it was a huge mistake and he only called her because he was trying to get me out of his head, or something lame like that."

"Okay," my mom says. "I can see why that would be upsetting. But why do you think you did something stupid?"

"Because I fell for him. And I shouldn't have!"

"That doesn't make you stupid. And what if he's telling the truth? What if he made a mistake? What if he does really like you?"

"How can you tell, though?" I ask. "You believed Dad, didn't you? And then he cheated on you. And whenever you took him back, he'd swear blind that he'd never hit you or cheat on you again . . . and he always did."

My mom stares at the horizon for a few moments before turning back to me. "Not all men are like your father, Zoey."

I shrug. "All the men I meet seem to be."

"They're not," she tells me firmly. "And you shouldn't think that, because if you do, you're going to miss out on so much."

I shrug again. "Doesn't seem like I'm missing out on anything worth having."

My mom takes my hand again. "I'm sorry," she says. "This is all my fault. I've made you believe that all relationships are doomed, that all men are like your dad, and that's all you can expect, but it's not true."

I pull a face. "Look at Aunt Chrissy," I say. "It's the same with her. You know Javi made a pass at me when he took me to buy a car?"

"What?" my mom exclaims. Then she shakes her head furiously. "I always knew he was a worthless, horrible—"

"It's not just him," I interrupt. "Every guy I meet seems to take advantage. Or tries to."

My mom looks at me in horror. "Who? What's happened?"

"A customer groped me at work."

My mom's face turns livid. "Who?" she demands.

"Some guy. It was fine." I don't tell her that Kit and Tristan had to intervene. "I'm sick of people thinking they can get away with behavior like that. What is it about me? Do I just attract people like that?"

My mom sighs and once again strokes my cheek and smiles

wistfully. "I understand." Her smile turns sad. "Mine and your aunt Chrissy's father, your grandfather . . . You know what he was like."

"An angry drunk."

She nods. "Yes. And we were so starved of attention, so hungry for love, that we both said yes to whatever man looked our way. We were looking for an escape. So we both ended up marrying the first man who asked us. Men who turned out to be worse even than our father. You never met Chrissy's first husband, but he was a piece of work. And I didn't choose much better," my mom continues. "I married your father."

What she's telling me confirms that I'm right. I'm just like my mom and Chrissy. I attract assholes; whether it's because I'm desperate for escape or approval or because I seem like a victim or don't feel I deserve better, I don't know, but the one thing I do know is that needing someone is a huge mistake that will cost you dearly. "So I am doomed," I mutter angrily.

My mom puts her hand on my chin and turns my head so she can look at me. "No, Zoey. You aren't the same as us," she says. "You're stronger. You have a self-belief I never had. You're not doomed."

I frown at that, because, honestly, I don't know what she's talking about. I'm not strong. I don't have self-belief.

"The way you stood up to your father," she says, "was braver than anything I could ever do. You saved us. Don't think I don't pray to God every night, giving thanks for you. There are many things I can't forgive your father for, but I will never regret marrying him because of you children."

I feel my eyes start to well up with tears and my throat constrict. "Why did you stay with him so long?" I ask. It's something

I've never asked her before, and I realize it's something I've needed to know, something I've wrestled with for years. Every time she took him back, it was as if she was choosing him over us.

She sighs. "I think because it felt like a choice," she says, confirming my fear. "And making a choice felt like I was the one in control, not him." She shakes her head as though laughing at her own stupidity. "But I was wrong. It wasn't a choice. I was trapped. I was afraid. And . . ." She sighs again. "I didn't think I could be alone. I thought I needed him."

I don't know how to react because how can you love someone who hits you? How can you need someone who hurts you so badly? How can you think so little of yourself that you think that's all you deserve? I can't make the same mistakes as her.

"Zoey," she says, "you're so beautiful, inside and out, and you don't need a man. You're strong and capable and independent in a way I've never been, and I couldn't be more proud of you for that." She wipes away a tear as she looks at me, and I wipe away my own tears, which have started to spill down my cheeks.

"But let me tell you this," she goes on, her voice becoming fierce. "Though you will never need anyone to make you happy, or complete you, don't cut yourself off from love or the possibility of it because you think all men are bad or because you're scared to get hurt."

"BOOOOOOO!"

I almost jump out of my skin. Cole leaps onto my towel, spraying me with sand. I squint up, shielding my face with my hand, and see Tristan walking toward us. Shit. I turn my head and blink rapidly, swiping at my tears, feeling hugely self-conscious in my bikini and reaching for my T-shirt and shorts. What the hell is he doing here?

My mom catches my look. "I told him to drop Cole here after soccer," she says to me with an innocent smile.

"Hey," Tristan says. He stops a few feet from us, hands thrust into his pockets, looking awkward as all hell.

"Thanks so much, Tristan," my mom says, standing up. "We're so grateful. Cole, why don't we go and get some ice cream?" she says.

I make to scramble to my feet to go with them and start pulling on my shorts.

"You stay here," she tells me.

I'm too flustered to say anything, and before I know it she's grabbed her bag and her towel and Cole's hand and is waving good-bye. Tristan moves to follow her.

"What are you doing?" she asks him. "Stay! Hang out with Zoey."

Oh God, so much for subtlety.

Tristan seems to waver for a moment and then nods reluctantly. I don't know if I'm angry or happy.

# TRISTAN

Bikini. Zoey almost naked. Zoey's skin. Zoey's breasts. Zoey's legs. Zoey's face.

Try. Not. To. Stare.

I squint into the sun instead, trying to burn the image of Zoey in a bikini off my retinas. I almost blind myself. Excuses rattle around my head, reasons I should leave—I've got work to do, a nonexistent dog to walk, a wall to paint, a parking meter to feed—but my body isn't listening. Instead, I find myself sitting down beside her in the sand, not too close but close enough that my peripheral vision is filled by the sunflower-yellow splash of Zoey's bikini, which she quickly covers with a T-shirt.

As she pulls it on over her head, I turn my head for a split second, regretting it immediately because now I have an image of Zoey that will no doubt stay with me forever: her near-naked body, the inviting curve of her breasts and her smooth, perfect stomach, and her hip bones, which direct my gaze like an arrow southward. I'm so used to seeing her in baggy T-shirts and sweaters that my brain is struggling with this overload. It's all I can do not to groan out loud. But that would make me seem like a monumental pervert, and I already seem like a monumental asshole. Not wanting to further weaken my case, I manage to silence whatever noise is trying to escape my lips and pull my knees toward my chest. I lean my arms on them, casual-seeming, but actually trying to hide the very obvious situation in my pants. I stare at the ocean and try to imagine being immersed in the cold and, when that doesn't work, I think of *Jaws*.

Neither of us speaks, and Zoey is staring off into the distance, an enigmatic expression on her face. I wonder how angry she still is and if she hates me, and once again I wish I could travel back in time and not send that text to Brittany. I can't help but think how different things might be if I hadn't. Would Zoey and I be lying here on the sand together, no T-shirt barricade between us, my skin against hers, my hands tracing patterns across her sun-kissed stomach. Would we have . . . ?

Okay, stop right there. Don't think it; don't go there. It's not helping my situation imagining those things.

She hasn't said anything, and I can feel her tensing beside me, as though weighing her own excuses for leaving, and I know if I want her to stay then I need to say something. Should I bring up what happened again? Apologize once more? Make a joke? No, bad idea. She reaches for her bag, and I know that I have mere seconds before she gets up and leaves.

"I need to talk to you about Cole," I blurt.

Zoey lets go of her bag, and her head snaps toward me. "Is everything okay?" she asks, worried.

"He knows your dad is out of prison. I wasn't sure if you'd told him or if he'd overheard something."

"Oh," she says, shaking her head, confused. "No. We haven't told him."

"Maybe Kate did?" I suggest. "He also said he doesn't want to try out for the soccer team because he isn't going to be staying." I pause. "Maybe it's because he thinks you'll be going back to Vegas."

I watch Zoey, realizing I'm holding my breath. I want her to say that they won't be leaving, that they've decided to stay. But she just keeps frowning.

"The arson investigator completed their report," she finally whispers. "Apparently, the accelerant used on the car was acetone."

"Nail polish remover?" I ask.

Zoey nods. "My mom always has a stash of it, from her job—she does makeup and hair. There was a big bottle of it in our bathroom." She chews her lip. "The fire department told me that it's an open case, but they also said it would be almost impossible to prove who did it. . . ." She lets that hang.

"Did you ask Cole if it was him?"

She nods. "He says he didn't do it. But I think he's lying."

"Have you told your mom or anyone?" I ask.

She shakes her head, chewing on her lip. I can tell that she's been bottling all this up, wanting to speak about it. The fact that I'm the one she's confiding in shows me that she must be really short on friends.

"I just don't know why he would do it," she says, and her voice cracks with emotion. "Why would he set fire to my car? He knew how hard I worked to pay for it."

"Maybe he was just messing around with fire," I suggest. "Kids do that."

"But it wasn't just matches," Zoey says. "It was acetone. What kid knows to use acetone to start a fire?"

A phone rings, and Zoey startles. She rummages in her bag

and pulls it out, frowning at the display. I guess she must have bought a new phone with her wages. She lets it ring a few more times and then finally answers. "Hello?" she asks, putting it to her ear. There's a beat, and then she asks, "Who is this?" After a few more seconds, she hangs up, looking unhappy.

"Who was that?" I ask.

She stares at the phone. "I don't know. They keep calling. That's the third one today."

"Probably just spam. I get those too."

She doesn't say anything, but I can see there's something troubling her. "What is it?" I ask.

"I think it's my dad," she blurts.

"What?" I ask.

"Before the car was set on fire," she says, "I got these weird calls—three of them, all anonymous. I don't know if it's him, but there was someone on the other end of the line. They're always there. I can hear them, breathing."

"How would he have gotten your new number?" I ask.

"Yeah, you're right," she says, blushing and shoving the phone in her bag. "I'm being stupid."

"No," I say quickly. "I don't think you're being stupid. I don't want you to worry—that's all."

She nods and starts gathering up her things. I don't want her to leave. But I don't know how to get her to stay. "Robert bought an alarm system for the condo," I tell her. Robert seems as invested as I am in keeping the family safe, and I think it might have something to do with Gina.

"I'm going to install it later today. It links up to your phone, so if someone comes to the door, a motion sensor will alert you via text."

Zoey nods. "Thanks," she murmurs. She stands up, and I scramble after her. She slides her feet into her flip-flops and stumbles. I catch her by the hand. That moment of contact between us makes the memory of kissing her explode in my brain. She quickly pulls away, throws her bag over her shoulder, and starts walking. I jog quickly after her.

# ZOEY

Even after everything, even after the hurt he caused, every time I'm with him I feel like I can let out the breath I've been holding and inhale again. I hate it.

I shouldn't have told him about Cole or about the phone calls I think are from my dad. It's just that he's easy to talk to, and I have no one else I feel like I can talk to so openly. I don't want him telling Will, though. He's got enough to worry about, living in a war zone. We've been e-mailing back and forth for the last ten days and things are back on an even footing. I've said sorry. He's said sorry. I haven't told him about the calls or about what happened with Tristan. The first because there's nothing he can do about it and the second because I'm worried what he'd do about it.

"Do you need a ride somewhere?" Tristan asks as we hit the street.

I shake my head, but then I see I'm late for work and need to head home and shower quickly first. I nod at Tristan. "Thanks."

He gives me a faint smile, and we head up the street, coming to a stop by his bike. Tristan pulls a helmet from some hidden compartment and hands it to me. I stare at it as though it's an alien object.

"Here," he says, taking it out of my hands and then putting it on me. I don't say anything, but as he does up the strap, his fingers graze my chin, and I have to stop myself from remembering the last time he touched my face and where it led. But it's too late, and now I'm staring at his lips, remembering how soft they were and how desperately we kissed, like time was running out. I didn't know a kiss could feel that way.

Immediately, the image of Tristan kissing Brittany appears in my mind's eye, erasing my sentimentality. I wonder if, since I told him I wasn't interested, he went back to her. Did he call her up and arrange another booty call?

"Okay, you ever ridden on the back of a bike?" he asks when he's done fixing the helmet.

I shake my head, the helmet so heavy it feels like I'm wearing a bowling ball as well as earmuffs. Tristan swings his leg over the seat, and I get a lurch in my stomach at the sight. He's so comfortable in his body, his movements so certain and so fluid. I notice the ripple of muscles in his forearms as he grips the handlebars and get another pang that I don't want to admit is desire and longing.

I climb on the bike behind him, but I'm not sure where to put my feet, and they dangle until he reaches back and puts his hand on my calf and guides my foot to a peg. I want him to do the same to my other foot, but he doesn't.

He's not wearing a helmet, and I'm about to ask him about it, realizing that I must be wearing the only one he has, but he shouts over his shoulder, "Hold on," and then revs the engine and pulls out of the parking space.

The movement makes me almost fall backward off the bike, but he anticipates it and reaches his hand back, around my waist, holding me in place as he steers one-handed.

I don't need telling twice. I look for something to hold on to, but there's nothing I can see, and when Tristan revs the engine again and drives down the street, the only thing I can do is wrap my arms around his waist to hold on. I'm fiercely aware of how I'm pressed up against his back, aware too that my thighs are wrapped around his. I can feel his abs through his T-shirt and remember how it felt to lift that same T-shirt and run my fingers along the ridges of muscle and feel his skin contract into goose bumps at my touch. He brakes at a stoplight, and I'm thrown even farther against his back. He puts his feet on the ground to steady the bike, and I start to do the same, but his hand falls to my leg, just above my knee. "Keep them where they are," he shouts over his shoulder, indicating my feet. "I've got it."

He takes his hand away and rests it back on the handlebars, and my leg starts to tingle where he was touching me.

The light turns green. Tristan speeds off again, and I feel a rush of exhilaration, laughter bubbling up inside me, threatening to burst out. I get it now—the obsession he and Will have with bikes—because it feels like nothing else on earth, except perhaps kissing Tristan. It's the same rush of adrenaline, the same dizzy feeling of letting go, of escape. And the best thing is the feeling I have of ceding control, letting Tristan take charge.

I close my eyes, letting my body mold to his. His broad back shelters me from the wind, and whenever he brakes, I'm driven even harder against him, but I notice I'm not doing anything to resist it.

He takes the long way home, but I don't say anything, and

he slows when we turn the corner onto our street—as if trying to drag it out. I want to keep going, keep driving, but I can't tell him this, so I close my eyes and breathe in deep, eking out every last second.

When I open my eyes, something catches in my vision, and I startle, lurching sideways on the bike, which then swerves dangerously. Tristan fights to keep the balance, righting the bike with his body weight, as I cling on to him for dear life.

My heart is thumping, my whole body shaking when Tristan pulls up in front of the condo. He turns off the engine and kicks down the stand, then turns to me. "Are you okay?" he asks, worried. "I'm sorry about that. . . ." He gestures to the street, where there are visible tire marks streaking the road where we swerved.

He says something else, but I'm not hearing him. I'm trying to pull the helmet off, but I'm hyperventilating and my fingers are clumsy. Tristan helps, unstrapping it for me, and I yank it off, then try to get my leg over the seat so I can get off the bike, but I'm panicked, and I stumble.

"Careful," he says, catching me just before my leg brushes the scorching-hot exhaust pipe.

I stagger back, away from him, glancing up the street.

"I'm sorry," he says again. "You moved suddenly. I wasn't expecting it. I don't usually ride with a passenger. . . ."

He thinks I'm angry and blaming him for the near accident. I shake my head. The words are jumbled in my head. I can't get them out. Instinctively, I move behind Tristan so his body acts as a shield. "N-no," I stammer, staring over his shoulder and up the street. "It's my fault. I thought I saw something."

Tristan glances where I'm looking, but all there is to see is a row of parked cars beside another apartment block. There's no one lurking between the two palm trees on the sidewalk; there's no one hiding in the shadows.

"What did you see?" Tristan asks.

I shake my head, trying to brush it off. I must have imagined it. I almost caused an accident over nothing.

"Zoey, what did you see?" Tristan presses.

He's not going to drop it. My eyes fly back to the street, to the shadows between the cars, searching for movement, searching for proof I'm not losing my mind.

Finally, I turn back to Tristan. "I thought I saw my dad," I tell him.

# TRISTAN

I sit on my bike and wait for Zoey. I told her I'd wait for her to shower and then drive her to work because she's so late. She glanced up the street and then at my bike, weighing her choices, and then nodded.

I took a walk up the street to see for myself if there was anyone lurking around, but there wasn't. Did she imagine it? Or did she see something and her imagination filled in the blanks? Her dad can't be here. He'd be breaking his parole terms by crossing state lines. But then what about those phone calls she received? If her dad is here, what does he want? I don't like to think about it.

A few minutes later, Zoey comes running out of the apartment. Her hair is wet, and her makeup-less face has caught a fresh smattering of freckles from the sun. She's glowing, and as I watch her walk toward me, my gut tightens. I'm a fucking idiot—that's what the drill-sergeant voice in my head is yelling. A big fucking idiot. She's the most beautiful person I've ever known, inside and out, and I had to go and screw things up.

I tear my eyes off her and swing my leg over the bike, holding it steady as she climbs on behind me and puts on the helmet, needing no help from me this time. She adjusts her body weight to keep the bike balanced and then wraps her arms around my waist, keeping a rigid distance between us, but even so, just being this close to her is making my brain spin out. I kick up the stand and rev the engine and feel her legs grip mine. I glance down, seeing the smooth, bare skin of her thigh, and have to resist the urge to put my hand on it.

A couple of times when I brake, the forward momentum pushes her against my back—giving me a few stolen seconds of contact before she rearranges her body to keep the distance. I try to brake slowly because it's pure torture and a major distraction when I'm trying to keep from plowing into vehicles.

When we get to her work, she hops off and hands me the helmet. "Thanks," she says.

"Want me to pick you up?" I ask, hoping she'll say yes, but she shakes her head.

"No. I'll be okay."

I try to hide my disappointment. She heads inside, and I see her, through the large front window of the restaurant, smiling and waving at the chefs and other waitstaff, and feel both happy that she's making friends and jealous that I'm not part of her world. Because you're a capital-A asshole, the voice yells.

A part of me wants to sit out here all night, but I realize that's perhaps not the best solution, and besides, it's probably time I tried to go cold turkey and weaned myself off her. It is pretty damn clear she has no interest in reliving what happened between us last week. But before I can start the engine, I hear someone yell my name.

I turn around. It's Dahlia.

"Hey," I say, surprised to see her. "What are you doing here?"

"Meeting Didi and Jessa," she explains. "We're going to get dinner, and then we're heading to a party at Emma's."

"Emma Rotherham's?" I ask.

She nods, grinning ear to ear. "Yeah, she told me to bring people. You should come. What are you doing here, anyway?" she asks, and glances at the restaurant just as Zoey walks past the window. "Oh my God," she says, turning back to me. "Are you stalking her?"

"No!" I protest. "I gave her a ride, that's all. I was just about to leave."

She notices something in my expression and narrows her eyes. "Did something happen between you two?" she demands. "Tell me you didn't have sex with her."

That's my sister. Direct as a missile. "I didn't have sex with her."

"But something happened," she states, a detective grilling a suspect.

"No, yes, kind of."

"Which is it? Yes or no?" she demands.

"Yes." I cringe inwardly and outwardly.

"What did you do?" she asks.

"I might have kissed her," I admit. "Well, she kissed me, actually."

"But you kissed her back."

"I might have," I admit.

"Then what happened?"

I don't answer. I'm worried she might kick my bike over, with me on it, if I tell her.

"What happened?" she growls again.

She's not going to let this go. "I fucked things up, just like you said I would."

"You didn't sleep with her and then dump her, did you?" she shrieks.

I shake my head. "But you were right. I shouldn't have gone there. I wasn't thinking straight."

"You weren't thinking with your brain is the problem," she says, coming to lean beside me on the bike. We perch there in silence for a beat, and my eyes track back to Zoey inside the restaurant. Dahlia watches her too.

"Can you fix it?" she asks me after a minute.

I shake my head. "Don't think so."

Dahlia studies me for a moment, but I don't look at her. I can't take my eyes off Zoey.

"My God," she says. "I haven't seen you like this since the last time you were in love."

That gets my attention. I spin around to face her. "What are you talking about? I've never been in love."

Dahlia smirks at me. "Miss Cornwell, third grade."

I laugh. "Okay, one time." Miss Cornwell was my universe. Forget the twenty-year age difference.

"I had a crush on her too." Dahlia laughs. "I think that's when I first realized I liked girls."

I smile and poke Dahlia with my elbow.

"Why can't it always be that easy?" she asks.

"What?"

"Love," she answers. "It seems so simple when you're a kid. You think you'll grow up and find someone to love, and that when you do, the person you love will love you right back and you'll live happily ever after. It's never that easy, though, is it?" She sighs and leans her head on my shoulder.

"I guess not," I say, looking at Zoey, who is carrying a tray of drinks to a table.

Dahlia sighs again and stands up. "Come tonight. To the party," she says.

I shake my head. "No. I have to be up early. I've got work. Drowning people to save."

She gives me a pleading look. "Oh, come on. You used to party all night with me in college, then go play football. You took your finals on no sleep and you still aced them."

I laugh under my breath. That was then. This is now. I'm definitely not a kid anymore.

# ZOEY

It's weird to think it, but this is the first party I've been to since I was ten and Michaela Gemballa had a murder-mystery birthday pajama party. Everyone loved it but me, because while all the other girls were going around trying to figure out who the murderer was, I was thinking about how my dad had beaten my mom half to death the week before.

The music is pounding. It's not coming from a playlist but from an actual DJ, standing behind a booth set up beside the torch-lit pool. The palm trees in the garden are strung with fairy lights and lanterns, and beneath them there's an actual bar— with white-shirted waiters in rolled-up sleeves tossing bottles of liquor in the air as they mix cocktails.

I'm wide-eyed with it all, having never seen a house this big in all my life. It must have at least eight bedrooms and just as many bathrooms, and the gates at the front are wrought iron and twenty feet high with an entry pad and cameras. That's the part I envy the most. The gates and all the security.

"Do you want something to drink?" Dahlia asks me.

I shrug, unsure, and tug self-consciously at my dress, which feels way too short and too tight. Dahlia notices. "You look great," she reassures me. "That color really suits you."

It's one of Emma's dresses—a blue bodycon one with cutouts at the waist, which I would never have dared wear even a week ago and definitely wouldn't have tonight if I'd known she was going to be here. What if she recognizes it as her old castoff? But Dahlia has already taken me upstairs and shown me Emma's walk-in closet, which is the size of our apartment and stuffed to the rafters with clothes, and reassured me that Emma won't notice and wouldn't care anyway. She's apparently very sweet; she only plays bitches on-screen.

I glance around the garden. There are hundreds of people dancing, making out, or posing for Instagram photos. I feel like an outsider—everyone is so glamorous and model beautiful and seemingly at home in this world. But then Dahlia tugs me toward the bar, and I see Jessa and Didi smiling at me and waving us over. It's then that I realize my insecurity might just be a mind-set and that maybe I should make an effort to feel differently. This is what I wanted, after all: new friends and a new beginning. All those thoughts about my dad, and about Tristan, are thoughts I can park outside those wrought-iron gates and deal with later.

"Here," Didi says when we reach the bar. She hands me a glass of something neon orange–colored with a paper umbrella stuck in it.

"What is it?" I ask. It looks like liquefied Cheetos.

"Just a little concoction I like to call a Didi Surprise. I had the bartender mix it."

"What's the surprise?" asks Jessa skeptically as Didi hands her a glass of it too.

"Just try it," Didi says, handing the last one to Dahlia, who raises her eyebrows.

"What's the green stuff floating at the bottom?"

"Does it have alcohol in it?" Jessa asks.

"Maybe," Didi says with a wink. "Just a splash."

Jessa hands her glass back.

"Why aren't you drinking it?" Didi asks her, narrowing her eyes.

Jessa flushes, and I look between them, remembering that Jessa is pregnant. Does Didi not know? It seems by the look she's giving Jessa, a kind of knowing wink-wink-nudge-nudge, that she does know and that the whole drink thing has been orchestrated as a way to make Jessa fess up.

"Okay, fine, I'm pregnant," Jessa says, smiling as the secret is let out of the bag.

Didi throws her hands in the air and tips her head back laughing, then swoops Jessa into a hug. "I knew it!"

"How many weeks?" asks Dahlia, who is almost as excited as Didi.

"Eighteen. We didn't want to tell anyone, in case it came out in the press."

"The secret is safe with me," says Didi, who is still clapping her hands like a seal and making gleeful squeals. She hands Jessa a sparkling water and clinks her glass against it. "To babies and baby-making!" she says, then adds, "You are making me god-mother, right?"

"Of course!" Jessa laughs, which only sets Didi off on another exciting round of squeals.

Didi turns to me and raises a toast to Jessa and the baby, and I clink my glass against hers and then take a sip of the Cheeto juice. It doesn't taste anywhere near as bad as it looks, and the alcohol quickly floods my bloodstream. I take another sip and smile, feeling the knots in my shoulders ease. I hadn't even realized how tense I was.

I know I probably shouldn't, given I don't have much tolerance for alcohol, but I keep taking sips, and it doesn't take long before all the cares I've been carrying around evaporate almost as fast as the drink does up my straw. I look around at all the swirling colors and the laughing people and feel like Alice in Wonderland. I've slipped down a rabbit hole, and this drink I'm holding is like a magic potion, making me feel bigger and more confident. The drink is also in a magically refilling glass. I point this out to Dahlia, and she prizes it out of my hand, asking me how much I've drunk.

"I'm not sure," I admit to her.

"She needs to enjoy herself," argues Didi. "Let her hair down."

Jessa, the only one of us who I think is sober, smiles at me. "Are you okay?" she asks.

I nod, grinning. "I'm so good," I tell her.

"Let's dance!" Didi says, pulling me toward the dance floor.

# TRISTAN

When I pull up outside, the music is pounding so loudly the house is shaking on its foundations. The driveway is clogged with cars, and the front door is open, people milling around. Most people look drunk or high or both, and a few couples are practically having sex in the living room when I peer my head around the door, looking for Dahlia.

I push my way through a crowded kitchen and onto a terrace that overlooks a pool full of people. If I didn't know I was in the midst of a party, I'd assume a shark was prowling the shallows thanks to the screams and wildly splashing limbs.

When a couple of girls make eyes at me on the terrace and ask if I have anything to smoke, I shake my head. A month ago, I would have stopped to talk to them—I'd probably have been in the pool already—but tonight I'm not interested. I try Dahlia again, but she's not answering her phone. Where is she?

My gaze lands on someone in the middle of the dance floor. She's a pinpoint of light, outshining everyone. She's dancing in her own world, oblivious to everyone around her, though no one at the party could possibly be oblivious to her. Her dress clings to her like a second skin, accentuating her incredible body, athletic and lithe as a dancer. My jaw drops open as I realize it's Zoey, and it takes me a few seconds to really comprehend it. Her hair, which is normally tied up, is down and forming a wild, curly halo around her head. It even looks like she's wearing makeup.

I stare at her for a good two or three minutes, watching her. If everyone else is a star in a galaxy, then Zoey's the sun. There's something totally free about the way she moves—uninhibited and unafraid. It contrasts so completely with how she normally is that it takes my breath away to watch it, as though she's undergone a metamorphosis.

Someone bumps her, and she stumbles, almost losing her balance and giggling. Is she drunk? I move toward her instinctively, but a guy dancing right beside her takes her arm to steady her, and she laughs at that, too. There's both a flutter in my heart at the sight of her laughing and a kick in my stomach that someone else is making her laugh. The guy is chatting to her, eyeing her up so obviously, I want to leap across the lawn and drag him away by the neck.

He's an actor type—sculpted and chisel-jawed as a Ken doll and wearing a blue Hawaiian shirt with the buttons strategically undone, the better to show off the chunky gold chain around his neck. He's holding out his hand to shake hers, leaning in close to tell her something (what could he possibly have to say?), and she throws her head back and laughs some more. My hands coil into fists, and I spin on my heel. I need to get out of here. Now. Before I march over there, throw him in the pool, and see if the gold chain is heavy enough to drown him.

"Hi!"

Dahlia appears in front of me, flushed and excited, like she just took a spin on a roller coaster.

"Hey," I mumble. "I've been looking for you."

"I'm sorry to call you out so late," she says, breathless. "My car won't start. I think it's the battery."

"You couldn't get a jump from anyone here?" I ask her, letting my irritation seep into my voice. "It's like a Formula One lineup out front. I'm sure you could have found someone to give you a jump."

"Yeah, I didn't think of that," Dahlia says nonchalantly.

Annoyed, I stalk past her. "Come on, then, let's just do this. We might need to borrow cables. Are you sure it's the battery?"

"No," she says. "It might be the carbonara."

"You mean the carburetor?"

"That's the one," says Dahlia.

"You're drunk," I tell her.

"No . . . Okay, maybe a little."

"You shouldn't be driving," I say, annoyed with her. "I'm taking your keys."

She rolls her eyes at me. "I wasn't planning on driving. I'll crash here tonight."

"So why did you need to call me to come fix your car, then?" I say, even more annoyed with her.

She pulls a face, then shrugs. "Why don't you come and dance?"

I pull my arm out of her grip. "I don't want to dance," I tell her. I don't want to look in the direction of the dance floor, even though I'm itching to see if Ken boy is still talking to Zoey. What if they've moved past talking and laughing and are already making out?

"Why not?" Dahlia pushes. "You're here now; you may as well stay and have some fun. Come on . . ."

The light bulb that goes on in my head is searchlight bright. "You did this on purpose," I say, feeling outraged. "There's nothing wrong with your car, is there?"

Dahlia gives me what she hopes is a winsome smile. "No . . . But I got you here, and look, Zoey is right over there. . . ." She gestures toward the dance floor, but I refuse to look.

"Why have you suddenly changed your mind about me and Zoey happening? Before, you couldn't stop warning me off her!"

Dahlia scrunches up her face like she does when she knows she's guilty of something and feels bad. "Okay, look, I'm sorry. I was wrong. I didn't realize how much you liked her. And I didn't know how much she obviously likes you. I shouldn't have interfered. It wasn't my place."

I grind my teeth, irritated at this too-late confession. But it doesn't even matter now. "D, I already told you . . . Zoey and I, it's not happening. There's more chance of the Pope showing up and going skinny-dipping in the pool, so if that's all, I'm leaving." I turn and walk off, slipping inside the house, hoping I can lose her in the mass of people.

Dahlia catches up to me as I stride across the hallway toward the front door. "Please stay," she says.

A girl with elfin-cropped white-blond hair and large brown eyes floats down the stairs just then and intercepts us. "Are you leaving?" she asks Dahlia.

I know Emma Rotherham from posters and from movies but have never met her in the flesh. She's beautiful. Tiny. Ethereal as a fairy.

"I'm trying to convince my brother to stay," Dahlia says. Then she looks at me. "Tristan, meet Emma."

Emma holds out a hand to me, and it looks like she expects me to kiss it, but I shake it. "Nice to meet you," I say.

"Nice to meet you," she says, emphasis on the *you*.

She's clearly the kind of girl who's used to being fawned over and adored, but I'm not interested in playing the role of fanboy.

"Why are you leaving?" Emma asks us. "The party hasn't even started."

"Things to do," I say.

"What things?" she asks, cocking her head to one side.

"Baseball cards to alphabetize."

Emma thinks I'm being funny, and her nose crinkles in amusement, but I'm not. When I can't sleep, that's what I do. I categorize my record collection and my baseball cards

"Are you leaving too?" she asks Dahlia.

Dahlia shakes her head. "No way. I'm going to be the last to leave."

Emma smiles at her. "I hope so." She gives her a long, meaningful stare, and my sister's cheeks start to turn a shade reminiscent of boiled lobster.

I look between them and have another light bulb moment. Emma Rotherham is into my sister. And my sister, it seems, might also be into her.

Emma finally looks away from Dahlia. She puts her hand on my arm and turns the full wattage of her smile on me. "It was really nice to meet you, Tristan."

"You too," I say, but she's not really listening. She's too busy smiling at Dahlia.

# ZOEY

Didi and Jessa want to find the bathroom, and they insist I go with them, which I'm quite happy to do because this guy with teeth so white they're brighter than the gold chain around his neck won't stop talking to me, and all I want to do is dance.

I used to take classes as a kid—ballet and jazz—but around eleven I stopped. My dad refused to pay for the lessons. But tonight I'm remembering just how much I used to love it and how free it made me feel.

The girls steer me inside and into the kitchen. My body is slick with sweat from dancing, my dress sticking to me like cellophane, but I don't care. Jessa leads me toward the fridge, which she yanks open.

I gawp at the fridge's vast interior filled with every variation of water a person could ever dream of. There are dozens of sleek glass bottles containing spring water, alkaline water, pH-balanced water, and even crystal geyser water. Jessa stares, confounded, then grabs the nearest bottle.

"Artesian water?"

I shrug. "Okay."

"Check out this fridge," says Didi, coming over with a plate piled high with mini burgers that she offers to us. "Is there nothing in here but water?" she asks in astonishment.

"No," says Jessa, pointing at the salad drawer. "There's salad, too." She shuts the fridge door. "We shouldn't spy; it's rude."

I stuff a burger in my mouth. "Delicious," I say with my mouth full, thinking how much Tristan, in his quest for the perfect burger, would like it, though he'd complain that it's too small.

"Let's go," Didi says, checking the time and pulling me out of the kitchen and into the hall.

"Where are we going?" I ask, looking back over my shoulder. The party is in the opposite direction, and I wouldn't mind finding the waiter with the tray of burgers because I'm suddenly wildly hungry.

"This way," says Didi, marching across the hallway to the front door. "There's something outside you need to see."

"Outs—" I hiccup, the word dying on my tongue and my hiccups vanishing as I spot Tristan. He's standing at the bottom of the sweeping staircase with Dahlia. They're talking to a small blond girl I instantly recognize as Emma Rotherham. I track immediately to her hand, which is resting on Tristan's arm. She's smiling up at him adoringly, like she's the fan and he's the film star.

"I'm going to dance," I mumble, turning around and pushing my way back toward the thumping beat of the music.

"Wait," Didi says, catching me by the arm before I even reach the kitchen. "Don't go."

I look between her and Jessa. My mind is slow from the

alcohol, but not *that* slow. "Did you bring him here?" I ask, realizing too late I'm gesturing wildly in Tristan's direction. "You did, didn't you?"

"Tristan likes you," Jessa says.

"Yeah, of course he does," I mumble sarcastically, glancing over at him talking to Emma. He just jumps from one girl to another. I can't believe I almost fell for it.

"And we know you like him too," Didi adds.

"No, I don't," I say. "Besides, he looks like he's moved on."

Didi frowns and looks over at him and Emma. "What? Oh no, that's not what you think."

I glance at Tristan. He's no longer talking to Emma, who is walking off arm in arm with Dahlia. He's looking at me. Our eyes meet, and I feel a jolt all the way through my body. I see the longing on his face, the hurt, too, as he turns away and makes for the door, and as I watch him go, I remember what my mother said about not thinking all men are my father. Maybe Jessa and Didi and my mom are right. Maybe I should stop being so obstinate and listen to them.

"I came really close to losing Kit," Jessa says, interrupting my thoughts. "I was scared of getting hurt and I was angry. It's a long story," she says in answer to my frown. "But the point is that I decided to take a risk and follow my heart, and it's the best decision I ever made." She pats her bump.

"Same with Walker and me," Didi adds. "If there's one thing I know, it's that life is short. You have to live every single day of it so you don't have regrets."

"But," I start to argue, "what if it doesn't work out?"

"You don't have to believe in fairy tales," Didi says gently, "but you don't have to only believe in horror stories."

# TRISTAN

I kick up the stand of my bike and rev the engine before taking off down the driveway, tires spitting up gravel. The gate at the end of the drive is shut, and I have to wait for the security guy to open it. As it rolls back, I hear the sound of someone screaming and turn my head. What the hell?

It's Zoey.

She's taken off her shoes and is barefoot. I tear off my helmet, suddenly afraid that something bad has happened. Why else would she be screaming at me?

"Tristan!" Zoey shouts.

"What's wrong?" I shout back, panic welling.

Zoey skids to a stop, breathless, at my side.

"What's wrong?" I ask again, seeing the terror in her eyes.

She takes a deep breath of air, almost a gulp. "I, um . . . I just wanted to . . ." And then she throws her arms around my neck, and before I can say anything, she presses her lips to mine.

I'm so taken aback I almost fall sideways off the bike but just manage to keep my balance, my arms wrapping around Zoey's waist, as though I'm afraid she's going to change her mind and run off. I can't help but smile, and I can feel Zoey smiling against my lips, and it makes me pull her even closer and kiss her even harder.

After a minute, I pull back an inch and look at her. I want to ask her why she's changed her mind, but suddenly there's a honk. A car is trying to get past. They honk again impatiently. I turn around. "We're having a Nicholas Sparks moment here; could you give us a minute?" I look at Zoey. "You want to stay?" I ask her.

She shakes her head at me. "No. Take me home," she whispers.

# ZOEY

We drive home, my arms wrapped around Tristan's waist, my chin resting on his shoulder. I lean in to his body on every curve and press against him every time he brakes, and this time I'm wishing the ride would take seconds, not the thirty minutes it does.

When Tristan parks outside our apartments and we get off the bike, there's a moment of awkwardness. We stand there looking at each other. Tristan seems nervous.

"Do you . . . ?" he starts before breaking off.

I put him out of his misery, taking his hand and leading him toward his place. He shuts the door behind us, and then he's pushing me up against it. I loop my arms around his neck, and we kiss for what feels like an eternity. We finally come up for air, and Tristan steps back, taking me by the hand and leading me into the living room. I take my first real glance at his place. Shelves line one wall—filled with books and vinyl records. Books! I'm tempted to rush over to them like they're long-lost friends, but that can wait.

My heart is beating fast, my body humming. I look at Tristan

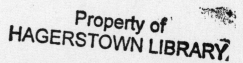

over my shoulder. He's watching me carefully, and I know he's wondering what next.

"Do you, um, want something to drink?" he asks.

I hesitate and then shake my head.

"Want to watch a movie?" he asks, clearing his throat and nodding at a collection of old DVDs lying on the floor by the TV.

I shake my head again, amused, because I don't think he really wants to watch Indiana Jones.

"So what do you want to do?" he asks, and I know he's checking in with me about how far I want to take things and how fast.

In answer, I loop my arms around his neck and pull him down so his lips meet mine. All I know is that I don't want to think. I want to feel. I want to be with him in every possible way. But I feel him tensing a bit, realizing something, and he instantly pulls back to look at me. "How drunk are you?" he asks.

"I'm not drunk," I say.

He looks at me skeptically.

"Okay, maybe a little," I admit.

He takes a deep breath and starts to disentangle himself. "Zoey, I think we should take it slow," he says. "I don't want to screw things up again. I don't want you to think I'm using you. And I don't want you doing anything you'll regret in the morning."

"I won't regret anything," I whisper, and try to kiss him again. But he's not having it.

"Zo," he says. "I'm serious."

I frown at him. "So am I."

"I don't think we should have sex."

I flush. "Okay," I mumble, feeling embarrassed. It feels like rejection. I try to pull away, but he holds on to me tightly by the shoulders.

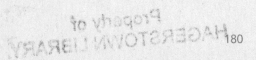

"Don't get me wrong. There's nothing I'd like more than to make love to you, but I want to wait until you really know you can trust me. I want it to be special."

"Okay," I say slightly tentatively, because what does that mean? His hands drop from my shoulders. I glance down at the DVD pile. Does that mean we're watching Indiana Jones after all? But Tristan takes my hand before I can move to the sofa. He starts leading me down the small hallway and into his bedroom. I'm confused, even more so when he lays me down on the bed and then hovers over me, holding his weight on his arms. "So . . . what do you want?" he murmurs, kissing me.

What do I want? What does he mean?

"Tell me," Tristan whispers.

I am so confused.

"Just because we're not having sex doesn't mean we can't do other things. So tell me what you want."

I draw in a warm breath of the air he's just exhaled. "I don't know," I stammer. "I . . ." I've never been asked that question is the simple truth. Not by a guy. I mean, there's only been one guy anyway, and he was never interested at all in what I wanted.

Tristan studies me up close. "I think you just aren't used to asking for what you want. You've put other people first for so long, you don't know how to put yourself first."

I start to protest, but he cuts me off. "Zo, you always find it hard to accept it when people want to do things for you. You've been like that with me since the beginning. So this time you're going to tell me what you want and I'm going to give it to you."

I feel a warmth spreading from my navel to the top of my thighs. Maybe it's the way he said my name, shortening it like that to Zo. Or maybe it's the idea that actually this is not what

I expected, but it's somehow better. It means something.

"So," he says again, a glimmer in his eyes. "What do you want?"

I shake my head. I don't know.

He tilts his head and leans in close, his lips by my ear, his breath tickling my neck. "Do you want me to kiss you?"

I nod.

He kisses me lightly where my ear meets my neck. I close my eyes and take a deep breath. He kisses my neck, lower down, closer to my collarbone. I shudder in response. "You want me to kiss you here?" He kisses the hollow at the base of my neck. "What about here?"

I don't respond.

He kisses my jaw right by my ear. My breath becomes uneven. He smiles. "You like it there?"

I nod.

He kisses me there again. Then my lips. And slowly his hand slides down over my dress, tracing every inch of my waist and hips. I think I've stopped breathing altogether by the time he stops and looks at me. He's reading me, my expressions, my breathing or lack of, as his fingertips trace my bare skin.

He peels off my dress, and then he lies beside me, his gaze drinking me in. I shiver even though it isn't cold.

"Tell me what you want," he says again.

"You" is all I can say, my face burning as I say it.

He narrows his eyes at me. He wants me to say more. But I don't know what to say. And I would never know how to ask for it even if I did.

He starts tracing his fingers over the lace edge of my bra, then lowers his head and draws my nipple into his mouth, pulling through the silk material of my bra until he makes me gasp. I should feel self-conscious. This is Tristan. Will's friend. And I do. I feel exposed, vulnerable, but not in a way that scares me—in a way that excites me.

He's kissing me again, and I bite his bottom lip, feel the heat of his hands. He groans as I press against him, and I wonder at whether he's as in control as he thinks. I tug at his T-shirt, my palms running over the smooth expanse of his chest and back, drinking him in with my touch, the way he did with me, and finally he relents and pulls the T-shirt off over his head before expertly removing my bra and then pulling me close so we're skin to skin.

After a few moments, I pull back to study him—holy shit. He's way more ripped than I thought, even though I had some idea from sitting behind him on the bike. The lines of his stomach muscles are ridges, his pecs defined, his chest so broad it's like a wall.

I look at his face, at his strong jaw, at his kind eyes with the curling lashes, at his beautiful skin.

"You're so beautiful," I say, the words falling out of me before I can stop them.

He smiles, bemused. "You're beautiful," he says, and gently pulls me toward him, his hands holding my face. He kisses me and starts stroking my arms and my stomach, until I'm so turned on I have to bite my tongue to stop from begging him for more.

He looks at me slyly, his pace slowing, so by the time his fingers trace the top of my underwear I'm practically hyperventilating. His hand slides beneath the elastic, and I raise my hips, but he stops, teasing me.

"Tell me what you want," he says again.

I shout the words in my head, but they don't make it past my lips. He puts his ear to my lips.

"What was that?" he says, almost laughing.

Annoyed, I press my hips upward. He frowns at me. "What?"

"I want you . . . ," I whisper.

He cocks his head to one side. "Want me to do what?"

"Make me . . . ," I say, scrunching my eyes shut, too embarrassed to get the rest out.

He kisses my eyelids. When I open them, he's smiling at me. Not smugly or annoyingly, but with total adoration. It makes my throat tighten.

"Do you want me to make you come?" he asks, relieving me of having to ask.

I nod. *Yes.*

He kisses me on the lips, then slowly pulls my underwear off. When I'm completely naked, he kisses me on the spot where my jaw meets my neck. It sends lightning bolts through me, making my whole body shudder, and as I gasp from his kiss he slides his hand between my legs. My eyes fly open as my back arches off the bed.

"You need to tell me how you like it," he says.

Oh God, he's not going to do anything until I tell him. I open my eyes. He nods at me, smiling encouragement. He really wants me to tell him. I realize it's not a game. He's not teasing me. He wants to know so he can give me exactly what I want.

"Like this?" he asks, gently touching me.

I nod.

"Or like this?" he asks, moving faster.

I nod again. "Yeah, like that," I say in a gasped whisper.

He grins, happy to finally receive a response.

I should be embarrassed, I think to myself, self-conscious at the way my body is responding to his touch, and so quickly, too, but I can't be. I'm floating; nothing exists beyond this moment, and this moment, and this moment, and . . .

Then there are no moments, just one infinite-seeming moment.

I fall back to earth with the softest of thuds, Tristan scooping me up and gathering me against his chest.

# TRISTAN

She curls into me, her breathing slowing, and I close my eyes, focusing everything on the feel of her skin against mine, the softness and warmth of her naked body, her thigh flung over my waist. I hook my hand under her knee and stroke the silky-soft skin behind it. She inhales and lets out a sigh, and I think to myself that if we could just stay like this forever I'd be happy. This is what I've been looking for all along. This feeling of not wanting to let someone go. I wasn't sure I'd ever find it, if it was even something that was real, rather than something invented by Hollywood. But it is real; it does exist.

"How are you doing?" I ask after a few minutes. She's not said anything, and I'm not sure if she's falling asleep. I want her to. I want her to stay the night, but I want to check with her.

"I feel bad," she whispers.

"Why?" I ask, alarmed. I pull back to look at her face, but she's hiding, her head bowed beneath my chin.

"Because you didn't . . . ," she mumbles.

I laugh, relieved that it's about that. "Don't feel bad," I tell her. "It was great for me. You need to know that when I do things for you, I'm not doing it to get something in return. I like making you happy."

She looks at me skeptically. My hands can't help but trace down her waist and over the rounded curve of her hip. "Believe me," I tell her, letting my gaze follow their path. "I loved every second of that."

Beneath the covers, I feel her hand reach for me, and it takes a monumental effort to push her away. I take her hand and squeeze it. "It's okay," I tell her.

"But . . . ," she argues.

"It's not quid pro quo." I prop myself up on one elbow. "I want to prove to you that I'm serious, that I'm not using you."

"I know you're not," she says, trying to sneak her hand from my grasp and reach for me again. I hold it tight.

"You're really bad at accepting anything from anyone, Zo, whether it's help or even a gift. Maybe it's time you learned to." She frowns, and I prop myself up on one elbow and look down at her, stroking a strand of hair out of her face. "Thirty days. That's what I'm going to do."

"What?"

"I'm going to teach you how to accept a gift. I want you to learn that it doesn't mean you're beholden and it doesn't make you weak. You do so much for other people. It's about time someone did something for you. For thirty days, I'm going to put all the focus on you."

She smiles at me suspiciously but then seems genuinely overwhelmed. "I don't get it. You don't want to . . ." She blushes furiously.

"Hell yeah, I do"—I laugh—"more than anything, which should tell you something."

She gives me a shy smile, and when I let go of her hand she doesn't try to reach for me again. I slide my hand to her inner thigh, and she inhales sharply, her eyes fixed on mine, her pupils dilating.

"I should call your brother," I say.

Zoey sits bolt upright. "What?"

I shake my head at my bad timing. "Sorry," I say. "I was just thinking about what Kit said to me. When he and Jessa got together, they hid it from Riley and he lost his shit when he found out. I figure we should tell Will."

Zoey turns pale, and I reach a hand and trace it up her neck, pulling her down into the bed, feeling the warmth of her skin against my body and wondering how it's possible I'll ever get out of bed again if she's in it.

"What's there to tell?" she asks quietly.

"Well, I want to date his sister. I kind of like her. A lot."

"You don't need his permission for that," she says, annoyed.

"I know," I say, turning serious and looking her in the eye, "but it's the right thing to do. If he were dating Dahlia, I'd want to know."

"Okay," Zoey says tentatively. "I'll call him and talk to him. But later."

I arch my eyebrows. "Promise."

"Promise," Zoey says.

"Where were we?" I ask, my hand inching even farther up her thigh, tracing the silky warmth between her legs.

She bolts upright in a panic.

"Oh God," she says. "I need to get back. My mom'll be waiting up for me. She'll be worried. I need to get going." She leaps out of the bed and starts gathering her clothes up.

"Is that what you want?" I ask her.

She stops, holding her clothes against her body. She shakes her head, biting her lip. "No," she says.

I reach across the bed and pull her toward me. "So text her and tell her you're with me."

She considers this, and I can see the silent argument going on in her head, but then she silences the voice of duty and smiles at me. "Okay," she says.

I grin, then pull her back to bed.

A phone buzzes around dawn, waking me. For a moment I think it's my alarm and reach for it, not wanting to wake Zoey, who's sleeping with her head on my chest, but it's not my alarm. I squint at the time, annoyed that I have to get up in a few minutes and get ready for work when all I want to do is stay in bed with Zoey. It's the first time a girl has ever stayed over in my bed, the first night I've slept the whole night through with someone in my arms, and I wonder now how I'll ever go back to sleeping alone.

Zoey stirs too, stretching her limbs, pushing up against me so I have to take several deep breaths to get ahold of myself. She opens her eyes and smiles a drowsy smile.

I kiss her. "Morning, beautiful," I say.

She smiles even wider, and I notice the mauve shadows beneath her eyes. I guess we didn't get much sleep.

"I've got to get to work," I tell her.

She pouts and then tilts her head and kisses me again. Her fingers tiptoe up my torso. I snatch them in my hand and grip them tightly. I really can't be late. But then the sheet falls back, and every ounce of willpower is sucked away by the sight of her nakedness. I'm going to be late.

The phone buzzes again. Zoey's phone this time. She frowns and reaches for it, picking it up from the floor, where it lies buried in her clothes. She sits up, pulling the sheet around herself as I take the opportunity to get up. I hear her gasp and turn. Her face looks stricken, the blood running from it.

"What is it?" I ask.

She swallows, then hands me her phone. I take it and glance down at the text on the screen.

**WHORE.**

# ZOEY

gain," Tristan says.

I look up at him, out of breath, sweating, and swipe my hair out of my eyes with the back of my arm. "I'm hot," I say, reaching for the water.

"Take your T-shirt off," he says with a smirk.

I look around. There's no one here. The gym is empty. Tristan managed to sweet-talk the owner into letting us borrow it after hours so he could run me through some self-defense moves.

I tear off the T-shirt so I'm left wearing just my sports bra and leggings. Tristan grins almost as wide as Cole did when Tristan gave him his Xbox. "And the rest," he quips.

I shake my head at him but can't help smiling. I still can't get used to the way he looks at me, but I also don't want to. I don't want to stop feeling that eruption of butterflies in my stomach. It's been a week since the party—a week that feels like a year for all we've crammed into it. Neither of us has slept a great deal; we're both so busy with work and life that the hours we spend together are too precious to use for sleep. We're catching up on each other's lives, learning each other in a whole new way: not just the likes and dislikes, the books and movies we both love or love to hate, but the inside things too: the secrets, the hopes, the fears—all things I've never voiced out loud before to anyone.

And when we're not talking, we're doing other things. Tristan has stuck to his promise—despite all my attempts to tempt him otherwise.

"Okay, once more," Tristan says. He's wearing gray sweat-pants and a black Coast Guard T-shirt. "Remember, use your voice first. Scream, shout, yell, do whatever you can to call attention to your situation."

I nod.

"And remember your fight stance."

I step my left foot slightly forward and raise my fists like he showed me. He makes me repeat the same move over and over: a simple hand strike followed by an elbow strike. "It's about muscle memory," he told me when I complained about the repetitive nature of the lesson. "So if anything happens, your body acts on instinct."

He says it seriously, with a studied look of concern. I know he's worried and he's trying to hide it. I know it's my dad call-ing and texting. That word—"whore"—it's a clue. And it's too coincidental that he sent the message then, just as I was wak-ing up with Tristan. It makes me wonder if he's spying on me. Tristan keeps trying to reassure me that he isn't, but I'm not so sure. After he sent the text, I was so hysterical and so para-noid I could barely leave the house. We called my dad's parole officer, and he told us that he only checks in with my dad in person twice a week, which means there's plenty of time for him to drive to Oceanside and back between check-ins.

Tristan installed a camera by our front door—one that

connects to our phones and lets us see whoever comes to the front door. Then he insisted on teaching me self-defense, so even though he's telling me not to worry, his actions are belying his words. I know he's spoken to Will, too, because Will keeps calling me and texting every day to check in. He hasn't asked me much about what's going on with Tristan. I think he's too weirded out about me dating his friend and probably doesn't want too many details.

Tristan said that when he called Will to tell him we were dating, he didn't say much to him, either, only that he was cool with it.

"I'm going to come at you from behind," Tristan tells me, bouncing on the balls of his feet.

I grin at him in the mirror. He rolls his eyes. "You have a dirty mind, Zoey Ward." He comes up behind me and puts his hand on my shoulder. "Try to fight me off."

He spins me around. I grab his arm with both my hands and try to break free, but I can't.

Frustrated, I drop my arms to my sides. "I can't do this," I sob. "It's stupid. I won't have a chance." I close my eyes, trying to banish the thought of my dad pummeling my mom with his fists, dragging her by her hair down the hallway. My breathing hikes, and the tears start flowing. I feel trapped but in the worst possible way, because the walls aren't visible and they surround me wherever I go.

Tristan wraps his arms around my waist from behind.

"I won't ever let him hurt you," he tells me, whispering the words into my ear before kissing me on the jaw.

I shiver against his body and lean into him, closing my eyes, wishing I could believe him.

"Okay, take me down," he whispers in my ear.

I slide my leg behind his, lever his weight, grab him by the knees like he showed me, and topple him backward, throwing my weight with a thump across his chest. He feigns as though I've winded him, so I roll fully on top of him, straddling him, and start to tickle him until he's crying with laughter. He wraps his arms around me and rolls me, pinning me to the floor and then kissing me.

"Am I interrupting?"

I freeze. Tristan scrambles off me and to his feet. A tall, good-looking guy with dark hair and stitches through his eyebrow, stands in the doorway, a gym bag slung over his shoulder and a skeptical, unamused look on his face.

"AJ," Tristan says, walking toward him.

I get to my feet too, embarrassed, and reach for my T-shirt, feeling AJ studying me as I walk toward him. I shake his hand, noticing how ice blue and utterly unreadable his expression is.

"This is my girlfriend, Zoey," Tristan says, and I swell with pride inside at the way he's said it so casually but also with such affection.

"Good to meet you," AJ says without a smile.

"AJ owns the gym," Tristan says by way of explanation.

I raise my eyebrows in surprise. Like Kit, he seems young to own a business—not even twenty-four, I'd guess. "Thanks for letting us use it."

"Well, I thought you were using it to work out," he answers dryly, tossing his bag in a corner alongside a pile of workout gear.

My cheeks turn bright red.

"Sorry," Tristan says, looking awkward.

"It's cool," AJ answers, glancing our way with a slight smirk. "I'll get out of your way." He heads toward a door in the back of the gym. "Just lock up when you leave." He glances my way and nods. "Nice to meet you, Zoey." And then he's gone before I can answer.

"He's a good guy," Tristan says, noticing my curious frown in his direction. "His girlfriend died eighteen months ago. In a car crash. She was with his best friend. They were having an affair. It's a long story. Come on, let's go get a burger," Tristan says, putting his arm around me. "There's this place nearby that I haven't taken you to yet. The relish tastes almost as good as you." He pauses. "Or," he says, "we could skip the relish and go back to my place?"

# TRISTAN

'm going to shipwreck us if you're not careful."

Zoey's standing on deck, holding on to the mast with one hand, shielding her eyes with the other, and all she's wearing is that yellow bikini. I could stare at her forever, but there's a serious chance I might sail us into something—rocks, a cliff, another boat.

She's definitely grown more confident these last weeks. Turns out her father said something to her when she was fourteen or fifteen and that's why she was hiding under all those baggy clothes. Like I didn't hate him enough already. I told her he said it because he could see the writing on the wall: Zoey was growing up, and when she became an adult she wouldn't be so easy to control. That's why he called her that name. It was a way to make her doubt herself, a way to tie her with invisible chains that he would hold the ends of.

Zoey scoffed when I first suggested it, but I think she's starting to believe me. I also told her it was a crime that she was hiding behind layers of clothing. She should be wearing what she wants, what makes her feel good. Anyway, I've made it my mission to make Zoey see herself the way she really is. I want her to see herself as beautiful, of course, but more than that, I want her to see how brave and strong she is.

When I told Will about Zoey and me dating, he went very quiet on the end of the phone. "Are you cool with that?" I pressed, anxiety making me hold my breath. For a horrifying moment, I thought maybe I was going to lose his friendship, but then he said, "Okay, just please don't hurt her."

I promised him I wouldn't, reassured him that it wasn't a passing flirtation, that it was serious, and I hope I convinced him.

I watch Zoey stumble on land legs across the deck, clinging to ropes and railings, until she reaches me at the helm. I reach one hand out to catch her as she jumps down and pull her sun-warmed body against mine. She fits like she's part of me, her head reaching to just beneath my chin. I kiss her neck, and she shivers in response. My hand is pressed to her stomach, and I think about inching it lower, but Kate and Cole are sitting a few feet away. Cole is practicing tying knots in a piece of rope. I told him if he learned three different knots by the time we got back, I'd buy him ice cream. I've discovered there's nothing Cole won't do for ice cream, or a chance to play Xbox.

Kate, on the other hand, is staring morosely at her phone, willing it to get a signal. I warned her that she'd have more luck spotting a mermaid, but that hasn't stopped her from desperately trying. She keeps staring up at the horizon, as though counting down the time until we reach land and cell phone range. I notice how tired she looks and how much weight she's lost.

"How's Kate doing?" I ask Zoey quietly.

"Okay, I think," Zoey answers, a hint of doubt in her voice.

"She seems distracted."

Zoey laughs. "Have you met my sister? I think if the boat started to sink, she'd seriously consider saving her phone before any of us." She chews on her lip, and I regret having brought it up. She doesn't need any more problems weighing on her shoulders. The anonymous phone calls have stopped, but I can't shake off the feeling we're in a lull and there's a storm coming. But at least out here, at sea, it feels like we're far from all that.

Zoey takes over the wheel, and I stand behind her, arms around her waist, trying not to get distracted by her nearness as I attempt to teach her how to navigate when all I want to do is navigate her down into the little cabin belowdecks.

"I see why you love this," she says to me.

"It's the closest thing to flying," I tell her. "The freedom."

"Is that why you joined the Coast Guard, so you could do both?"

I nod. "Mainly. You're at the mercy of nature, something stronger and more powerful than you can imagine—wind and rain and storms—it takes skill to beat them and stay alive."

She goes quiet. I wonder if she's thinking of her father. I know I am.

She shakes it off and turns to me, grinning. "Imagine sailing this across the ocean," she shouts over the noise of the wind.

"Where would you go?" I ask.

She shrugs. "I don't know. Italy. Maybe the South Pacific!" She gazes at the horizon. "There are so many places I want to see. I guess the one place I've always dreamed of going is this little island in Greece called Milos. I read about it in a book once."

"A book on Greek myths?" I ask.

She smiles. "You're such a nerd." I laugh.

"Says you, baseball boy."

"I'll take you there one day," I murmur in her ear. "To Milos. We'll go to all those places."

She turns to stare at me, unblinking, her expression halfway to shocked.

"What?" I ask.

She shakes her head, a small smile teasing her lips. "It just . . . I don't know . . . we're talking about a future. You said 'we.' I've never really thought about a future before, and when I did I was always by myself."

"Oh," I say.

"No," she says quickly, hearing the note of worry. "I like the 'we.' I like it a lot."

"While we're on the subject of futures, have you looked at those brochures yet?" I ask, referring to the college information packs we picked up last week.

She nods. "Yeah, I'm going to sign up this week for classes."

It's my turn to smile. "Which ones?"

Her expression turns serious. She looks nervous, as though she doesn't want to tell me. "What?" I press, curious.

"I think I'm going to choose courses that can help me get into law school."

I stare at her. "Seriously?" She wants to be a lawyer?

Her cheeks flush, and she looks at the ground. "You think it's a dumb idea."

I shake my head. "No! It's great. I just had no idea you were even thinking of becoming a lawyer."

She looks up at me, tentative and uncertain. "I mean, I don't know if I'll make it. It's competitive, and it'll take years, but . . ." She breaks off.

"But what?"

She looks at me again, a shy smile on her lips, and shrugs. "I feel like maybe I can do it." She pauses, narrowing her eyes at me. "Are you crying?"

"Me?" I say. "No. It's the wind." She doesn't buy it and shakes her head at me like I'm a giant dork. But I'm so happy for her, that she's finally making plans for the future, and not just plans but setting herself goals—and ambitious ones too. "I know you'll do it," I tell her.

She shrugs. "I want to be able to help people who are in situations like the one I was in."

I nod. I get it. Zoey can never accept help without wanting to pay it back, so it's no surprise to me that this is her motivation.

Zoey turns serious again, her smile fading. "I don't know how I'll afford it," she says, "but I'm going to try. Maybe I can get a scholarship in a couple of years to a state college."

"In California?" I can't disguise the hope in my voice.

She nods, starting to smile as she sees the grin taking over my face.

"You're staying?" I ask, my hand tightening on her stomach.

"I think so. My mom really loves her new job, and . . . we really like it here." She gestures at the ocean and the blue sky. "Actually, I *love* it here."

I think about what that means. It means we have a future together.

"Do you think Robert will let us stay in the apartment long-term?" she asks.

I nod, feeling a surge of happiness. I want to pick her up and swing her around the deck. Scratch that. I want to take her downstairs into the little cabin, lay her on the bed, and forget the fact I have six days still to go before I'm allowed to sleep with her.

Stupid self-imposed rule. What was I thinking making her agree to a thirty-day moratorium on sex?

But it doesn't even matter because we're not up against a clock anymore—she's staying. We have all the time in the world. I squeeze her tight and kiss her on the lips. She smells of coconut and sunshine and tastes of honey, and once again I get the image of laying her down and stripping off that bikini and—

"What were you just talking about?"

I pull away from Zoey. Kate is looking up from her phone, staring at us.

"Huh?" I say.

Kate's glaring at Zoey. "You said something about Robert letting us stay long-term."

Zoey's smile fades. "Yes," she says. She hands me back the wheel and goes over to Kate, sitting down beside her. "I wanted to talk to you. Mom and I have been thinking that maybe we should stay here. Things are going well. Cole likes school. I have a good job. It seems like it makes sense."

Kate's face transforms into a look of visceral hatred and fury. "For you!" she yells. "I hate it here."

Zoey's jaw drops. "Wh-what?" she stammers. "I thought . . . I thought you liked it."

Kate rounds on her. "Well, I don't. I hate it." She's shaking now. Her voice trembling with pent-up anger.

Zoey's as surprised as me at the outburst. "I don't understand," she says. "What's going on?"

Kate's turned bright red, fury twisting her features. "What do you care?" she shouts. "All you care about is him." She jerks her head in my direction.

"That's not true," Zoey answers, her voice quiet and calm

but holding a trace of frustration. "You know it isn't."

Kate glares at her, then storms past, toward the stairs and down into the cabin. Zoey watches her leave in shock, then turns to look at me. I shrug blankly. I have no clue what that was about. Kate has always been a mystery to me. Maybe it has to do with the cat?

Zoey goes after her, and I hear the sound of raised voices in the cabin below.

"I did it!" Cole shouts. He's been busy this whole time, sitting on deck by the mast, trying to tie the frayed piece of rope I gave him into a bowline.

"Well done," I tell him, half-distracted by the shouting coming from Kate inside the cabin. She's yelling at Zoey to leave her alone.

"Do I get ice cream now?" Cole asks, scampering across the deck.

"Sure," I tell him. "We'll all get ice cream."

"Not Zoey," he answers matter-of-factly.

"Why not Zoey?" I ask.

Cole shrugs. "She's been bad. She doesn't get ice cream."

I smile, confused. "What do you mean, she's been bad?"

Cole squints at me. "She's a liar. Liars don't get ice cream."

Astonished, I stare at him. "She's not a liar," I say. "What are you talking about?"

Cole squats down and busies himself, untying the knot he just made. He murmurs something I can't hear over the noise of the wind flapping the sail.

"What did you just say?" I ask, aware of Zoey walking up the steps from the cabin behind me.

Cole looks up, eyes flashing. "Zoey's a lying bitch."

# ZOEY

"Cole!" I say. "Where did you learn that word?"

"But you are!" Cole hisses at me. "You're a lying bitch."

Still reeling from my fight with Kate, I can only blink at Cole in shock, my heart hammering. He sounds like my dad, and the thought of it makes tears spring up.

"Apologize," Tristan says to Cole, his voice firm.

"No!" Cole shouts. His eyes glint with defiance, and I can see just where this is going to lead, so I intervene.

"Cole," I say quietly, kneeling beside him, trying to get a grip on my emotions, "tell me why you think I'm a liar. What have I lied about?"

"Everything," he mutters, not meeting my eye.

I don't understand his accusation. "What do you mean, 'everything'?"

"My dad went to prison because of you. You lied."

"Who told you that?" I ask, my heart starting to race.

Cole picks furiously at the knot in the rope. "Cole?" I press. He ignores me. I glance up at Tristan, feeling lost. Cole doesn't know the details of what happened between our parents or the trial, so how could he know what my testimony was? Tristan stares at Cole in confusion too.

"Your sister isn't a liar," he says, but Cole ignores him as well.

"Cole," I say, "it isn't true. I didn't lie. I've never lied. Who's telling you otherwise?"

His mouth purses even tighter, locking his secrets away so he doesn't spill them. I need to prize them free, even though a horrifying thought has burst into my mind—the only person who would seed that idea into Cole is my father. But how would my father be in communication with him? Cole doesn't have a phone or e-mail. There's only one way. And that's in person.

"Cole," I say. I take him by the shoulders when he refuses to look up at me, frustration and fear making me snap. "Cole," I repeat, shaking him until he looks up at me, his eyes flashing furiously. "Have you seen Dad?" I demand.

"No!" he spits, wriggling free and darting toward the stairs. He vanishes down inside the cabin, and I'm left squatting on the deck, feeling that the waves punching the side of the boat are punching me. I almost topple, and it's Tristan who helps me stand, pulling me against his strong, broad chest.

"Do you think he's seen your dad?" he asks.

My legs are shaking with more than just the unfamiliar motion of the waves. I know Cole, and I know he was lying when he said no. His answer came too fast, and he couldn't look me in the eye.

"Zoey?" Tristan presses.

I nod. He's seen our father.

# TRISTAN

After work, I hurry to Zoey's place and find Gina sitting at the table with Robert. She startles when I walk in and knocks over her cup of tea.

"Sorry," I say as Robert hurries to the kitchen for a towel to mop up the spill.

"It's fine," says Gina. "I'm just a little jumpy these days."

Robert soaks up the spilled tea and then dabs at a little spot on Gina's shirt. She smiles and blushes. Robert also blushes, and I do a double take. Okay, it's like that, is it? I shake my head, wondering how I didn't see it already, though it's been staring me in the face. Robert's been coming by every day or so to do odd jobs: finishing off the exterior paintwork and installing locks on the bedroom doors and the windows. At first I mistook his attentiveness for landlord diligence, but now I realize it's something else. He certainly doesn't come by my apartment every day to fix things. And he doesn't bring me flowers, either, I think, eyeing the bunch of sunflowers on the table. Man's got moves.

Robert, in a crisply laundered blue shirt, thanks Gina for the tea and moves to the door, gesturing for me to follow. I do. Once outside, I turn to Robert, still grinning. "Nice shirt," I say. "You never dress up for me, Robert."

Robert blushes all the way to the roots of his gray hair. "It's not like that," he mumbles. "Gina's a lovely lady, and I don't like to think of her ex-husband out there, making threats."

"Me neither."

We both turn serious, contemplating the unsettling feeling that the threat still exists and is hanging over them. I scan the parking lot and the street, thinking back to that almost-accident on the bike when Zoey thought she saw her father in the shadows. At the time I thought she was seeing things, fear making her imagination spin out of control, but now I think she really did see him. The thought that he has been here, spying on us the whole time, is beyond troubling. Mainly I worry for the times I'm not around, like now, when Zoey is at work. But along with worry, I feel anger—anger that he can do this to them, terrorize them like this.

Ever since the boat trip, Cole has buttoned his lips and refused to say another word about his dad, despite Zoey's pleas. We've tried to figure out how they've been in contact and have spoken to the school, the parole officer, and the mailman, but haven't gotten any answers. We've checked Zoey's phone, as well as her mom's and Kate's, to see if Cole has been using them to make calls or send texts, but we haven't found anything suspicious.

I rang the cops and spoke to someone, telling them that Zoey's father was breaking the terms of his parole, but the cops told me I needed evidence if I was making a claim like that, proof that would stand up in court. That's why I installed a camera by the front door, hidden in a hanging flower basket. If only we can get some footage of him at Zoey's door, then we can prove he's broken the law, and he'll go back to prison.

Robert sighs and shakes his head. "I don't know what else to do," he says. He looks as frustrated as I feel. "What happens if either of us isn't around?"

I nod. It's my worry too. Zoey's also kept up with the self-defense classes. But none of it feels enough. It's like battening down the hatches and filling sandbags, waiting for the hurricane to reach shore. There's a sense that we can prepare all we like but there's no knowing if any of it will make a blind bit of difference when the hurricane actually hits. Will keeps calling to check in, and I keep reassuring him that everything's okay, that I've got it all under control and won't let anything happen to his family in his absence, but it's a huge promise to make, and his anxiety is rubbing off on me.

I check the time. Zoey's working tonight, but once she finishes it will be past midnight, which makes it officially the end of my thirty-day promise, which also makes it a month since we started dating. Zoey's been teasing me about it, trying to push me to breaking the deal early, but I've held fast. It's been hard, but worth it. Not just getting to know her on a level that's more intimate than anything I've ever experienced with anyone before, but seeing her trust grow day by day too, along with her confidence.

She now tells me exactly what she likes and doesn't like, without any prodding on my part. I've been playing it cool about tonight to Zoey, making out like I could wait another thirty days no problem, but the truth is that I'm far from cool. On a scale of one to ten, I'm at about a fifteen.

I'm nervous as hell too, more nervous even than I was before I lost my virginity. I'm worried that when it comes down to it, it won't be all that—not for me, but for her. Big-game nerves.

I have the evening to tidy the apartment, make the bed, shave, shower, and choose the right music, but it doesn't feel like very much time to get ready, so I say a fast good-bye to Robert and run off home.

A few minutes before midnight, apartment shipshape and smelling of cedarwood and sage—thanks to a candle that Dahlia gave me a while ago—I run to pick up Zoey from work. I won't let her walk there or back here alone. She's aiming to buy a car soon—tips are good at work, and she's already set aside more than a thousand dollars for one. But even when she has a car, I'll still be accompanying her, because there's no way I could sleep in peace knowing her father is out there.

After she received that first text message from her dad, she told me everything her father had done, all the names he called her and the threats he made in court. At the time she didn't think he meant it when he threatened to kill her, and she still doesn't fully believe it. But I'm not prepared to give him the benefit of the doubt. He was in prison for three years for beating his wife almost to death, and he clearly didn't have a come-to-Jesus moment sitting in his cell. It seems like instead he used those three years to tend to his resentment at the person who'd put him there. The question is, how far will he go to get revenge?

But he's an ex-cop, and he's not stupid. He knows what he's doing, and he's being careful—and that suggests a man who isn't acting in the heat of the moment. It suggests someone with a plan, someone willing to take his time, and that scares me a whole lot more.

Zoey called the courthouse two weeks ago and asked for the file on her father's case to be sent to her. I read her statement, taken just after the attack, and marveled at how she was only fifteen but sounded so much older. What struck me most was the prosecution's argument that Zoey's father was a sociopath of unusually high intelligence who had been drawn toward police work as it played into his idea of himself as superior to others. They brought an expert to the stand to give their opinion. I read it several times, feeling sicker with each rereading. He's a man with a god complex who sees himself as the ultimate arbiter of justice, and who feels no empathy.

As a result, when I step outside my apartment it's with unusually heightened awareness, my ears pricked for every noise. I pause and scan the darkness for any unusual shadows, relying on that base animal instinct that's always triggered whenever I sense danger. Those are the instincts we are trained to hone and to rely on in the military, but I also know that Zoey's father will have much the same instincts. On top of that, he has the weight of years on me, three of them spent in prison, where, as a former cop, he must have become even more indomitable in order to survive.

Not sensing anything out of the ordinary, I jog over to my bike. I pull on my helmet and notice a long, uneven scratch carved into the body from handlebars to exhaust. I crouch down to examine it, a string of curses erupting. Goddamn it. Someone used a key or a screwdriver to do this. They've gouged it with force—scoring through the paintwork to the metal. It's going to cost a fortune to fix.

I straighten fast, my neck prickling. It feels as if someone is watching me. Turning slowly, I scan the street for movement. Is someone out there? Did I imagine it? I realize I'm going to be late to get Zoey, so I get on the bike and turn the key in the ignition. The engine makes a loud clattering sound before a series of loud bangs makes me leap off. The engine gives out with a loud splutter. What the hell? I just had the bike serviced. It makes no sense . . . unless . . . Zoey's dad's done something to it. Maybe he's sabotaged it somehow by putting something in the tank.

I yank off my helmet and have to restrain myself from kicking the curb. Damn. I check the time again. I'm going to be late. A thought pushes through the silent rage in my head: Maybe that's the point? Maybe he did this on purpose. . . .

Before I can fully finish that thought, I'm running.

# ZOEY

The restaurant is closed. Only the dishwasher and the manager, Tessa, and I are still here. I wait by the reception area, alternating between checking my phone to looking out the window. Where's Tristan? He's never late. I try calling again, but he doesn't pick up. My skin feels prickly—as though spiders are crawling over me.

I go to dial him again, but before I can, my phone rings, startling me. I look down at the display, expecting to see Tristan's name pop up, but instead it says: UNDISCLOSED ID. My heart almost bursts out of my chest like the alien in that movie Tristan made me watch the other day. My finger hovers over the answer button, a voice in my head warning me not to pick up. I ignore the voice and put the phone to my ear. "Hello?"

Silence.

Then breathing.

It's him. I know it's him.

"I know it's you," I finally say, my voice coming out as a harsh and broken whisper.

The breathing becomes heavier, as though he's smothering laughter.

"Leave me alone!" I hiss before hanging up.

I gaze out at the dark street, willing Tristan to arrive. Where is he? The phone next to me on the reception desk suddenly rings, making me leap several feet away from it. I stare at it, frozen.

"Can you get that?"

It's Tessa, sitting at the other end of the bar. I shake off my terror and reach for the phone, which seems to be trying to leap off the receiver and right into my hand.

"Good evening, Riley's," I say, trying to keep my voice light.

Silence. My stomach clenches tight as a fist.

"Good evening, Zoey."

I open my mouth to draw in air, but my throat closes up and my lungs refuse to work. I can't breathe. I grip the edge of the desk. "What do you want?" I hear myself ask my dad.

A sound rumbles down the line. It takes me a few seconds to realize he's laughing, a low, throaty noise that makes vomit leap up my throat.

"Why do you look so scared, Zoey?"

His words hit me like bullets. My head flies up. I stare out the window, but I can't make anything out. It's too dark. Another laugh rumbles down the phone. He's out there, I think to myself. He's watching me right now.

"What do you want?" I manage to say again, fighting the urge to sink to the ground and take shelter behind the desk. Where is he?

"I want three years of my life back," he says, bitterness lacing his words. He sounds more than bitter, though. His words are loose, his tongue slurring the edges of them. He's drunk. "You going to give them to me?" he demands.

It's not my fault, I want to say, but the words don't come; they're trapped in my throat.

"Yeah, didn't think so," he mutters.

My eyes strafe the street outside. There are a handful of cars—is he in one of them? Or hiding in the shadows of one of the storefronts opposite?

"Three years is a long time, Zo-Zo," he says, using my nickname from when I was a kid. "Long enough for me to think of how I'd pay you back for putting me inside." He snorts. "My daughter, my own daughter, putting me away. Hard to believe. There's a word for people like you where I come from. 'Snitch.' Know what happens to snitches in prison?"

I have an idea.

"You're worse than your bitch mother," he spits. He's on a roll now. This is how it always goes with him. Once he gets going, it's like a stopper removed from a bottle. I should hang up, but if I do it will only make him angrier, and what if he decides to come inside?

I look over at Tessa, head bent over the books at the end of the bar, oblivious to what's happening.

"And you're taking after her too, aren't you? Becoming a slut, just like her."

I turn around so my back is facing the window and he can't see my face. I want to hang up. I want to cover my ears and sink to the ground and crawl somewhere safe. I want to let out the horrified scream that is trapped inside. But I don't do anything. I just stand there, frozen, and listen mutely as he continues speaking.

"I've seen you with that man, in and out of his apartment at all hours."

Tristan. He's talking about Tristan. He's seen us together. He's spying on me. Ice chills my veins.

"Are you sleeping with him?" he asks.

I squeeze my eyes shut, trying to block the horror of his voice.

"He know what a slut you are?" he asks. Then he pauses for a beat before answering his own question. "Of course he does— that's why he's with you, always running after you like you're a bitch in heat. . . ."

The door behind me bursts open. Spinning around with a yelp, the phone still pressed to my ear, I expect to see my father standing there in the doorway, but it's Tristan, out of breath and sweating. He sees the horror on my face and stops midstep.

"What's the matter?" he asks.

I drop the phone. It clatters to the floor. I stare past Tristan, out through the open door and onto the street. "He's watching me," I whisper.

# TRISTAN

I wanted this evening to be something special, but Zoey and I are both too on edge to do anything besides sit on the sofa and watch a movie—*The Breakfast Club*—though neither of us is able to focus on it. Zoey keeps jumping at every sound that bursts out of the speaker, and I'm restless. I keep wanting to get up and check the locks on the doors and the video feeds of the security cameras.

I told her that my bike broke down, but I didn't tell her that I think her father was responsible for it. She's freaked out enough without me adding to her panic. He was watching her at the restaurant, lurking somewhere outside. What kind of a psycho does that? He probably followed us back here. We called the police, but they said unless there was an actual crime or an actual threat, there was nothing they could do. It's maddening.

What's he planning? I wonder. And how did he find them? Did he somehow find a way to contact Cole? Did Cole tell him Zoey's number, and tell him where she worked? I stare blankly at the TV, wondering what I can do to protect Zoey. The simple, frustrating fact is that I can't do anything—not until he makes a move.

As the credits roll, Zoey stays staring at the screen. I'm not even sure she's noticed that the movie is over. I lean over her for the remote and switch off the TV. "Let's go to bed," I say instead, getting up and holding out my hand to her.

# ZOEY

'm not letting my father win. I'm not letting him ruin tonight. I roll toward Tristan, who is lying staring up at the ceiling with his eyes open, and start kissing him. Trying to banish all thoughts of my dad from my head, I squeeze my eyes shut so I stop staring at the door, which I'm terrified is going to fly open at any point to reveal my dad standing there.

Reluctantly, it seems, Tristan starts kissing me back. I pull him over and on top of me. He hovers above me, holding his weight on his forearms so as not to crush me, but I wrap my arms around his neck and tug him down on top of me. "Make me forget," I murmur against his lips.

Tristan freezes, then rolls off me, frowning. His fingers stroke my cheek, brush a strand of loose hair out of my eyes. "Zo," he says, "I don't want to make you forget. I want you to be here, with me. I mean . . . this night . . . I want it to be something you remember. That we both . . ." He breaks off. "I want it to be special."

I draw in a breath, knowing he's right, but frustrated that my dad has ruined this, too, now. I feel the pent-up fury spilling out of me in tears that roll down my face.

"Shhhh," Tristan says, pulling me close and cradling me against his chest. "It's okay. I've got you."

I squeeze my eyes shut and try to stop crying, and Tristan wipes away the tears, then holds my face in his hands and kisses my cheeks. "Don't cry."

BANG!

I bolt upright in alarm, as does Tristan. Someone is pounding on the front door. I freeze, but Tristan is on his feet, already moving for the door. "Stay here," he warns me. "Lock the door."

I fumble out of bed. No way I'm staying here and letting him answer that door alone. The banging hasn't let up, and now I hear someone yelling my name too. "Zoey!"

It's my mom.

I reach the living room in time to see Tristan yanking open the door. My mom is standing there, nearly hysterical. "It's Kate," she cries. "She's gone."

"What?" I rasp.

"I went to check in on her and Cole, and she's not there. She's not anywhere."

"Wait," says Tristan. I turn to look at him. He's holding his phone. "A camera detected motion. It sent me a text thirty minutes ago." My heart plummets to my stomach. "I missed it."

My mom and I crowd around Tristan and watch the video. It's Kate, sneaking out the front door. The time on the bottom is stamped 2:58 a.m. "Where's she going?" I ask as we watch her scamper down the stairs.

"She's got a bag with her," Tristan says as she vanishes out of sight. He hits play again, and we watch the video one more time.

"Let's go back to your apartment," Tristan says to me.

I nod and grab my bag and phone, then follow my mom across the courtyard and up the stairs to our place. We let ourselves in.

"Where do you think she's gone?" my mom asks me, clutching my hands. She's speaking in a whisper, trying not to wake Cole.

I rub my hands through my hair, aware I must look a mess, but there's no time to think about it. "I don't know," I say. "Did you check her room for clues?"

"I didn't want to wake Cole, so not really. But she's taken her toothbrush and hairbrush, and I think she went through my purse. I found it on the table."

That makes my eyebrows shoot up. "Your purse?"

"Did she take any money? Cards?" Tristan asks.

My mom shakes her head. "I only had a twenty. She took that. But not the cards."

Something strikes me then. "Oh God," I murmur before rushing to the bedroom I share with my mom.

My mom follows. "What?" she asks, worried.

I drop to my knees in front of the closet and pull out a shoe box that I've been using to store a few things—my community college paperwork, a handful of letters from Will, receipts and movie theater tickets I've collected from dates with Tristan, as well as the notes he leaves me on the pillow every morning. I rummage around until I find the envelope I keep stashed at the bottom. I pull it out and feel my heart sink.

I open it, feeling a mix of fury and disappointment, the latter immediately snuffing out the former when I see it's empty.

"What is it?" my mom asks again.

"I had almost a thousand dollars in here," I say. "It was all the tips I've saved. I was going to use it to buy a car."

"Oh no," my mom says, sinking down on the edge of the bed. "Why would she take it? What for?"

"She's run away," I say.

"But why?" my mom asks, confused.

I stand up, checking the time. It's almost four in the morning. "Where could she have gone?" I wonder out loud.

"I'll call the police," my mom says, coming up behind us.

"I'll go and look for her," Tristan says.

"I'm coming too," I tell him. I can see he wants to argue with me but doesn't.

"I have to stay here with Cole," my mom says.

I take her hand. I'm scared to leave her. But I don't want to tell her. She smiles at me. "I'll be okay," she reassures me.

"We'll check the bus and train stations," Tristan says.

"What if she took an Uber?"

"Do you think she's gone back to Vegas?" he asks.

I shake my head. "I don't know. I thought she hated it there."

"What's going on?"

We all turn. Cole stands in the door to his bedroom, rubbing his eyes with his fists and yawning.

"Nothing," I say. "Go back to bed."

"What time is it?" he asks, looking among us all, confused.

"It's late. Or rather, it's early," I tell him, moving his way.

"Where's Kate?" Cole asks.

I look at my mom. She kneels down in front of Cole. "Kate's gone," she tells him. "Do you know where she might be?"

Cole stares at her, and I study his reaction. It hits me for the first time, like a slap to the face, that there's a chance Kate might be the one in touch with my dad and not Cole. What if it was her who told him where we were living? This whole time we've been focused on Cole, but what if it was Kate? What if she's gone to meet him now?

"Cole," I say, also kneeling alongside my mom. "We need to know: Did you speak to Dad? It's really important to tell us if you or Kate have."

Cole looks between us. His face turns red and blotchy—his very own Pinocchio tell. "I haven't spoken to him! I don't know where Kate is," he shouts.

My mom takes Cole's arm. "Cole, tell us!" she cries.

Cole snatches his arm back. "Get off me!"

I stand up, seeing that this conversation is only going one way, and that's toward a screaming match with Cole, but then Tristan interrupts. He's in the kitchen, standing by the trash can. He's holding a crumpled piece of paper in his hand after rummaging through the garbage for clues.

"Look," he says, offering me the piece of paper.

I take it. It's a MISSING CAT poster with Romeo's photo plastered across it and Kate's phone number written at the bottom. "You think she's gone to find Romeo?" I ask.

"It's a possibility, right?" he says with a shrug. "She's been really upset about him and about you guys staying here in Oceanside."

He's right. At least, I think he's right. And it's a way better prospect than the thought of her going off with my dad.

Tristan kneels down by Cole. "We need you to stay here and look after your mom while Zoey and I go look for Kate."

Cole pulls a face and then glowers daggers at my mom. "Why do I need to look after her?" My mom visibly flinches, and I wonder if for her it's like seeing a miniature version of my dad appearing in Cole.

"Because that's what real men do," Tristan tells him in a calm voice. "They take care of their families. They watch over them and protect the people they love. And your mom needs you."

I look at Tristan as he says those words, and my heart swells. Cole nods at him, his expression serious, and I wonder, will he turn out like my dad? Or will he learn by Tristan's example?

# TRISTAN

I t's dawn by the time we get to Emma Rotherham's house to pick up Dahlia's car so we can make the trip to Vegas. Dahlia comes down the stairs wearing a satin robe, which piques my curiosity, but with Kate missing I don't have time to ask questions about the status of Dahlia and Emma's relationship.

"Are you okay?" she asks Zoey, hugging her.

Zoey nods, distracted. She just wants to get going, and Dahlia can see that, so she hurries to fish her keys out of her bag.

"You sure it's okay to borrow it?" I ask again, taking the keys she offers.

"I can borrow one of Emma's if I need to go anywhere, and besides, I'm kind of staying here at the moment." She brushes her hair behind her ear as she says it, and a blush spreads up her neck. It's clear from her expression and the glow on her face that she and Emma are officially . . . something.

"Drive safe." She turns to Zoey. "And I hope you find her."

"We'll find her," I say to Zoey an hour later as I drive east, reaching across to squeeze her hand. She squeezes mine back and doesn't say anything. I hope she can't tell how worried I am.

I don't think their dad is involved, but I do worry about a kid of Kate's age out there all alone, a possible target for anyone. The only way she could have gotten to Vegas from here is by bus or hitching, and neither of those options is particularly safe. But Zoey has enough to worry about without me bringing that up.

Every few minutes she tries calling Kate, but Kate's phone is switched off and it's going straight to voice mail.

"What about her friend Lis?" I ask.

"I don't have her number," Zoey answers. "I'm going to try calling her school office when it opens."

"How about Instagram?"

"Her account's set to private. I can't see what she's posted." She starts tapping something into the search bar of her phone. "I found Lis's account. I'll send her a message." Once she's done, she starts scrolling through Lis's feed. "There are loads of photos of her and Kate and . . ." She trails off.

I glance over quickly and see Zoey is frowning. "What?" I ask her. "What is it?"

She shakes her head. "I don't know. There are photos of the two of them together."

"And?" I ask, overtaking a semi that's hogging the center lane.

"It's not the photo. It's the comments below. Someone's commented that they make a perfect couple. And there's another one—a hashtag 'love goals.'"

I turn to Zoey, who looks over at me. "Oh my God."

"They aren't just best friends."

"I think Lis is her girlfriend," Zoey finishes. She turns back to the photos and keeps scrolling. "Why didn't she tell me? Why would she hide that?" She asks it plaintively.

"A lot of people have trouble coming out to family," I tell her. "Even my sister. Even in *my* family, where we were already flying a rainbow flag from the house during Pride week. She only told me after I found her kissing this girl I liked at a party. And she didn't tell our parents for another year after that."

A deep frown line runs between Zoey's eyes. "But she knows I wouldn't care."

"When we find her, you can ask her why she didn't tell you," I say, reaching my arm across her headrest and stroking the back of her neck.

Zoey nods unhappily.

# ZOEY

I look at the bare brick facade and think of how it resembles a prison rather than a school. But Kate was happy here. She had Lis, who was more than just her best friend, and I tore her away from that. It's no wonder she's been so unhappy since we left. How could I not have seen it? Kate was right to accuse me of not caring about anything except myself. I've been so focused on Tristan that I didn't bother to notice the pain my own sister was going through.

I suppress the whispering voice of panic in my head when I think about her out there in the world, all alone. I try too to suppress the annoyance I feel when I picture her using all the money I've saved.

The bell rings, and kids start streaming out of the buildings—most heading for the football field and the bleachers. Lis spots us straightaway and comes jogging over, wearing multicolored leggings and a cropped top. She has several ear piercings and a nose stud, and her eyes are lined with dark purple kohl. Her backpack is covered in pins, most of a political persuasion. I remember Kate saying Lis was into art and politics.

"Hey," she says when she reaches us, eyeing us warily.

I introduce Tristan to her, and she shakes his hand. "I don't have long," she says, fidgeting from foot to foot.

"Thanks for meeting us," I say. "We're trying to find Kate. We think she might be in Vegas. Have you heard from her?"

She nods. "I saw her this morning."

"What?" I say, relief making me light-headed. "You saw her?"

Lis nods. "Yeah, at recess. She was here."

"How did she get here?" I ask.

"She caught a bus from San Diego. It left at, like, four thirty this morning."

"Where is she now? Do you know?"

Lis's gaze darts to our feet. "I don't know." She digs the toe of her scuffed Vans sneaker into the asphalt. "We got in a fight." She shoots a nervous glance at me and then at Tristan.

I look at Tristan. He reads my mind and takes a few steps away, giving us privacy.

"I know you guys were dating," I say as Lis glances at her watch.

Lis looks up, alarmed. "How did you find out?"

I shake my head. "Can you tell me what happened?"

Lis's eyes brim with tears. "We broke up. I told her I couldn't do the long-distance thing anymore."

"So she came here to try to change your mind?" I ask.

Lis nods, her slender shoulders shaking.

"How long were you guys dating for?" I ask.

Lis swipes at her eyes, smudging the mascara across her cheek. "Six months." She pauses. "She told you?"

I shake my head. I can't believe Kate held on to this secret for so long. It's no wonder she was so upset about leaving. "Do you know why she didn't tell me?" I ask.

"She didn't want to tell anyone, at least not at first. She had just come out to a few people when . . . you left."

I take a deep breath. So much was happening in Kate's life, and I've been oblivious.

"Do you know where she might have gone?" I ask, racked with guilt.

"She said something about going to find the cat."

I squeeze Lis's arm. "Thank you."

She tries to give me a smile, but it comes out wobbly. "I'm sorry," she says. "Can you tell her that?"

I nod, and she turns and jogs back toward the school entrance. Tristan comes up behind me and puts his arm around my shoulder. "What did she say?" he asks.

"That I win the award for worst sister ever."

Tristan double-takes. "She said that?"

"No," I admit, "but she might as well have. They were dating, and I didn't even know it. How could I not know something so important about my own sister? She came out to strangers before me."

"That's normal," Tristan says. "Don't take it personally. Dahlia did the same."

I move toward the car, and Tristan follows, opening the door for me.

"Where are we going?" he asks. "Did Lis know where she was?"

"You were right. She's gone to find the cat."

# TRISTAN

Romeo, Romeo, wherefore art thou, Romeo?"

Zoey arches her eyebrow at me, and I mumble, "Sorry." Not the time. Or the place. Speaking of which, it's hard to picture Zoey living here, and not only because the house is boarded up but because everything is beige and brown and gives off an air of dereliction—from the peeling paint to the dirt-bowl front yards and the dust-covered cars. The only signs of nature are the brave blades of grass forcing their way through the heat-cracked asphalt.

We approach the front door, which has been replaced with a thick piece of plywood, put in place by someone who obviously likes their nail gun. I guess the authorities wanted to keep it from becoming a crack den. The whole front of the house is blackened with soot, and in the driveway there's a patch of charred concrete where I'm guessing Zoey's car once sat.

"There's no way in," Zoey says, examining the door and then stepping back to check the plywood that's also been nailed over the window frames.

Dejected, she looks around wondering, like I am, if Kate's

already been here, and if so, where she might have gone next. "Let's go around the back," Zoey says, and I follow her around the side and into a deserted courtyard. It's midday and about a billion degrees, so no one is outside, though I notice a curtain flutter in a house across the way.

The back of Zoey's house is boarded up too, but one of the boards has been pried away and is hanging loose.

Zoey races over to it, and together we rip it off. Inside, I catch a glimpse of a bedroom—though it looks like it's been ransacked. There are clothes and blackened sheets strewn across the floor, and unless Zoey's mom let Cole paint the walls with graffiti, then it's safe to say we aren't the first people to find our way inside. I heave myself over and jump down. My foot immediately crunches on a broken beer bottle. Whoever pried off that plywood had themselves a little party. I turn and help Zoey through the window. She jumps down and stands stock-still, staring in horror, as I get out my phone and shine the flashlight.

"Kate?" I shout.

I step in front of Zoey and push open the bedroom door, which leads into a living room. It's worse than the bedroom. Green mold speckles the sofa, and the smell reminds me of a urinal inside a mushroom factory. I cover my nose and try to breathe as shallowly as I possibly can without passing out.

There are beer cans and misshapen spoons and torn pizza boxes lying all around. Zoey makes a sound—an exhalation that sounds like a sob. I turn and see she's holding something in her hand, and when I shine the torch on it, notice it's a broken mug.

"Cole made me this," she says.

I scan the ground and spot the missing handle lying in a pile of ash. Zoey turns the mug upside down and empties it of cigarette ends and blunts. "Here," I say, taking it from her and picking up the handle. "We'll fix it."

The skin on the back of my neck prickles just then, and I hold a hand up to Zoey, warning her to stay quiet. There's someone here. I can feel it.

There's a quiet rustle from one of the rooms, and Zoey moves toward it, but I step in front of her again. I'll be the one to open the door. It might just be a kid with a paint can, painting graffiti on the walls, or even a rat, but either way I'd rather it was me confronting it.

I set the mug down on the edge of the sofa and then open the door. It's another bedroom, with a bunk bed pushed against one wall. I shine the torch on the bottom bunk. The bedding is filthy—stained with God knows what, but by the smell of it, nothing good—and it looks like a campfire might have been lit and then smothered in the corner of the room.

The closet door is open, and all the clothes have been ransacked, so the shelves are empty, barring a few pairs of Spider-Man underwear and a child's sock. I shine the light onto the top bunk, and both Zoey and I jump back in fright.

Kate is sitting, knees pulled to her chest, her head bowed and resting on her arms.

"Kate?" Zoey whispers. She lets go of my hand and moves toward her, climbing the ladder and gingerly crawling onto the top bunk beside her. She puts her arm around Kate's shoulders, and they both start to cry.

# ZOEY

It's going to be okay," I tell Kate as she sobs in my arms.

She shakes her head against my shoulder. "No, it's not," she says, her voice muffled.

"It is," I reassure her. "I know it doesn't feel like it now, but it will be." Tristan has left the room, and I can hear him moving around the apartment, probably looking to see if anything is salvageable, though I wouldn't bet a cent anything is. "Why didn't you tell me about Lis?" I ask Kate, once she's calmer.

She tenses, and I wonder if she's about to deny things, but finally she says, "I don't know."

"You know I would have supported you."

She leans back at that to look at me, her face all blotchy from crying. "You didn't tell me about you and Tristan."

Okay, she has me there.

Kate cuts me off. "You never tell me anything. You didn't tell me about Dad being out of prison either."

"I was trying to protect you."

Kate looks at me, offended. "I'm fifteen. I'm not a kid. You don't have to protect me."

"I'm sorry," I say again, seeing for the first time that she's right. Because I've always thought of her as my little sister, someone I needed to look after, it's difficult to think of her any other way. But the fact is, she's only a year younger than I was when my dad went to jail. "I guess I didn't want to upset you or make you worry over nothing," I say.

Kate narrows her eyes at me. "Is it nothing?"

I open my mouth to answer her but pause. Here's my chance to be straight with her, but I honestly can't. "It's nothing to worry about," I tell her.

"Don't lie to me," she says angrily. "I'm not an idiot. If there's nothing to worry about, why did Tristan install that camera by our front door? Why won't he ever leave your side? He's worried about you. *I'm* worried about you." Her voice cracks on this last part, so I take her hand and squeeze it.

"Honestly, it's fine," I tell her, the lie clogging my throat.

Kate's eyes brighten again with tears. "Don't lie," she growls.

I stare at her for a few moments before taking a deep breath. "Okay, yes, Dad has been calling me, making threats."

Kate's face pales beneath the blotchiness. "What kind of threats?"

"Nothing specific," I say vaguely. "He's mad at me. He blames me for testifying against him. But it's just threats. He won't do anything."

"What do you mean? Look what he did to Mom! He almost killed her. He *would* have killed her if you hadn't . . ." She starts crying, fat tears falling fast down her cheeks. "And if you don't think he's going to do something, why the need for all the cameras? Why did Robert buy Mom pepper spray?"

This is exactly why I didn't want to tell her what was

happening. I can't bear seeing how afraid she is. I should have kept lying.

"Have you told the cops?" Kate asks. "Can't they do something?"

I shake my head. "No. There's no proof. That's why Tristan installed the camera by the door."

"He's been to the house?! He's in Oceanside?" Kate asks, shrinking away from me in terror. "How did he find us?" she demands to know.

"I don't know." I don't tell her I think Cole might have told him.

Kate's lip trembles, and the tears start to come even faster. "Why can't he leave us alone?" she cries.

There's nothing to say to that. I wish he would too, but I think the only way he's going to leave us alone is if we catch him on camera breaking his parole terms and the cops arrest him and throw him back in jail. But he won't be in jail forever; they'll let him out . . . and what will happen then? Sometimes it feels like I'll never escape him.

"Are we going to have to leave Oceanside?" Kate asks, wiping her tears with the back of her hand.

I don't say anything. The truth is, I've thought about leaving, and every time I do, Tristan enters my mind and I dismiss the idea out of hand. But is that selfish? Am I putting everyone in danger by staying? Am I putting Tristan in danger as well? My dad has his sights on Tristan now too, and the knowledge makes me sick with fear.

"I don't know," I tell Zoey, because I can feel her hanging on my answer.

"I like it there," she says quietly. "I don't want to leave."

"I thought you hated it?" I ask, surprised. "I thought you wanted to come back here."

She gives a gentle shrug. "I just miss Lis. I don't miss the place." She casts a glance around the room, at the wreckage and debris of our previous life, and as I stare at the trashed mattress and broken toys and stained walls, it's as if I'm viewing someone else's belongings. These things feel like they belong to a different life, one I'm happy to let go of. We were given a new start, and that new start involves Tristan.

"Do you love him?" Kate asks.

"Huh?" I ask, turning to stare at Kate. "Dad?"

"No," she says. "Tristan."

I open my mouth and then shut it. I don't as a rule talk about myself or my feelings, not to anyone, but before I can stop it, the word "yes" tumbles out of me. For a moment, I want to snatch it back and swallow it. It's scary to admit it out loud when I haven't even admitted it to myself.

Kate smiles at me and rests her head on my shoulder. "Good," she says. "He's nice."

"Yeah," I say with a smile, thinking how "nice" doesn't cover it. "He is.

"Did you love Lis?" I ask after a while.

Kate sniffs. "I don't know. I think so. How do you know for sure?"

I laugh. It's not like I have any experience of love apart from what I feel now with Tristan and what I've always felt toward Mom and my siblings. But that's a different kind of love. What I feel for Tristan is like fire: almost too bright to look at, warming, comforting. But terrifying, too—as though it could consume me if I let it.

I sense Kate waiting. "I guess it's knowing you'd do anything, risk anything, sacrifice everything for them," I tell her.

Kate takes that in, then stares at me with an intense, unhappy look. "That's sad."

"What is?" I ask, confused.

"You think love is sacrifice."

"Isn't it?"

Kate struggles with that, her nose wrinkling. "I guess it's part of it," she admits, "but it shouldn't be all of it. You shouldn't sacrifice your own happiness or your own dreams to make other people happy."

"But I'm not . . . ," I argue.

"Yes, you are," Kate argues back. "At least, you have done that for us. You didn't go to college, you're having to work now to pay the rent and bills, and . . . it's not fair. You're the smart one. You should be in school."

I shrug, staring at Kate, who suddenly seems older than her fifteen years. It is what it is, though. Who said life is fair? "But I *am* happy," I tell her, trying to reassure her.

"*Now* you are," she says. "Because of Tristan."

I can't argue with that.

Kate rests her head on my shoulder. "I'm sorry," she says.

"What do you mean?" I ask.

"That you've had to do so much for us."

"I don't mind," I say, kissing her forehead. "Honestly."

Kate hugs me tight. "I love you."

My throat tightens with emotion, a lump rising up from my chest. I can't remember the last time we said we loved each other. I can't remember the last time we spoke like this. "I love you too," I tell her.

"I'm sorry I stole your money," she says in a small voice. She sits up and starts scrambling around in her bag, pulling out the tattered envelope of cash I've collected from tips. "Here," she says, thrusting it at me. "I only spent sixty dollars. I promise I'll pay you back as soon as I can."

"It's okay," I say.

She rests her head again on my shoulder. "I didn't tell you about Lis because I was ashamed," Kate says after a while.

I turn to look at her. "Why?" I ask.

Kate takes a deep breath. "It sounds stupid, but when I was little, I remember Dad seeing a couple in a restaurant, and they were holding hands—that's all they were doing. It was two guys and they weren't kissing or doing anything. They were just holding hands. And Dad said something to them. He told them they were disgusting and started cursing at them. It was awful. I wanted the ground to swallow me up."

I'm not even surprised. I remember him saying homophobic, sexist, horrible things all the time. "He hates everyone," I tell her.

"I know. He's an asshole. But it still stuck with me, you know?"

I nod, thinking ruefully of the word "whore" and how that stuck with me my whole life too. "You can't let him have that power over you," I tell her.

"I know," she says, "I just . . . I hate him."

I shake my head at her. "No. That's what *he* does. He hates. Don't be like him, or he's won."

"How can you not hate him, though?" she asks me, incredulous.

I take another deep breath and let it out slowly. It's hard. I have to admit that. "Because hating him doesn't do anything," I eventually say. "It doesn't change anything. It just makes me angry and sad. And I don't want to be those things. I don't want to be anything like him. I just want to be happy. And I don't think you can be both."

Kate frowns. I can see her struggling with knowing I'm right and with processing the anger she feels. It isn't so easy to stop being angry and to stop hating. All those feelings have to go somewhere, and where are you supposed to put them? I think I buried all my feelings down deep, keeping busy, not thinking about him, and now . . . and now I guess there's no room in me for all that old, squashed-up anger. The good has displaced it.

"Don't let him win," I tell Kate, repeating the exact same words the district attorney told me all those years ago, before I took the stand. "He wins if you let him dictate your life and your choices." As I say it, I realize I'm actually talking to myself as much as to Kate. I'm not leaving Oceanside, I realize. I'm not running anymore. I'm not letting my dad have that power over me or letting him take my happiness away. I'm not leaving Tristan. And with that knowledge, I turn to Kate. "Shall we go home?" I ask her.

She blinks away the last of her tears, then nods.

When we leave the bedroom, there's no sign of Tristan, but I assume he's waiting outside.

I give Kate a boost, and as she climbs out the window ahead of me, I hear her squeal.

"What is it?" I ask, alarmed and scrambling quickly after her.

As I straighten up, I spot Tristan walking toward us, holding something in his arms. It's a writhing, spitting fur ball of white and black.

Kate sprints toward him, arms outstretched. "Romeo!"

I run after her, watching as she scoops the protesting cat into her arms and smothers him in kisses, all while he tries to claw her face off. Somehow Romeo looks more bobcat-size than house cat–sized, and I wonder what he's been eating.

"Where was he?" I ask Tristan in amazement as Kate ignores Romeo's frenzied slashing and squeezes him even harder.

Tristan smiles at me and nods his head over his shoulder. I glance past him and see Winston, our old neighbor, the man who helped us the night of the fire, walking toward us, grinning ear to ear.

"Saw you climbing in the window," he says, jerking his head in the direction of the house. "I was about to call the police. We had a few problems with people breaking in," he says by way of explanation. "Then I saw it was you." He grins at me, then points at Romeo. "I found your cat. Been taking care of him these last few weeks."

"Thank you," I say, watching Kate finally get a spitting Romeo to settle down, albeit grumpily, in her arms.

"I tried to find you," Winston says, "but there's no record of you online. Couldn't get your number, either, from the police. I hoped you'd show back up one day."

"Thank you," Kate says. "Thank you so much."

"You gonna be moving back in?" Winston asks, nodding at the house.

Kate looks at me, beaming, then at Winston.

"No," we both say in unison.

# TRISTAN

haven't slept in thirty-two hours, and I'm almost seeing double. It's not safe to drive all the way home, and after calling Gina to assure her Kate is with us and everything is fine, I suggest that we stay the night in Vegas before heading back home in the morning.

Zoey, almost as exhausted as me, nods, and before she can worry about the cost, I tell her I've got a contact at the MGM Grand who'll comp me a room.

Whatever happened in the house, it seems that Zoey and Kate talked things out. And seeing Kate's face when she saw the Tasmanian devil was almost worth the drive here. But it's hers and Zoey's reactions when we walk into our suite at the MGM an hour later that *definitely* make the drive here worth it.

Kate's jaw hits the swirly carpeted floor as her gaze takes in the chandelier the size of a car that's suspended from a two-story ceiling. Zoey walks slowly through the living area to the enormous window and the panoramic skyline view of the city.

I go to stand by her, and she slips her hand into mine. "This is amazing," she whispers.

"Manager owed me a favor."

"What did you do for him?" she asks.

"Saved his life," I say smugly. "And his boat from sinking."

Zoey stares at me in wonder.

"Oh my God!" we hear Kate shriek from upstairs. When we look up we see her leaning over the railing above us. "There are THREE bathrooms. Three!" she exclaims. "And they have robes!" she squeals, before showing us her hands full of miniature bottles of toiletries. "And free shampoo!" She runs back into one of the rooms, and we hear more squeals of delight.

"Want to explore?" I say to Zoey.

She nods, and we run around the suite, opening up doors and discovering a dining room, a study, two bedrooms, and the three bathrooms that Kate already informed us about.

"My friend told me we can order anything we want from room service—it's all complimentary."

At that, Kate's eyes grow even wider, and she throws herself across the bed and toward a table where a room-service menu sits. "I'm starving!" she yells. "How much can we order?"

"Whatever you like," I tell her. "The burgers are really good, I hear."

Zoey leans her head on my stomach, and I put my arm around her, feeling sleepy as Kate takes over and starts ordering the food, including three burgers with all the trimmings, a milkshake for her, onion rings, fries, a Caesar salad, and a fruit platter. When she's done, she hangs up and rolls off the bed. She opens up a cabinet, revealing a flat-screen television.

"What shall we watch?" she asks, jumping onto the bed beside us. "Oh my God, look: there's every channel under the sun. Okay, maybe not that one," she says, scrolling past an adult channel. "No romance, that's for sure. How about *The Hangover*? There's a tiger in it. Romeo will like that."

Zoey shakes her head.

We settle on *Ferris Bueller's Day Off* because Zoey and I both feel like Kate's '80s movie education is severely lacking, and also it will appeal to her, given she's skipped school, just like the main character.

Kate pulls Romeo into her lap like a toddler hugging an American Girl doll, only one that's possessed by Satan. Romeo slashes his way out of her arms, then positions himself on a throne of pillows.

As we settle down to watch the movie, I stretch out on the bed and sigh, feeling relaxed for the first time in a while, understanding that it's in large part to do with the insanely comfortable four-hundred-thread-count sheets and feather pillow at my head, but also because for tonight I don't need to worry about Zoey's dad.

# ZOEY

The room-service trays are scattered around Kate's room like a bomb has exploded. Kate lies at the epicenter of the blast, arms flung out, legs splayed, clutching her stomach and groaning. "I'm so full I think I might throw up." She sighs.

Tristan finishes the last morsel of burger on his plate, then piles his plate on top of the other empty ones on the closest tray. I check the time. It's only seven in the evening, but not having slept for what feels like days, I'm so spaced.

"Okay," says Kate, rolling herself off the bed in the manner of a beached whale trying to throw itself back into the surf. "I'm going to take a bath, and then I'm going to pass out." She staggers to the bathroom, pausing in the doorway to look back at Tristan and me, still lounging on the bed. She smiles at us. "You two are welcome to snuggle up with me, but just in case you forgot"—she gestures at the door—"we are staying in a palace one hundred floors high, and right next door is your very own California King."

"Hint taken," I say, getting up. I turn toward Tristan, but he's already on his feet, holding out his hand. He needs no encouragement, and I smile. I know exactly what's on his mind.

In the next second, he's pulling me out the door and into our room—the master suite. The view from the window is just as impressive as it was down in the living room, but neither of us is interested in looking at it. Tristan kicks the door shut, and I lock it. When I turn back, Tristan pulls me toward him. He holds me by the top of the arms and looks down at me, and my heart gives a wildly violent kick. I'm holding my breath in anticipation, as though I'm about to get my very first kiss. I'm so nervous I have butterflies, a riot of them, spinning and dancing in my stomach. I lift my hand and run it over his jaw, which is stubble dark, with two days' worth of beard. "I like it," I say.

He squints at me, unsure if I'm being serious, but I am. He looks unkempt, sleepy, shadows under his eyes, his T-shirt rumpled like he just got out of bed.

"You want to take a shower?" he asks.

I nod.

He grins and pulls me into the bathroom. I brush my teeth as Tristan tries to figure out the many taps and switches that turn on the shower. He succeeds, and I watch in the mirror as he strips off his shirt.

Toothpaste drool falls out of my mouth to the marble floor. I've seen Tristan with his shirt off before, but that's as far as I've seen. As he starts to undo his jeans, he catches my eye in the mirror and gives me a one-sided smile that almost makes me fall over. I have to balance myself against the basin. Now I really can't stop staring. As his fingers reach the final button of his jeans, I realize I've been holding my breath for so long I'm about to pass out and that I still have a mouth full of toothpaste froth.

I spit it out in a hurry and rinse.

When I turn around, though, I find Tristan's jeans and boxers on the floor and the door to the shower open, the glass already steamed up.

I strip out of my own clothes in record time, feeling no embarrassment because he's seen me naked a hundred times already. Even a month ago, I was so embarrassed to be naked in front of him I'd close my eyes and cringe, but now it's another story.

When I walk into the shower, he has his back to me and is leaning with his hands on the wall, letting the hot water pummel the hard, knotted muscles in his back. I walk up behind him and run my hands over his back and around to his chest. He takes my hand and presses it over his heart, and I kiss his shoulder blade as the hot water sluices over us both.

Tristan turns then and takes my face in his hands, tilting it up and bending down to kiss me on the lips. I press up against him as the water cascades over us and between us like we're standing under a waterfall.

He groans, and my hands start to wander. It's the first time he's let me, and I can't help myself. I want to trace every inch of him, and I'm so hungry for him I can't slow down. He grips my shoulders and then nudges my head aside so he can kiss my neck, drawing my slick hair out of the way. One hand cups my neck and the other slides between my legs, making me gasp even louder. He kisses me hard, and I wrap my leg around his waist and pull him nearer so he's pressed against me and groaning.

What was a dull ache has become a burning sensation in my core, spreading down my limbs. I don't want to wait a single second longer for this, and I can tell that he doesn't either. His breathing is ragged, his kisses hungry. He bites my neck, grips my arms and holds them above my head, then kisses my breasts and shoulders. I arch my back and try to reach for him, but he holds me fast and shakes his head.

He kisses me some more, until my legs dissolve and the only thing keeping me upright is his weight pushed up against me, pressing me to the wall. With the water falling in my eyes and blinding me, and his mouth on mine, I'm dizzy. It feels like drowning and being saved at the same time.

"Zo," he whispers in my ear, holding my face in his hands. "You want to go to bed?"

I shake my head. "Here," I say, and I realize I can't wait another second. I'm aching so badly for him.

He nods and pries himself free of me for one second to reach into his wallet on the bathroom floor and grab a condom.

He cups my knee in his palm and slides into me. I cry out in surprise and pleasure at how good it feels. My fingers bite into his shoulders as he pushes into me again, gently at first, slowly, as though scared he might hurt me. My name is a sigh on his lips, which are pressed close to my ear. When I run my fingers through his hair and whisper his name, he moves faster, pushing harder, until we're both groaning. This is what it's meant to feel like, I realize. Now I get it.

I open my eyes to find him staring into mine. Neither of us says anything. We just move together in perfect sync, no need any more to ask what the other wants because we both know intuitively, can read each other's bodies, every sigh, every touch. He knows exactly how to touch me, exactly how to kiss me to make my body arch and my skin burn and every nerve sing, and I can read the map of his body, can sense from the tension in his arms, the shudder down his spine, and the murmur of his breath, exactly what he likes too.

He waits for me until I'm on the verge of coming, and then he grips me tight and comes too—his eyes fixed on mine—and when we finish, hanging on each other as though keeping ourselves upright, out of breath and shaking, I want to laugh and sing and let my hammering heart explode for happiness, but all I actually do is burst into tears.

# TRISTAN

"Why are you crying?" I ask her.

I turn off the shower and lift her face to mine in a panic. Did I hurt her? Shit.

She shakes her head and buries her face in my shoulder.

"Zo, what's the matter?" I ask, getting even more worried. "I'm sorry."

She looks up at that, surprised. "What?"

"You're crying," I say. "Did I hurt you?"

She shakes her head in astonishment. "No. God, no." She smiles, takes my face in her hands, and, seeing the worry on my face, kisses me on the lips. When she pulls back, I'm still frowning, not understanding.

"It's just . . . ," she says with an embarrassed shrug, "I don't know. It was good, that's all."

"It was?" I ask, still worried but starting to think maybe she's telling the truth. "It was okay for you?"

She grins at that, hooking her arms around my neck, and nods. "It was better than okay."

"So why are you crying, then?"

"Because I'm happy, you idiot," she says. "And freezing. Could I get a towel?"

I snatch a towel from the rail outside and wrap her up in it, then wrap another around my waist and quickly bundle her out into the bedroom and toward the bed. We burrow under the covers, and within minutes the towels are lost, kicked to the ground, and Zoey's still-wet body is on top of mine. I hold her in place, not wanting to ever let her out of my arms.

"Was it okay for you?" she whispers in my ear, and I hear the note of worry in her voice.

"Are you kidding?" I ask, laughing. She has no idea how good that felt. The thirty-plus days of waiting were worth every second. I honestly didn't know sex could feel that good.

"Do you want to go again?" she asks.

"Do you really need to ask?" I say, kissing her.

I roll her off me and hover over her, holding my weight on my arms and looking down at her. "I know I say it all the time, but you're so beautiful," I tell her.

She smiles in a way that makes my heart swell to fill my chest, her eyes filling with tears again. I slide my hand between her legs, to the place I know makes her moan. She bites her full bottom lip and reaches for me hungrily, like she doesn't want to wait. I don't want to make her sore, but she's impatient. Her hands grip my forearm, her skin no longer cold but feverish, and she moans. I take that as a sign to keep going. I stroke her, and it's like watching her unfurl. She opens up—without embarrassment, without self-consciousness—and it's more of a turn-on than she could ever know.

She pulls me down on top of her, and this time I go slowly, even as she arches her back to meet me and wraps her legs around my waist. I want to savor the feeling, an intimacy of knowing and belonging that I've never experienced before. A whole new connection is forged between us—one I know won't ever be broken—because this girl belongs to me just as much as I belong to her.

When Zoey cries out again and buries her head against my shoulder, that's all the signal I need. It's as if every cell in my body is receiving five thousand volts. I collapse down on top of her, my arms and legs shaking, and she holds me in place, not letting me move or unglue myself from her until we're ready to go again.

# ZOEY

raise an eyebrow as Tristan lifts the silver dome off his sixth breakfast plate and grins at the sight of a stack of pancakes and bacon drizzled with syrup.

He and Kate are competing to see who can eat the most. "I need the calories," Tristan says by way of explanation, giving me a wicked grin. He's eating with gusto, a starving man tearing into the bacon like it's his first meal in days.

My limbs are floaty and a little achy, and I'm so relaxed it's an effort to lift the spoon and stir my coffee. I watch Tristan eat, though, smiling when he looks up and catches me staring at him. He shoots me a smile, a new smile, one I haven't seen before—one that seems to reflect this new intimacy between us, like we have a secret no one else knows, something that only we share.

Butterflies start to jostle in my stomach as I remember the details of last night. They're pressed indelibly in my mind. I can still feel him: feel the rough stubble burn on the inside of my thighs; the scorched sensation of my skin where his lips traced a path along my collarbone to the hollow at the center of my neck;

the sweet, dull ache inside me that makes me long to crawl back into bed with him and press repeat.

I stifle a sigh with a strawberry.

"Earth to Zoey."

Startling, I look at Kate.

"You eating that strawberry or trying to seduce it?" she asks me, one eyebrow arched.

Tristan snorts as I pop the strawberry in my mouth. "Eating it," I mumble.

"I was asking you if you slept well," Kate asks.

"Huh?" I ask, cheeks flaring as red as the strawberry I just ate. Did she hear us? I tried to keep it down, burying my face in the pillow when I had to, but maybe she did. Kate's looking at me innocently, but is that the hint of a smirk behind her blank expression?

"Yeah," I mumble again, stuffing some cantaloupe in my mouth. "Really well," I say, thinking of how sleep was easily sacrificed and wondering how many days I could physically keep going without sleeping. I'm willing to try it.

She cocks her head at me. "You look like you haven't slept a wink." She points a finger at me. "And what's that on your neck?"

Panicked, I tug at the collar of the bathrobe to see where she's pointing. Did Tristan leave a mark?

"Gotcha!" Kate yells. She stands up. "Well, I'm going to find Romeo and feed him this smoked salmon. Then I'm going to take another bath and see how many free toiletries I can sneak in my bag. See you downstairs in an hour?"

Tristan checks his watch and nods. We have to check out by nine to make it back for his shift at work. I've got work too this evening, but I'm already dreaming about afterward and the six hours we'll have before dawn.

When I glance at Tristan, I see he's pushed his half-finished pancakes out the way and is on his feet. I stare at him questioningly.

"We have an hour," he says with a grin. And with that, he grabs my hand and pulls me toward the stairs.

"Second Helpings." Tristan announces the name of the store, pulling into the parking lot in front of a large brick building with a rusty old garment railing and a few armchairs sitting outside the door. "I already had those," he remarks, grinning at me.

"And fifth and sixth," Kate remarks. She's talking about breakfast, but I know Tristan is talking about something else entirely.

Kate throws open her door and makes a dash for the thrift-store entrance. I smile watching her, happy to see her happy.

"Thanks for the detour," I say to Tristan.

He nods. "Who doesn't love thrifting?" he asks.

I follow him, clutching at my sixteen-ounce coffee like it's the antidote to all my body's woes. I down the final dregs and toss it into the waste bin by the front door to the store.

Tristan throws his arm around me, but I shrug it off. He looks at me, wounded. "It's a competition," I tell him. "You're on your own."

"Wow," he says, "I thought you were joking."

I give him an arch look. "We don't joke in our family about this," I answer, already scouring with one eye the rack of clothes by the door for any likely contenders. The purpose of the competition is to find a gift for everyone, but the gift must be the most hideous and awful item in the store and cost less than five dollars.

We walk inside and survey the aisles of donated clothing and household detritus. It's my Mecca. I'm a thrift-store queen, an expert at speed sorting. Give me a thrift store, and I'll dig out the designer jeans, cellophaned Xbox game, and almost-new hardback copy of a bestselling novel.

Necessity made me this way after we landed in Vegas, broke and furniture-less and cutlery-less. It's where I have bought my clothes for the last four years and where we've all shopped for birthday presents. One year before Christmas, I turned it into a game so we could make it more fun for Kate and Cole. I could tell they both felt ashamed that everything they owned was "pre-loved," as my mom liked to call it. And now the game has become a family tradition.

"Wait," says Tristan, pulling me back just as I'm about to take off down the aisle marked MEN'S CLOTHES. I look at him impatiently, aware that Kate is already speeding through aisles ahead of me, with one eye on the prize. I can't relinquish my title.

Tristan gives me a funny look. "You really want to win this," he says, surprised.

"Hell yeah." I laugh.

He stops my mouth with a kiss, then just as abruptly pulls away, leaving me reeling. By the time I recover, he's already halfway down an aisle, ransacking the hangers. Amateur move.

I race off down the men's aisle. My tactic is to head for the rail with the brightest clothing, ignoring the beiges, browns, blacks, and grays. Bingo. I find a selection of ugly Christmas sweaters. These always deliver. And lo and behold, within seconds I'm pulling out a red wool sweater with a white cat knitted on the front, along with the words MEOWY CATMUS.

Perfect for Kate.

Next comes Tristan. I skip back toward the men's clothing aisle and to the shirts, but instinct tells me to ignore the meager offerings there and instead head toward the shelves with the junk. As I scan the shelves I notice the word BACON. I pull the box down. It's a puzzle, possibly the weirdest puzzle ever created. A five-hundred-piece photo of a man wearing a suit of bacon, lounging on a sofa while a woman in a taffeta ball gown stands over him. I grin and shove it under my arm. Two minutes left, and I decide to spend it finding something for Cole so he doesn't feel too mad about missing out on a trip.

I head straight for the shelf of Xbox games. There are dozens, and I wonder why anyone ever buys them new when you can pick them up for a fraction of the price secondhand. I pick up a Lego superhero game, figuring that at least it won't have any guns or soldiers in it. Carrying all my finds, I decide to spend my spare time browsing. I crouch down in front of a couple of dusty old boxes, one containing vinyl and another containing junk from what looks like a house clearance. There's a broken music box and some old *Life* magazines from the '70s, and beneath those I unearth a tin box, dented and rusty and once used to store tobacco, by the smell of it.

When I pop it open I find a baseball card. I laugh out loud and carry it over to the cash desk, where I'm met by Tristan and a flustered but beaming Kate.

She hands me something on a hanger, and I take two steps back in fright. "What the hell is that?" I ask in horror.

It's a swimsuit in a garish neon green, with giant red lips splashed all over it.

"Now you can be a Kardashian," she tells me.

I take it as if it's made of radioactive fibers. Used undergarments make me shudder. It's so hideous I think Kate might have won.

"And this," she says, turning to Tristan, "is for you." She hands him a Hawaiian shirt in banana yellow and tangerine orange.

"I think I might wear this to Kit and Jessa's wedding," Tristan says, holding it up against his chest to check the measurement.

Kate isn't sure if he's joking, and neither am I.

It's Tristan's turn. He unloads his pile of goodies on the counter. "For you," he says to Kate, handing her a Chinese waving cat.

She grabs it in delight. "I love it!" she says. "These are super lucky! They're supposed to bring you money. And I could use money. I need to pay Zoey back."

Tristan frowns, not having expected such a positive reaction. "This is for you," he says to me, handing me a Medusa wig, green nylon hair woven through with plastic snakes. "Figured you could wear it on Halloween," he says. "I know how much you love those Greek gods."

"Medusa was a monster, not a goddess." I pull on the wig.

"Still beautiful," says Tristan, kissing me.

"Disgusting," grumbles Kate, though I can't tell if she means the display of affection or the wig.

"I also got you this." He picks up a box from the floor and hands it to me. It's the Game of Life. I start laughing, taking it from his hands. "I'm going to thrash you," I tell him.

"That a promise?" He smirks.

"Okay, my turn," I say, rolling my eyes at him. I hand Kate the MEOWY CATMUS sweater.

"This isn't hideous," Kate says, holding it up. "I would totally wear this."

"Oh, really?" I ask. "Go on, then."

"At Christmas," she prevaricates. "Obviously, I can't wear it now, because it's summer and people would look at me weird."

"I think they would look at you weird regardless of when you wore it," Tristan counters.

I hand Tristan his bacon suit puzzle. He stares at it quizzically, Kate peering over his shoulder. "That's so wrong," Kate finally says.

"I think it looks quite tasty," Tristan remarks. "A suit you can eat. That's actually quite clever."

"Who wins?" Kate asks, looking between Tristan and me.

"I don't know," I say. "Shall we call it a tie?"

Kate sighs. "Okay, I guess so. "What's that?" Kate asks, pointing at the other goods in my hand. I show them the tin I discovered and the baseball card inside it.

Tristan frowns at the card, then takes the tin as though it's the Ark of the Covenant. Holding it in both his hands, he stares at the card in awe, and Kate starts laughing at him.

Tristan looks at me, his smile vanished, his face turning pale. "Do you know what this is?" he asks in a hushed tone.

"A baseball card," I say. "I thought you might like it."

"No," he says, thrusting the tin back at me with urgency. "You have to keep it."

I take the tin, confused, as he glances furtively over his shoulder at the cashier, but she's busy ringing up another customer's items.

"I think it might be worth something," Tristan says quietly.

Kate's eyes light up. She stares at me, then at Tristan. "How much?" she asks.

Tristan shrugs. "It's a signed 1959 Willie Mays. I don't know for sure, but something."

The customer is done at the desk, and before I can stop him, Tristan walks quickly over to the cashier with all our things. "How much is this?" he asks, nonchalantly holding up the tin.

The cashier pulls the glasses down off the top of her head and peers at it, befuddled. She glances at the card but seems to consider it a piece of trash. "It didn't have a price on it?" she asks.

"No," I interject. "I found it in a box under that shelf." I point, and she looks over at where I'm pointing.

"Oh, those items are all on sale. Give me a dollar and we'll call it a deal."

Kate spears me between the ribs with her elbow and looks ready to burst like an overfilled helium balloon. I ignore her and look at the lady holding out her palm and Tristan pulling out his wallet, rifling through it for a dollar bill. Is that fair? Are we defrauding the thrift store by not admitting we're in possession of something that could be valuable? But Tristan is already handing over the dollar. Plus another ten for the wig and the waving cat.

Kate keeps digging into me even harder with her elbow. I turn to her. She shoves her phone under my nose and jabs her finger at the website page she's called up. It's a baseball card forum, and there's a picture of the exact card from the tin alongside a figure that makes me blink twice to make sure I've read it correctly.

"You ready?" the cashier asks me. I'm too stunned to reply, so Kate dumps all our stuff on the counter and hands over a twenty-dollar bill, before grabbing the change and all the items and hustling me outside.

Once we're inside the safety of the car, Tristan hands me the tin.

"But I bought it for you," I tell him, refusing to take it.

"No," he says, shaking the bacon suit puzzle in my face, "you got me this. That's yours," he insists, pushing it into my hands.

"But," I start to argue.

"Don't argue with him!" Kate hollers from the back seat. "It's worth almost ten thousand dollars!"

"How much?" Tristan asks, whipping around.

"Ten thousand dollars," Kate repeats, showing him her phone.

He takes the phone and studies the website and then shakes his head in astonishment. "I knew it was worth something, but I didn't know it was worth that much."

I take a deep breath and then push the card back toward him. "Have it," I tell him.

He shakes his head at me, grinning. "Seriously, Zoey, stop offering it to me. I'm not taking it. Think what you could do with the money."

# TRISTAN

P ayday," I say when Zoey lands on another green square. As I hand over the money from the bank, she narrows her eyes at me. "You're letting me win," she says.

"Never," I answer, and it's true. "I had a ski accident and got screwed on my taxes," I point out.

"You also have four kids." She laughs, nodding at the four plastic pegs in my little plastic car. "And children are expensive."

"But I want four kids," I argue.

"Well, I hope they figure out a way for men to give birth, because no way I'm having more than two." She slams her mouth shut and flushes a shade of beetroot. I pause, dice in hand. Zoey flusters and starts rearranging her stack of fake money, then glances up at me nervously. "I didn't mean . . . ," she begins, but before she can finish, I take her hand and pull her across the board toward me, scattering money, plastic cars, and my four tiny pink and blue babies across the living room floor.

"What are you doing?" Zoey shrieks, laughing as I pull her into my lap.

"Nothing," I say, kissing her.

"But we were in the middle of a game. I was winning."

"I forfeit," I tell her, my mouth on hers. Truth is, I can't get enough of her lips or her body, and there's a limit to how long I can play a board game without my imagination weighing the throwing of dice against the stripping off of Zoey's clothes and deciding I'm wasting my time.

As my hands start to dive inside her clothes, Zoey sighs. "I have to get to work."

"I'll drive you after," I murmur, my lips on her neck.

"No," she argues, her breath catching. "That's why I bought the car."

I know she's right. The silver RAV4 was secondhand and cost five thousand dollars. Zoey struggled with using the money from the baseball card sale on herself, but her mom and I and Kate persuaded her the car was necessary and to put all the rest of the money in the bank for her college tuition.

"I'll be fine," she says, sensing my hesitancy.

I don't want to say anything because I don't want to bring the shadow into the light. Zoey's dad lurks always in the periphery of my thoughts, like a monster under the bed. Although we haven't heard anything from him for a week now, that might be more to do with the fact Zoey has changed her phone number. His probation officer says he's always in Scottsdale on the days he needs to check in and that he also has a job now, working as a security guard for a construction company. But still, I don't like taking chances.

"I'll follow you," I say. I'm not a fan of Zoey parking and having to walk the short distance to the restaurant by herself.

"My very own protection detail," she jokes.

"Always," I tell her, nuzzling her neck. Then I grin. "What do you call security guards at the Samsung store?"

She groans, and not with pleasure.

"Guardians of the Galaxy."

She groans louder, but she's laughing as well, her breath tickling my neck. "Your jokes are terrible." She sighs.

"And you love me anyway," I say, smiling.

She pulls back and looks at me, her hazel eyes serious all of a sudden. "I do, you know," she says. "I love you."

It's the first time she's said it, and my heart stills in my chest. I freeze, taken aback. I hadn't expected it, have never had anyone say it to me this way before and have never said it to anyone either. There's that vulnerable look in her eye, the exact same look she had just before I kissed her for the first time, and I realize she's waiting for me to say something. I cup her cheek.

"I love you too," I say, and then I kiss her, the shock of it hitting me. I do love her. The knowledge fills me up like helium, making me light-headed. I love her. I don't want to live without her.

After a few minutes, before things get too out of hand, she struggles out of my arms. She's late for work and, despite my protests, won't call in sick. Standing up, she disappears into the bathroom. I wait a few seconds, then pull the letter out of my back pocket, where it's been burning a hole, and turn it over in my hands, wondering what to do with it—time's running out. I should tell her, I think, but there's never a good time, and how am I ever going to break it to her? I should stop being a coward and do it, but I know once it's out of the bag, everything will change. And I don't want things to change. That's the problem.

I hear the sound of the bathroom door opening and shove the letter under a pile of magazines.

# ZOEY

"K ate, be ready in two minutes, okay?" I shout through the bathroom door, where Kate has been ensconced for the last hour. We're running late for Jessa's bridal shower.

I race through the kitchen, where my mom is making lunch for Cole, who is playing on his Xbox. "I'm just running over to Tristan's," I tell her, unlocking the front door. "I think I left my phone there."

My mom nods, and I race out the door and down the stairs before sprinting across the courtyard to Tristan's door. I knock, but he doesn't answer, which is weird because his bike is parked out front, so I use the key he gave me and unlock the door. When I step inside, I hear the shower running. I'm going to be late, but I can't help myself. I push the bathroom door open and stand grinning, watching Tristan shower. He has his back to me and is busily soaping up while singing a Drake song—badly. Tristan has many skills, but singing isn't one of them. I manage to hold in the laughter for about 3.2 seconds before it bursts out of me.

He leaps around in fright at the sound, though his startled expression quickly gives way to something else. "You going to stand there and get a free peep show or come over here and kiss me?"

I eye the steamed-up bathroom, which I know is already messing with my hair, turning it frizzy, but then the sight of naked Tristan is too much to walk away from. I step across the wet tile toward him, and he pulls open the glass shower door. I kiss his wet lips and try to pull quickly away before I get all wet from the spray, but it's too late. Tristan has his arms around me.

I scream and dance back out of his octopus arms. "No," I yell as he tries to pull me into the shower. "You're getting me all wet."

"That's the plan." He grins lasciviously at me.

"You're incorrigible," I tell him.

He shrugs, still grinning. "Pass me a towel, then," he says.

I do, reaching blind for one on the rail beside me, because I can't tear my eyes off his ripped torso. He steps out of the shower and takes his time wrapping the towel around his waist. He knows full well that he's tormenting me, but I'm already running late, and now my hair is really screwed.

Tristan cocks his head toward the bedroom. "You want to . . . ," he starts.

"No," I tell him firmly, trying to ignore the way my body is responding to the sight of his slick, smooth chest and the water dripping down his neck, which is begging to be dried off. I wonder if we'll ever lose this physical craving for each other. "I'm just here for my phone," I say, backing out of the room.

"I think I saw it in the living room," he shouts after me.

I search down the sides of the sofa and on the coffee table, picking up a pile of magazines. A letter falls out from between them, and I stoop to pick it up, then freeze. I hear Tristan shouting something to me from the bedroom, but I can't make out the words because my ears are filled with screeching white noise.

"Zo?" Tristan asks, entering the living room.

I glance up at him, dazed. He's wearing jeans and pulling on a shirt. "I found it," he says, holding up my phone. "It was in the bedroom."

He pauses when he sees my face. "What's the matter?" he says, but then he breaks off as his gaze drops to the letter in my hand.

He looks up at me, his smile gone. "I was going to tell you," he says.

"When?" I say, my voice shaking.

He takes a deep breath and bites his lip. "I don't know." He takes a step toward me. "Look," he says, "I haven't decided if I'm going."

"What do you mean?" I say, waving the letter at him. "It's pilot school. It's what you've always dreamed of. You have to go."

"No, I don't," he argues weakly.

I blink at him, astonished. "Tristan, you told me that spots never open up, that you'd have to wait years. You can't say no to this."

"But it's in Florida," he says. "That's the other side of the country."

There's a lump in my throat, and I try desperately to swallow it. I can't show how I feel about this. I can only let him see how happy I am for him. This is what he wants. "You have to go," I say.

His shoulders slump as he stares at me, his caramel-colored eyes filled with worry. "But what about you?"

I take a deep, shuddering breath and try not to let the tears fall. He didn't even really try to argue with me. I know I didn't want him to, but the words reveal he's already decided, without even talking to me. That hurts. I give him a shaky smile. "I'll be fine."

"No," he says, stepping toward me. "I don't want to leave you."

"I'll be okay," I say, but I can't look him in the eye.

He steps closer, and I feel his fingers beneath my chin, gently raising my head so our eyes meet. "Zo, I can't leave you."

Can't. Is that because of the promise he made to my brother? Or because he's worried about my dad?

"I love you," he says, his voice cracking.

A piece of my heart breaks, because I hear in his voice how much he wants to go and I know how much it means to him and how he's torn over the decision because he doesn't want to hurt me. I need to make the decision for him. The lump in my throat is so big I can't swallow, but I force myself to speak. "I love you too," I say. "And that's why you're going. Because I want the best for you."

Tristan pulls me into his arms, my cheek against his bare chest. I squeeze my eyes shut, but the tears still come, leaking out the sides and sliding down my cheeks. I've just found him, and now I'm going to lose him. It's two and a half thousand miles between here and Florida. I'll never see him. And I know what happens with long-distance relationships. All I need to do is look at Lis and Kate and Tristan's sister, Dahlia, and her ex Lou. Time and distance wear holes in even the closest relationships. It won't work out.

All these thoughts flash through my mind in a matter of seconds as I stand pressed to Tristan's chest, my brain already trying to imprint the memory of his arms wrapped around my waist, the feeling of his lips pressed to my forehead, the husky sound of his voice saying my name. I try to hold on to all those things because I know I'm going to lose them.

This is why it was so dangerous to open my heart. This is what I was afraid of, and I was right to be. I should never have let myself fall for him.

No, a voice in my head says with fervency. It was worth it, worth every single second.

I can't let Tristan see, though, just how much it hurts. He might not go if he suspects. "It's just a few thousand miles," I say to him, forcing a smile to cover my lie. "We'll find a way to make it work."

Tristan takes me by my shoulders and stares at me. He shakes his head. "No," he says. "I don't want to do a long-distance relationship."

My breath catches in my throat. He doesn't want to even try to stay together. He wants to break up.

"Come with me," Tristan whispers, his arms tightening on my shoulders.

"What?" I whisper.

"Come with me," he says.

I stare at him, and it takes a second to realize that he's not breaking up with me. The relief almost bursts out of me in a sob, but then the reality of what he's asking sinks in. How can I come with him? How can he even ask me to? He knows I can't leave my mom and Kate and Cole, especially not now. But, oh my God, it would be a lie to say I'm not tempted.

He's staring at me, an almost desperate, pleading look in his eye, and I'm momentarily caught up in a dream of what that life might look like. Florida. The two of us, living together in a little house that's just ours. I can picture it as clear as daylight. The cozy bed with clean white sheets, the vase of flowers on the kitchen table, the coats and shoes by the door. Tristan waking up each morning and heading off in his uniform to pilot school, me packing my backpack and heading to college. I think of waking up in his arms every morning, my head on his chest, and going to sleep with him every night, curled on my side, his arm flung over me, anchoring me in place. But it's just a fairy tale. And just like a spell cast by an evil witch, it all evaporates before my eyes.

"Please," Tristan says. "Just think about it."

I shake my head sadly. "I can't go," I tell him.

His jaw tenses as he grits his teeth in frustration. His arms drop from my shoulders, and it feels as if he's left invisible weights behind, pressing down on me.

Tristan backs away, an expression on his face that breaks my heart all over again. He looks hurt beyond measure, and angry, too, as though I've wounded him. I've never seen him look that way before, and it shocks me. He can't expect me to choose between him and my family, though. That isn't fair. And besides, he's the one choosing to leave, not me. I don't blame him. He's choosing his career over me, just as I'm choosing my family over him. And maybe that's it. Maybe that should tell us something.

"Maybe," I say to him with a shrug, "it's for the best."

Tristan frowns at me, and instantly I regret saying it. The hurt in his eyes grows, and he takes another step back from me. He doesn't say anything, and we're disturbed by a knock on the door. We both startle, but neither of us moves to answer it. We keep staring at each other, words pressing against our lips but neither of us saying anything. Both of us too afraid, perhaps, and reeling too hard. How has this conversation veered so far from where it started to end up here, at this dead-end place?

"Zoey?"

I turn. Kate has opened the door and is peering around it. "We're late," she says. "I thought you said two minutes." Her smile fades as she takes in the look on my face, and then, frowning a little, she glances toward Tristan before turning back to me. "I'll wait for you outside," she says.

"No," I say, finding my voice at last. "I'm coming." And with that I run after her, not even glancing back at Tristan or saying good-bye.

# TRISTAN

She just broke up with me. Or did I break up with her? What the hell just happened? I pick the letter up from the floor where Zoey dropped it. The problem is I want one as much as the other. I want Zoey, but I also want this. I've wanted to be a pilot since I was a kid. I've been waiting on a spot at pilot school for a year. It's a rare opportunity, and if I turn it down it's unlikely they'll offer it again. I know Zoey gets that, but I don't get why she can't come with me. It's the perfect solution. As soon as I said it out loud, I knew it was the only one that made sense, but I'd do long-distance if I had to. It's not what I want, but it's better than breaking up. I never wanted that.

I'm so confused. What did she mean that maybe it was for the best? Has she been having doubts about us? Was I just a means to an end for her? Did she just need someone to make her feel safe?

My phone buzzes. I'm hoping it might be Zoey as I reach for it but see that it's not her; it's Walker. He's outside waiting. Shit. I'd forgotten. Kit's bachelor party starts in twenty minutes. I race around, grabbing clothes and my wallet and keys, my mind too distracted to remember what I need. I almost think about bailing, because I'm not sure I can sit all day and pretend happiness when I feel like the world just got ripped out from under my feet. But I can't bail. It's been planned for months, and what kind of a friend would I be if I did?

When I rush outside a few minutes later and see Walker in his Jeep, which is loaded with fishing poles and coolers, I decide that I need to put on a brave face. I can't ruin Kit's bachelor party, so I force a smile as I jump in beside Walker.

"Let's get this show on the road!" I shout as he guns the Jeep's engine.

# ZOEY

What happened? Did you guys argue?" Kate asks as I drive.

I shake my head. "No."

"Is everything okay?" Kate presses.

I take a deep breath, unsure whether to tell her, not because I want to keep a secret from her, but because I'm afraid if I talk about it I'll start crying, and I really, really can't afford to cry.

"Did you break up?" Kate asks.

I don't answer.

"Oh my God," Kate whispers. "You broke up. Why?"

"One of those things," I say, blinking away the tears and focusing on the road. How can I tell her the truth—that I couldn't leave and he couldn't stay? That she and Cole and Mom are the reason?

"But you guys seem so happy," she says in shock. "You're so good together. I don't get it."

"He's going to Florida," I say.

"What do you mean?" Kate asks.

"He got into flight school, and it's in Florida."

Kate looks at me, confused. "So?" she asks. "It's not like it's a one-way mission to Mars. There are these things called planes. They're long metal tubes that fly through the sky and take you from A to B, B being Florida." She reminds me of Tristan when she says things like that. It's like she's picked up his humor by osmosis.

"It's not that," I say. "I don't want to do long-distance, and neither does he."

"Why not?" Kate asks.

"It never works," I say, looking at her pointedly.

Kate shuts up at that, unable to argue with me.

"Besides, it's for the best," I say, repeating myself from earlier, though the words sound hollow even to my ears.

"How is it for the best?" Kate asks.

Now it's my turn to shut up, because I have no idea how to answer.

We ride the rest of the way in silence. Kate seems sulky, her arms crossed over her chest, her mouth pursed. My hands grip the wheel so tightly, and I'm trying so hard not to cry that it hurts every time I breathe. I wonder how I will get through today as we pull through the gates at Emma's house.

Kate breaks her silence finally as I round the bend and the house appears. She lets out a gasp. "Oh my God . . ."

I look up at the pink- and champagne-colored balloons bedecking the pillars, making the house look like it's wearing a frothy tutu.

"This is the most amazing house I've ever seen," Kate says, amazed.

I park. Kate nervously smooths down her dress, one that I bought for her as a gift. It's turquoise and brings out the brilliant copper tone of her hair. She looks stunning, and for a brief moment the happiness I feel at seeing her giddy excitement cuts through my unhappiness and makes me smile.

As we get out of the car and walk across the gravel driveway toward the house, the door flies open and Dahlia and Didi rush out, throwing handfuls of confetti over us, as though we're the bride and groom. They sweep us up and carry us inside, across the cool entrance hall and toward the French doors at the back of the house that lead to the garden.

Kate drags her heels, staring around in wonder. Dahlia links her arm through Kate's and starts peppering her with questions as they walk. This is the first time they've met, but Tristan must have told her all about Kate, because I can tell she's determined to make sure Kate feels welcome. I watch Dahlia introduce her to Emma, and I see Kate blush and stammer a hello, feeling another surge of happiness for Kate rush through me. Vegas and Lis might be becoming distant memories for her. I wonder if that will ever happen to me. Will I ever forget Tristan and move on? I don't think so. It feels as if a fundamental part of me has shattered.

The back of the house has been decorated with balloons as well, and a variety of floaties cover the surface of the pool, so that I can catch only the vaguest glimpse of glittering blue water between them. There's a unicorn, a giant pair of red lips, and a flamingo. A dozen sun loungers surround the pool, and on each of them rests a neatly folded pink bathrobe with our names embroidered in gold thread.

Vases filled with stargazer lilies are set on tables alongside cupcakes decorated with sprinkles. There's a chocolate fountain and a tray of sparkling champagne flutes. Didi offers me one.

"Nonalcoholic this time!" she says when she sees me hesitate.

I take it from her and force another smile, realizing my happy face slipped for a moment.

"What's going on?" Didi asks, narrowing her eyes at me in suspicion.

"Nothing," I say lightly, and then, changing the subject, I gesture brightly at the sun loungers. "Did you organize all this?"

"Dahlia and me," she says, grinning. "Just wait until you see what we've got planned for later. Jessa's going to love it."

She turns to me, and I smile so hard my cheeks ache. "It's amazing," I tell her.

"Have you been crying?" she asks.

Damn. I should have worn sunglasses. "No," I say, lying through my teeth, feeling the acid sting of more tears gathering behind my eyes.

"It's not your dad, is it?" she asks, worried.

I shake my head. "No. Everything's fine. I haven't heard from him. I think he's decided to leave us alone." I don't know if I believe this, but it sounds good to say it out loud. Thankfully, before Didi can pepper me with more questions, Jessa appears on the patio. She's wearing a pale pink sundress, and her baby bump is starting to show. She looks so radiant and glowing that my breath, still catching painfully every time I inhale, gets stuck somewhere in my chest. I tear up as I watch her walk toward us, smiling a little shyly, her cheeks dusted pink. She's rushed by all of her friends, and in that moment, I turn and run, not wanting anyone to see the tears that are now falling freely.

I find myself by the pool house. The door is open, so I run inside, closing it behind me. I sink down on the sofa, and suddenly all the pain and hurt I've been holding in comes bursting out of me like an avalanche. There's no way of holding it back.

It was the sight of Jessa that set me off, acting like a final hammer thwack to the crack in my heart that was damming all the tears. She and Kit are so in love, and I'm jealous. I'm jealous of their happy-ever-after. I felt a kick in the chest of anguish that I'm about to lose not just Tristan but his friends, too. I was just getting close with all of them, but the truth is they only invited me because of my connection to Tristan. I don't know them well enough yet for our friendship to endure when they find out Tristan and I are no longer together.

The door clicks behind me, and I startle and look up. It's Didi and Dahlia. "There you are," Didi says.

"I'm sorry," I say, avoiding their eyes, hoping the dim light will hide the state of my face. "I was looking for a bathroom," I add, turning away as though pretending to look for one.

Didi comes toward me, blocking my path. "What's the matter?"

I look up at her, my lip trembling. I thought I could hold it together, but I can't. "Tristan," I say, my voice cracking. "We broke up."

Dahlia's face twists in shock. "Oh no, I'm so sorry." She purses her lips. "What did my brother do?"

I shake my head and sink back down onto the sofa. They sit beside me, one on either side, and put their arms around my shoulders. "He's going away to Florida for pilot school."

"Oh," Didi says.

"What?!" Dahlia exclaims. "He never told me this."

"Me either. I only just found out. But he's known for a month."

"I don't get it," Dahlia says. "Why are you breaking up?" She sounds like Kate did with her reaction back in the car.

I shrug. "I don't know," I admit. I feel like I've lost track of the arguments we both made. "It just seemed too far to make it work. He wanted me to go with him."

Didi and Dahlia exchange a look. I make to stand up and put an end to the conversation. We need to get back to the party before Jessa wonders where all her guests have gone. "I'm fine," I tell them. "I don't want Jessa to—"

The door opens again. This time it's Jessa.

"There you are!" Jessa says. "I was looking for you."

Jessa's smile fades the moment she sees Dahlia and Didi with their arms around me. "What is it?" she asks, concerned, rushing toward me the same way Dahlia did. I feel completely overwhelmed that I came in here to escape and now they're all here and making a fuss.

"Nothing," I say, smiling furiously, trying to bat them all away and walk to the door. "I'm absolutely fine. Let's go."

Jessa stops in front of me, hands on her hips. For a softly spoken, sweet-hearted girl, she suddenly reveals an inner core of steel. "You don't seem okay. What happened?"

"She and Tristan broke up," Dahlia explains.

"What?" she says, aghast and looking at me. "Why?"

"He's going away to Florida, to pilot school."

Jessa shakes her head. "Why are you breaking up?" she asks, confused.

I open my mouth, and then I shut it again. Every time someone asks me this, I realize I don't honestly know the answer anymore. If I ever did. "I don't think it will work," I say lamely.

Jessa makes a tutting sound. "That's nonsense," she says. "Kit was away for months and months when we first started dating."

I cringe. How could I have forgotten that? My own brother

is away for months at a time too. That's the cost of being with someone in the military.

"We made the choice to stay together," Jessa tells me. "It wasn't even a choice, if I'm honest." She says it gently, but I can't help but blush. I feel so stupid to be talking about this in the face of what she went through with her brother and Kit. "It's difficult," she goes on. "I won't lie. But at least you'll be able to see Tristan. It's only Florida."

"Why don't you go with him?" Didi asks.

"I can't go. I've got my job here, and"—I shrug, embarrassed—"I've got friends." *For the first time in my life*, I want to add but don't. I like it here in Oceanside. It feels like I've finally found a home, but how much of that feeling is because Tristan is here?

"You'd make friends somewhere else," Didi says.

"Especially if you started college," Dahlia adds.

"And you'd come back and visit all the time," Jessa says. "And it wouldn't be forever. Just a year or so."

"Plus, Florida is just like Oceanside. There are beaches everywhere! Just a few more alligators."

I bite my lip, considering it, then shake my head. "I can't leave Kate and Cole and my mom. They need me. I don't know how my mom would cope without me. Not just paying the bills but taking care of Kate and Cole too. I can't just run off and leave them, no matter what I want."

As I say it, I realize that it is what I want. It's the first time I've voiced it, either in my head or out loud. I do want to go with him; even though it's terrifying and feels like a huge leap, I know that I want to be with Tristan wherever he goes. The thought of traveling, of living with him and not being responsible for anyone else, is amazing. But it's impossible.

"What?"

I whip around.

Kate is standing in the middle of the doorway. "What did you just say?" she asks. "Are you breaking up with Tristan because of me?"

"No," I say quickly, "that's not—"

"I heard you," Kate shoots back. "You said you couldn't go because you didn't want to leave us, but that's stupid. I don't want you to stay because of me. You don't need to."

I don't know what to say. I look at her and then around at the others, who are all silently watching me. I didn't think I had a choice, but maybe I was wrong. Maybe I do.

# TRISTAN

Kit, Walker, and I are sitting at the back of the boat, lines cast. Behind us, Kit's dad and Jessa's dad are arguing politics, but in a way that tells me they've known each other for decades and can each take as much ribbing as the other is capable of doling out. They're preparing the fish, gutting them like true experts, readying them for the grill. As I watch Jessa's dad fling the fish guts into a bucket by his feet, I feel like I know exactly how the fish feels.

I stare at the choppy waves and the achingly blue sky and think about my choices. Sea or sky. I can't have both. Or I can't have both *and* Zoey. I get it—I understand why she can't come to Florida, but I'm hurt she broke up with me because of it. It doesn't feel real. It feels like one giant mistake I should be able to rewind. Maybe if I had a do-over, I could say the right things and they wouldn't add up to a breakup.

I need to speak to her, but of course, out here, miles from land, there's no cell phone reception. And besides, I shouldn't be pleading with my girlfriend over the phone when I'm meant to be helping Kit enjoy this weekend. He seems to be having a good time so far—his feet are kicked up on the rail, there's a beer in his hand, and he's grinning like he's delighted these are his last days of single life. It's wrong to feel jealous, especially after what he went through. Kit told me once that Jessa's the reason he made it home, the reason he's still alive. I know that he and Jessa have faced a lot, but they've weathered it. They've survived and come out stronger on the other side. They're getting married and having a baby, for God's sake.

It's only then that I admit the dreams I've been dreaming and the thoughts I've been allowing to percolate in the back of my mind. They are idle thoughts, whispers really, of what could be: taking Zoey out on a boat and getting down on one knee, turning around at an altar and seeing her walk toward me in a white dress, her holding our baby in her arms, smiling up at me. I've allowed myself to think these things, imagine them in more detail than I'd care to admit to anyone. Was it stupid? Was I jumping the gun? She's so young. We're both so young. I know it's senseless to imagine marriage and kids at my age, unrealistic even, but I did. And I never laughed at those imaginings because they seemed so natural, so obvious. Of course I'd marry her one day. I knew it almost from the very first time I kissed her. I don't do things by halves. When I commit, I commit, and I committed to Zoey with all my heart and all my soul. I don't know how to undo that. In fact, I know I can't. And more than that, I know I don't want to.

I stare at the sea so long I feel like I'm in a trance. I can't leave her. How can I leave her after I promised Will I'd keep her safe? After I promised myself all those years ago? And it's not just the promise I made to him. It's the promise I made to her: that I wouldn't ever let her dad hurt her. If I go away, I can't keep that promise.

There'll be other opportunities, I tell myself, other shots at becoming a pilot, even though I know I'm kissing this one good-bye for good. But really, it's nothing compared to knowing Zoey is safe. If I left, even if we agreed to try the long-distance thing, I wouldn't ever be able to relax. I'd constantly be thinking about her and worrying. I'd be worrying even if we weren't together. So there's really only one option; there's only ever been one option, and that's to stay.

"Tristan," Walker says, "did you bait your line?"

"Huh?" I ask, blinking at him, dazed.

"You're not getting bites because you didn't bait your line."

I stare at him for a few seconds before I figure out what he's talking about. "Oh," I say.

"You okay?" Walker asks.

"Yeah, I'm fine."

He squints at me. Walker's got a nose for things, an alert to nuance and tone that others don't see, and can always tell when someone's not being truthful. He has a wisdom beyond his years that I appreciate as much as I do Kit's humor and devotion to the people he loves and Will's quiet resoluteness. I'm lucky to have such friends. I decide to be honest. "Zoey broke up with me," I tell him, "because she found out I got into pilot school in Florida."

"What?" Kit asks, lurching around to face me and almost upending the cooler of beer beside him.

"You're moving to Florida?" Walker asks, surprised.

"No, I'm not going," I say, shaking my head. "I can't. I can't leave her here. And she can't leave her family. So . . . I have to make a choice."

They both take that in, sharing a glance. They know how

much I've wanted this, how long I've been waiting on a spot to open up at pilot school. I shrug. It's easy enough to give it up when I weigh it against losing Zoey.

Kit digs around in the melting ice and pulls out a beer. He pops the cap and hands it to me. "Stupidest thing I ever did was walking away from Jessa," he says. "Straight-up almost lost her because of it."

"Same with me and Didi," Walker adds, kicking his feet up onto the railing and adjusting his cap. They get it. And their understanding does something to ease the ache of giving up a dream I've nurtured and held on to since boyhood.

Life's a series of choices, I guess. We set goals, dream dreams, make plans, but sometimes something comes along unexpected and knocks us off one path and onto a different one. The new path might be good, but it doesn't mean you can't regret the view you'll miss seeing from the other path. Staying here in Oceanside doesn't mean giving anything up, not really. I can live with not becoming a pilot. I can't live without Zoey.

# ZOEY

can't wait to tell Tristan I'm coming with him. Now that I've made the decision, it's all I can think about. It's not forever, and all the fears I had about losing friends and not being there for my family are things I can deal with. I can deal with anything so long as I'm with Tristan. Also, If I'm in Florida, I'll be even farther away from my dad, and as I'm the one he's angry at, I'll make it safer for my mom and the others by moving. I tell myself this, but I might just be fooling myself.

I sneak away from the girls when everyone is getting massages and try to call him, but of course his phone is off. He's sailing and out of cell phone range. I almost leave him a message, but I don't because what I want to say needs to be done in person, face-to-face. After I hang up, though, I call my mom and explain to her that Tristan has been accepted to pilot school in Florida. "Do you love him?" she asks.

"Yes," I say, feeling the truth of it all the way to my bones.

"Did he ask you to go with him?"

"Yes."

"Then you should go," my mom says.

"But—"

"No buts!" She cuts me off. "I mean it, Zoey. I know you're young, but you need to follow your heart." It's not what I expected to hear. I thought when I told her my decision she'd caution me to not rush in, advise me to follow my head and not my heart, to not make the same mistake she did: following a man offering her escape. But she doesn't. "He makes you happy, and you deserve happiness," she says.

"But what about you?" I ask.

She laughs gently. "Stop worrying about me, Zoey. I'm fine. And we'll manage. We'll miss you, of course, but we'll be fine."

Will they? Is she just saying that to make it easier on me? I don't know what to believe.

"I'll be fine," she says again, as though hearing my silent concerns.

"What about Dad?" I whisper, giving voice to my greatest fear, the thing we try never to talk about.

There's silence on the other end of the phone. "Let's not talk about him, okay? We can't let him dictate our lives anymore. I want you to go. And I want you to live your life and have adventures and no regrets."

"I can start college there," I say wistfully. "I'll need to find another job."

"You will," my mom says. "You'll be fine. And if you're not, you can always come home."

"Mom," I say, my voice thickening with emotion. "I love you."

"I love you too," she says, and I hear the tears in her voice.

"I'll see you soon," I say.

I hang up and wipe away a tear. It's going to be so hard to leave them, but my mom is right. I can't let my dad dictate my life anymore. I need to set myself free. And I do want to follow my heart. And my heart belongs to Tristan.

# TRISTAN

A half mile from shore, I get reception and check my voice mail. There's nothing from Zoey, and disappointment sinks its claws into me. I'd hoped she might have left a message, and her silence hurts. My shoulders sag for a moment before the phone buzzes in my hand.

But it isn't Zoey. It's a security camera sending me a text alert. It does it every time it detects motion outside Zoey's front door. It happens at least a dozen times a day. Usually, it's Zoey's mom or Zoey entering or leaving the house, but this time when I hit play I see a shadowy male figure move in front of the camera. My pulse leaps. Is it Robert? No. He's too tall, too broad to be Robert. The video is grainy, and I can't see the guy's face because he's wearing a trucker hat, pulled low. Maybe it's a deliveryman, but he's not wearing a uniform. Or maybe it's her dad.

With a shaking hand, I open the app and hit the button on the camera, pulling up the live feed. It takes a while to load, though, and when it does, the man is nowhere in sight. I rotate the camera and catch a glimpse of an arm in the corner of the frame. What's he doing? I check the time. Almost seven. Is Zoey home already? Is her mom?

I switch to another camera—one I installed on the lamppost right beside where I park my bike. I put it there after I got my bike fixed at exorbitant expense thanks to the concrete mix he poured in the gas tank. This camera gives me an angle on the bottom of the stairs leading to Zoey's apartment and a stretch of the parking lot. There's no delivery van in sight.

I catch movement in the corner of the frame. It's a car—Zoey's car. I watch the silver RAV4 pull into the spot beside my bike, and a few seconds later I watch her and Kate get out. Shit, I think to myself. What do I do? Where's the man disappeared to?

I hit the button on my phone to switch camera views back to the one by the door and get a full-face view of him. He's standing right in front of the camera, which is hidden in a hanging basket of flowers Zoey's mom planted.

Panic pounds loudly through me. It's Zoey's dad. I'd recognize him anywhere, even though the years in prison have filled him out and hardened him. My heart stops in my chest. He looks down at the parking lot—he must have seen Zoey and Kate—and then he ducks out of sight. Where's he going? There's a long balcony running the length of the condo—has he run to the other end of it and down the far stairs, or is he waiting to jump them? I need to warn Zoey. Frantic, I turn to Kit. "Give me your phone," I shout.

He turns, startled, but pulls out his phone without a word. He's an ex-soldier. He knows from my tone I'm not messing around, and his reactions are fast and unquestioning. "Call Zoey!" I yell at him. "Get her on the phone."

"What's going on?" Jessa's dad whispers as Kit and Walker press in around me to see.

"I saw her dad," I say, staring at the feed on my phone, willing him to appear. "Is it ringing?" I ask Kit.

He shakes his head, then hands it to me. I press it to my ear using my free hand. "Come on," I say as it rings and rings. "Why isn't she picking up? Where is she?"

I flip to the other camera feed on my phone, still holding Kit's phone to my ear. She and Kate are nowhere in sight. Where did they go? "They were right there," I say, confused.

"Shall I call the police?" Walker asks.

"Yes. Give them the address. Tell them they're in danger. A domestic violence situation. Tell them the suspect is likely armed."

"Is he?" Kit's dad asks.

"It'll make them take it seriously," I answer, my nerves stretched taut. Who knows if he actually is armed?

Suddenly, Zoey and Kate appear in the line of sight of the camera, walking past my bike. They must have gone to my place first, I realize. Why isn't Zoey answering her phone? Can't she hear it ringing? "Pick up!" I hiss.

I watch as Zoey and Kate start walking up the stairs to their condo. I want to reach out and grab them both, stop them from climbing the stairs, where their dad is waiting for them, but all I can do is watch helplessly, frustrated, listening to Walker behind me speaking to a police dispatcher. He's struggling to make himself understood, and time is running out. It's like watching a horror movie in slow motion.

I need to do something, but when I stare around me, all I see is ocean. We're a half mile from shore. Goddamn it. My eyes fly back to the screen.

Zoey and Kate have disappeared from sight.

# ZOEY

can't believe how cool Emma is. She said I can come over any-
time, and she even gave me her number!" Kate shoves her
phone under my nose to prove it.

"I know," I say, laughing, "you already told me this fifty times."

"When people at school see this photo of me and Emma,
they're not going to believe it," Kate says, showing me the photo
of her and Emma in matching pink robes, which she's now made
her lock screen image.

We reach the door, and Kate dramatically falls against it.
"That was the best day of my life." Her phone suddenly rings.
She answers it as I fish the keys out of my bag. My mom and
Cole are out—she's taken him for pizza. I glance up at the camera, hidden in the flower basket, its dark eye peering out at us,
and wonder if Tristan is watching me, having been alerted by
text message.

"Yes, she's with me," Kate says. "Do you want to talk to
her?" She turns to me, offering the phone. "It's Tristan," she
says. "I think he wants to talk to you, but I can't hear him. He's
breaking up."

I take the phone, confused. Why's he calling Kate? Then I remember my phone is in the car, where I forgot it. "Hello?" I say as Kate starts to open the door.

"Get out of there!"

"What?"

"Your dad's there. I saw him on the camera. Get out of there! Now!"

I grab Kate's hand just as she's opening the door and yank her away. She lets out a gasp of surprise and a yelp as I drag her to the stairs. "What's happening?" she says, her voice halfway between fear and laughter.

"Move!" I say, pushing her down the stairs, tripping over myself in my hurry to get away.

"What is it?" Kate cries as I keep my hands on her back and force her to move faster.

"Dad," I say, breathless. Kate pauses for a fraction of a second, then takes the stairs three at a time. I'm right behind her, not even daring to glance back. He was here. He's still here. We run to the car. I fumble for my keys. Kate pulls on the door handle to the car, trying anxiously to get it open.

"Hurry!" she says.

I can't find the keys.

"Come on!" Kate yells. Then her voice drops to a whisper. "Oh my God," she sobs.

I feel a chill up my spine. A voice in my head tells me not to turn around. My hand keeps scouring my bag, frantically looking for the keys. Panic makes me shake from head to toe. A sob is rising up my throat.

*Run*, I think to myself. *Get Kate and run.* I turn, but before I can take a step, a shadow falls over me. My way is blocked. I look up.

"Hello, Zoey," my dad says.

All the air inside me leaves in one massive exhalation that turns my legs to Jell-O. "What do you want?" I ask, feeling Kate grip my hand.

My dad smiles at me. He looks old, like someone has etched lines in his skin with a scalpel. His hair is longer than I've ever seen it and showing strands of gray. He's still a good-looking man, imposing, and bigger than I remember him. He was intimidating before, but now he's even more so. Prison hasn't whittled him; it's sharpened him.

"How did you find us?" I ask.

He smiles, and I notice his front tooth is chipped and that he has a scar down the side of one cheek that I'd mistaken for a crease. "Never you mind," he says, his eye glinting with amusement.

He nods at the house. "Nice place."

Kate whimpers behind me.

"Hey, Katie," my dad says. "Look at you, all grown-up. No hi for your dad?"

I hear Kate make a sound—something between a grunt and a whimper. Her hand squeezes mine so hard, I feel the bones crunch.

"You wearing makeup now?" he asks Katie, seeming amused, though his eyes harden.

She doesn't answer, and I tense, aware I'm using my body to block his view of her, trying even now, after all these years, to protect her, just like I did when she was little.

How can I keep him calm? His eyes have a wild intenseness to them, and so similar in color to Cole's. It's disconcerting.

"Should you be here?" I ask, phrasing it as a question, trying to keep my tone light and nonaccusatory so as not to spark him into a rage.

"Your mom home?" he asks, his gaze turning to the house.

I shake my head, praying she doesn't choose now to arrive home with Cole.

"Is she out on a date with that *man*?" my dad asks, practically spitting the word.

"Mom's not home," I say to him quietly, wondering if he means Robert. "And you're not supposed to be here."

"Not supposed to be here," he repeats, smirking. "I'll be wherever the hell I like," he hisses.

I flinch backward, bumping into Kate, who whimpers.

"You're breaking the law being here," I tell him, keeping my voice as even as I can. "You could get arrested." I try to act like I'm concerned for his welfare. Whatever I do, I can't show fear. Fear is what he feeds on. I remember how Mom's terror excited him, made him even crueler. All I need to do is keep him here long enough for the cops to arrive. Tristan must have called them. They must be on their way. They'll arrest him. He'll go back to prison for at least the remainder of his sentence, possibly longer.

"Who's going to tell?" he says, eyeing me with so much menace that my whole body starts to shake. "You?"

I swallow dryly, trying not to glance at the street. How long would it take for the cops to respond? The time he beat my mom so bad he almost killed her, it took forever, the seconds stretching into lifetimes.

"They won't believe you," he goes on, starting to smile, though the smile never reaches his eyes. "I've got a friend who'll vouch for me, say I was with him all day. It'll be my word against yours."

"They believed me last time," I say.

I'm not sure why I spoke the words out loud. One moment they were in my head, and then I heard myself speaking them. Am I a total idiot, antagonizing him like that? Maybe I want him to react because if I can get him to react, get him to hit me, they'll charge him with assault. It would be worth it to have him hurt me if it meant it would keep him away from us for longer.

"They will believe me," I say, defiantly lifting my chin. "You're not supposed to be here. You're not allowed to come anywhere near us. We don't *want* you anywhere near us. We hate you."

My dad raises his arm so fast it's a blur. I bring one arm up instinctively to block the blow, the muscle memory from all the sessions with Tristan kicking in, but his fist doesn't make contact. It remains level with my face for a few seconds before he drops it. I'm breathing hard, aware that Kate is crying behind me, and he smiles, happy to have frightened me.

"You tell your mom I came by to see her," he says, and makes to turn away.

"Why?" I ask, throwing the question at him in an attempt to stop him from leaving, willing the cops to arrive. "Why can't you leave us alone?" I ask.

"You put me in prison," my dad says, turning back toward me. "Your lies took away three years of my life."

I didn't send him to prison, I think to myself; his own actions sent him there.

"You know what they do to cops in prison?" he continues before I can point this out to him.

Whatever they did to him in prison, whatever he suffered, was just a fraction of what he deserved. Any sympathy I might have vanishes when I remember the crack of my mom's cheekbone as it shattered, the wet smack of her head against the banister, the terror he put us through.

"Leave us alone."

It's Kate who says it. Her voice trembles, but she spits the words at him.

He looks at her, half-amused and half-saddened. "Oh, Katie, what have your mother and your sister been telling you? Whatever it is, it isn't the truth. They're lying to you. Poisoning you and Cole against me. Your mom was having an affair. I got upset. It was that one time I lost my temper, and your mom was to blame. She was threatening to take you kids away from me. I didn't mean to hurt her. I love her. And you. Don't you want to hear my side of the story, Kate? Don't you want to have your dad back in your life?"

Kate's mouth falls open. She doesn't answer. Oh God, is she buying it?

"We don't want you back in our lives," Kate says, her eyes flashing with fury. "You're a liar, and I hate you, and I never want to see you again."

My dad's face contorts. I move to block Kate, knowing that a blow is coming. My dad's gaze whips to me. "You—you bitch," he says. "You turned them all against me with your lies."

His hand is suddenly circling my wrist. He yanks me toward him, but instinctively I react the way Tristan taught me in our self-defense classes, twisting my arm, gaining my freedom in a move so fast it surprises my dad. He lunges for me, and I scream and shout at him to back off. I manage to smash him in the nose with the heel of my hand, and he grunts as blood sprays. But he somehow gets a grip on my wrist and starts to yank. I lose my footing. He drags me forward, away from Kate, who follows, hanging on to my other arm, screaming at him to let me go. I feel like I'm being ripped in two.

Just then, the wail of a cop car siren cuts through Kate's screams. My dad lets go, and Kate pulls me away. The cop car screeches into the parking lot, its blue and red lights swirling, as my dad takes off toward the back of the condos. Two cops exit the car and race after him.

Shaking, Kate and I huddle against the car, holding each other tight. "It's going to be okay," I whisper to her as she sobs.

# TRISTAN

'm running down the dock at a sprint, bag slung over my shoulder, phone pressed to my ear, panic fueling me, when she finally picks up. "Zoey?" I shout into the phone at the sound of her voice. "Are you okay?"

"Yes," she whispers.

I'm so relieved, I almost collapse to my knees. "Jesus, I thought . . ." I trail off, fighting back tears. "I saw you on camera. Saw him grab you . . ." I relive that moment, watching her dad accost her and Kate by the car, the awful powerlessness of not being able to intervene, of having to watch him raise his fist to her, the utter terror and frustration of not being able to do anything. I've never felt so useless in my life. "I didn't know what had happened."

"The cops arrived. They caught him. He's been arrested."

I cover my eyes, feeling a welling of emotion from deep inside, a wave that feels like it might burst up and out of me. For the last twenty-five minutes I've been living with the fear that something had happened to her, something bad. I couldn't get through to her or Kate; neither was picking up.

I feel a hand on my shoulder and whip around. It's Kit. Behind him are Walker and the others. *She's okay*, I mouth to them, and see the relief spread across their faces. "I'll be there in ten minutes," I tell Zoey.

"Okay," she says, her voice so soft I almost can't hear it. Then she hangs up.

I stare at the phone for a few seconds. Did it sound like she wanted me there? In all the panic and confusion and fear, I'd forgotten our earlier conversation, our breakup. Either way, though, I don't care. I need to see her.

"What happened?" Walker asks.

"They arrested him," I say.

"Thank God," Kit's father says. He pats me on the shoulder.

"Why you still standing here?" Kit asks, staring at me like I'm a lunatic and pressing his car keys into my hand. "Go!"

For a dazed second, I stare at him, and then I turn and run.

# ZOEY

My mom arrives home with Robert and Cole just as Kate finishes giving her statement to the police and ten minutes after they took my dad away in the back of a patrol car.

"What's going on?" she asks in a trembling voice, clutching Cole to her side. Robert comes around the car quickly and walks toward us.

"Officers," he says, nodding at the police officers. "What happened?" He looks at me and Kate. "Girls, are you okay?"

We both nod. My mom rushes over to us, pulls us into her arms. "He was here?" she asks, looking in terror between us and the cops.

I nod. "Tristan saw him on the security cameras and called the cops."

"Who was here?"

We both turn around. Cole is standing a few feet away, staring at us. "Was Dad here?" he asks.

I break away from Mom and approach him. "Yes," I tell him.

"Where is he now?" Cole asks, looking around, his face

lighting up with hope before he frowns in confusion at the sight of the cop car and the police officers.

"They arrested him, Cole," I say.

"What?" he shouts. "Why?"

"Because he shouldn't be here. He's not allowed to be. He broke the law."

"Why?" Cole asks again angrily. "How's that breaking the law? He just wanted to see us."

I narrow my eyes at him. How does he know that?

"You got him arrested!" Cole shouts, stepping away from me, his face scrunching up in fury. "It's your fault. He didn't do anything."

"Cole," my mom says weakly.

"I hate you!" Cole says, his eyes flashing so angrily they remind me of my dad's and make me flinch backward.

"That's not fair—" I say as Cole starts running up the stairs to the apartment.

I watch him go. He's right on the one hand. I did get Dad arrested and sent back to jail. I'm not going to be sorry for it, though. I just wish Cole understood the reasons.

My mom slips her hand into mine. "He doesn't mean it."

Robert puts an arm around my shoulder. "How are you doing?" he asks.

I nod, unsure what to say.

"The police say he'll be held overnight and arraigned in the morning." He glances with concern at my mom. "Let's go inside, make a cup of tea."

My mom lets Robert lead her upstairs, his hand in hers. I stand and watch them and Kate, feeling a strange light-headedness overcome me as Robert ushers them inside. A bubble of laughter rises up. I struggle for a moment to figure out what it is I'm feeling—shock, maybe? No. It hits me finally with a jolt. It's not shock. It's relief. I'm free. My dad is going back to jail. I don't have to be afraid anymore. I don't have to worry. At least, not for a few years. And my mom has someone who obviously cares about her. I won't be abandoning her. I laugh out loud.

"Zoey?"

I look up. It's my mom, standing by the door to our apartment. She's beckoning me up the stairs. "Are you coming?" she asks.

# TRISTAN

tear into the parking lot in Walker's Jeep, throwing it into the only available spot before jumping out and racing toward the stairs to Zoey's apartment.

I'm halfway up when I hear her call my name. I spin around and see her. She's standing in the doorway to my apartment. Seeing her is like seeing land after being lost at sea for months. It's relief and wonder all rolled into one. I leap down the steps three at a time, not taking my eyes off her.

As I get closer, I slow down because I don't know what to say. I don't know where we stand. I thought I did, but now, seeing her there, looking so unsure and unsmiling, I'm on guard again. But then she takes a step toward me, saying my name and reaching for me. The next thing I know, I'm pulling her into my arms, feeling her fingers digging into my back as she clutches me so tight her body is pressed into mine, as though she's trying to burrow into me.

I can feel her shaking in my arms, and when she lifts her tear-stained face to mine, I kiss her before she can get a chance to say a word. She kisses me back, trying to talk between kisses, saying my name, saying sorry, saying words I don't hear because all

I want to do is run my hands over her, make her stop shaking, let her know I'm not going anywhere, ever. I don't know what I would have done if something had happened to her, and that thought makes me want to hold on to her and never let her go.

We tumble back through the door into my apartment, tangled in each other's arms. I kick the door shut with my foot, and Zoey pulls me back with her onto the sofa, kicking off her shoes as she goes, tearing at my shirt and my pants as I do the same to her dress, until we're both breathless and naked and she's pulling me inside her. "I love you," I tell her, kissing her, needing her in a way that feels desperate and out of control. But when I try to slow down and pull back, she locks her legs around me, clings to me tighter, her mouth on mine, swallowing my words.

"I thought I'd lost you," I murmur against her lips.

She shakes her head, strokes my face.

"I can't lose you," I tell her.

She pulls me in even closer, deeper, holding me there so I can't move. "You're not going to," she whispers.

"I'm not going anywhere," I tell her, holding my weight above her on my arms and looking down on her. She's still shaking, her eyes welling. "I'm staying right here," I tell her, wanting to reassure her.

"No," she says, shaking her head at me.

I nod. "Yes."

"No," she argues. "I'm coming with you. We're going to Florida."

I stare at her. "What?"

She nods, and before I can respond, she pulls me back down, my full weight on top of her. I can't process anything more than her last words. We're going to Florida.

But then all thoughts flee from my mind until all that's left is *right now*.

# ZOEY

do."

There is not a dry eye in the house, except for the ring bearer's—Jessa's nephew, little Riley Jr., who pulls a face when Kit's dad, officiating the ceremony, tells his son he can kiss the bride. Kit pulls Jessa into his arms, lifts her veil, and kisses her to everyone's delight, except little Riley's, who says a resoundingly loud "Yuck."

We all laugh and cheer. I turn to Tristan, and he pulls me into his side and kisses me on the lips. For some reason, ever since Tristan and I got back together, I haven't been able to keep my hands off him. And it's not like I had an easy time of it before. Every single second I'm with him or even close to him, I feel an ache deep inside me, one that often needs to be filled there and then. And he's been more than happy to oblige. Every night we fall asleep in each other's arms, only to wake again an hour or so later, reaching for each other, and then again, before dawn.

It's not a hunger, because hunger can be satiated. It's a need. I think it's because I'm no longer afraid. With my dad locked up until he can be tried on further charges of assault, I feel for the first time fully free of fear. The shackles are gone and I'm making up for lost time.

I'm smiling all the time too, as are Kate and my mom. It's only Cole who acts surly and angry, even more so than before. With Robert at her side, my mom is more able to handle Cole, but still, he blames me. He calls me a liar, refuses to talk to me, and mutters under his breath when I try to talk to him. It hurts, but Tristan says he'll get over it in time, when he's older and can understand the truth. I still wonder how my dad was able to communicate with him and fill his head with so many lies. Cole refuses to say, but I'm hoping now that Dad's in prison it will stop. I'm also talking to Didi about arranging some therapy for him.

Kit finally breaks away from kissing Jessa, and they turn to the assembled guests. Behind them, the Pacific glitters like a million diamonds have been sprinkled on its surface. None of them could outshine Jessa, though, who looks like a Pre-Raphaelite painting, her long hair hanging loose in waves, her dress a beautiful, romantic lace-and-silk creation.

Kit shakes hands with guests who rush to congratulate them, while refusing to relinquish his grip on Jessa with his other hand. He beams with pride, glancing every few seconds at his bride, as though he can't quite believe she's real.

Behind them, Didi and Jo, Jessa's sister-in-law, are dressed in dusky pink bridesmaid dresses. Didi wipes away a tear, and I see Walker, Kit's best man, squeeze her waist and whisper something in her ear, which makes her gasp and press a hand to her heart.

I wonder if they'll be next. I look at Tristan, and even though we're way too young to talk of marriage and there are so many things to do first—graduate college and start and finish pilot school, for a start—I know that there's a chance that one day it will be us. I can see it, silly as that might seem. There's a deep sense of knowing that this is it, that we belong together. I've heard people talk before of soul mates, usually in books, and I never believed it was real. Love for me always seemed dangerous, but now I know it doesn't have to be that way at all.

We take our seats at white-linen-covered tables set under flower-strewn pergolas dangling with fairy lights. As the sun sets into the sea and the band plays, we eat until we are stuffed and drink until the laughter can probably be heard all the way in Malibu. I lean back into Tristan's arms, looking around the table at all our friends, and feel like the luckiest person alive.

"Are you all packed?" Dahlia asks us as we toast the happy couple.

"Yes," I tell her. I was packed days ago. I can't wait to leave, to finally head off into the horizon. There's freedom beyond it.

After Kit's speech, when he calls Jessa his North Star and reduces everyone to tears by mentioning Riley, Jessa's brother, and how much they all miss him and wish he were here, they cut the cake, and the party gets into full swing. Tristan pulls me to my feet and leads me to the dance floor. I'm self-conscious at first, but soon the dance floor is crowded and the joy is infectious, and I kick off my shoes and throw back my head and decide to let go. Dancing is a lot like sex, I think to myself: the less you're inhibited, the better it feels. Tristan, it turns out, is a great dancer, which shouldn't surprise me when I think about how good he is in bed.

He has pulled off his tie and undone the first three buttons of his shirt, and by the time a slow song comes on and he reaches for me, we're both slick with sweat. As soon as I'm in his arms, I start thinking about getting somewhere private, somewhere we can be alone, and he does too, because he bends his head and nuzzles my neck and whispers in my ear, "Want to get out of here?"

I nod, catching the glint in his eye, his desire fueling my own. And suddenly the need becomes urgent. I start pulling him off the dance floor. It's past midnight. Jessa and Kit have slipped away, heading off on their honeymoon. Walker and Didi are dancing in each other's arms, Didi still clutching the bouquet she caught earlier.

I spot Dahlia and Emma sitting under a bower of flowers, heads pressed together, taking a photo, and I smile. Dahlia waves at us and blows a kiss in our direction.

Tristan leads me to my car, walking at a fast clip. He offers to drive and we jump inside. He starts the engine, then pauses. It's a thirty-minute drive home, and I know he's wondering if he can wait that long. I lean back against the door and bite my lip. His gaze falls to my body, becomes glassy with desire. "God, I want you," he whispers.

"Drive," I tell him.

He puts the car in gear with a sigh. The wedding venue is a private estate on a bluff over the ocean, and once we're through the gates and onto the road, there's not a single car for miles. It's a straight run, and Tristan drives at seventy—not too fast but fast enough. We're both in a hurry to get home.

"Shit," Tristan murmurs.

"What?" I ask.

"There's some guy riding my ass," he says, frowning as he looks in the rearview mirror.

I turn around. He's right: there's a maroon-colored truck right on our bumper, practically on top of us.

"What's he playing at?" I ask, my heart beating fast and adrenaline flooding my system.

The road is empty. If he wanted to overtake us, there's nothing stopping him. "Why don't you pull over?" I say to Tristan.

Tristan's slowing down, trying to move to one side to let him pass. "He's driving like an idiot," he mumbles.

"Pull over," I say again, feeling my anxiety build. "Let him pass."

Tristan moves his hand to the indicator, but before he can press it, we lurch forward violently as the truck rear-ends us. There's a screeching, grinding sound of twisting metal and smashing glass.

"Oh my God!" I scream, and grab for Tristan across the divider.

"Shit!" he yells, stamping on the gas, trying to put distance between us and the truck.

I turn around. The truck is on our tail, matching our acceleration, its bumper touching ours. "What's he doing?!" I shout in terror.

In answer, the truck rams us again. We swerve across the road, and Tristan struggles to right the car.

It's my dad. The thought launches itself into my head with as much force as the truck ramming us. It has to be him. Who else would do this? I turn around in my seat and try to see out the window, but the dazzling glare of the truck's headlights blinds me. "He's still coming!" I cry as the headlights fill my vision.

Tristan speeds up and manages to put us ahead of the truck. Tears streaming down my face, I scramble in my bag for my phone.

Tristan's gaze locks on the rearview mirror. "Shit," he says.

I look in the side mirror and see the truck roaring up behind us. I dial 911, my fingers shaking, but before I can press call, the phone goes flying out of my hands as we lift up in the air. The grinding crunch of metal fills my ears, along with my own screams.

I clutch at the door and the seat in terror as we spin across the road, and all I'm aware of is Tristan yelling at me to hold on, struggling to keep control of the wheel. As he fights to stay on the road, the truck slams into us one more time. We spin across two lanes, down a ditch, and the last thing I see is Tristan wrenching the wheel hard to the right before we slam into a tree.

For a while, all I can register is the tink-tink-tink of the engine and then the fact I'm lying at a slight angle. The car has come to a rest on a slope. The front windshield is smashed. In the distance, through the cracked glass, I see the lights of the truck disappearing over the horizon. Thank God.

I turn to Tristan. "He's gone," I say, a sob bursting out of me.

He doesn't answer. I reach for him, feeling a twinge and a stiffness in my neck. I must have pulled a muscle or gotten whiplash from the crash, but I ignore it and reach over to shake Tristan's arm. "Tristan?"

He groans. His side of the car took the brunt of the crash. He turned the wheel deliberately, I realize, so he'd be on the side that hit the tree. His window is smashed and the door of the car crumpled.

"Are you okay?" I ask him, starting to panic.

He grunts, then turns to me, his face a grimace. "Are *you* okay?" he asks.

"I'm fine, I'm fine," I say. "I think it was my dad."

"Yeah," Tristan says quietly.

The thin sliver of moonlight coming through the shattered

windshield bathes him in a milky glow, but I can make out a gash on his forehead that's spilling blood down the side of his face. He wipes at it with his sleeve and then looks at it in surprise before touching his fingers to his head and wincing. He then notices something wrong with his other arm. I follow his gaze. His whole shirt is soaked through, the blue cotton now a deep purple color, sticking to his skin.

"Oh my God," I say, staring in horror at the blood. A shard of glass from the window or a piece of metal from the door has slashed his arm by the looks of things. Tristan looks too, then swallows. "It's fine," he says unconvincingly.

I stare at him before frantically searching for my phone and am on the verge of hysteria by the time I finally find it under my seat. When I try to dial 911, nothing happens. "There's no reception!" I cry in a panic.

Tristan has his head shoved into the back of the headrest and is breathing deeply through gritted teeth.

"We need to get to the hospital," I say, but how? The road is deserted.

"You need to help me stop the bleeding," Tristan says.

I turn my attention to his arm, ignoring the wave of dizziness I feel.

"Do you have a scarf or something we can use as a tourniquet?"

I shake my head.

"Use my belt," Tristan says.

With shaking hands, I struggle to get it out of his belt loops. As I fight with it, Tristan starts talking. "A man's in a car accident, and he really hurts his arm."

I glance his way, wondering if he's lost so much blood he's

turning delirious. He's gritting his teeth against the pain and is pale beneath the blood smearing his face, but he seems alert. "And the doctors take him into surgery," he goes on, "and they tell his wife they'll do their best."

I realize he's telling a joke, and I laugh despite myself because the circumstances are so terrible, but I also know that he's trying to distract himself from the pain by making me smile.

"He gets out of surgery, and the doctors go and speak to the wife and they say, 'Good news. We managed to save his arm.'"

I'm finally able to tug the belt through the final loop and free it.

"'Bad news,'" Tristan continues through gritted teeth. "'We didn't manage to save the rest of him.'"

"That's not funny," I say, crouching almost on top of him in order to tie the belt around his arm.

He grimaces at me. "You're laughing," he says.

I'm actually crying, but I don't point that out to him. "Tell me what to do," I say as I loop the belt and pull, trying not to focus on the blood soaking his shirt. There's so much of it, my hands are sticky.

"Tighter," Tristan tells me. "Tight as you can go."

"I don't want to hurt you," I tell him, almost sobbing.

"Well, then don't break up with me ever again," he says.

"Stop joking," I half sob, half laugh. I finish tying the belt. What now? We can't stay here. He needs to get to the hospital. "Do you think the car will start?" I ask Tristan.

Tristan reaches with his good hand and turns the key. The engine growls. "Yeah. The engine's fine."

"You turned the car," I say, "so you'd take the brunt of it."

He nods. "Don't say I'm not a gentleman." He tries to smile, but he's gritting his teeth too hard, and it comes out as a grimace.

"I'm going to climb over you," I tell him. I scoot over onto his lap, and then he shunts himself over the gear stick into the passenger seat with some difficulty, even though I help him as much as I can.

I put the car in reverse and press the gas, but the wheels just kick up dirt, and we don't move.

"Try again," Tristan grunts.

I nod and then try again, this time gunning it as hard as I can. The car lurches backward up the slope with a screeching sound as the side scrapes along the stand of trees.

Once on the road, I floor it, one hand gripping Tristan's, trying to will him to stay alert and awake. I talk to him, but he's drifting in and out, and when I ask him to tell me another joke, he doesn't answer.

"Tristan!" I shout as his eyelids flutter. "Stay awake!"

His eyes snap open, but he stares at me glassily, as though he doesn't recognize me.

"You told me you weren't going to leave me ever. You promised." I sob the words, and Tristan seems to hear them as his eyes fly open again and this time they fix on me. He sees me. Focuses on me hard, his breathing coming short and fast. I hold his gaze, willing him not to succumb as I grip his hand and force him to stay awake.

Finally, I pull off the highway and drive to the nearest hospital, swerving up to the ER.

"We're here," I say. "It's going to be okay." But when I look at him, his eyes are closed and he's gone.

# TRISTAN

Darkness presses in on me as though I'm sinking underwater, dark cold water. I feel Zoey's hand grip mine and pull me back.

"Stay awake," Zoey says. "Stay with me."

I force my eyes open and smile at her. She looks so beautiful. I want to tell her how beautiful. She strokes my face. I try to speak, but my mouth won't work. It's as if my tongue is numb. My eyes start to droop again, my vision blurring.

"Tristan," someone says sharply. Not Zoey. He shouts something else, too, but I can't make out the words.

I can feel a coldness leaching up my arm as though it's being dunked in dry ice. It flows up my arm, moving snakelike toward my throat.

"Zo," I start to say.

She leans over me, tears glittering at the corner of her eyes. Why's she crying?

"Tristan!" she sobs.

I try to reassure her I'm going to be okay, but then the darkness lunges up like a monster yawning and swallows me whole.

# ZOEY

The doctors whisk Tristan away on the gurney, submerged in a tide of white coats, racing along beside him through the doors and into the ER.

I try to follow, but I'm not allowed past a set of double doors, so instead I turn and give my details to the receptionist, then take a seat in the waiting room. I call Dahlia, who picks up and immediately jumps into action, telling me she'll call their parents and be there within the hour, and then I call my mom, who doesn't answer. Neither does Kate. Feeling anxious, unable to shake the sense of something terrible having happened to them, I text Robert. Next, I call the cops to report what's happened, even though I have no confidence they'll care or even do anything. They say they'll send someone to take a statement from me at the hospital.

I still don't understand how my dad isn't in jail. He broke the terms of his parole. The cops arrested him outside our apartment. Did they let him go and just not tell us?

I know it was him who set my car on fire—it had to be—and I know it was him who tried to run us off the road and who's done this to Tristan, but I can't prove it. They'll never put him in prison. He'll be out forever, hunting me down wherever I go.

As I dwell on this, a man and a woman walk over and stop in front of me. "Zoey?" one asks.

I nod, gripping the sides of the seat. The woman flashes something in front of my face. A police badge. "Detective Roper," she says. "This is my partner, Detective Fredericks."

They sent detectives? I was expecting someone in uniform. "Are you here to take my statement?" I ask. "Because I think it was my dad who ran us off the road. Is he out of prison?"

They glance at each other. "Yes," Detective Fredericks answers. "They tightened his parole, but he wasn't required to serve more time."

If I weren't sitting, I think I'd fall to the floor. It was him. I thought I'd been certain, but it isn't until I hear it from their lips that I fully accept it was him.

"Perhaps we can go somewhere more quiet?" the female detective says.

I gesture at the ER. "I can't leave. I need to be here. My boyfriend's in surgery."

"We know," the woman, Detective Roper, says. She's about forty, with short black hair and kind eyes.

"We need to talk to you urgently," her partner says, and something about his tone and his expression pulls me up short, chills my blood.

"What is it?" I ask, looking between them.

"Let's find somewhere quiet to chat," the woman says, giving me a smile. It's a fake smile.

I follow them through endless white corridors, our heels squeaking on the linoleum tile, my mind blank. Something terrible has happened to my mom, or to Kate and Cole. I know it in the depths of my being. Why else would they be here? Why else would they need to talk to me? My feet drag, the voice in my head urging me to turn and run, run as fast as I can so I don't have to hear whatever it is they are about to tell me.

Somehow, though, I keep following them, and then somehow again I find myself in a room with brown carpeted floors, a sagging sofa, and a watercolor of sunflowers on the wall. I'm on the sofa, unsure how I sat down, and the two detectives are sitting opposite me, wearing expressions I can already read.

"Has he hurt my mom?" I hear myself ask.

Detective Roper takes a breath, pauses, and in that pause I live a million lifetimes.

"He tried," she says, reaching across the table to take my hand.

"What?" I gasp, looking between them. What does that mean? I can't breathe; I can't think. The walls are closing in. Someone presses something into my hand. A plastic cup of water. They urge me to take a sip. I do. It rushes cold down my throat and settles me. I bow my head over my lap and take several deep breaths, trying to process everything, but nothing makes sense.

Detective Roper is sitting beside me with her arm around me, and a nurse has appeared out of nowhere and sits on the other side, holding the cup of water.

"What did he do?" I finally think to ask.

"We think he tampered with the water heater. They were poisoned with carbon monoxide. Your mother's boyfriend found them. Your mom was meant to meet up with him and didn't show, so he went to the apartment. When he couldn't get an answer, he broke the door down. They were lucky they were found when they were."

"Are they going to be okay?" I ask.

"Yes, but they need to stay overnight."

I take that in. Tristan. My mom. Kate. Then I remember Cole. I look up in alarm. "Cole," I say. "Where's my brother?"

The detectives exchange a look. They've clearly been anticipating this question. "We can't find him."

I look between them in disbelief. "What?" I ask dully. "What do you mean?"

"He wasn't there when Robert found your mom and sister. His room was empty."

"Where is he?" I ask, getting to my feet, the ground unsteady and tilting beneath them.

"We're looking for him," Detective Fredericks says. "There's an Amber Alert out. We'll find him."

"My dad," I say. "He's got him."

They exchange a glance. The man takes out a little notebook and a stubby pencil. "We need to ask you a few questions, Zoey, if that's okay, about what happened."

"A truck ran us off the road. I think it was my dad driving—"

Detective Roper interrupts. "Can you describe the truck, the color, the make? Do you remember the license?"

I shake my head. "No. It was dark."

"We should be able to get the color of his truck from the paint that will have been left behind on your bumper. And if we're lucky, the make and model too." She nods at her partner, who gets up, pulling out his phone. "And we'll be looking for a vehicle with a crushed bumper and damage to the front end."

But what if he's ditched that vehicle? What if he's already in

Mexico? What if he's done something to Cole, too? What if I lose my whole family, and Tristan?

"We're going to go and make some calls," she says. "We'll be right back."

I watch them go, feeling helpless and more alone than I ever have in my life. "What's happened to Tristan?" I ask, turning to the nurse who's stayed with me. "Is he going to be okay?"

She pats my hand. "He's still in surgery. I'll get someone to find out and let us know as soon as he's out of the operating room."

I nod, feeling frustration bubbling up. I want to burst into tears, but I can't. I need to stay strong. "I want to see my mom and sister," I say.

She nods and walks me through the hospital's endless corridors until we reach a room that says NO ENTRY on the door. There's a window, and through it I can see my mom and Kate lying on beds.

"Can I go in?" I ask.

"I'm afraid you can't. We have to wait outside," the nurse tells me.

"Why?" I ask.

"It's a hyperbaric chamber. It's how we treat carbon monoxide poisoning. It helps draw the toxins out of the body. They're going to be fine. Don't worry. You'll be able to speak to them soon."

I feel the tears sliding down my face. This is my fault. If I hadn't taken the stand and been a witness for the prosecution, my dad wouldn't have gone to jail, and if he hadn't gone to jail, he wouldn't blame me and he wouldn't have taken it out on the people I love.

"I'm sorry," I whisper out loud.

"It's not your fault."

I turn around. Robert is standing there with a steaming cup of coffee in his hand. The nurse smiles and leaves as I notice how tired and haggard Robert looks under the unforgiving lights, worry etched across his face. He sets his coffee cup down on a nearby table and opens his arms. I fall into them, and he holds me tight, smelling of coffee and old-man aftershave. "It's going to be okay, Zoey," he says. "Your mom's a fighter. She might not look it, but she is. That's where you get it from."

I look at him, and my lip trembles. "I got Tristan hurt," I tell him, sobbing.

He shakes his head firmly at me. "No, your dad got Tristan hurt. You saved him." He pauses. "Is he going to be okay?"

I shrug, my limbs shaking. "He's in surgery."

"Why don't you go and wait for him? I think he'll want you there when he comes around. I'll stay with your mom and Kate. The doctor says it will be a while before they wake up."

I look at them uncertainly through the thick glass of the door.

"Go on," he urges. "I'll keep an eye on them, let you know when they wake."

"Thank you," I say.

He nods and wipes my cheek with the back of his hand.

# TRISTAN

My eyes hurt when I open them, but not as much as my arm, which feels as though someone's had a go at hacking it off with a blunt saw before giving up halfway. I feel someone squeeze my hand, and I know before I open my eyes that it's Zoey. I'd know that touch anywhere, can sense her presence even with my eyes shut.

I force my eyes open and see her leaning over me, her eyes wide with worry.

My mouth feels too dry to speak, so I reach my hand up to press the back of her head closer, and I kiss her instead. When she pulls back to look at me, I can see her eyes are wide with fear and red from crying.

"Please don't scare me like that ever again," she says.

I grin at her through the pain. "I promise," I croak, then frown at her expression. There's no relief, only angst. "What's the matter?"

"My mom and Kate," she says, swallowing hard. "They're here in the hospital too. My dad messed with the water heater, so there was a carbon monoxide leak."

I struggle to sit up. "Are they going to be okay?"

She nods. "The nurse says they will be."

"Did they catch him?" I croak.

Zoey shakes her head. "And he's taken Cole."

"Taken him where?" I ask.

"I don't know."

I reach for her, and she tumbles forward, across my lap, and into my arms. I suppress a howl of pain when I move my bandaged arm. "I don't know where he is," she cries. "They've put out an Amber Alert. We just have to wait."

I squeeze her hand.

"Your parents and Dahlia are here. They're outside talking to the doctors."

"What if Cole left a note?" I say. It's a struggle to talk. My brain still feels groggy from the anesthetic and my eyelids are heavy as lead.

"You think he would?"

"I don't know. But you should go and check. If he knew he was going with your dad, he might have wanted to say good-bye."

"But the police were at the apartment. If there was a note, they would have found it."

"Maybe, maybe not."

"I don't want to leave the hospital," she says, but I can tell she's mulling on it.

"Go," I urge her. "Just promise me you won't do anything stupid. If you find a note, call the cops."

She nods, but as soon as she's out the door, I start to regret the idea. What if her dad is there waiting for her? No. The last place he'll be is the apartment, which has been crawling with cops. He's probably crossed state lines already. I glance at the IV line into my arm, which hooks up to a bag of blood. Damn it, I think to myself as my head sinks back into the pillows in frustration. I shouldn't have sent her out there alone.

# ZOEY

Crime scene tape crisscrosses the water heater by the front door. It's been dusted for fingerprints, and so has the door. I wonder if that's what my dad was doing—tampering with the water heater—when Tristan spotted him that time on camera. Or if he noticed it then and came back later to mess with it.

Inside, everything seems normal. I keep the door open and notice that the cops, or maybe Robert, have opened all the windows to air out the place. I turn on the lights and run into Cole's room, searching for a note. I come up empty but do discover he's taken his schoolbag and most of his clothes. I check my room too, hoping Cole had left a good-bye of some kind at least to my mom if not to me. But I find nothing in there, either.

Disappointment hits me hard, and I sink to the sofa, clutching my hands together as though praying. I've heard it said that the first few hours are key in a child abduction, that after twenty-four, the chances of ever seeing the child alive again are almost nil. I know he's gone willingly, and I don't think my dad plans to harm him—Cole is the only one of us who believes his innocence—but still, the statistic terrifies me.

What if the police don't find him?

Think, Zoey. Where might he have gone? But I can't think of anywhere. I don't know. Cole never said anything, never gave anything away. He and my dad have been communicating somehow, ever since Vegas. I should have pushed Cole to find out how. I should have made him tell me. If I had, then I could have stopped all this from happening.

But how did they talk? Cole doesn't have a phone. He doesn't have an iPad or access to a laptop, and I have checked with the school to make sure about that. He never gets mail. I look around the room, frustrated that I can't figure it out. I'm staring at the Xbox for a good minute before I realize I'm staring the answer in the face.

Isn't it possible to send e-mails or messages via Xbox games?

I turn on the console and watch the TV screen come alive. I've played a handful of times with Cole, so it doesn't take me long to find the inbox. It's full of hundreds of messages, all of them between "daddysback" and "Colestar."

I want to read them all, trace this toxic relationship and its path and find out how it started, but there's no time, so I open the last message, sent today at 5:51 p.m. **See you there, buddy,** my dad writes.

I click back to the previous message. **Are we going to go fishing and on the wheel like you promised?** Cole writes.

**Sure thing bud,** my dad responds.

What are they talking about? A wheel? I start flicking through all the other messages, but there's nothing about a wheel or fishing. I stand up and start pacing the living room, gnawing my already bitten fingernails. I think back to my childhood, digging through memories I've long since buried. Anything I can think of.

We went on a road trip once. My dad told us we were going to the beach—to LA—but we never made it that far, since we got stuck in Vegas, where he lost all our money gambling before driving us home to Scottsdale in a stinking rage. I think Cole was probably about four at the time.

But Vegas isn't near the ocean. So I don't think they are talking about going back there. He must mean somewhere near the ocean if there's fishing, or maybe a lake, I guess. What if he means Mexico? Then I remember that on that same trip we were meant to stay in a hotel on the beach in LA, by the Santa Monica Pier. My dad told us all he'd take us on a wheel over the ocean and then fishing.

*Like you promised?* Cole's words in his message to dad ring in my mind. On the trip to LA, Cole was so excited he wouldn't stop talking about it in the car. He'd never seen the ocean. Never been on a Ferris wheel. None of us had.

That's where they're going.

# TRISTAN

Zoey," I say, "I'm calling the police. You can't go on your own."

I hear her beeping open her car door. Damn it. She's not listening. I know how she feels about the police, so pushing her on the subject isn't going to help.

I stare again at the IV in my hand. I wish I weren't stuck in this damn bed. My parents are just outside in the hall, talking to the hospital's insurance person, and my sister has gone to get me something to eat. For some reason, I'm starving after waking up from the anesthetic.

"Zoey, don't go on your own."

"I have to do this, Tristan."

I grip the phone tightly in my hand. There's no reasoning with her, and I know I can't stop her from going. "Please be careful," I say to her.

"I will," she says. And then she hangs up.

Straightaway, I call the detectives who gave their cards to Zoey. Detective Fredericks answers on the first ring. I explain to him what Zoey told me, about the messages she found on the

Xbox and her guess as to the hotel in Santa Monica they might have gone to. I explain everything to him, and he says he'll pass it on to the LAPD and get right back to me.

As I hang up, Dahlia walks into the room carrying a take-out pizza. "Extra pepperoni," she says, laying the box on the bed. Then she stops and stares at me. "What the hell are you doing?"

I'm struggling out of bed and yanking the IV out of my hand. "I have to go," I tell her.

"Where?" she asks, jumping backward as the blood spurts out of the IV line and splashes her high heels and gold sheath dress. She must have come straight from the wedding. The wedding that already feels like it happened a decade ago.

"Where are you going?" she asks again, trying to get me back into bed.

I'm woozy and light-headed from standing up too fast, and dots dance in front of my eyes. "Zoey's going to LA to find Cole."

"What?" Dahlia hisses, propping a shoulder under my arm to stabilize me.

"She thinks she knows where he is."

"I thought her dad abducted him."

I nod, looking around for my clothes. My shirt must have been put in the trash, unsalvageable thanks to the blood. I don't know what happened to my jacket, so all I can do is pull on the bloodstained white T-shirt I was wearing beneath my dress shirt. It'll have to do. I bend down and rummage in the little closet by the bed for my shoes and pants, almost passing out from the effort.

"Tristan," Dahlia says, trying to force me back into bed. "You need to stay here. You just had an operation."

"It was just a few stitches," I say.

"It was not *just* stitches! You lost a load of blood. This is stupid."

"I can't let her go alone," I say, sitting down on the bed to pull on my pants, but one-handed and with pain shooting arrows up my injured arm, it's all but impossible.

"The doctor won't let you leave," Dahlia says, staring at me with her hands on her hips. "Get back in bed."

"I'm not asking permission," I tell her, straining to pull up my pants.

Dahlia glances at the doorway, where our parents are still talking to the doctor. "Shit," she murmurs, glowering at me.

"Either help me or don't," I tell her, knowing that she doesn't have a choice. She's my twin. We're in this thing together.

She rolls her eyes at me. "Fine," she hisses, grabbing my pants and helping me on with them. She then hurries to help me with my shoes. We don't need to discuss the plan. Dahlia and I have been covering for each other since we were toddlers, helping each other out of binds, distracting our parents while the other one hid their vegetables in the dog's bowl, stole the ice cream from the freezer, or snuck down a drainpipe to go out and party. She stands up, nods at me, her face still set in a disapproving scowl, then turns and yanks open the door.

"Mom, Dad," she says, exiting in a flourish from the room, holding the pizza. "Tristan's asleep. Want some pizza?" She opens the box lid, which is large enough to provide a screen of sorts while I slip out the door, and through sheer force of her personality, Dahlia manages to distract everyone while I hobble on weak legs down the hallway toward the exit.

Two minutes later and out of breath, Dahlia meets me by the exit that leads to the parking lot. I'm leaning against the wall, out of breath, struggling to stay upright, my arm throbbing like it just had a bullet shot through it. I can tell by the angry purse of Dahlia's lips that she's still mad at me, but she says nothing, just takes my hand and half drags me toward her car.

"You forgot the pizza," I say as she unlocks the doors.

She glares at me. "You want to go back for it, feel free."

We get in the car, and I painfully stretch the seat belt across my body with my one good arm as she starts the engine. Her phone starts chirping. I glance down at it, sitting in the seat well between us. It's Dad.

Dahlia gives me a look—it's my problem to deal with. I press the ignore button. She checks her mirrors, wipes a smudge of lipstick. "Well, at least you have one mighty good-looking getaway driver," she remarks, stepping on the gas.

# ZOEY

've plugged Santa Monica Pier into the app on my phone, and I arrive before dawn. As I pull into a beach parking lot alongside the pier, I get a call from Detective Fredericks, letting me know that LAPD detectives have visited almost all the hotels in Santa Monica, trying to find my dad and Cole. They've put out an APB, and all units are on alert, but they haven't found them. He tells me I need to turn around and head back to San Diego and let the police do their job.

"But you haven't found him," I point out.

He hasn't got an answer to that, so I hang up and get out of the car. The beach is empty at this hour, and the broad expanse of sand stretching to the ocean seems desolate and barren.

I glance up at the pier and the funfair frozen on the end, the wheel stationary. It's closed now, of course, but I imagine in the daytime the pier swarms with tourists.

It's cold, and I rub my bare arms. I changed last night into jeans and a T-shirt and a pair of sneakers but forgot to bring a sweater. Standing here reminds me of the first time I ever saw the ocean: when Tristan took us to the beach on our first morning in Oceanside. He didn't know it was my first time see-ing the ocean, and I was too embarrassed to tell him. I remem-ber him giving me his sweater, and the memory makes me wish he were here now.

I scan the row of hotels facing the beach. The cops apparently checked all of them after I called and didn't find my dad or Cole. What if I got it wrong? I wonder. What if they're not here after all? Should I still double-check? Pulling out my phone, I do a search of nearby hotels. Most of the ones on the beach cost five hundred dollars or more a night. No way my dad is spending that much on a hotel room. He'd always save money wherever possible so he could spend what he saved on beer and gambling.

I expand the search radius, and the farther back from the beach, the cheaper the hotels get. If my dad promised Cole a hotel right by the pier, I'm sure he chose the cheapest one he could find. There's a motel called the Pierpoint Inn a couple of blocks back from the ocean.

It's worth a shot. If I can't find them, I can always come back to the pier and hope to spot them later. It's a long shot, and hope is rapidly fading, but I may as well try. I have to do something.

I get back in my car and drive the mile to the motel, pulling up a little way down the street. If he is here, I know my dad will be watchful. He just snatched a child, and although he won't expect anyone to be looking for him here, he's an ex-cop, and he isn't stupid. It's possible he has a plan to lie low for a while until the coast is clearer and it's easier to drive long-distance without so much risk.

I walk toward the motel's reception, scanning every truck in the parking lot as I go. I skid to a stop in shock by the second one. The front bumper is completely mangled, and one of the lights cracked. I didn't get a real look at the truck last night, so I don't know for sure if it's the same one, but what are the odds? It feels too easy though to have found it this fast.

I spin around, feeling a shiver run up my spine. Is he here with Cole right now? Are they in the room behind me? The curtains are drawn. I cup my eyes and peer inside the dark interior of the car. Fast-food wrappers and empty Coke cans litter the back seat, and on the floor, I spot a waving cat. It's a toy just like the one that Tristan gave Kate. I wonder if Cole picked it up at the last moment and stuffed it in his bag as some kind of memento.

I jog past the car and hurry into the motel's office. There's no one around, so I ring the bell, and a sleepy woman in her sixties with platinum-blond hair and skin like a tortoise comes out of a back room.

"Looking for a room, hon?" she asks me.

I shake my head. "No. I'm looking for my dad," I say, forcing a smile. "He's staying here with my brother. I want to surprise them."

She smiles back at me. "That's sweet. Where are they visiting from?"

"Arizona," I stutter. "I'm at college here. At UCLA. They've come for the weekend. I thought I'd surprise them and take them for breakfast."

"What name?" she asks, glancing at her computer screen. I hesitate, not sure if my dad would have given a false name. I'm almost certain he would have.

"That's their car out there," I say, pointing through the window and hoping to avoid answering her question. "The maroon truck."

"Oh yes, they got in a few hours ago," she says, nodding and checking the screen. "They're in room one-thirty-four. They're probably still sleeping, though. Your brother looked tired."

Her words sink in. They *are* here. Oh my God. I've found them. For a second all I can do is stand there, mute. "I'll come back later," I finally garble. "Thanks." And with that, I hurry outside and rush around the corner of the building. As soon as I'm out of earshot, I pull out my phone to dial 911, but before I can, it rings. It's Tristan.

"I found them," I blurt.

"What?" he asks.

"I found them. At a motel."

"Where? What's the address?" he asks.

"The Pierpoint in Santa Monica."

"Stay right there," Tristan says, his voice anxious. There's a pause, and I hear the muffled sound of him talking to someone. He comes back on. "I'll be there in less than ten minutes."

"What?" I ask in surprise. "Who are you with? Where are you?" I ask.

"I'm with Dahlia. She broke me out of hospital—"

"Tristan!" I say angrily. What's he thinking?

"Zoey," he interrupts. "Wait for me. Promise me you aren't going to go charging in there. Call the police."

"I was just about to," I tell him.

"Okay," Tristan says, sounding relieved. "And wait for them. Don't do anything stupid. Promise me."

"I promise," I tell him.

"I love you," he says.

My heart kicks in my chest, as it does every time I hear him say the words. Tears spring to my eyes. Last night, I really thought I might lose him. "I love you more," I tell him.

"Not possible," he whispers back.

I hang up and call Detective Roper. When I explain I've found my dad and Cole, she doesn't hide her irritation that I've gone against their orders to stay put and let them handle business. She puts me on hold for thirty seconds before coming back on the line to tell me LAPD officers will be with me shortly. "Get somewhere safe and hang tight. I'll call you when the situation has been locked down."

I murmur in agreement, but when I hang up, I stay put. I'm not leaving. I'm staying until I know Cole is safe. I hide myself next to the ice machine in a little recessed alcove. Standing in the shadows, I bounce on my tiptoes and check the time repeatedly. What's taking so damn long for the cops to get here?

I hear a clanging metal sound and peek my head around the corner. The little metal door to the pool has just opened and banged shut behind someone. I see a small blond head on the other side of the railings, and my breath catches. Cole.

My first instinct is to shout his name and run to him, but I stop myself. What if my dad is with him? I edge closer to get a better view. Cole's walking along the edge of the pool, gazing down at the water. Maybe Dad told him he could swim in the morning, and he woke up at the first sign of light peeking through the curtains and decided that it was time to swim. He has a towel in one hand, dragging along the ground behind him.

Is my dad still asleep? I wonder. Should I call Cole's name? Should I approach him? But what if he yells? I know my dad has been spewing poison in his ear about me, so I shouldn't risk it. He's already chosen my dad over us. But something propels me forward anyway. He's my brother, and he's right there, in reach.

I step out of the shadows. "Cole," I say quietly.

He startles and looks up. He's stunned to see me, and his first reaction is surprise. Then happiness bursts across his face in the shape of a smile before a scowl replaces it.

"What are you doing here?" he says so loudly I wince and glance over my shoulder toward the room. Shit. I should have stayed quiet. But it's too late now. I hurry toward him, ease open the metal gate, and gently close it behind me. "I came to see you," I tell him in an anxious half whisper.

He's at the other end of the pool. He doesn't move toward me. He stands frozen, still scowling at me. "Cole," I say with quiet urgency, holding out my hand to him. "You need to come with me."

"No," he says defiantly.

My pulse leaps. I want to turn and look at the room, but I don't want to take my eyes off Cole. "Why did you run away?" I ask.

"I want to be with my dad," he says. "He's taking me to Disneyland. And fishing." He pauses. "How did you find us, anyway?"

"It doesn't matter," I say, inching toward him like he's a wild animal I'm trying not to startle. "But Mom and Kate are in the hospital. They're really sick. And Mom wants to see you."

Cole frowns at that. "What do you mean?" he asks. "Why are they in the hospital?"

I take a deep breath. I can't tell him the truth—that Dad tried to kill them. He won't believe me anyway.

"You're lying!" Cole suddenly yells. "I don't believe you."

"I'm not lying," I say, trying to get him to calm down. "They are in the hospital."

Cole's expression turns from wide-eyed shock to narrow-eyed anger. "You're a liar."

"Cole, I'm not a liar. And I love you. That's why I'm here. Mom and Kate love you too, and they need you. We want you to come home."

I can see him struggling to process what I've told him, trying to figure out if it's lies or truth. "Dad needs me," he says, his bottom lip trembling. "I'm all he's got. We're going to live by the beach. He's going to buy me a dog and take me fishing, and we're going to go on the Ferris wheel later today."

I take that in. "But if you go with Dad, he'll never let you see Mom or Kate or me ever again."

Cole's lip trembles some more, his eyes welling with tears.

"I know that's not what you want," I tell him, pushing my advantage, one eye on the door to the room. I step toward him so now I'm in touching distance. "I know you love Dad," I say, "but, Cole, he wants to take you away from us forever."

"Because you won't let him see me!" Cole yells, startling me.

"No," I answer firmly, terrified that all the yelling must have woken up my dad. I glance again over my shoulder. Where the hell are the cops? "It's the judge who told him to stay away from us. Because he hurt Mom and he tried to hurt me."

Cole stares at me, and I see how torn he is, how much he's fighting against his own better judgment. "Is Mom okay?" he finally mumbles.

"I don't know," I tell him, relieved that he's believing me. "But I do know that she'll get better a lot faster if she knows you're there. Kate, too. Come with me. Let's go."

Cole stares at me, his eyes filling with tears. I hold my hand out to him. After a beat, he takes it. I want to pull him into my arms and hug him, but there isn't time, and I'm too afraid. I pull him through the gate, which slams loudly shut behind us.

Wincing, I start rushing toward the street, but Cole suddenly starts fighting against me, yanking on my hand.

"No," he says, digging in his heels. "I have to say good-bye."

I stop and look at him. "You can't say good-bye, Cole. We have to go. Right now."

"Why?" he asks.

"Because—" I start to say, but before I can finish, he springs out of my hand and dashes toward the room.

"Cole!" I hiss.

He stops by the door. "I need my bag," he whispers, opening the door and slipping inside.

Oh God. I tiptoe after him, waiting outside the door, adrenaline making my heart race. What the hell is taking so long? Where is he? I inch forward and peer into the gloomy interior of the room.

A shape lunges out at me, grabbing me by the arm and yanking me inside the room. I stumble, hit the side of a bed, and fall forward with a cry, and then my dad is on top of me, pulling me upright by my hair. "Look what we found here," he says, his snarling face pressed to mine. "Did you call the police?" he demands to know.

I'm so afraid, but instead of fighting like Tristan taught me, I'm frozen. All I can do is shake my head. I'm not an idiot. If I tell him I called, he might hurt me, snatch Cole, and run. I have to buy however many more minutes I need.

"Did you come alone?" he asks, falling straight into cop interrogation mode.

I nod. He narrows his eyes at me. "How did you find us?" He turns to Cole. "You tell her where we were?" he yells.

Cole, shocked, shakes his head. "No," he hiccups. "I didn't tell. I swear."

"I found all your messages on the Xbox," I tell him.

He scowls grimly at the mistake that has screwed things up for him. Then he shoves me backward so I collapse on the bed.

"Cole," he says, without turning away from me, "get your bag. We're leaving."

Cole has started to snivel. "Where are we going?" he asks. "I want to see Mom."

"Get your damn bag!" my dad roars at him. Cole jumps in fright, grabs for his bag on the end of the bed, and looks at me, his eyes wet with tears and fear. A surge of anger rushes through me. "Go wait by the car," my dad says to Cole, trying for a more gentle tone. "I'll be right there."

Cole looks between my dad and me, lying sprawled on the bed. I see him open his mouth as though about to argue, but I shake my head at him. I don't want him here to see whatever is about to happen. I want him out of the way. Cole backs away toward the door.

"Good boy," my dad says to him. "Go on, now."

"Go," I tell Cole, trying to smile at him reassuringly. "It'll be okay. Just go wait by the car. Dad and I are just going to talk."

Cole seems only slightly reassured, but he does leave, shutting the door behind him.

I wonder if he'll run for help. It's my only hope right now. That or the cops arriving. After he's gone, I scan my dad, looking for the telltale bulge of a gun. When I was a kid, he'd carry concealed all the time, on his ankle or shoulder if he was wearing a jacket. He's wearing only jeans and a T-shirt right now. I wonder if he's got a holster on his ankle.

It doesn't matter—I'm not going to go down without a fight.

"HELP!" I shout, remembering that the first thing Tristan

taught me in self-defense was to use my voice. As I open my mouth to shout again, my dad lunges toward me and grabs me by the neck, choking off the scream.

"You shouldn't have come," he hisses.

"You shouldn't have taken him," I croak.

"He wanted to come."

"He's a kid," I whisper, struggling to breathe. "He doesn't know the truth."

My dad frowns at me, but it quickly turns into a sneer. "You took him away from me. Your mom took you all away from me. Poisoned you against me." His fingers tighten.

My hands squeeze his wrists, and I tug at them, trying to loosen his grip. I can't breathe. My vision is swimming. "You did that all by yourself," I whisper, wondering where the cops are. It feels like hours since I called them, but perhaps it's just a few minutes.

I wonder if this is how I'll die. I'm gasping for air, trying to get him off me, but my efforts are wasted. His hands are iron vises. I can feel my strength ebbing, and I close my eyes, not wanting to see the black rage and hate in his eyes. Tristan's face fills my mind.

And then white light. I'm flung away and land hard on the ground, dizzy and gasping, sucking in air. I glance up, blinking against the harsh white light that fills the room. The door is wide open, daylight streaming in.

Tristan stands there, pale, wearing a bloodstained shirt, his eyes dark-circled and his one bandaged arm held against his chest. "Leave her alone," he shouts, rushing toward us.

My dad blocks his path, and in his hand is his gun. Tristan freezes. My dad looks at me, though he keeps the gun pointed on Tristan. "You said you came alone. Always knew you were a lying bitch."

"Please don't hurt him," I say, looking in panic at Tristan. "Let him go."

"I can't let you go," my dad mutters, angrily crossing to the door and slamming it shut, plunging us back into darkness.

Tristan glances at me. What have I gotten him into? My dad gestures for Tristan to move, and he does, crossing quickly to me. Our hands find each other, our fingers linking, squeezing tight as we eye the gun in my dad's hand. Tristan moves himself in front of me.

"I'm your daughter," I say to my dad, trying to move out from behind Tristan. "I love you," I tell him, almost choking on the lie. "We can fix this. We can work it out. Please don't do this."

I see the decision get made—the resolution crossing his face, and then his finger squeezing the trigger—all in slow motion, and in the same instant I slide in front of Tristan to shield him.

There's a deafening bang, followed closely by a second bang, and I fly sideways and hit the ground. Tristan falls too.

Pain shoots through me like comets streaking across a black sky. My vision turns starry.

I look up and see the monstrous shape of my dad looming over us, the gun still in his hand. He blinks, seemingly astonished. Maybe it's shock at what he's done. Maybe it isn't. Light bursts around him in a dazzling halo. The room is suddenly ablaze with light. I can't breathe—the pain is almost as bright as the light.

I've been shot, I realize. But what about Tristan? Is he okay? Thoughts flit like eels through my mind, so fast and so slippery I can't grasp on to them. The only thing I can hold on to, like a beacon in the darkness, is the thought of Tristan. Please let him be okay. I don't care if I die. Just let him be okay.

My dad drops to his knees in front of me like a dark avenging angel. For a moment, I think he's about to beg forgiveness for what he's done. As the blood starts to pool around me, soaking my shirt, I stare up at him, but his expression shows no remorse, not an ounce of sorrow. He's baring his teeth like an animal about to shred his prey.

My ears are ringing so loudly from the crack of the bullets that all other sounds are dulled. Time has slowed to a near stop. My heart seems to be following suit.

Tristan is all I can think of as the light starts to fade. I led him here. This is all my fault. Where is he? I desperately want to see him. I can feel something behind me. Something heavy and unmoving. A body? His body? I want to roll over and reach for him, but I'm paralyzed.

I desperately need to know that he's okay.

But what if he isn't?

What if he's dead?

What if I'm dying too?

I'm so dazed I can't put it all together.

But in the very next second, my father, who is still staring into my eyes, falls sideways, his head slamming into the floor beside me. He blinks at me in shock.

And next thing I know I'm being hauled to my feet and dragged away. I stare in wonder at the person doing the dragging. It's Tristan. I would sob with relief if I weren't in so much pain. He doesn't seem hurt; that's all that matters. He's holding my face in his hands, and he's shouting something. I can't make out the words. But he's alive!

Suddenly, everything ramps sharply up, as though someone has turned a tuning knob and finally hit the right frequency. "Zoey! Are you okay?" Tristan is shaking me by the tops of my arms.

I take a breath. My chest hurts but not too bad. I think I was just winded in the fall, maybe cracked a rib. I nod at him, still confused, though. What happened?

I glance down at my dad, who is clutching at his stomach, gasping, his eyes rolling back in his head. I stare in astonishment at the red stain on his shirt and the rapidly spreading pool of blood beneath him. It was *his* blood. Not mine. He's been shot. The bullet he fired hit the wall behind me. And though I tried to throw myself at Tristan, to shield him, he must have pushed us both to the ground. We saved each other.

Behind Tristan, I see police in uniform, holding guns. They lower them, and I race past them and outside, ignoring the police yelling, because I can see Cole standing in the doorway right behind them. He's seen it all happen.

"Cole," I say, dropping to my knees in front of him, wrapping him in my arms and spinning him away from my dad, who has been swarmed by paramedics.

I bury Cole against my shoulder. "It's okay," I say over and over, rocking him. "It's okay." But how can it ever be okay? I think as the police force us up and hurry us out the room. I feel myself being pushed from person to person, still clutching Cole to me, until I find Tristan again and Dahlia, too, and they circle us and hold us tight as commotion roars around us.

Cole starts to sob, clinging to me. There's so much noise—sirens and shouting and van doors slamming, but Tristan and Dahlia block it out so that I can sink to my knees on the concrete parking lot and hold my baby brother while he cries.

# Epilogue

**Three weeks later . . .**

Y ou good?" Tristan asks, worried.

I nod, though I think I'm lying. I have a lump in my throat, and my chest feels tight. I don't know how I'm going to say good-bye.

"Last chance to change your mind," Tristan says, looking at me nervously.

I loop my arms around his neck, then reach up and kiss him on the lips. "I'm never changing my mind," I tell him.

"Good," he mumbles, kissing me back.

I lose myself in the kiss. Ever since that day three weeks ago—the day of the accident and the shooting—I've become hyperaware of every single moment, focused much more on the present than dwelling on the past or worrying about the future.

Every kiss, every touch is imbued with a newfound magic—with gratitude and hope and even wonder. We're alive. We're here.

And so is my dad. Currently, he's in prison, awaiting trial for attempted murder as well as a litany of other crimes, including kidnapping. The lawyers say there's no chance he'll be let out this time, not until he's an old man at least, and though it took me a while to actually believe them, the district attorney reassures me it's so. I'll have to take the stand again as a witness, but this time I'm not afraid to do so. I'm going to look him in the eye and show him that he didn't win. I did.

Cole has been seeing a child therapist, and he's been doing much better as a result of their intensive sessions together. The thought makes it a little easier to leave, even though I'm sad to be moving away from my new friends and my family. We'll be back for Thanksgiving, in time to meet Jessa and Kit's new baby. Didi and Walker will be visiting soon because Walker's brother lives in Miami. And Will is coming to see us as soon as he's back from deployment, something I'm both nervous and excited about. He wanted to come home right when he heard the news about Dad, but the military wouldn't give him leave. But once he's back, he'll be back for good.

"I'm ready," I say to Tristan, turning to the trunk full of our belongings. I don't have much in the way of belongings, so mostly it's Tristan's things: bags of clothes, a box of '80s DVDS that he refuses to part with. The Game of Life has made it in too, and the bacon suit puzzle. We're shipping his bike and a few other things, like his surfboard.

"What about your baseball cards?" I ask him, looking for the old shoe box he stores them in.

He shakes his head when I turn to look at him. "I don't have them," he says.

"What?"

"I sold them."

"You what?" I say, astonished. "Why?"

He pulls something out of his back pocket. It's a slim white envelope. He hands it to me.

I take it tentatively. "What is it?"

"Open it."

I do. Inside are several sheets of paper. "I don't get it," I say flicking through them.

"I sold the cards," he tells me. "They were sitting in a box in my closet. Figured I could put them to better use."

I hold up the pieces of paper. "But what is this?"

"It's an itinerary." He smiles at me and winks. "We are going to Greece."

I'm so confused. "We're driving to Florida. How can we go to Greece?"

"I'm taking you to that island you wanted to go to," Tristan says. "We're going to visit ruins and eat moussaka and philoso-phize like ancient Greeks."

I stare at him in astonishment. "But I don't have a passport" is all I can think to say.

He hands me another envelope. I tear it open. A blue pass-port tumbles out. "But . . . how?" I ask, opening it up and seeing my own photo staring back at me.

"Remember that apartment application form I told you that you needed to sign?"

I stare at him in shock. "That was a lie?"

He shrugs and pulls a face. "You didn't read it. You just signed. It was easy. And your mom helped me get all the other documents I needed."

I stare at the passport, then up at Tristan, amazed and giddy with excitement. "We're going to Greece?" I say, finally starting to process it.

"Yes," he says, grinning at me, delighted by my delight. "We're going for three weeks. We're going to sail around the islands. Go to Crete and that other place you wanted to go, where the gods hang out. Milos."

I throw my arms around him and hug him until he grunts, and I realize I'm hurting him. His arm is still recovering. Tristan tells me that they set back the dates of his pilot school training because of it, and I guess that's one good thing—it means we have almost a month of vacation!

My thoughts are interrupted by shrieks of laughter. I look up. My mom, Kate, Cole, and Robert are on the balcony by our front door. Kate is filming me on her phone. They're in on it, I realize.

They walk down the stairs, and I notice they're all carrying bags. "Where are you going?" I ask, confused.

Tristan hands Robert my car keys.

"We're taking a road trip," he tells me, putting his arm around my mom.

"We're going to drive your car to Florida," my mom says.

"And then we're going to Disney World!" Cole yells.

"You are?" I ask, thoroughly and completely discombobulated.

"Yes," says Kate.

"We figured we'd have a vacation too," my mom says, beaming up at Robert, who kisses her gently on the lips. My heart almost bursts with happiness at the joy on her face and the love I see radiating from both of them.

"We'll move your things into your new apartment so it's ready for you when you get back," my mom adds.

I look among them all, choking up with emotion. "I don't know what to say."

"Try 'good-bye,'" Tristan says. "We have a flight to catch."

I'm going on a plane? For the first time. Oh my God.

I look at my family and have to bite my lip hard to stop the tears from welling up.

"Good-bye," I say.

They throw their arms around me, pulling me into the center of their circle, and I breathe in deep, not wanting to let go.

"Here," says Cole, pulling away. "I made you something." He pulls a piece of paper out of his pocket. I unfold it and see it's a drawing, but this time there are no guns and no blood. There's a yellow circle in the sky and a boat on the ocean. I recognize myself and Tristan on the deck. We're waving and smiling at four figures on the beach, all holding hands: my mom, Cole, Kate, and someone else. "Who's that?" I ask.

"That's Robert," Cole answers, blushing a little.

I think I might cry, but I manage to blink the tears away. "Thank you," I say. "I'm going to frame it."

Cole grins at me. "Bring me back a present," he tells me.

I hug him again.

"You're going to miss your flight," my mom says, crying for the both of us. She squeezes my hand and kisses me on the cheek. "Go, have fun," she whispers, smiling at me. "Make memories."

"I will," I tell her, reaching backward out of the circle and finding Tristan's hand.

He links his fingers through mine and squeezes, tugging me toward the horizon. "Let's go."

# Acknowledgments

Many, many heartfelt thanks to Nicole at Simon & Schuster for the wonderful editing advice that helped me shape the novel.

Amanda, my book agent, whose honesty, hard work, and support over the last decade are so appreciated. I would be nowhere without you.

John and Alula, who show me the real meaning of love every day.

When a marine chaplain knocks on her door, Jessa's heart breaks—someone she loves is dead. Killed in action. But is it Riley or Kit? Her brother or her boyfriend . . . ?

COME BACK TO ME

MILA GRAY

Read on for a sneak peek into Mila Gray's heart-wrenching romance.

# Jessa

A whorl in the glass distorts the picture, like a thumb-print smear over a lens. I'm halfway down the stairs, gathering my hair into a ponytail, thoughts a million miles away, when a blur outside the window pulls me up short.

I take another step, the view clears, and when I realize what I'm seeing, *who* I'm seeing, my stomach plummets and the air leaves my lungs like a final exhalation. My arms fall slowly to my sides. My body's instinct is to turn and run back upstairs, to tear into the bathroom and lock the door, but I'm frozen. This is the moment you have nightmares about, play over in your mind, the darkest of daydreams, furnished by movies and by real-life stories you've overheard your whole life.

You imagine over and over how you'll cope, what you'll say, how you'll act when you open the door and find them standing there. You pray to every god you can dream up that this moment won't ever happen. You make bargains, promises, desperate barters. And you live each day with the murmur of those prayers playing on a loop in the background of your mind, an endless chant. And then the moment happens and you realize it was all for nothing. The prayers went unheard. There was no bargain to make. Was it your fault? Did you fail to keep your promise?

Time seems to have slowed. Kit's father hasn't moved. He's standing at the end of the driveway staring up at the house, squinting against the early morning glare. He's wearing his Dress Blues. It's that fact which registered before all else, which told me all I needed to know. That and the fact that he's here at all. Kit's father has never once been to the house. There is only one reason why he would ever come.

He hasn't taken a step, and I will him not to. I will him to turn around and get back into the dark sedan sitting at the curb. A shadowy figure in uniform sits at the wheel. *Please. Get back in and drive away.* I start making futile bargains with some nameless god. If he gets back in the car and drives away, I'll do anything. But he doesn't. He takes a step down the driveway toward the house, and that's when I know for certain that either Riley or Kit is dead.

A scream, or maybe a sob, tries to struggle up my throat, but it's blocked by a solid wave of nausea. I grab for the banister to stay upright. Who? Which one? My brother or my boyfriend? Oh God. Oh God. My legs are shaking. I watch Kit's father walk slowly up the drive, head bowed.

Memories, images, words, flicker through my mind like scratched fragments of film: Kit's arms around my waist drawing me closer, our first kiss under the cover of darkness just by the back door, the smile on his face the first time we slept together, the blue of his eyes lit up by the sparks from a Chinese lantern, the fierceness in his voice when he told me he was going to love me forever.

*Come back to me*. That was the very last thing I said to him. *Come back to me*.

*Always*. The very last thing he said to me.

Then I see Riley as a kid throwing a toy train down the stairs, dive-bombing into the pool, holding my hand at our grandfather's funeral, grinning and high-fiving Kit after they'd enlisted. The snapshot of him in his uniform on graduation day. The circles under his eyes the last time I saw him.

The door buzzes. I jump. But I stay where I am, frozen halfway up the stairs. If I don't answer the door, maybe he'll go away. Maybe this won't be happening. But the doorbell sounds again. And then I hear footsteps on the landing above me. My mother's voice, sleepy and confused. "Jessa? Who is it? Why are you just standing there?"

Then she sees. She peers through the window, and I hear the intake of air, the ragged "no" she utters in response. She too knows that a military car parked outside the house at seven a.m. can signify only one thing.

I turn to her. Her hand is pressed to her mouth. Standing in her nightdress, her hair unbrushed, the blood rushing from her face, she looks like she's seen a ghost. No. That's wrong. She looks like she *is* a ghost.

The bell buzzes for a third time.

"Get the door, Jessa," my mother says in a strange voice I don't recognize. It startles me enough that I start to walk down the stairs. I feel calmer all of a sudden, like I'm floating outside my body. This can't be happening. It's not real. It's just a dream.

I find myself standing somehow in front of the door. I unlock it. I open it. Kit. Riley. Kit. Riley. Their names circle my mind like birds of prey in a cloudless blue sky. Kit. Riley. Which is it?

Is Kit's father here in his Dress Blues with his chaplain insignia to tell us that my brother has been killed in action or that his son—my boyfriend—has been killed in action? He would come either way. He would want to be the one to tell me. He would want to be the one to tell my mom.

Kit's father blinks at me. He's been crying. His eyes are red, his cheeks wet. He's still crying, in fact. I watch the tears slide down his face and realize that I've never seen him cry before. It automatically makes me want to comfort him, but even if I could find the words, my throat is so dry I couldn't speak them.

"Jessa," Kit's father says in a husky voice.

I hold on to the doorframe, keeping my back straight. I'm aware that my mother has followed me down the stairs and is standing right behind me. Kit's father glances at her over my shoulder. He takes a deep breath, lifts his chin, and removes his hat before his eyes flicker back to me.

"I'm sorry," he says.

"Who?" I hear myself ask. "Who is it?"

# Jessa

Three months earlier . . .

Oh dear God, who in the name of heaven is he?"

Didi's grip on my arm is enough to raise bruises. I look up. And I see him. He's staring at me, grinning, and I have to bite back my own grin. My stomach starts somersaulting, my insides twisting into knots.

"Kit," I say, half in answer to Didi, half just for the chance to say his name out loud after so long. My eyes are locked with Kit's, and when he hears me speak his name, he smiles even wider and walks across the living room toward me.

"Hey, Jessa," he says. His eyes travel over me, taking me in, before settling on my face. He rubs a hand over his shorn head, a self-conscious gesture that makes the somersaults double in speed. He's still grinning at me but more sheepishly now.

"Hi," I say, swallowing. I'm nervous all of a sudden. I haven't seen him in nine months. I wasn't sure he was going to be here today, and though I've run through this moment dozens—hell, thousands—of times in my head, I find I'm completely unprepared for it now it's actually happening. In all those imaginings I never once factored in the way he'd make me feel—as though

I've just taken a running leap off a cliff edge. I'm breathless, almost shaking, finding it hard to hold his steady blue gaze.

He looks older than his twenty-one years. His shoulders are broader, and he's even more tanned than usual, both facts well emphasized by the white T-shirt he's wearing. I can feel Didi squeezing my arm with so much force it's as though she's trying to stem an arterial bleed, and I know if I turn around I'll see her drooling unashamedly. She might go to a convent school, but Didi's prayers center around asking God to deliver her not from trespassers but from her virginity.

"Happy birthday," Kit says now. He hasn't taken his eyes off me the whole time, and my skin is warming under his relentless gaze. I can feel my face getting hotter.

"Thanks," I manage to say, wishing I could come up with a better response, something flirtatious and witty. I know I had something planned for this moment, but my brain has chosen to shut down.

"Hi!"

It's Didi. She has let go of my arm and now thrusts her hand out toward Kit. "I'm Didi, Jessa's best friend. You must be Kit. I've heard a lot about you."

Plenty of emphasis on the *lot*. I make a mental note to kill her later. Kit glances over at me, clearly struggling to contain his amusement, before turning his attention fully back to Didi. He shakes her hand, introducing himself properly, and it gives me a chance to mentally pull myself together and really get a look at him. He's six foot but he seems taller, maybe because he's standing so straight. I recognize the ink marking on his arm, poking out from beneath his sleeve. It's the same tattoo that Riley has. A Marine Corps emblem. My fingers itch to trace it. Oh God. For months I've been telling myself to get over Kit, ordering myself to forget him. Didi rolls her eyes at me every time I mention his name. She's even added my name on Urban Dictionary under the word *pathetic*. But now, as I watch Kit casting his spell over her, I can see she may finally be ready to cut me a break.

She's firing questions at him like she's a Chinese match-maker, asking all about his job and his uniform. I wouldn't be surprised if she starts asking him next how much he earns and whether he has a girlfriend. I would interrupt, but I'm still trying to gather my wits and formulate a sentence, and, truth be told, I'm kind of hoping she does ask him whether he has a girl-friend. Though another, bigger part of me doesn't want to hear the answer. Because what if he does? Taking a breath, I remind myself he's been in Sudan for the last nine months living with a bunch of guys, sleeping in a room with a dozen other men, eat-ing in a mess hall. It's not like he's been going to parties or out clubbing every night, so it's highly unlikely he's managed to find himself a girlfriend in that time.

Kit answers Didi's questions politely, nodding and giving the standard-issue responses that they're trained to. In other words, no detail whatsoever. All I know is that he and Riley have been in Sudan along with the rest of their marine detachment, protecting the US embassy in Khartoum. That's all. They only got back yesterday.

As I listen to Didi and Kit talking, Didi telling him all about how she only moved to Oceanside six months ago and how her big ambition is to finish school and move to LA (thankfully she omits to mention her other big ambition—to lose her virginity), I realize I'm fixating on Kit's lips, imagining what it would be like to kiss him.

Nothing has ever happened between Kit and me, nothing ever could, so imagining is all I can do. He's my brother's best friend and has been since they were fourteen. We've known Kit since we moved to California when I was eleven. He and my brother have been inseparable since the day they met at baseball try-outs. It's the kind of bromance you see in the movies. Not the *Brokeback Mountain* kind, luckily for me, but something I was always a little envious of. Kit and Riley have probably not gone a day since meeting without seeing each other. They're closer than brothers. It's a friendship that persists despite the fact that my father hates Kit and has tried everything in his not inconsiderable power to pull the plug on it.

I glance through the window out into the garden where my father and Riley are firing up the grill. As though operating on some kind of sixth sense, my father's head snaps up. He was a marine sniper in his day, and he has an eerie ability to sense whenever he's being watched. He has me in his sights. Then I see him register Kit. A dark scowl passes over his face before Riley ignites the charcoal, sending flames soaring as high as the nearest palm tree, and my father turns back around to bark orders at him. Honestly, only in my house does a birthday party get turned into a military operation.

It's never been exactly clear why my father hates Kit so much, but I know it has something to do with his father, who is also a marine, and who served in the same company as my father back in the eighties. It could also be that my father blames Kit for some of Riley's more questionable life choices—namely signing up as an enlisted marine, rather than going to college and becoming an officer, which is what my father had expected him (read: preached at him from birth) to do. Then there was the time they burned down the garage while setting off fireworks. And the time they both streaked across the bleachers during a televised football game. Yeah, now I think about it, there are maybe a few reasons why my dad holds a grudge against Kit.

Kit's father is now a marine chaplain, having found God after a long battle with grief and the bottle following Kit's mother's death. My father meanwhile climbed the ranks and is now a colonel, a role that he inhabits even out of uniform, probably even in his sleep. That could be why Kit is still in the kitchen with us and not out making fire with the men. Or maybe it's for some other reason?

Kit turns back to face me and takes a deep breath. Behind him I catch sight of Didi making a "check him out" face. I try not to laugh.

Just then my mother comes bustling through from the kitchen carrying plates laden with food.

"Kit!" she exclaims delightedly. My mom doesn't hold the grudge toward Kit or his father that my dad does. In fact she's almost as fond of him as she is of me and my brother. She treats him like her second son. Whenever Riley and Kit come back on leave it's like the Second Coming. My mom throws off the depression that she's been shrouded in since they left and buzzes back to life. I know that no matter how proud she is of them she hates the fact they're marines as much as I do. I've always suspected too that she's trying to make up for my father treating Kit like he's some sort of pariah. It gets kind of embarrassing at times. Like now.

She sets a couple of bowls of salad and marinated chicken down on the table and grabs Kit into a fierce hug. She only comes up to his shoulder, but he looks like he couldn't prise himself free even if he tried. Which he doesn't because he's far too polite, and I think he secretly likes the fuss she makes of him.

Didi takes the opportunity while my mother is hugging Kit to sidle up to me. "Oh man, I didn't even recognize him from the photos. He's so much hotter. I want to see him in uniform. Just imagine. If this is how hot he looks in normal clothes."

I ram my elbow into her ribs. I've already seen Kit in uniform. And Didi's not wrong. It rendered me speechless.

"Or naked," Didi whispers. "Actually, yes, forget the uniform. Imagine him naked."

"Shhh," I murmur, not admitting to her that I have. Many times.

"He is *so* into you."

"Shut up," I mutter as my mother lets Kit go. My pulse spikes, though. Is Didi right? Or is she just saying that because she knows it's what I want to hear?

"No, I'm serious, he can't take his eyes off you," Didi says, covering her words with a cough as Kit turns to stare at me again. "See." Didi swings toward my mom. "Mrs. Kingsley, do you need a hand?" she asks in an exceedingly loud and exceedingly obvious voice.

My mom looks up, flustered. "Oh, that would be great, thanks, Bernadette."

"Didi," says Didi abruptly. She hates anyone calling her by her given name. She grabs for the chicken and heads for the doorway, where great wafts of smoke are billowing thanks to the lighter fluid my brother has just thrown on the grill. She shoots me a look over her shoulder as she goes—eyes bugging, head tilting in Kit's direction. From this I deduce she's telling me to go and talk to Kit.

The trouble is I've never had to force myself to make conversation with Kit before. It's always come naturally. Until now. For some reason my throat suddenly feels as though it is stuffed with rocks. I can barely think a coherent sentence, let alone speak one.

"So, Jessa, how you been?" I hear Kit say just behind me.

I turn around, my heart shooting like a rocket into my rib cage.

"You know . . . good. Fine. Okay." Waffling. I'm waffling. He's laughing at me. I can see the way he's trying not to smile, biting his lips together. His lips. Okay. Focus. Don't stare.

I take a deep breath. As no one but Didi knows, I've liked Kit for years, have had a crush on him since I was about fourteen and he was seventeen, but the last time he was back on leave was the first time I felt it might be reciprocated, maybe, possibly. Possibly not. It's this *maybe, possibly, possibly not* that has kept me awake most nights for the last nine months. I kept on replaying the interactions we'd had over and over until the memories were so worn I wasn't sure if I was patching them with invented events, imagining things that hadn't happened. Had his fingers lingered in mine that time he pulled me to my feet? Did he hold me extra close when he hugged me good-bye? Did he look at me with burning intensity because he was imagining kissing me or because I had food stuck in my teeth? We've e-mailed each other regularly while he's been away, and the e-mails have been lighthearted, veering sometimes into flirtatious before just as quickly scooting back onto more solid *just friends* ground.

"That's good," he says now. Is that a smirk?

Why can't I stop staring at his lips? Why do I have to lose my train of thought so completely when he stands so close? And did he always smell this good? What the heck is with me?

I manage finally to find my voice and construct a whole sentence with verbs and nouns and pronouns. Incredible. "What about you? How was it over there?"

I catch the slight flicker as his smile fades momentarily before brightening once again. He rubs a hand over his head. "Yeah, you know . . ." He shrugs as he trails off.

Stupid question, I think to myself. Damn. For a moment neither of us says anything. I start twisting the end of my ponytail, something I do when I get nervous, then, realizing what I'm doing could be construed as flirtatious as well as ditzy, I drop my hands to my sides. Kit stands there waiting, watching me, that half smile still on his face. His expression is hard to read. He seems to be enjoying my discomfort, but there's something else about the way he's looking at me. He opens his mouth as though to ask me something, but then closes it again. The air around us feels charged, but that could be because I'm hyper-aware of every gesture I'm making and also of the fact that my father is standing not fifty feet away holding something that could be interpreted as a weapon.

"How long do you have?" I finally ask, feeling my cheeks starting to burn almost as hot as the chicken that's now smoking on the grill.

"Four weeks," he answers.

I nod and stare down at my feet. Four weeks. A month. And then he's gone again. Why am I even wanting something to happen between us? It wouldn't be worth it. He'd be gone before I knew it.